For Jan

ACKNOWLEDGMENTS

I must thank Jane Hawk and Catherine Yoes for their encouraging feedback, and Catherine Cresswell for her excellent suggestions. My greatest debt is to Jane Austen, who created such wonderful characters.

The flaws that remain are my own.

CAST OF CHARACTERS

Mrs. Annesley: Companion and chaperone to Georgiana Darcy.

Mr. Bennet: Proprietor of Longbourn, husband to Mrs. Bennet, father of five daughters – Jane Bingley, Elizabeth Darcy, Mary Bennet, Kitty Bennet, Lydia Wickham. "A mixture of quick parts, sarcastic humor, reserve and caprice."

Mrs. Bennet (née Gardiner): Wife to Mr. Bennet, sister to Mrs. Philips and Mr. Gardiner, daughter of an attorney (deceased) of Meryton, mother of five daughters – Jane Bingley, Elizabeth Darcy, Mary Bennet, Kitty Bennet, Lydia Wickham. Her business has been to get her daughters married; she has succeeded with three of the five. "A woman of mean understanding, little information, and uncertain temper."

Miss Catherine (Kitty) Bennet: Fourth daughter of Mr. and Mrs. Bennet, she is delicate and slight and misses her younger sister, Lydia, very much.

Miss Mary Bennet: Third daughter of Mr. and Mrs. Bennet, she has the misfortune of being the only plain one of the five, and compensates through her accomplishments – music and reading. "A young lady of deep reflection who reads great books and makes extracts."

Miss Caroline Bingley: Unmarried sister of Mr. Bingley and Louisa Hurst (née Bingley), she has a fortune of 20,000£. "A fine woman, with an air of decided fashion."

Mr. Charles Bingley: Tenant of Netherfield Park, husband of Jane Bingley, brother to Caroline Bingley and Louisa Hurst (née Bingley). "Good-looking and gentlemanlike; he had a pleasant countenance, and easy, unaffected manners."

Mrs. Jane Bingley (née Bennet): Wife to Mr. Bingley, eldest daughter of Mr. and Mrs. Bennet. According to her sister Elizabeth, Jane is about five times as pretty as every other woman and never sees a fault in anybody.

Miss Anne de Bourgh: Heiress of Rosings Park, daughter of Lady Catherine de Bourgh and the late Sir Lewis de Bourgh. "She looks sickly and cross."

Lady Catherine de Bourgh (née Fitzwilliam): Proprietor of Rosings Park, widow of Sir Lewis de Bourgh, mother of Anne de Bourgh, aunt to Mr. Darcy, Miss Georgiana Darcy, Colonel Fitzwilliam and others.

Patroness of Mr. Collins, she is arrogant and conceited, dictatorial and insolent.

Brown: Undergardener on the Netherfield estate.

Mr. Henry Clarke: From the family that owns Clarke's Library, this young man is clerk to Mr. Philips.

Mr. Thomas Clarke: Older brother of Mr. Henry Clarke.

Mrs. Charlotte Collins (née Lucas): Wife to Mr. Collins, daughter to Sir William Lucas and Lady Lucas, mother of Lewis William Collins, sister to Maria Lucas and others. "A sensible, intelligent young woman."

Lewis William Collins: Infant son of Mr. and Mrs. Collins, grandson of Sir William and Lady Lucas.

Mr. William Collins: Heir to the entailed Longbourn estate, husband to Mrs. Charlotte Collins, father of Lewis William Collins, cousin of Mr. Bennet and his five daughters. Mr. Collins is a clergyman in Hunsford, his living afforded him by Lady Catherine de Bourgh. "A tall, heavy looking young man ... his air was grave and stately, and his manners were very formal."

Mrs. Elizabeth Darcy (née Bennet): Wife to Mr. Darcy, second daughter of Mr. and Mrs. Bennet, sister to Jane Bingley, Mary Bennet, Kitty Bennet, and Lydia Wickham. "She had a lively, playful disposition, which delighted in anything ridiculous."

Mr. Fitzwilliam Darcy: Proprietor of Pemberley, husband to Elizabeth Darcy, brother and guardian to Georgiana Darcy, nephew of Lady Catherine de Bourgh. "Fine, tall person, handsome features, noble mien, and the report of his having ten thousand a-year ... was looked at with great admiration ... till his manners gave a disgust which turned the tide of his popularity."

Miss Georgiana Darcy: Sister to Fitzwilliam Darcy and an heiress with 30,000£. "Her figure was formed and her appearance womanly and graceful."

Colonel Fitzwilliam: Younger son of an earl, nephew to Lady Catherine de Bourgh, cousin to Mr. Darcy and to Miss Georgiana Darcy; he shares joint guardianship of the latter. "Not handsome, but in person and address most truly the gentleman."

Mrs. Ford: Mrs. Collins's previous nursery maid.

Mr. Edward Gardiner: Brother to Mrs. Bennet and Mrs. Philips, he grew up in Meryton but is now a man of business living in London on Gracechurch Street.

Mrs. Gardiner: Wife of Mr. Gardiner and a favorite with her two oldest nieces.

Mr. Goulding: A neighbor.

Mrs. Goulding: A neighbor.

Hannah: Maidservant of Miss Mary King.

Hill: Housekeeper at Longbourn House.

Mr. Hurst: Husband to Louisa Hurst (née Bingley). "Merely looked the gentleman."

Mrs. Louisa Hurst (née Bingley): Wife of Mr. Hurst, sister to Charles Bingley and Caroline Bingley. "A fine woman, with an air of decided fashion."

Jeanette: Mrs. Elizabeth Darcy's French maidservant.

Mrs. Jenkinson: Companion and chaperone of Miss Anne de Bourgh.

Joan: Mrs. Collins's current nursery maid.

The elder Mr. Jones: Apothecary in Meryton.

The younger Mr. Jones: Son of the elder Mr. Jones and apothecary in Meryton.

Miss Mary King: She inherited 10,000£ from her grandfather in Meryton; Lydia described her as "a nasty little freckled thing."

Lady Lucas: Wife to Sir William Lucas, a neighbor of the Bennets at Longbourn. "A very good kind of woman."

Miss Maria Lucas: Second daughter of Sir William and Lady Lucas.

Mr. Will Lucas: Eldest son of Sir William and Lady Lucas, brother to Mrs. Collins, Maria Lucas, and others.

Sir William Lucas: Owner of Lucas Lodge, husband of Lady Lucas, father of Charlotte Collins, Maria Lucas, and several others. He was knighted when mayor of Meryton. "... all attention to everybody ... by nature inoffensive, attentive and obliging."

Mr. Morris: Young relative of a real estate agent, he is a clerk to the attorney Mr. Philips.

Mrs. Nicholls: Cook for the Bingleys at Netherfield Park.

Jim Page: Son of Mrs. Page.

Mrs. Page: Meryton milliner whose shop is across the street from the house/office of Mr. Philips.

Frank Perkins: Son of Jailer Perkins.

Jailer Perkins: Jailer in Meryton.

Mr. Philips: Attorney in Meryton, former clerk to the father of Mr. Edward Gardiner, Mrs. Philips and Mrs. Bennet. "Broad-faced and stuffy."

Mrs. Philips (née Gardiner): Wife to Mr. Philips, sister to Mrs. Bennet and Mr. Gardiner, aunt to the Bennet girls.

Reeves: Housemaid at Netherfield.

Richard: Footman to Mr. Philips.

Old Mr. Robinson: A neighbor.

Young Mr. Robinson: A neighbor.

Mr. Selby: Betrothed to Miss Mary King, from Liverpool, nephew to a baronet.

Mrs. Smith: Tenant of Mr. and Mrs. Philips.

Colonel Thorne: Commander of George Wickham's regiment in Newcastle, and a friend of Colonel Fitzwilliam.

Reverend Wallace: Vicar with the living at the village of Kympton, near Pemberley.

Lieutenant George Wickham: Husband to Lydia, son of the former, deceased steward of Pemberley, he grew up with Mr. Darcy but did not turn out well. "He had all the best part of beauty – a fine countenance, a good figure, and a very pleasing address."

Mrs. Lydia Wickham (née Bennet): Wife to George Wickham, fifth and youngest daughter of Mr. and Mrs. Bennet. "A fine complexion and a good-humored countenance … high animal spirits and a sort of natural self-consequence."

Wilson: Pemberley coachman.

Mrs. Annabelle Younge: Former companion and chaperone of Miss Georgiana Darcy, in whose character Mr. Darcy was unhappily deceived.

CHAPTER I

When a single man with a good income moves into a neighborhood, especially when he leases a large estate, the people rejoice and speculate. They are impatient to learn everything about him, such as his preferences for hunting, whether he likes to dance, what sort of horse he rides and whether or not they can persuade him to take an interest in one of their unmarried daughters. He is the subject of conversation, the recipient of eager visits, and the object of hopes and dreams.

But when a middle-aged widow of modest means hires a few rooms in a market-town, her arrival is barely noticed. She is too old to cause excitement among the men, and too plain to provoke jealous gossip among the women. Even the tradespeople sigh with disappointment, for a widow of modest means cannot be expected to provide much custom for bread, meat and millinery. So when Mrs. Smith took lodgings in Meryton, her appearance mattered to only a few: to the attorney Mr. Philips, who was the landlord of Meryton's newest resident; to those in his office, who were in charge of the details; and to his wife, Mrs. Philips, who welcomed any increase in their income, and had long regretted the vacancy of the apartment on F— street.

Mrs. Philips, calling on her sister Mrs. Bennet at Mr. Bennet's Longbourn estate, about a mile from Meryton, shared news of the new lady and neighbor, expressing the hope that her tenant would join them occasionally for an evening of cards. "I have called on Mrs. Smith and she has returned the visit. She seems an agreeable, genteel sort of lady."

"Does she now?" asked Mrs. Bennet, who was distractedly peering out the window in search of Kitty, her younger unmarried daughter. She turned to Mary, another single daughter and asked Mary if she knew where Kitty was; Mary replied that she was ignorant of her younger sister's whereabouts.

Mrs. Philips attempted to be philosophical. "You know, sister, at our time of life, with the departure of the militia and the marriages of your daughters, we should welcome every new acquaintance."

One might have expected that Mrs. Bennet, not too distant in years from Mrs. Smith, would be sympathetic to the middle-aged woman and her situation. "I hope she is a good tenant for you and Mr. Philips," Mrs. Bennet said valiantly, before resuming the subject that she cared for most:

single young men who she might convince to marry one of her two remaining daughters. The eligible bachelors in Meryton were few and well known, but Mrs. Bennet, devoted to her daughters' welfare, observed them assiduously. "How is Mr. Philips's new clerk?"

Mr. Philips, once a clerk to Mr. Gardiner, the long-deceased father of Mrs. Philips and Mrs. Bennet, had recently hired a new clerk of his own, in addition to Mr. Morris, an extremely plain fellow who had worked for Mr. Philips for the last two years. "His name is Mr. Clarke," said Mrs. Philips, "which makes me think he must come from a long line of clerks."

"He is connected to the Clarkes at the library," said Mary, the third of the five Bennet daughters and the only one in the room. A dedicated reader, she was a patron of the local circulating library. "He has returned to Meryton after working in London."

"Yes, yes, but what are his prospects?" inquired Mrs. Bennet, who did not think well enough of any business based on people reading books to rely on them to support her daughters. "Does Mr. Philips think he will advance? Does Mr. Philips really have enough work to support *two* clerks?" Before Mrs. Philips could answer either of these questions, Mrs. Bennet continued. "He might do for Mary, if he is of a serious nature. On the other hand, laying a good table and looking fine is important for an attorney, so Mr. Clarke might be more suitable for Kitty."

Without waiting for an answer, Mrs. Bennet moved on to other prospective husbands. "Perhaps the eldest Lucas boy. At least Lucas Lodge is in the neighborhood. It is so hard to have children move away. I cannot tell you what I have suffered, Sister, in being separated from my dear Lydia and my dear Lizzy."

Mrs. Bennet could rejoice in her great success in having already married off three of her five daughters. Lydia, the youngest and Mrs. Bennet's favorite, had been the first to marry. Her husband was Lieutenant George Wickham, whom the Bennets had met when the —shire Militia had been quartered in Meryton. Mr. Wickham was handsome, charming, and unreliable; he had only consented to marry Lydia after a scandalous elopement and pressure from interested parties. There was no question but that Mrs. Bennet certainly missed Lydia, even though she and her favorite daughter had not been parted long, as Mr. and Mrs. Wickham had recently stayed at Netherfield, with Mrs. Bingley, the eldest of the Bennet daughters.

Mr. Charles Bingley, Jane's husband, was the tenant of Netherfield Park, located about three miles from Longbourn, Mr. Bennet's estate. The match between Bingley and Jane was one that that everyone could celebrate, for Bingley was reliable, handsome, good-humored and rich. The only flaw in his character was that he had taken a rather long time to propose, those months of hesitation causing deep anguish to Mrs. Bennet and to her daughter Jane – but since they had married ten months ago, all was forgiven.

Mrs. Bennet's last married daughter was Elizabeth, the second of the Bennet daughters. She had married Mr. Fitzwilliam Darcy, Mr. Bingley's great friend. No one could complain about Mr. Darcy's looks, for he was a tall, handsome man; nor could anyone object to his fortune, for he was the owner of Pemberley, a great estate located in Derbyshire. Mr. Darcy, however, was *not* a charming man, and when he had first arrived in Meryton in the company of Mr. Bingley he had been generally disliked due to his pride and his continual giving of offense, and to falsehoods that had been spread about him by George Wickham.

Mrs. Bennet was obliged to say that she missed Elizabeth, because that daughter was now Mrs. Darcy, by far the richest of her three married daughters. Before the marriage, however, Elizabeth had been her least favorite, as Elizabeth was quick enough to see and to occasionally object to her mother's excesses. These remonstrations had irritated Mrs. Bennet, who felt that such interference was inappropriate. With her second daughter at a distance, the source of her vexation was gone, and expressing affection was much easier for Mrs. Bennet. She very much enjoyed talking about, if not talking with, Mrs. Darcy.

Mrs. Philips had heard all these things so often that all she had to do was to make the usual sympathetic noises as she stirred more sugar in her tea, while Mary, who had heard them even more frequently, ignored her mother as best she could.

"The eldest Lucas might do for either Mary or Kitty. And that would make up for what they have taken. I still have not forgotten how Lady Lucas stole Mr. Collins from me!"

The eldest Lucas daughter had married Mr. Collins, a cousin to Mr. Bennet, a clergyman in Kent and the heir to the Longbourn estate. Longbourn was entailed, in default of male heirs, and Mr. and Mrs. Bennet had no sons. Mr. Collins had come to Longbourn in search of a wife, but the Bennet daughter he had chosen, Elizabeth, had refused his offer of marriage – another reason that daughter had fallen out of her mother's good graces for a period. As Elizabeth's marriage to Mr. Darcy was far better than the match that she could have made with Mr. Collins, Mrs. Bennet might have been expected to forgive Elizabeth this refusal. Sometimes she was successful, but other times the resentment, so habitual, if not the memory of the cause, reasserted itself. For Mr. Collins, affronted by Elizabeth's refusal, had consoled himself by marrying one of Elizabeth's closest friends, Charlotte Lucas.

"It would be a way to even the situation between us, and at least Lucas Lodge is nearby. Ah, Mr. Bennet, there you are!"

Mr. Bennet, husband to Mrs. Bennet and the proprietor of Longbourn, emerged from his library in order to join them and to take a cup of tea. Besides, his sister-in-law, although not a great wit, was at least a slight change from the sameness of the relatively small circle in which they now lived.

"Do you have any news for us, Mr. Bennet?"

Before Mr. Bennet could answer, the final member of their reduced family party arrived: Kitty, fresh from a walk to the Lucases, the family who had caused so much grief for Mrs. Bennet.

Mr. Bennet accepted a cup of tea poured by Mrs. Bennet and answered his lady's question.

"Mr. Collins has sent us a letter," Mr. Bennet announced, who enjoyed sharing this information because he knew it would irritate his wife.

"Mr. Collins writes many letters," observed Kitty, who shared her mother's dislike of Mr. Collins, but not because he was the future proprietor of Longbourn. After meeting so many officers, as she had during the —shire Militia's stay in Meryton, Miss Catherine Bennet could not imagine settling for a clergyman, especially one so long-winded and dull.

"He has not written so many recently," Mary corrected. "What does Mr. Collins say?"

Mr. Collins, Mr. Bennet announced, had written his letter to inform them that he and his dear Charlotte and their little son were planning to visit Meryton in the near future, so that little Lewis Collins could meet his grandparents, his aunts and uncles and his cousins.

"I hope they are not planning to stay here," said Mrs. Bennet.

"No, Mamma, they will be staying at Lucas Lodge," said Kitty, then explained that Lady Lucas had also received a letter from Charlotte.

"Then I will not share the details of their impending journey with you. Most of Mr. Collins's letter is devoted to the birth and christening of his son," said Mr. Bennet. He adjusted his spectacles and read aloud:

You may already be aware, through my dear Charlotte's relations, that we have chosen, with the acquiescence of Lady Catherine de Bourgh, to christen our son Lewis William Collins. If the child had been a girl we would have chosen Catherine Anne, to honor my noble patroness and her distinguished daughter, but the child, as you know, is a boy – not that we are the least disappointed, especially as he is a strong child, with healthy lungs and appetite. The first reason for choosing this name was to honor Lady Catherine's late husband, Sir Lewis de Bourgh. The second name, William, is a family name honoring Mrs. Collins's father and happens to also be my own. We also considered Lucas, or even Bennet, to carry on the name that you have not been able to bequeath, and I feel I must apologize for giving the preference to those who are at hand. We hope to have many children, and if we are so blessed, be assured, my dear Mr. Bennet, that we will honor you when the time comes, although I must say that having just one child requires a great deal of effort, especially as we were unfortunate with our initial choice of nursery maid. The change in domestic circumstances experienced by many new parents will excuse my tardiness in composing this missive to inform you of my son's name, and the reasons supporting the choice, but as you and Mrs. Bennet are parents yourselves you will certainly comprehend the difficulties and forgive us. Be assured, however, that Mrs. Collins and our son are all well, and we hope to introduce you soon to Lewis William Collins, and continue to heal the breach between the two branches of our family.

Mr. Bennet read the page to the feminine members of his family, in the hope that they would enjoy the pompous formality of his cousin's manner. Unluckily, this was an appreciation that he could not share; only Elizabeth had inherited his delight in others' foibles – one of the reasons that Mrs. Darcy, although the least preferred of Mrs. Bennet's children, was Mr. Bennet's favorite. As Mr. Bennet read, Mrs. Bennet fidgeted impatiently, Kitty attempted and failed to hide several yawns, and Mrs. Philips stared at the plate of muffins and wondered if she would appear too greedy if she took another. Only Mary attended to Mr. Collins's epistle with any interest, but her interest was completely serious.

Mr. Bennet, realizing the limitations of his audience, stopped reading and resumed drinking his tea.

Mrs. Bennet proved that she had been paying attention by responding to the letter's contents if not its style. "So, Mr. and Mrs. Collins have a healthy son! Of course we already know about it, as Mrs. Collins wrote to Lady Lucas long before your cousin wrote to you. I suppose that they wish to show Longbourn to Lewis so that he can claim it as his own."

Mr. Bennet knew that his wife still felt guilty about never producing a son and cutting off the entail. That increased her resentment of Mrs. Collins, who had achieved with her first child what Mrs. Bennet had failed to do with five. Mr. Bennet attempted to reason with his lady. "Mrs. Bennet, even if Mr. and Mrs. Collins had been able to honor Lady Catherine by having a daughter to name after her, the property would still be entailed on Mr. Collins. Once I die, Longbourn will go to him. There is nothing that we can do about it. Is that not true, Mrs. Philips?"

Despite being both the daughter and the wife of an attorney, Mrs. Philips was ignorant of most legal matters. She was also not accustomed to being appealed to by her brother-in-law on any point. Her mouth full of muffin, she mumbled something unintelligible but fortunately for her, no one paid any attention.

"And if Mr. Collins should die?" asked Mrs. Bennet.

"Then little Lewis Collins will inherit."

Mrs. Bennet spoke without enthusiasm. "Lewis William Collins! I will not have him staying here, breaking everything! We will have to place all the fine things on the highest shelves."

"Mamma, Lewis is only a few months old," Kitty protested. "He cannot possibly be walking."

Mr. Bennet reminded Mrs. Bennet that they would soon have grandchildren themselves, and that they might as well prepare the house for it.

Mrs. Bennet, however, was not to be dissuaded from voicing displeasure. "I do not see why an infant, who no one cares anything about, should be heir to Longbourn!"

Mr. Bennet said that he expected that many people cared about Lewis Collins, including their neighbors, Sir William and Lady Lucas, the boy's grandparents, to say nothing of Mr. and Mrs. Collins, who were certainly delighted by their son. "Mr. Collins has written four pages on the subject," said Mr. Bennet, waving them.

Mary asked if she could read the rest of the letter, and Mr. Bennet passed the pages to his third daughter.

"Mary, how can you *want* to read anything written by that man?" asked Kitty.

"There are many reasons to like Mr. Collins, or at least to show him respect. He is a clergyman; he is our cousin, and he is the heir to Longbourn."

"And one of the dullest men that ever breathed!"

Mr. Bennet said, "For once, Mary and Kitty, I am in agreement with both your sentiments."

Mr. Bennet's remark was confusing to Mrs. Bennet, who upbraided him for talking nonsense.

Kitty, leaning back in her chair, voiced a different complaint. "The weather is so warm, and I am so bored. I wish I could visit Lydia, Papa. I do not see why she should be allowed to visit my aunt Gardiner in London while I stay here."

"We *all* wish we could visit Lydia," said Mrs. Bennet, who missed her youngest daughter's liveliness and good humor. "But London in August, Kitty, would be even warmer than Hertfordshire. I do wish Lydia and Wickham would write. We have not even learned if Wickham reached Newcastle safely."

Mary began sharing other items of news from Mr. Collins's letter.

"I will finish my tea in the library," said Mr. Bennet. He was reminded, as he had been so often, that a small dose of his family was sufficient to renew the great appeal of the solitude and serenity of his books. Besides, *he* had already read Mr. Collins's letter; he did not need to be informed of its contents again.

"As you please, Mr. Bennet," said Mrs. Bennet.

"Who is that?" asked Mrs. Philips, who, as a guest, had been seated with the best view of the window, but whose eyesight was not so good that she could distinguish much at a distance.

They could all hear the sound of horses' hoofs and an approaching carriage. Mrs. Bennet told Kitty to take a look, and even Mr. Bennet delayed his escape and waited to learn the identity of the arrival.

Kitty bounded over to the window and pulled the curtain to the side. "It is Jane!" she said. "Or – at least it is Mr. Bingley's carriage." Kitty continued to gaze out the window and to make her report. "The carriage has stopped – the man is opening the door – he helping Jane out."

"Anyone else, Kitty? Has Mr. Bingley come calling too? Or Miss Bingley?" inquired Mrs. Bennet.

But Kitty reported that Jane had arrived alone.

The mother still took action, telling Kitty to ring the bell and to order a fresh pot of tea and another plate of muffins. Mrs. Philips and Mary Bennet looked more alert, and even Mr. Bennet, on the threshold of departure for the sanctuary of his library, sat back down with the others. His eldest daughter might not be quite his favorite, but he valued her highly. Jane's calm demeanor and good sense were always welcome after the high spirits and querulousness of the others.

But Mr. Bennet was disappointed in his expectation for rational, intelligent conversation, for when Mrs. Bingley entered the room, instead of greeting them calmly, she sat down and burst into tears.

CHAPTER II

A young matron who sinks into a chair and cries must be comforted. The occupants of the Bennet parlor were united, at least, in their desire to help dear Jane, although not in agreement in how to go about it. Mrs. Philips tried to loan her niece her recently acquired little glass flask of smelling salts, which was inappropriate as Mrs. Bingley was weeping and not faint. Mary tried to think of something pertinent and profound to say; Kitty prepared a muffin and a cup of tea; Mr. Bennet pulled out a large handkerchief and silently handed it to his eldest daughter; and Mrs. Bennet, pushing aside Mrs. Philips, loudly demanded to know what was wrong.

"Are you ill?" inquired Mrs. Bennet. "Should we send for Mr. Jones?"

These questions were relevant because Jane expected to become a mother in about six weeks.

Jane wiped her face with her father's handkerchief and surveyed the large party hovering before her. "Mother, I assure you, I am not ill. There is no need to send for the apothecary."

Mrs. Bennet continued with her theories. "Is it that Miss Bingley? Has she been unkind to you? If so, she should go and live with Mr. and Mrs. Hurst, wherever they are these days."

Miss Bingley, Mr. Bingley's sister, was petitioning for her brother to purchase an estate in some other neighborhood, and had listed Mrs. Bennet as chief among her reasons for suggesting a removal to another county. Miss Bingley's opinion of Mrs. Bennet had somehow traveled from Netherfield to Longbourn, and the mistress of Longbourn had taken great offense.

"No, Mamma. Please, please, forget about it." Jane gazed around her at all the anxious faces. "It is nothing, really. Forgive me for disturbing you. And thank you, Kitty, for the tea and muffin. I am certain it will restore me."

But the others in the Bennet parlor could not cease speculating. Mrs. Philips wondered if a servant had been giving her trouble, for her new acquaintance, Mrs. Smith, had just told her a horror story about servants. Mrs. Bennet wanted to know if they were having money troubles, and if so, Bingley should discuss it with Mr. Bennet.

Mr. Bennet was silent. He was not sure what he could do in such a case – Longbourn was a fine estate, for their area of Hertfordshire, but he did not have the means to compensate for any shortfall of Mr. Bingley's, whose income was more than twice his, and included fewer dependents – but again Jane shook her head. Although he said nothing, Mr. Bennet observed his daughter carefully.

Mary had finally determined what sort of consolation she could offer. "Would you like me to play for you on the pianoforte? Music can be a great comfort to a distressed spirit."

"No, Mary, thank you. Just tell me how all of you are."

A valiant attempt was made to change the subject; the names Mr. Collins and Lady Lucas were offered, but the curiosity regarding Jane's situation was too strong. Mrs. Bennet and the other ladies could not resist inquiring what was wrong – so frequently that Jane took the desperate step of asking Mary to play the pianoforte for her after all.

Mary entertained them for half-an-hour. Then Jane departed, and Mrs. Philips as well, grateful to accept a lift back to Meryton in the Netherfield chaise.

Mr. Bennet then observed to his lady: "I suspect that Jane came in order to tell us something and then decided against it."

But Mrs. Bennet, in the habit of disagreeing with her husband on everything, was inclined to believe Jane's assertion that nothing was wrong. "We asked her what the matter was, and she said nothing, several times! Why would she come to tell us something and then not speak? What could ever stop her from confiding in her parents, especially her mother? And her sisters? It is very good of you, Mr. Bennet, to take such an interest – but Jane has already denied it, and she is the most trustworthy of our girls." Mary and Kitty, both still in the drawing-room, frowned at this reflection, but their mother obliviously continued. "I will tell you what it is. Jane will soon be having her first child and a young woman in her condition can easily be fanciful. Things, even little things, can upset one. I should know. My nerves have always been sensitive, and Jane, after all, is my daughter. Perhaps Miss Bingley said something, and Jane needed an hour or two away from her. I am sure it is nothing. What could be wrong?"

"I do not know," said Mr. Bennet, and added, unusually gravely for him, "I hope, Mrs. Bennet, that you are right and that it is all it is." He returned at last to the solitude of his library but he was so concerned that he considered writing a letter to his second daughter. His anxiety persisted, so he actually wrote the letter that evening and sent it via the post the following morning.

It was this note that Mrs. Darcy opened, just two days later, when it reached her at Pemberley. She read it aloud to her husband, a procedure that took less than a minute.

Dear Lizzy,

Your sister Jane is out of spirits. She was in tears at Longbourn this afternoon. She needs your help. Yours sincerely, etc.

"What do you think is wrong?" Elizabeth asked of her husband.

"Dear Elizabeth, you must know better than I."

"I wonder that she has not written. Perhaps she is too distressed to write. Or could she be ill?"

"Everything you say is possible," said Mr. Darcy.

"But if any of those things were true, my father should have mentioned it. Could something be wrong with Bingley? Have you heard anything from your friend?"

But Darcy had received no communication from Mr. Bingley for several weeks. The men, though good friends, did not keep up the same sort of chatty correspondence far more common to females.

"I wish my father had said more," said Elizabeth, passing the letter to her husband.

"Your father rarely says more," said Darcy, for terseness was Mr. Bennet's custom. "But since he has actually taken the trouble to write, he is obviously concerned. It is possible that he has not said more because he does not know more. What I believe your father *wants* is for you to visit. Also, his letter indicates that Jane needs *you*, and not that Bingley needs me. So do you wish to travel to Longbourn – or perhaps, if you go, you should stay at Netherfield?"

Elizabeth could not disagree with anything that her husband said, and was impressed at his eliciting so much meaning out of so few words. Moreover, she wished to be with her sister during this most interesting time, but she did have more to add. "And I believe what *you* want, is for *me* to make the journey and for you to remain at Pemberley. You are avoiding Longbourn."

"My dear, do not accuse me."

But they both comprehended that their marriage fared better when Mr. Darcy was not reminded too often and too strongly of his wife's mother. Not only was Mrs. Bennet an irritant in herself; the prospect that Elizabeth might grow to resemble Mrs. Bennet would strike fear into any rational man. Elizabeth sometimes experienced anxiety herself with respect to the possibility, even though Darcy had assured her that she would have to change a great deal before she acquired the manners of her mother.

Darcy said genially, "If you insist upon my going to Netherfield, I will, but I believe that your sister will be more likely to confide in you if I am not there. Especially if it is a matter concerning her condition."

"Your arguments are too good," said Elizabeth. "Besides, you have the Grangers to take care of"– Darcy was overseeing some improvements being made to some of his tenants' property – "and Georgiana is returning from London next week. You will want to be here to welcome your sister, and Colonel Fitzwilliam is coming too. Wilson is the most reliable coachman in the country, so you have no fears for my safety."

"And the weather has been dry, and the roads between Pemberley and Longbourn are excellent. Georgiana, however, will miss you."

"And I will miss Georgiana – and her music." Elizabeth did not add, that it was a penance to trade Georgiana Darcy's glorious music for the pedantic efforts of Mary Bennet, because she did not need to remind husband of yet another way in which the Bennets were inferior to the Darcys. He had known of all these deficiencies – her want of connection and fortune, not to mention her mother – before he had asked for her hand, and yet his affection for her was so great that he had done it anyway.

"And I will miss you," said her gallant husband. "You must promise me not to stay away for long, and to return as soon as you are assured of Jane's safety. And if you miss me, or if you think I could be of any use, I will come immediately, even if it means leaving visitors to their own devices at Pemberley."

The question then became whether she should stay at Netherfield Park, with her sister, or at Longbourn, with her parents. "If Jane will have me, I would rather stay at Netherfield. But perhaps it would be indelicate for me to invite myself, whereas my father has invited me."

"Elizabeth, you know very well that you will be welcome at either house. But my recommendation is that you choose Netherfield. First, if Jane needs assistance, you can supply it more easily if you are under the same roof. Second, given her condition, it is natural for you to wish to be near her."

"And, if you do join me, you would much prefer to be at Netherfield than at Longbourn," said Elizabeth.

"Do not take that into account. I know how much Jane means to you, and I would endure much more to put your mind at ease. But I think my other reasons are sufficient."

So Elizabeth wrote the appropriate letters, including sending a note of apology to some friends with whom she had become acquainted since becoming mistress of Pemberley, and made the other necessary arrangements. Two days later she set out to spend some time with her sister and to visit the neighborhood of her youth.

CHAPTER III

Elizabeth had been in Hertfordshire but once since her marriage, when she and Mr. Darcy had been journeying somewhere else, and so had only spent two nights there in the past ten months. On that occasion she was still so newly married, with all the attendant fuss granted to every bride – something that she could not avoid as her mother had been determined to exhibit her to everyone – that Elizabeth had neither time nor leisure to ponder the difference in her situation before and after marriage. On this visit she planned to spend several weeks at least, so she would have opportunity for assessment and reflection.

Nearly everything looked as it had the summer before; the hedgerows were familiar, the usual rosebushes flourished in the warm sun and her carriage was even barked at by the same dogs. Yet there was a difference to her eyes; and she was wise enough to realize that the neighborhood had not changed; *she* had. When she lived here she had been Miss Eliza Bennet, the second daughter of a gentleman with five daughters, with only modest expectations with respect to money and marriage. Now she was Mrs. Darcy, whose future and fortune were assured, with a splendid carriage, a trunk full of fine clothes, and even a personal maidservant, Jeanette, riding beside her. These trappings signaled rank and riches to every person she encountered, and guaranteed her the best treatment – even when she did not need it.

Elizabeth told Wilson, the coachman, to first go to Longbourn so she could call on her parents before continuing to Netherfield Park. The stop would allow her to stretch her legs and to refresh herself. It would also be an act of courtesy to her parents, with whom she was not staying. Finally, she hoped to have a moment with her father to see if he could tell her anything more about Jane.

She descended from the carriage and was met with noisy affection by her mother. "My dear Lizzy! Mrs. Darcy! How was your journey? My, that is a fine carriage, but you now have the best of everything, do you not? Do not worry, your father's man will see to the horses and Hill will give your maid and your coachman something out of the kitchen. Come in, come in; make yourself comfortable. There, my dear, I must give you a kiss."

In the vestibule Elizabeth greeted the rest of her family. Even though it was not his hour to leave the library, Mr. Bennet had appeared to welcome his favorite daughter, and Mary and Kitty were also embraced in turn. Elizabeth, still standing, made the usual inquiries about everyone's health, and she received assurances with respect to nearly everyone, although Mary lugubriously warned her that Jane had been in tears.

"We are all well, quite well," said her mother, louder than everyone else, as she answered the question again. "True, Jane seemed a little out of sorts a few days ago, but I called yesterday at Netherfield and all was well. In her condition, nerves are so delicate."

"What have you brought?" inquired Kitty, for Elizabeth had a basket on her arm.

"Do not be so hasty, Kitty," said Mrs. Bennet.

"I have brought a few small presents," said Elizabeth.

"How thoughtful and generous of you. Is not Lizzy thoughtful?" said Mrs. Bennet. "Come in, sit down; and Kitty, ring the bell for tea."

They entered the parlor, and then Elizabeth distributed the gifts, passing several books to her father, a handsome reticule to her mother, some sheet music and a metronome to Mary, and an elegant little parasol to Kitty. As she glanced around she detected that the silver had been polished, the finest tea cups brought out, and she had been ushered to the best chair in the room, the one usually sat in by her mother.

Everyone expressed gratitude at being remembered; Elizabeth only hoped that the presents were sufficient, and then Elizabeth showed Mary how to use the metronome. Mary, however, was dubious. She was the most old-fashioned of the Bennet sisters, and was generally suspicious of new devices, and despite Elizabeth's assurance that metronomes were used by the finest young ladies these days, including her sister-in-law Georgiana, Mary seemed to view the gift as criticism of her musical ability. Mary's attitude was reinforced when Kitty, intrigued by the ticking device, observed: "This will keep you from changing the pace when you play for our dances, Mary. You cannot understand how difficult it is to dance when the tempo keeps shifting."

"And you do not understand, Kitty, how difficult it is to play the pianoforte at all, especially when people do not appreciate it."

"If you do not change the tempo, then perhaps the dancers will be grateful!"

"Girls, stop quarreling! And turn that thing off. It is assaulting my nerves," exclaimed Mrs. Bennet.

Elizabeth smiled; despite the polished silver and the best tea cups, at least her family was behaving normally around her. Her mother and sisters resumed speaking with their usual fretfulness, and told Elizabeth the neighborhood's most recent news: Mr. and Mrs. Collins were planning a visit soon to Lucas Lodge, which meant that Elizabeth would have the opportunity to see her friend Charlotte; Miss Bingley had behaved rudely to Mr. and Mrs. Wickham when they were visiting, but that did not surprise Mrs. Bennet at all, as she had taken a great dislike to Miss Bingley (Elizabeth was a little dismayed to discover that she shared many of the opinions of her mother, although she consoled herself that she expressed them differently). An acquaintance of theirs, Mary King, was betrothed to a Mr. Selby from Liverpool, and was back in Meryton to take care of some business before her nuptials, and Aunt Philips was desperate to see Elizabeth and planned a reception in her honor at her house during Elizabeth's visit.

When they finished their tea, Mr. Bennet, who had been relatively silent so far, invited his just-arrived daughter to enter his library with him and to help him decide where to put his new books. As they left the noisiness of the parlor, Kitty resumed fidgeting with the metronome and telling Mary that she really ought to try it while Mary disagreed. The voices grew louder, only drowned out by Mrs. Bennet and then the closing of the door.

Elizabeth stood in front of a bookshelf, reading titles of stories and histories that had amused and educated her throughout the years. "I am sorry that a gift of mine should cause my sisters to quarrel."

Mr. Bennet sat in his usual chair. "My dear, it has nothing to do with your gift; *everything* causes those two young ladies to quarrel."

"I had hoped that with the rest of us married, Kitty and Mary would become close friends," remarked Elizabeth, "but I suppose their dispositions are too different."

"Longbourn House is not as noisy as it used to be," said Mr. Bennet. "Or perhaps my hearing is not as good. I thank you for these volumes, I am sure they will give me many pleasant hours."

"They were selected by Mr. Darcy."

"Mr. Darcy is a very clever son-in-law, but even if he were to give me ten times as many books, I would still come to see you and his library at Pemberley."

Elizabeth laughed, then changed the subject. "So, Papa, you know why I am here. Your letter about Jane worried me. One reason I came to Longbourn first, was to ask if you could tell me more about her situation."

Mr. Bennet obliged her by describing the weeping that Jane had done a few days before, as Mary and the others had mentioned.

"And you had no success in determining the cause of her tears?"

"None at all. But if it is a private matter, in whom can she can confide? She knows we all love her, and that may give her comfort, but she may not be assured that we will be discreet or give good advice."

"Papa, your advice is often excellent."

"You are too kind. We both know that I have made many mistakes in my life."

"And you have not seen or heard from Jane since?"

"No. Mrs. Bennet visited her yesterday, as she said, and you have heard her report. We also received a note, but it was just about your visit, Lizzy, assuring us that they had plenty of room and were looking forward to seeing you. It is up to you to discover what is bothering Jane."

Elizabeth thought that her father could have made a greater effort. True, Jane had not explained to her father what was bothering her during her visit to Longbourn, which could be taken as proof that she did not plan to take him into her confidence – but Mr. Bennet could have taken the carriage and made the hour's trip to Netherfield, instead of expecting Elizabeth to travel for two days. It was like her father, she thought, to let others labor so that he could be left in peace. On the other hand, he had a point; *she* was the best person to speak to Jane. Furthermore, they were both married women now, with independent means; they should not depend on their parents. Most of all, if Jane was suffering, Elizabeth wanted to be with her. "Then it is time for me to see Jane," she said to her father. Elizabeth then left the library, and gave the orders to summon her coachman and her maid. She told her family that she would visit Longbourn frequently while she was in the area, then climbed into the Pemberley carriage and continued to Netherfield Park.

CHAPTER IV

It was a relief to leave the tumult of Longbourn and to arrive at the relative calm of Netherfield. Elizabeth was welcomed by everyone: affectionately by Jane; heartily by her brother-in-law Mr. Bingley; and with resigned politeness by Miss Bingley. They exchanged the usual queries about health and then Elizabeth was taken through the house. She had stayed once before at Netherfield, but that was before the marriage between her sister and Mr. Bingley. This time she had different and better rooms: the suite occupied by her husband when he visited Netherfield. But of most interest to Elizabeth was the newly outfitted nursery, and she admired its arrangements.

Civility demanded that Mr. and Miss Bingley both spend some time with Mrs. Darcy. Mr. Bingley did not seem to mind, but he did appear distracted and Elizabeth detected puffy dark circles beneath his eyes. For Caroline Bingley, the effort was more penance than pleasure, and her only genuine smile was when the clock struck five and they could move to their rooms in order to dress for dinner. Jane's options with respect to her wardrobe were few, so she joined Elizabeth in making her toilette, and when the maidservants were dismissed the sisters could indulge at last in a tête-à-tête.

"Lizzy – my dearest Lizzy, I am so glad that you have come."

"And, I, too, am happy to see you in such good health. But my visit is not merely social – I am concerned." Elizabeth showed the letter that she had received from their father, then inquired tenderly: "What is wrong, Jane? Are you unwell?"

Jane looked away for a moment as her lips trembled and she considered what to say. "I am well, or as well as any woman can be in my condition. But I will confess to you, because I know you will be discreet, that I am worried."

"Can you tell me the nature of the problem?"

Jane nodded. "Charles – Bingley – has been behaving strangely."

"How so?" asked Elizabeth.

Jane related how her husband had canceled an order for a horse, had been drinking several more glasses of wine than was his custom at dinner, and had not been sleeping well, instead pacing back and forth as if worrying about something. He had been irritable with Jane when she asked him about something for the nursery, and then had become downright angry when she had inquired what the matter was.

Elizabeth said she could not imagine the mild-tempered Bingley becoming angry with anyone, let alone his beloved wife.

"He raised his voice with me, Lizzy! I am not imagining it. He actually raised his voice, told me to stay out of things that do not concern me and even ordered me to get out of the room. And then he threw a book at one of the dogs – he did not hit her, but the book was damaged."

"That does not sound like Bingley."

"No, it does not, but what if his character has changed? I understand that marriage does that to some people, and that others are transformed when they become parents. Bingley has always been so sweet-tempered, that I have loved anticipating him as a father. No man could be gentler! In the past, when I have seen him upset, it was for a reason that has made me proud to be his wife. He was angry, once, when Mr. Hurst was curt with a scullery-maid. But what if I have been wrong? What if Bingley does not want to be a husband or a father? I could endure his being bad-tempered and cross with me, Lizzy – I am sure that many wives endure far, far worse – but what if he is unkind to our child after it is born? That I could not bear."

Elizabeth considered. "It sounds as if something is troubling him, something he does not want to share with you."

"It does, does it not? And that is distressing too! We are husband and wife; we are supposed to help and comfort one another, in both prosperity and adversity – but for some reason he will not talk to me. What secret could he have, so terrible that he could not tell me? Anything could be better than what I have been imagining."

"If he cannot confide in you, could he speak with someone else?"

"Who?"

"Darcy?" Elizabeth hazarded.

Jane hesitated. "Perhaps."

"I agree that confiding in you would be easier for most people than confiding in Darcy. My husband can be intimidating."

Jane gave a small smile. "That is true, while no one fears losing *my* good opinion. However, if Bingley believes that he has been a fool, or that he has been weak, then he could be reluctant, even ashamed, to confide in Darcy. He looks up to him so!"

"I love and esteem my husband, but it is not as if Darcy has never made an error of judgment himself. He is not infallible."

"I am sure of that, and although Bingley may agree with that statement on a rational basis, his feelings could prevent him from consulting his friend."

"You know your husband best, and as my husband is not here at present, we will have to find someone else. What about his sisters? Could he confide in either of them? It is difficult for me to imagine, but you know Bingley best."

Mr. Bingley's sisters, Miss Caroline Bingley and Mrs. Hurst, were neither of them especially sympathetic women, although it was possible, nay probable, that they were more likely to be kinder to their beloved brother than almost any other person, with the exception of each other. Again, Jane hesitated; over the past few months of living with Caroline, even she had learned to detect the occasional unkindness in her, and Mrs. Hurst was with her husband at their own house in London.

"What about turning to Papa? Could Mr. Bingley confide in him?"

Jane considered. "Perhaps. But if the problem is that Charles has fallen out of love with me, then the last person he will want to confide in – besides me, of course – would be my father."

"I am sure that Bingley is as much in love with you as ever, but even if it were true, Papa could give some advice about that," said Elizabeth. Mr. Bennet had been charmed by Miss Jane Gardiner's beauty and good humor before he proposed, only for him to discover her lack of restraint and weak understanding later.

"Lizzy, our parents are more content with each other than ever," said Jane, who, in her propensity to think well of everyone, did not take as dim a view of their parents' marriage as did her sister Elizabeth.

"Perhaps. You see them frequently, and I do not, so I will rely on your judgment. Besides, three of their vexations have been removed."

"Three of – you mean us, their daughters? If you speak this way you will make me think that Bingley *is* upset about the baby!"

Elizabeth responded seriously. "No, Jane. In our situation our parents had good reason to be concerned about our futures, because we were not well provided for, but now three of us are married, two advantageously. That would certainly be a reason why Mamma, at least, would be in a better humor now, and if her spirits are less irritable, then Papa's will be too. But this is not so for you and Bingley. His fortune is not entailed, is it?"

"No."

"Then let us continue. As I already said, but as I believe you need to hear again, it is simply not possible that Bingley has fallen out of love with you. No man in his right mind could do such thing, and although Bingley may be distressed about something, he is certainly in his right mind. But let us consider something else. Could Mr. Bingley be unwell? Could some physical ailment be causing him trouble?"

Jane reported that Bingley was drinking more wine, but she believed that was because he was perturbed, and not that the wine was perturbing him. He was eating less and sleeping less – Elizabeth confirmed that she had noticed new lines in his face and a puffiness around his eyes – but Jane had not noticed any injury or symptoms of sickness, such as fever or sneezing. And Mr. Bingley had not, as far as she knew, consulted one of the local apothecaries or a London doctor.

Elizabeth nodded and said that they would assume that his health was good for now, and only return to that if they exhausted every other possibility. Then she said, wishing there were a more delicate way to express it: "Could he have financial difficulties?"

Jane shook her head. "I have considered this, but I do not see how. I have reviewed our expenditures. And although we have spent a little more in making improvements to the nursery, we have not been at all extravagant. Nor has his income changed, either. I have looked over the letters from the bank from last month and there has been no diminution in either interest or principal."

"I am very glad to hear it," said Elizabeth. She had every confidence in Jane's comprehension of financial matters; as the eldest, Jane had assisted their father for years. "Now, forgive me some of these questions, but I feel as if I must ask them. Could Mr. Bingley be gambling?"

"Do not fear offending me, Lizzy; your questions can be no worse than the ones that I have been posing to myself. As for having gambling debts, I do not see how it is possible. We play cards sometimes in the evenings, and when the Wickhams were here, we wagered a little, but the amounts were always small. I know that men sometimes lie to their wives about such things, but Mr. Bingley has not been out at night with other friends. He has had no opportunity to lose a great sum."

"Very well. What about visitors? Letters? Has he received some troubling news?"

Jane reported that there had been no unusual visitors, and that when he had returned from making visits himself, either to their neighbors or even journeys to London, his mood had been excellent. She could not answer for *every* letter that had come into the house, but she admitted that she had gone into the library once when he was out and had carefully searched through the papers in his desk and had found nothing extraordinary.

"Perhaps he has some difficulty with one of his sisters or with Mr. Hurst? Could one of them be in debt?"

Jane paused. "I suppose that is possible. However, if it were Caroline, I would expect her temper to be affected, and in her I have noticed no difference. And as for the Hursts, I have seen no particular difficulties in the communications from them." She sighed. "I know you do not consider me suspicious enough in general, Lizzy, but I am telling you all that I know and have seen."

"I have every confidence in you. If nothing has happened recently, could Bingley be troubled by something from the past?"

"Such as?"

"That I do not know. Is anything different – other than his mood and his behavior? When did you detect a change in his behavior?"

Jane considered and said that it was about a fortnight after the departure of the Wickhams. And he had been at his most ill-tempered the day before she had burst into tears. "Do you have any notion as to what could be going on, Lizzy?"

"No, Jane, not yet."

"Then I am afraid he *has* fallen out of love with me."

"I do not know what is wrong, Jane, but I am sure that it is not that. Of all our conjectures, that strikes me as the least likely." Elizabeth took her sister's hand in her own. "We will determine what is the matter, and find a way to resolve it. You will see. Everything will be as it should be."

"Having you here is such a comfort!"

Their tête-à-tête was ended by a knock on the door; it was the guilty party himself, coming to tell them that they were wanted for the evening meal. The sisters had been talking a long time, and had failed to notice the hour. "I am sure that you both are hungry," said Mr. Bingley, offering his arm to his wife and assisting her down the stairs. Elizabeth followed, her mind full, wondering what could be distressing her brother-in-law.

CHAPTER V

During that evening and the morning of the next day, Elizabeth observed Mr. Bingley carefully. The opportunities were not so many, because Bingley did seem to be avoiding spending time with her and Jane. This could have been because he wanted to give her and Jane some time alone, a natural enough consideration given that the sisters had not seen each other for many months. Yet Elizabeth noted that he seemed distracted during dinner, failing twice to respond to her questions about a horse he had bought in the spring. She wondered if the simple explanation could be that he was going deaf – a circumstance that would certainly disturb the temper of a man so young and which could even cause him to raise his voice. She could imagine him not wanting to admit such an infirmity to Jane, especially not when a baby was coming and he did not want to worry her. Perhaps when hunting, a gun had fired too close to his head; Elizabeth had heard of this harming the hearing of some men.

That was her first theory. Elizabeth thought it extremely satisfactory, for it had the advantage of explaining much and blaming no one. Although it would cause some inconvenience to Jane and Bingley throughout the years, they would manage. Then someone dropped a pan in Mrs. Nicholls's kitchen, and everyone, including Bingley, started at the table, at which point Elizabeth decided regretfully that she would have to dismiss the notion. Besides, after further consideration she realized that Jane would certainly have noticed if Bingley's hearing were deficient. They had detected a little deafness frequently in their own father, although some of the occasions when he appeared not to hear could be explained by the habit he had formed of not listening to their mother.

Bingley made his excuses to leave the ladies alone, spending some time alone with his port after dinner, and then, after sitting with them a mere quarter of an hour, retreating to his library with several candles. This was unusual first because Bingley was generally quite sociable, and second because he was not a great reader. Yet he remained in the library almost the entire evening, apparently studying an old book. When the sun came up the next day he avoided them again, this time by wandering out of doors. It was a fine day, and so no excuse was needed for taking a walk – Elizabeth after so many hours in the carriage, absolutely needed some exercise and rejoiced in the flowers and the shrubbery – but Bingley turned when he saw, or rather, heard her approach, again disproving her little theory about his hearing.

On the other hand, Miss Caroline Bingley was not avoiding Jane and Elizabeth. Miss Bingley spent the morning with them, making inquiries about Pemberley and its inmates and with her acquaintance in Lambton. Elizabeth wondered a little at Miss Bingley's spending all her time with her and Jane, especially as Miss Bingley, Elizabeth was certain, disliked her as much as ever. But poor Miss Bingley had few other amusements available to her; she was not a great reader, nor an enthusiastic walker, and could only spend a few hours each day either practicing or sketching or horseback riding. Her own sister was in London, which meant that if she wished for companionship she had to settle for Jane and Jane's sisters. Elizabeth understood Miss Bingley's situation, and she pitied her, but she had not yet reached the point where she could honestly declare that she liked her. She found Miss Bingley's presence especially irksome as she wished to converse with Jane in private.

It was not till they were in the carriage again, this time traveling to Longbourn for tea, that Elizabeth was alone with Jane. She confirmed to Jane that she believed that Bingley *was* distressed by something. "I am so glad that I am not imagining it!" Jane exclaimed. However, beyond that comfort, Elizabeth could offer nothing except the idea about his losing his hearing – an idea that she had already rejected. Nevertheless, the subject was animating, even if they made no discoveries, and the time in the carriage passed quickly.

When Elizabeth and Jane descended from the Pemberley carriage, Mrs. Bennet made a renewed effort to treat her second daughter as an honored guest. Elizabeth was again given an excellent chair and offered the choicest dainties.

Mrs. Bennet asked if she had recovered from her trip. Mary and Mr. Bennet also appeared, but Kitty was out, which gave Mrs. Bennet the opportunity to complain about Kitty's tardiness.

"Where is she, Mamma?" Elizabeth inquired.

"Over at the Lucases. I do not know why she should favor them over her own family."

"Punctuality is a sign of respect and responsibility," observed Mary.

"Indeed it is, Mary, indeed it is," said Mrs. Bennet.

"It is not so very late," said the more tolerant Jane. "I am sure Kitty will be here soon."

"And there is no need to wait for her," said Mrs. Bennet, pouring out the tea. "Take this cup to Lizzy, Mary."

Mary protested that this task properly belonged to Kitty.

"But Kitty is not here!" Mrs. Bennet exclaimed.

"Do not trouble yourself, Mary," Elizabeth said, and in an effort to restore the family peace, rose to distribute the cups of tea herself. As she handed one to her father he observed that Mary managed to quarrel with Kitty even when she was absent.

"See?" Mrs. Bennet scolded Mary. "*Lizzy* does not consider the task above her. *She* does not make a fuss, even though she has dozens of servants waiting on her."

Mary appeared discomfited, while Elizabeth thought being held up as a paragon was not a good way to promote sisterly affection. "In truth I am glad to move a little," she said. "I am still stiff from the journey and I do not always have the opportunity to exercise."

"A little too much riches and respect, eh, Lizzy?" her father inquired slyly. "You did not expect that your marriage had any disadvantages."

"It is true that some aspects have surprised me," said Elizabeth, "but on the whole, Papa, I am very happy."

"I am glad to hear it," said Mr. Bennet. In a low voice he observed to his second daughter that Jane seemed more composed; Elizabeth nodded and indicated that she could not tell him more just then – but Mr. Bennet appeared content to let Elizabeth take care of Jane.

Mrs. Bennet said, "Of course you are happy, Lizzy, how could you not be happy? Not only are you richer than any of us, Darcy adores you, and you seem fond of him. And even if you did quarrel, Pemberley is so large that I am sure that you could avoid each other easily. Mary, if we could find such a man for you!"

"Mamma, let us change the subject," said Jane. As the eldest daughter, she had been the object of Mrs. Bennet's matchmaking efforts longer than any of her younger sisters, and she understood how mortifying they could be.

But Mrs. Bennet was not to be deflected. "Meryton does not have so many eligible men these days," and she went through the list. "So it is up to you, Jane, and to you, Lizzy, to find good husbands for your sisters. Mary would be best with a man who is fond of music but who does not care for dancing. Am I not right, Mary?" Mrs. Bennet did not wait to hear whether Mary agreed or not, and continued: "What about that cousin of Mr. Darcy's, Lizzy? The younger son of that earl? Does he care for music?"

"Colonel Fitzwilliam," said Elizabeth. She struggled to keep from smiling, for she could not imagine the colonel falling in love with either Mary or Kitty. "Colonel Fitzwilliam does care for music, but I believe he is interested in another young lady."

"What a pity," said Mrs. Bennet, relinquishing her claim on the young man whom she had only seen once in her life, at her daughter's nuptials. "Well, if Colonel Fitzwilliam's romance does not work out, you must introduce him to Mary. Music is balm to a broken heart. And Lizzy, you and Jane have to do better. It is your responsibility to find husbands for your sisters!"

"And what would *you* do, Mrs. Bennet, if they took over this project of yours?" inquired Mr. Bennet.

But Mrs. Bennet was spared having to answer her husband by the arrival of her fourth daughter. "Kitty! Where have you been?" she demanded. "How can you linger at Lucas Lodge when you know that your sisters are calling?"

Kitty would normally have been perturbed by such a remonstrance, but on this occasion she had an answer ready. "Because at the Lucases, there was such news! Have you heard? Mary King is dead!"

CHAPTER VI

Miss Mary King was a young lady whom the Bennet girls had often encountered at the Meryton assembly, a dance held once a month in the town (a pitiful affair since the departure of a regiment more than a year ago, when the hall had been brightened by officers in their redcoats). Miss King, small and freckled, had never been a general favorite, especially not compared to the Bennets, considered the local beauties. Then Miss King had inherited ten thousand pounds from her grandfather, drawing the attention of some of the lieutenants, a turn of events that had caused much grief to the Bennets, whose romantic expectations at the time had been rather bleak. But the improved circumstances of the Bennet daughters – Mrs. Bingley and Mrs. Darcy in particular – made even Mrs. Bennet more charitable towards other young ladies – especially as Miss King's death meant she was no longer competing for the few eligible single men.

The news was so startling and unexpected that everyone turned to look at Kitty. In her eagerness to hear the news, Mrs. Bennet herself brought her tardy daughter some tea and told Mary to make room for Kitty on the sofa – Mary was too dumbfounded to protest – and Kitty, the center of attention, sat down.

"Miss King is dead! How terrible!" said Jane.

Mrs. Bennet had a flood of questions. "Why, what happened? Was she ill? I never heard that she was ill. Has anyone else fallen ill? Perhaps we should send a note to Mr. Jones!"

"Was it an accident?" asked Elizabeth.

Mrs. Bennet shook her head. "You are right, Lizzy, it must have been an accident. The carriage I saw her in last week – it did not look safe – and the coachman had shifty eyes."

"You are all wrong. You will never guess!"

Mr. Bennet said, "If you tell us, Kitty, we will not have to guess."

"Very well," said Kitty. "Mary King, Lady Lucas says, took her own life!"

The others exclaimed in horror. Mrs. Bennet was the loudest, while Mary said something gloomy about the terrible sin of suicide. Even Jane, Elizabeth and Mr. Bennet, the more rational members of the family, were shocked. Jane wondered how it was possible that Mary King, a young woman who seemed to have everything to live for, who had inherited ten thousand pounds two years ago, making her one of the richest young ladies in Meryton, who had recently become betrothed to a young man from Liverpool, could be so desperately miserable as to kill herself, while Mr. Bennet remarked, rather sadly, that one never really knew people, and that they were always full of surprises. Elizabeth, however, doubted. "Is it certain that she took her own life? Absolutely certain?"

Kitty eagerly shared the details that had been imparted to her. First of all, there was a note from Miss King, directed to Mr. Selby, the man she had been supposed to marry. The note was short, explaining that she loved him but she could not marry him; that she would never make him happy. Second, Mary King had taken belladonna, purchased, not from Mr. Jones, the local apothecary, but during her last trip to London. A bill of sale had been found.

"But why? Why would she never make him happy?" inquired Elizabeth. "And if that were so, it sounds like a reason for *him* to take his life, but not for *her* to take hers!"

But Kitty could not supply a more satisfactory explanation. "Perhaps Mr. Selby no longer wanted to marry her, and she could not face life without him," said Kitty, but her only argument for making this suggestion was that her friend Maria Lucas had told her that Miss King had been violently in love with Mr. Selby. After several minutes of speculation, they realized their curiosity could only be satisfied with additional information.

"How did the Lucases learn all this?" asked Elizabeth.

Miss King's maidservant Hannah had discovered the dead Miss King in the early afternoon, when she had come to work after her morning off. The distraught maidservant, not knowing what to do or where to go, had hurried to beg for assistance at the Philips's house, as Mr. Philips was Miss King's attorney. Lady Lucas had happened to be calling on Mrs. Philips when Hannah arrived to make her desperate report.

Mrs. Bennet expressed her displeasure at Lady Lucas's learning the information before her. The Bennet females were at a constant disadvantage with respect to the Lucases regarding rumor and gossip, for Sir William Lucas enjoyed society while Mr. Bennet preferred solitude. And in this situation, as Mrs. Philips was *her* sister, Mrs. Bennet felt that *she* should definitely have learned this information before her neighbors.

"It is most unlucky," Mr. Bennet soothed his wife, "but I am certain that your sister will call on you soon and give you fresh details that you can impart to Lady Lucas."

The conversation of the Bennet daughters remained fixed on wondering why the young lady could have taken her own life. Jane was still shocked that anyone that they knew could be so desperate, and Mary was horrified by what this deed would mean to the fate of Miss King's immortal soul.

Mrs. Bennet changed the subject to a more practical one, and wondered if Mr. Selby was in need of consolation. All her daughters remonstrated, especially Elizabeth. "Mamma, it is far too soon to consider such a thing. The man must be grieving terribly."

Mrs. Bennet would have dismissed any suggestion like this from Miss Elizabeth Bennet, but she was more likely to listen, or at least *appear* to listen, to Mrs. Darcy. "Perhaps, Lizzy, you are right. Far from me to appear tactless. Although it would comfort him, at the right time, and life should be lived; we should make merry while we can. What do we know of Mr. Selby? Does he have a good estate? Of course, he is in Liverpool so we may never even meet him. I will have to call on my sister."

Mr. Bennet could not tolerate more discussion on the topic of suitors and removed himself to his library to escape it. Elizabeth and Jane looked at the time and realized that their visit had lasted long enough. They ordered the carriage, then bade their parents and sisters farewell for the day.

"What troubling news!" Elizabeth exclaimed as Wilson turned the carriage into the lane.

"Yes, it is," Jane agreed, and turned her face toward the window.

They passed by several houses, and Elizabeth wondered if any of their occupants were contemplating suicide. Perhaps, as her father had observed, one never knew other people as well as one believed.

In the dim light of the carriage, it took her several minutes to realize that tears were slipping down Jane's face. But when she did, she expressed concern. "Jane, were you particular friends with Mary King? I am so sorry."

"I am grieved about Miss King, of course, but these tears are not for her."

Elizabeth wondered if Jane's condition was making her more likely to weep, as her mother had maintained. Aloud, however, she said, as gently as she could: "Then is there a particular reason? Can you tell me about it?"

"What if – what if Bingley is so melancholic that he takes his life?"

CHAPTER VII

Elizabeth did her best to reassure her sister that Bingley was unlikely to kill himself. "He is a man with everything to live for," she told Jane warmly. "He is also a good man and a responsible man. He would never do that to you, Jane. Never!"

"But who could have ever thought that Mary King would take her life? She also seemed to have everything to live for. Can we ever know whether another person is truly happy?"

Although Elizabeth had had similar thoughts just moments before, she was quick to deny them. "We cannot know what is going on with distant acquaintances, perhaps, but Bingley is not a distant acquaintance. He is your husband, and he loves you. And what do he and Mary King have in common? They barely knew each other."

"They have danced together."

"That is not enough to make them both suicidal," Elizabeth said. With cheerful, confident, reassuring conversation, she was able to stop Jane's tears long before they reached Netherfield, where they were greeted by its master and his sister.

"At last!" exclaimed Bingley. "I feared that something had happened to the carriage."

"I was not afraid," said Miss Bingley, "for I know that Eliza could walk here if necessary."

Elizabeth was known for her love of long walks, and in the past had used her feet when a carriage was not available – an independent tendency that Miss Bingley had formerly dismissed as country town indifference to decorum.

"But Jane could not walk so far," said Mr. Bingley, offering his arm to his lady. His concern was reassuring to both his wife and his sister-in-law.

"As you see, we are in good health, and there is nothing wrong with the carriage or the horses."

"So have all the clocks in Longbourn stopped?" inquired Miss Bingley. "Did someone push over the sundial? Or was there another reason for the delay?"

Jane and Elizabeth explained that they had heard some shocking news, and after reassuring Mr. Bingley that nothing had happened to anyone at

Longbourn, the sisters related what they had heard about the death of Mary King. As in every other house in the neighborhood, the circumstances of her death were discussed that evening in Netherfield. Of their party, Mr. Bingley seemed most affected, possibly because he was the most tender-hearted among those present. "She was a pleasant young woman," he said, with a sigh. "I remember dancing with her."

"I barely recall her at all," said Miss Bingley, least touched by the matter. "It seems rather cowardly, does it not, to take one's own life?"

Jane observed her husband at these words, while Elizabeth in turn watched Jane watching Bingley.

"We cannot know what distressed her so," said Bingley.

"It is a pity," Elizabeth said, "that anything could be so terrible that she could not confide in a friend or a relative." She thought Bingley looked conscious at these words, although in the flickering candlelight it was not easy to distinguish expressions.

Jane pressed the point. "I was not well acquainted with Miss King," she said, "so I cannot judge her. I can only hope that anyone I know well – family member or friend – would feel free to come to me with any problems and have the confidence that I would listen sympathetically."

Bingley took his wife's hand and kissed it. "No one familiar with you, Jane, could doubt that you would listen with a generous and understanding heart."

Jane was fatigued, so she retired early, and Elizabeth likewise made her excuses. Jeanette prepared her for the night, then Elizabeth went to bed early herself, her head full of the day's conversations and events. After observing Bingley's gallantry towards Jane, Elizabeth was sanguine that all would now be well between Mr. and Mrs. Bingley. She was less confident, alas, that *she* would learn what the matter was, for Bingley could demand Jane's discretion in the matter. Elizabeth felt that she deserved to discover his secret, for she had traveled from Pemberley to Netherfield to be supportive of her sister.

"But I cannot importune Jane. If she is content, I will attempt to be as well."

These thoughts, and the troubling ones about poor Mary King, did not keep her awake long. Elizabeth slept well and woke refreshed and was outside before breakfast, enjoying the sunshine, the chirping birds and even her impatience. She had to wait till the others had risen and breakfasted before she could manage a moment alone with her sister. Miss Bingley was practicing the pianoforte – her disciplined dedication reminded Elizabeth of how much she had neglected her instrument since her marriage – Mr. Bingley was conversing with one of the gardeners, and Elizabeth and Jane sat together in a corner of the drawing room.

"You are smiling this morning, Jane," Elizabeth observed.

"It is terrible of me, I know. Poor Miss King!"

"But has Bingley told you what is troubling him?" And, with great self-command, she added: "There is no need to tell me if it is confidential. I assure you, that I can respect and understand that. However, if you wish to share – if it would ease your heart – I can assure you of my discretion."

"Dearest Lizzy!"

Elizabeth waited for her sister to continue, and assumed that the silence was due to Jane's putting her thoughts in order. But when Jane still said nothing, Elizabeth said, "Very well, I will content myself with your happiness. That should be enough."

"I would tell you if I knew anything, but Bingley has not informed me of any deep, dark secret. But last night he was so much more like himself that my heart is lighter."

"I suppose I should be glad that he seems to have no deep, dark secrets," said Elizabeth. "But are you certain nothing is distressing him?"

"He admitted something has been troubling him, but that it is of no consequence – he heard something distressing about someone he knew in the past, but the death of Miss King has shocked him into thinking about the present and the future."

"I see. And that is all?"

"Yes, Lizzy, that is all."

Elizabeth both admired and was vexed by Jane's lack of curiosity, for as Bingley had not confided in Jane, Elizabeth could not persuade Jane to confide in her. Even though she had been convincing herself that she would be content with ignorance, the serenity that Jane appeared to achieve so easily was only a matter of aspiration for Elizabeth.

Elizabeth decided to put temptation out of the way by changing the topic, returning to the unexpected demise of Miss King, which had also provoked her curiosity. The conversation at Netherfield centered on the practical: should they make a condolence call? If so, on whom? Miss King's local family was deceased – as a girl she had lived with her grandfather; it was from him that she had inherited her money – and although she had had an uncle in Liverpool, they had never met him, nor did they have his address. The fact that her death was a suicide made even the composition of a letter of sympathy a challenge.

But Elizabeth had a solution. Her first duties on a visit such as this were to her parents and to her sister, but she was staying with Jane and yesterday they had called at Longbourn. Now it was appropriate for her to make other calls. She would visit Mrs. Philips and Lady Lucas, both meriting attention, as Mrs. Philips was her aunt and Lady Lucas a neighbor of many years, and who were likely, given their positions, personalities and husbands, to have the most current information available.

"Oh, yes, Lizzy, do call on Aunt Philips," Jane agreed. "I know that she longs to see you."

Elizabeth went alone in the carriage, as Jane, despite her improved spirits, preferred to stay at home. Elizabeth told her coachman that the first stop would be at her aunt's in Meryton and that afterwards they would cross the bridge to visit Lucas Lodge.

Mrs. Philips greeted her niece affectionately but was particularly distracted, as Mr. Philips, Miss King's attorney, was still dealing with the awful details.

"We do not even know where she is to be buried," lamented Mrs. Philips. "The vicar says that she has to be buried on the north side of the church – a suicide, you know – but that it is extremely inconvenient because of the shrubbery. The service, too, will have to be amended. Still, we cannot put the body just anywhere! What are we supposed to do, leave it in a field? If we were on a ship we could put the body in a shroud and throw it overboard – I've heard that is what they do at sea, because at sea north and south do not matter."

Elizabeth thought that north and south, as well as east and west, were of paramount importance at sea, but she did not dispute the point. "So it was definitely suicide," Elizabeth remarked.

"It seems so, but Miss King cannot have been in her right mind, to kill herself like that. I saw her just two weeks ago – I introduced her to Mrs. Smith – and she seemed a little pale and thin, but I thought it was just because she was anxious about her upcoming nuptials. Poor thing, she did not have a mother to advise her."

"So no one knows why she took her life?"

Mrs. Philips confirmed that they did not, not completely, but this morning Mr. Philips had received a letter from Miss King's London bankers, actually sent before Miss King had died, requesting Mr. Philips to speak to Miss King and to ask her why she was withdrawing such large sums of cash.

"Large sums of cash?" repeated Elizabeth.

"Yes, a vast quantity, according to Miss King's banker. Unfortunately the letter arrived too late for Mr. Philips to give any advice to poor Miss King," said Mrs. Philips.

Mrs. Philips added that her information ought to be treated as confidential and it ought not to be repeated to anyone, although she had already told her sister, so if Elizabeth wished to discuss it with her mother, that would make no difference.

If, by the end of the day there were any people in Meryton who did not know these details, thought Elizabeth, it would be because they were either deaf or babes in arms. She did learn some additional information from her aunt. Mr. Selby, Miss King's bereaved betrothed, had been invited to Meryton to settle her affairs; Mr. Philips was suggesting that he stay at the Meryton Inn.

"Poor Mr. Selby," Elizabeth murmured sympathetically.

Mrs. Philips agreed that he had to be suffering terribly. She also had a second dilemma. She had planned to hold a little reception in her niece's honor; given the death of poor Miss King, should she proceed? "How long will you be at Netherfield, Lizzy?"

Elizabeth said the duration of her visit was yet unknown, but she imagined that she would wait to make sure that Jane was in no danger.

"Then I should wish to have it sooner rather than later – I have already consulted with the butcher and the bakers – in three days' time – but will that be insensitive?"

"If you invite me, I will come," Elizabeth assured her aunt.

Mrs. Philips expressed her satisfaction and said she would now issue other invitations. She also hoped the others at Netherfield would attend as well.

Elizabeth said she could not speak for the others. Jane might not be well, and Mr. Bingley would not leave his wife alone in her situation. As for Miss Bingley, Elizabeth doubted very much that she would wish to attend the evening party in the apartment of a Meryton attorney, especially not a reception held for Mrs. Darcy, but *this* she did not say to her aunt.

Mrs. Philips understood the reasons for her niece's caution, but requested her to convey her hopes anyway. Elizabeth then ordered the carriage, kissed her aunt, and then proceeded to Lucas Lodge where she was greeted with the friendly formality of Sir William Lucas and all of the family who was at home. The Lucases, as usual, were ready to talk. Sir William made his customary compliments, saying that with Mrs. Darcy back in the neighborhood, the brightest jewel had returned to Hertfordshire, and desiring to know if, since her marriage, she had been presented at St. James. Lady Lucas welcomed her with pleasure, and Elizabeth was delighted to see that Maria Lucas was blooming with health and good looks. The other sons and daughters also joined in the rather crowded drawing-room.

After Sir William informed Elizabeth that they expected Mr. and Mrs. Collins and their little boy to visit the following week – "how fortunate that you and your friend will be here at the same time!" – the topic of conversation switched naturally to the death of Miss King. For many years, Maria Lucas had been a particular friend of Mary King, so all the Lucases were distressed by the sad event. Maria was willing to share all she could about Miss King. She reported that Miss King had never appeared to suffer from melancholy, except when her mother had been ill, but that had been several years ago. She had been a little crossed in love now and then, but that was in the past, so could also not explain her swallowing a lethal dose of belladonna. The last few months she had had an expectation for a lifetime of happiness.

"Here is the last letter she ever sent me," said Maria. "That is, besides a note or two, arranging to meet. Feel free to read it, Mrs. Darcy."

Elizabeth unfolded the small, hot-pressed sheets and read the letter with curiosity, its uneven writing making the sentences look like waves on the page. It was dated several months ago and reported that Miss King had met a Mr. Selby at a concert in Liverpool, and then he had escorted her and another friend to a lecture. Mr. Selby was not especially handsome and he was rather conservative in his views, but that meant that he seemed, to her, steady and sensible. "Handsome men are not to be trusted," wrote Miss King, and Elizabeth knew that Miss King was referring to George Wickham, who had courted her after her grandfather's death. "But I feel as if I can rely on Mr. Selby. Moreover, he is in line to a baronetcy, not directly, but it is not impossible, for his cousin is extremely reckless. Imagine my being a Lady!"

Miss King came to life in these few words. It was shocking to realize that she was dead.

Elizabeth returned the letter to Maria Lucas. "I grieve for you, Maria."

Maria, who had not been close to Mary King for at least a year, murmured something unintelligible that seemed to express her thanks for Mrs. Darcy's sympathy.

Even though it was indelicate, Elizabeth — who did not have Jane's reticence — brought up the subject of Mary King's missing fortune. She attempted to introduce it in the mildest manner possible (she was not her mother either): "Have you heard that Mary King withdrew a large portion of her fortune? How is that even possible?"

The Lucases *were* aware of this, as Sir William Lucas had called on Mr. Philips this morning. Maria said that for exact figures Elizabeth would have to turn to her uncle Philips, who surely had the particulars, but Maria still had some information to give. When Miss King first inherited the ten thousand pounds from her late grandfather, she had invited Maria Lucas to lunch frequently, and had often made small presents, such as gloves and bonnets and lace. But these last few weeks — Miss King had returned to Meryton from her uncle's in Liverpool in order to settle some business before her wedding, and also because she had a favorite dressmaker in the town and she wanted her to prepare her trousseau — Miss King had not invited Maria to any lunches, nor had she given her any presents, and when Maria had last seen Miss King, only a week ago, Miss King had seemed exhausted, as if she were not sleeping.

"Perhaps she had doubts about her betrothed? Perhaps she had concerns about the character of Mr. Selby?" inquired Elizabeth.

But if Miss King had had these doubts, she had not shared them with Maria Lucas. And if that *had* been the case, it would have been far more practical for Miss King to have ended the engagement instead of her life, thought Elizabeth. The fact that she had left him the remainder of her fortune seemed to indicate that she had not been plagued by doubts regarding Mr. Selby.

Maria Lucas had given the substance of what she could contribute, but the Lucases were not ready to abandon the interesting topic. With little new to be said, all anyone could offer were generalities, repetitions and elaborations. Elizabeth noticed a tendency to exaggerate the importance of Miss King in their lives – which, for all of them save Maria, had really been very slight.

"A very sad business," said Sir William. "Before Miss King moved to Liverpool, my son was thinking of courting her."

"Father, please," said the eldest son, either because he did not want the past recalled – or because it was not true.

"Very well, no more of that," said the patriarch agreeably.

Elizabeth offered sympathy to Lady Lucas, as Lady Lucas had been with her aunt Philips when the discovery of the body was reported.

"Yes, it gave me quite a turn! So shocking, to see such a thing!"

"You mean you actually saw Miss King's body?" inquired Elizabeth, surprised that *this* had not been mentioned before.

"No, no, I suppose I did not, but with all this talk, I feel as if I had. Just a few houses away, you know, and if I had gone with Mr. Philips and Miss King's maid I *would* have seen where she died – where she took her own life."

Lady Lucas's readiness to embellish what she had actually experienced cast doubt on much of what Elizabeth had heard, but Sir William treated his wife with as much solicitude as if Lady Lucas actually had discovered Miss King's body herself. But when they had reached this level of speculation, Elizabeth decided it was wise to change the subject. "Do you know how long Mr. and Mrs. Collins will be staying?"

The Lucases informed her that Mr. Collins would only remain a day or two, as he wished to be back in Hunsford in order to read the Sunday service, so that Lady Catherine de Bourgh would not be discommoded by a substitute, but Mrs. Collins planned to remain several weeks. Lady Lucas was worried about the journey for her daughter and her grandson. "To travel with an infant is no easy thing," said Lady Lucas, while Sir Williams was certain that they would manage.

"Sir William, you do not comprehend the difficulty," said Lady Lucas.

"It is much easier than having us all go there," said the eldest son, for there were many Lucases, and conveying all of them to Kent was impracticable.

"You are right, Will," Sir William said to his son, "our carriage could never hold so many," and then to his wife he said, "and you are absolutely correct, my dear — we men do not always appreciate the hardships you ladies endure, with caring for children and putting up with husbands."

His charm soothed his lady's feelings. Elizabeth said that she looked forward to seeing Mrs. Collins and her little boy, and then — with less honesty, but earnest civility — that she hoped she would be able to see her cousin Mr. Collins while he was here, but that she would understand if he were too busy given the brevity of his visit.

"Oh! I am sure that Mr. Collins will call on *you*, Mrs. Darcy," said Lady Lucas. "You are, after all, the niece by marriage of his patroness."

"And undoubtedly, Mr. Bingley will be interested in hearing Mr. Collins's advice about fatherhood," added Sir William. "Great changes are coming to Netherfield! What a day of joy that will be! Although my lady will remind me that the event also comes with dangers, which ought not to be trivialized."

All the Lucases joined in their best wishes for the health and safety of Mrs. Bingley during the next few weeks, at which point Elizabeth, feeling as if her calls had lasted long enough, ordered the carriage and returned to Netherfield.

CHAPTER VIII

The next few days were enlivened only by minor amusements. It rained frequently, and even when it paused the skies threatened, discouraging most exercise. Miss Bingley played the pianoforte, and occasionally Elizabeth did the same. Miss Bingley sketched, Elizabeth read, and Jane did needlework. Mr. Bingley's uneven mood returned. He paced back and forth in his library. He practiced at billiards, and when he played poorly, complained vehemently. At one point he said he was ordering the carriage to go to London and then changed his mind. When they sat down to cards he was so distracted that he forgot which suit was trump, and then abruptly quit both the game and the room.

"We cannot play at whist with only three," said Miss Bingley. "Jane, do you mind if I open the instrument?"

Jane said she would welcome some music, and Miss Bingley, after inviting Elizabeth to precede her, an invitation declined by Elizabeth, sat down at the pianoforte.

Jane put away the cards. "Something troubles him," she said, keeping her voice low.

"He may have told you that it is something in the past, but whatever it was, it is obviously not forgotten," said Elizabeth. "Only when you discover what it is will you be able to truly help him." She was concerned for her sister, but at least now she believed that *her* curiosity on the matter had a better chance of being answered.

The next day, the rain was not so fierce, and the dullness of Netherfield was broken by a visit from Mrs. Bennet and her daughter Kitty. Even Miss Bingley was so tired of being cooped up within doors that she willingly joined them and partook of the conversation.

Mrs. Bennet and her daughter had brought more details about the demise of Miss King. The unfortunate had been buried in the north side of the local church. They also reported that Mr. Philips was advising Mr. Selby, who was now staying at the Meryton Inn. Furthermore, Hannah, the maidservant who had discovered Miss King's dead body, was being questioned because all of Miss King's jewelry, and even her jewelry case, were missing.

"Miss King had a lovely pair of amber earrings set in gold," said Kitty. "Her hair was reddish, but those earrings were very pretty. She had a gold cross, too, and a chain to go with it."

They all agreed that it was dreadful to contemplate that anyone could steal a cross, but Mrs. Bennet opined that if a thief was a thief, well, the thief was a thief. "But I cannot imagine what that girl Hannah would *do* with the jewelry. A woman of her station could not wear such things, and how could she sell them? No one would take such things from her without questioning her and wondering where she got them."

"I have heard that there are ways to sell such ill-gotten goods," said Miss Bingley. "Disreputable shops, managed by men who do not ask any questions. This Hannah could not expect to be compensated for what an item was worth, of course, but she could make a pretty penny."

Everyone stared at Miss Bingley, and Mr. Bingley asked her exactly how she had come by such information.

"Louisa told me," said Miss Bingley, referring to their sister. "Mrs. Hurst discovered that one of the jewelers that she had visited was engaged in these practices. He would purchase stolen items of jewelry, reset the stones so that no one could recognize them, and resell them. They were usually stolen by members of the lower class – maidservants, manservants, and so on."

They discussed this for a while, then Elizabeth inquired: "Yet is it certain, absolutely certain, that Hannah took Miss King's jewels?"

"Who else could it be?" asked Mrs. Bennet. "She is the one who discovered the body. She is the one who had the opportunity. And as Miss King's maidservant, Hannah would have known exactly where the jewels were kept."

Kitty, however, raised some objections. "But, Mamma, you know that Mr. Philips and Mr. Selby did not find the jewelry or the case in Hannah's room, so there is no actual proof. It seems that Mr. Selby gave the case to Miss King himself, so he would have recognized it, if it had been found."

"So she hid it somewhere else," said Mrs. Bennet. "With a friend, perhaps, or the men did not find it because they did not know how to search through a woman's possessions."

"Poor Hannah," remarked Jane. "Even if she took the jewels, it may have only been out of concern for her future."

Miss Bingley was appalled. "Jane, please! Your sweet nature does you credit, but how can you have sympathy for a thief?"

Mr. Bingley defended his wife. "We do not know that Hannah is a thief. She may have been falsely accused. And in that case, I also have sympathy for her, Caroline."

Although Elizabeth rather agreed with Miss Bingley in her suspicion of the maidservant, Elizabeth was pleased to see her brother-in-law speak so warmly on the subject, especially in defense of his wife. She also recalled a prediction that her father had once made: that all the Bingleys' servants would cheat them and hoped that, contrary to so much of her own experience, that Jane's and Bingley's confidence in the goodness of human nature would be justified. Then another idea occurred to her. "Was not Miss King having financial difficulties? Is it possible that she disposed of her jewelry and her case herself in order to raise cash?"

Mr. Bingley was particularly struck by this suggestion. The others, save Mrs. Bennet, conceded it was possible, but Mrs. Bennet raised objections. "And what could Miss King have spent her money on but jewelry and other fine things? She did not need her money to live on; she had a home with her uncle in Liverpool, and she had her grandfather's house here. It would not make sense to sell what she had, presumably for less, in order to purchase other jewelry and fine things. Besides, Mr. Selby had made her a present of a jewelry case, and she was just about to marry him! Do you think Miss King would part with that?"

Elizabeth admitted that her mother had a point.

"I barely knew Miss King," said Miss Bingley, in a tone that suggested that she did not regret this, "but others did, and they may be able to report the last time that they saw her wearing her favorite jewels – the earrings that you mentioned, Miss Kitty, or the cross?"

No one in the Netherfield drawing-room had met with Miss King recently enough to report on the jewelry that she had been wearing, but Kitty said that Maria Lucas might know more. "Those amber earrings were very elegant," Kitty remarked. "I wonder how much a pair like those would cost. Do you know, Mamma?"

As Mrs. Bennet could not recall the earrings in question, she could not know, but she told Kitty that she would have to ask her father for the funds herself, unless she wanted to pay for them out of her allowance.

Elizabeth decided that the next time she wished to make a present to Kitty, she would remember to consider earrings as a possibility, while Miss Bingley raised her eyebrows at the tenor of the discussion.

Miss Bingley was fortunate. The clock on the mantelpiece sounded and Mrs. Bennet realized that if she wanted to be at Longbourn in time for dinner, that she needed to leave immediately – and besides, she could continue scolding Kitty on the way home, if she so chose. She ordered the carriage and then said: "I hope it becomes dry before my sister's reception. You will attend, Lizzy, will you not? My sister is counting on you. Mr. Bennet and I will not be there, but Kitty and even Mary should be."

Elizabeth confirmed that she had every intention of attending Aunt Philips's party, while Jane said that she would attempt to go, but her condition sometimes made evening parties a little difficult. Miss Bingley simply smiled and said nothing. Mr. Bingley said that he had business up in London, business that unfortunately could not wait – even though he had been postponing it all week.

CHAPTER IX

The following day was dry. Mr. Bingley went up to London, on business that he wished to complete before the child was born. He would stay with his other sister and her husband, Mr. and Mrs. Hurst.

The ladies of Netherfield Park gathered to wish him well before his journey.

"I am glad you are here while I am gone, Elizabeth. You are good company for Jane."

"And what am I?" inquired his sister.

"You are also good company for Jane," said her brother diplomatically. "Between the two of you, I expect to find her in perfect health upon my return – which should be some time tomorrow."

Jane told him to give her love to Louisa, and told him to be careful. They stood on the steps and waved goodbye.

"Do you know what his business is?" Elizabeth inquired, as they returned inside.

"I assume that he is negotiating the purchase," said Miss Bingley.

"Purchase? Of an estate? Where?" Elizabeth demanded.

"I thought Charles wrote to Darcy about it. Did Mr. Darcy not tell you?" inquired Miss Bingley, delighted by Elizabeth's obvious ignorance in the matter. Elizabeth felt her cheeks redden.

But Jane explained. "Lizzy, you know that Charles has long planned to make a purchase, just as his father intended it before he died. There is an estate under consideration, but its purchase is by no means certain, as so many questions remain open – whether or not the heir will sell and whether or not we can come to terms. With negotiations so delicate, we have not wished to talk about it – what if Mamma were to learn that we wish to move? She would be seriously displeased, and possibly for naught."

"I understand," said Elizabeth, and she did, but she was not happy to learn that she had been excluded from the confidence in this matter while Miss Bingley had not. Then she mentally scolded herself for being so silly: Miss Bingley was living with Jane and Bingley, which meant that these negotiations could not be concealed from her even had they wished to do so. As for Bingley's correspondence with Darcy on the subject, the details could have been so trivial as to not make Darcy mention it – or he could have assumed that Jane would have written on the subject and that Elizabeth's knowledge was more complete than his. And Jane, naturally reticent, would be reluctant to write down her hopes when a matter was not a *fait accompli*. "Indeed I do," she reiterated, with such warmth that she convinced her listeners and almost convinced herself.

Miss Bingley, disappointed that Elizabeth was not more disappointed, excused herself, while Elizabeth and Jane seated themselves in the drawing-room and Elizabeth asked for more information about the estate under consideration. Jane explained that Rushburn Manor was in a county that neighbored Derbyshire – Elizabeth exclaimed that it would be wonderful to have Jane so close – but that Jane was by no means so sanguine about the purchase.

"Could that be the reason behind Bingley's bad temper?" asked Elizabeth. "Because he wishes to make the purchase, and because it seems unlikely to happen?"

Jane did not think so. "We told ourselves that we would not expect it, so if we are disappointed, we would not be downcast."

"Jane, just because a person, even Bingley, declares that he will not be distressed by something, that does not mean that he really will not. The desire for self-command is admirable, but few achieve self-command easily, no matter how earnestly it is wished. Disappointment on this matter could distress Bingley more than you realize."

Jane considered Elizabeth's words. "I believe that you are correct in general, Lizzy, for I recall how difficult it was for me to master my own temper when I believed that Bingley did not love me."

"Dear Jane! *You* were never ill-tempered."

"But Rushburn Manor is not the only estate that is expected to be eligible soon. The London agent informed us that there were several families who plan to sell over the next few years. Finally, Bingley made it clear that his being out of sorts was due to something in the past, not the present or the future."

Elizabeth doubted. She believed that a man could profoundly desire to purchase an estate before his children were born, and that such a desire could make him ill-tempered if thwarted. However, she said: "Your superior knowledge of your husband prevents me from disagreeing."

Jane continued. "Besides, despite what Caroline says, I do not think that Bingley's trip to London today has anything to with the purchase of Rushburn, for the agent informed us that he would be touring properties in the north during the next few weeks."

Elizabeth was certainly open to the possibility that Miss Bingley could be wrong. She introduced another idea. "Perhaps he is arranging a surprise for you or the child."

Jane appreciated this happy notion, although she thought it would be better if Bingley consulted her first. "Still, if it is not too extravagant I will not complain."

The day was fine. Jane took a nap shortly after noon, so that she would have strength to go to the Philips's that evening. "I grow fatigued so easily!" During that period both Miss Bingley and Elizabeth decided to walk in the Netherfield Park shrubbery. They had not intended to walk with each other but then they discovered they were both heading in the same direction, limited to a gravel walk by the mud in most of the paths. So they endured, somewhat unwillingly, a half hour together – even though Miss Bingley encouraged Elizabeth to overtake her if she wished. "Please, Eliza, if you wish to walk ahead, do not let my languid pace detain you." But Elizabeth was a little fatigued herself – too many days without exercise, she thought – and they civilly conversed about the weather, the path, and new fashions. They were both happier when they returned to the house.

Although Miss Bingley had seemed perfectly well in the morning, by the time they needed to dress in order to go to Mr. and Mrs. Philips's, she had developed a terrible headache. "I do not know what has overcome me," she said. "Perhaps I took too much exercise."

Elizabeth suppressed a smile, for their exertion had been very little, but Jane was sympathetic. "Of course, Caroline; you should stay home and rest. Lizzy and I will give your excuses to Mrs. Philips."

"Miss Bingley has developed a most opportune headache," said Elizabeth, after she and Jane were both settled in the Pemberley carriage.

"Yes, very convenient," agreed Jane. "Except this morning I heard her tell her maid that there was no reason to prepare her evening dress, and that she certainly would not be leaving the house today."

Elizabeth laughed.

"And I warned Nicholls this morning that she would most likely be expected to prepare Miss Bingley's favorite supper this evening. You do not feel slighted, do you? Miss Bingley would not have enjoyed herself much at my aunt's, whereas we will be with family. The hours which will fly by for us would seem long to her."

Elizabeth assured her dearest sister that she was not the least offended by Miss Bingley's choosing to stay at home. Why should she be affronted, when it was an arrangement that suited everyone? She remarked on its being a fine, warm evening, and the fact that the nearly full moon should guarantee them a safe journey home later.

CHAPTER X

Mrs. Darcy and Mrs. Bingley entered the Philips's apartment. Elizabeth surveyed the scene, with the familiar furniture, and the mostly familiar people. The ladies were almost all the same that she had known her entire life, and, compared to the days of when the last regiment had been quartered in Meryton, the gentlemen were unremarkable, at least at first glance. The absence of redcoats to brighten the room was palpable. But Elizabeth had learned to mistrust her first impressions – after all, she had first been charmed and lied to by George Wickham in this very room – and so she resolved on caution in forming any judgments.

Mrs. Philips pushed her way through her other guests to welcome her nieces. She hastily found a comfortable place for Jane, and then proceeded to present Mrs. Darcy to everyone at her party. Elizabeth, by virtue of her marriage to a rich man, had become a person of importance. She was treated, even by some of those she had known her entire life, with as much fawning deference as her cousin Mr. Collins had always shown towards his patroness, Lady Catherine de Bourgh. Elizabeth hoped this would not continue. She hoped, even more, that she would not acquire the autocratic manners of Lady Catherine, dictating to everyone and expecting them to dance attendance. Still, her presentation to the guests was a formality that had to be endured, for the sake of her aunt.

Her aunt presented her first to Mr. Henry Clarke, who had been hired by Mr. Philips only a few months ago. Mr. Clarke was a tallish man of average looks, and as a clerk, had only modest prospects. These qualities explained why Mrs. Bennet had never ranked him among the first tier of potential suitors.

Aunt Philips was less prejudiced against law clerks, however, for she had married her father's law clerk, who, due to his marriage, had inherited the local practice and was now the leading attorney in Meryton. Mrs. Philips described Mr. Clarke as the best clerk Mr. Philips had ever had. "Mr. Philips quite depends on him," she added, as the young man moved in their direction.

"Really? What makes him the best?" Elizabeth inquired.

But when asked to provide particulars of Mr. Clarke's talents, Mrs. Philips was at a loss. She mumbled something about his handwriting being excellent and his always being on time – both important attributes in a law clerk, Elizabeth supposed.

"Mrs. Darcy, I am delighted," Mr. Clarke said after Mrs. Philips made the introduction. "I have heard so much about you."

"Have you?" Elizabeth had seen Mr. Clarke before, when he had been simply called Henry, but she had heard little about him.

"Indeed, I have. You were celebrated even before you became Mrs. Darcy – praised for your beauty and your wit. I can see that your beauty, at least, exceeds the praise; I look forward to experiencing your wit."

Elizabeth wondered who had praised her, and then realized it must be her aunt or her uncle or both. Mr. Clarke, she decided, was also skilled at flattery – that might account for the high esteem in which he was held by Mr. and Mrs. Philips – and at least this young man was not intimidated by her elevated social standing.

They conversed several minutes, discussing commonplace topics such as the weather, travel and London. Elizabeth decided, in that short time, that she could not see him as a suitor for Mary, even though she was certain that Mary would value penmanship and punctuality. Mr. Clarke was quick, whereas Mary tended to be slow. Mr. Clarke would make a better match for Kitty – Elizabeth perceived that Mr. Clarke enjoyed society, as did Kitty – but she was still not certain if they had much in common.

Elizabeth smiled, apparently at one of Mr. Clarke's witticisms but actually because she realized she was behaving as badly as her mother, evaluating single men as potential husbands for her unmarried sisters. Her own husband would shudder, if he knew her thoughts! However, the exercise gave her something to consider during the evening, and married women *were*, as her mother often said, supposed to provide their unmarried sisters with opportunities. At least, Elizabeth thought, she regarded them rationally, and did not assume that every man was ready to fall in love, regardless of inclination or suitability.

Mr. Clarke stepped away to make room for another young man, Mr. Jones, the young apothecary, who had recently joined his father's practice. He was of medium height, thin and rather shy, stammering and blushing as he spoke. Elizabeth wondered if he had trouble speaking when he met with patients; she hoped not, for he did not generate much confidence. Fortunately their exchange was brief, and he quickly moved aside, joining his friend Mr. Clarke in a different part of the room. When Mr. Jones was with Mr. Clarke he seemed to relax, his spirits buoyed by one of the law clerk's ready compliments. The way that Mr. Clarke seemed to take care of the awkward Mr. Jones was charming, reminding her a little of how Mr. Darcy took care of Mr. Bingley.

Elizabeth could not imagine Mr. Jones as a suitor for either of her sisters; how could he ever have the resolve to make a proposal? On the other hand, Mary, who spoke so slowly herself, might tolerate him very well. And if Mr. Jones was not inclined to conversation, Mary could always play the pianoforte.

Alas, thought Elizabeth; she *was* turning into her mother.

Her aunt presented her next to Mr. Morris, Mr. Philips's other clerk. If Mr. Clarke was the best clerk that Mr. Philips had ever had, then Mr. Morris was *not* the best clerk – implying that his prospects were worse than Mr. Clarke's and therefore he was not worthy of either sister. He was a short, heavyset man with small but piercing dark eyes in his round face. He spoke with bland deliberation. "Welcome back to Meryton, Mrs. Darcy," he said, then added that he hoped that she would enjoy the evening and moved on to a table with fruit and cheese.

Elizabeth was then presented by her aunt to various Lucases, which, as she had not only known them her entire life but had already met them at Lucas Lodge, struck her as rather unnecessary. Sir William, however, behaved as if he appreciated the gesture and made his usual gallant compliments. His children were not quite so formal and they told her that Charlotte, her husband and her son were expected to arrive in three days.

Finally her aunt introduced her to a red-headed stranger, Mr. Selby, the man who had been betrothed to Mary King. Elizabeth was most curious about him, but his words were clipped and his manner dull. He did not reveal much in the two minutes that they spent together.

Aunt Philips, having done her duty to her niece Mrs. Darcy by presenting her to all the young men, was less thorough with respect to the women. This was understandable, however, as besides the Lucases, most of the women consisted of Elizabeth's sisters – Mr. and Mrs. Bennet had not come – and they were gathered around Jane, making sure that she had everything that she needed. The one exception was Mrs. Smith, Mrs. Philips's new tenant. Mrs. Smith was a middle-aged woman, respectably but not fashionably attired, with pleasant manners. Mrs. Smith said she appreciated this opportunity to meet Mrs. Darcy. "Your aunt speaks so highly of you, that I am honored to make your acquaintance."

"Are your rooms to your liking?" inquired Elizabeth. "It is many years since I have been in them." The apartment had belonged to Mr. Philips before he had married Mrs. Philips.

"Very fine, I thank you," said Mrs. Smith, "and Mrs. Philips is an attentive and considerate landlady. Still, I am afraid they are nothing compared to Pemberley."

"Do you know Pemberley?"

"Do you mean, have I ever been there? Alas, no, I have not; I have spent my time in other places. But your aunt and your mother speak frequently of the estate."

"I imagine they do," said Elizabeth. Her mother had visited only once, at Christmas, when frivolity could be best endured, and her aunt Philips had never made the journey at all, but Elizabeth was certain that Mrs. Philips gloried in Mrs. Bennet's descriptions, and passed them on freely.

Mrs. Philips, now that she had completed her duty in her presentation of her niece, released Elizabeth and attended to the wants of other guests. Elizabeth was content to join Jane again, who was seated with Kitty. "So now I have met the very best of Meryton!"

Jane smiled and said: "I know my aunt was anxious to make sure that you feel welcome. And it is not just that she wants to honor you, Lizzy, but she knows that these people desire to make a good impression on you."

It was yet more evidence of the consequence of wealth, thought Elizabeth. "And what do you think of Mr. Henry Clarke, Kitty?"

"He can be amusing," said Kitty, "but I believe he shows me attention only because I am the niece of his employer."

"You are not engaging in matchmaking, are you, Lizzy?" asked Jane.

"If Kitty and Mr. Clarke are indifferent to each other, then I will not encourage them," said Elizabeth. She then changed the subject. "So that is the bereaved Mr. Selby," glancing briefly in that bachelor's direction. "I am surprised that he would be at a party, so soon after Miss King's death."

Jane and Kitty agreed, but Jane added, "My uncle Philips told Mr. Selby that it would do him good to leave the inn, and that a quiet engagement such as this could not offend the memory of Miss King. In truth, my uncle Philips has been afraid that Mr. Selby might succumb to the same melancholia which overcame Miss King."

"I do not think that it is helping," remarked Kitty.

"I am sure that my uncle Philips's intentions were good," said Elizabeth, but she concurred with Kitty; the young man did not seem to be deriving any benefit from the gathering. Mr. Selby was not talking to anyone. The clerk, Mr. Clarke, made a good-humored attempt to speak with him but walked away after a minute or two. The ever-attentive Mrs. Philips made sure he was served with food and drink, but the plate before him was untouched. She could not devote much effort to him, however, for she had to usher her guests to places at the game-tables.

Most settled readily at one table or the other; Elizabeth was gratified to observe Kitty making sure that Jane had a comfortable situation in the group playing Vingt-Un, while Mr. Philips was in charge of the more dignified whist table.

No choice seats remained, yet not everyone in the room was at a table. Those without places were Miss Mary Bennet, Mr. Morris, Mr. Selby and Elizabeth herself.

Mrs. Philips was untroubled by the fact that Miss Bennet and Mr. Morris were not at any of the tables, for both were always at hand. She was slightly more concerned about Mr. Selby, who had been invited especially by Mr. Philips; she felt obliged to entertain him. He refused, however, saying that he thought cards and laughter would be inappropriate for him at this time, and Mrs. Philips did not argue, as his gloomy attitude might dampen the enjoyment of those around him.

But with Elizabeth not at a table, Mrs. Philips was almost desperate.

"Mrs. Darcy, we can easily make room for you here – or we can squeeze you in there; Kitty does not need to play – and if you wish to play at whist, I am sure that Mrs. Smith will gladly give you her place."

Kitty appeared alarmed at being told she would lose a few hours of pleasure, while Mrs. Smith readily put down her cards and began to rise. Elizabeth hastened to stop them. "Do not trouble yourself, Kitty – Mrs. Smith – I am very good where I am."

"But, Mrs. Darcy! I do not want your evening to be dull!"

"It will not be, I assure you. I am not inclined to cards," she said. "I can sit here very pleasantly and observe the games."

"If only we had an instrument, you could entertain us," Mrs. Philips fretted. "I will have to get one before your next visit." Her attention was then usurped by the cards dealt at her table.

47

Elizabeth could not see where or how a pianoforte could be squeezed in among the many tables and chairs. Her aunt would have to sacrifice the very comfortable sofa, at least, and then where would her guests sit?

"I, too, wish there were an instrument," said Mary. "But my aunt's friends usually prefer the noise of cards to the soothing sounds of music."

"Many people in the world have little taste," said Mr. Morris. "But we must make the best of what we have." He found a backgammon board, set it up, and invited Miss Bennet and Mrs. Darcy to join him.

"Very well," said Elizabeth, "I will play whoever wins this round. Mr. Selby, will you join us?"

Elizabeth had several reasons for declining to sit at one of the livelier tables. One was genuine fatigue. She rather wished that she had followed Jane's example and had taken a nap in the afternoon, in order to fortify herself for the evening. The second reason was her sister Mary. Miss Mary Bennet, as the middle sister, had so often been the odd one out, squeezed between the pairings of Jane with Elizabeth and Kitty with Lydia. Elizabeth, closest to Mary in age among the five sisters, had always felt some guilt on the matter, and decided to give her sister more attention. Finally, Elizabeth was both concerned for and curious about the bereaved Mr. Selby.

Mr. Selby sighed. "I suppose it would not be injuring Miss King's memory to play at backgammon." Laughter erupted behind them, as Mr. Clarke told a joke to Kitty and Maria Lucas. "Merriment, however, is beyond me."

"I did not know her well, but Miss King always seemed a good sort of girl," said Elizabeth, pleased to have this opening to the subject.

"She was," he said, and then his expression became so obviously pained that he was near tears, and Mary leaned over to her and reproached her in a half-whisper for her lack of tact.

In general Elizabeth considered herself a superior conversationalist to her sister Mary, and she did not think her words had been so very inappropriate, but given Mr. Selby's reaction, she felt compelled to change the subject. "You are not from around here, are you, Mr. Selby?" she inquired, hoping the question would not increase his sorrow.

He had grown up near Liverpool, which was where he had met Miss King. He had only come to Meryton because Mary King had named him as the beneficiary of her will. Mr. Philips and Mrs. Philips had been exceedingly kind and helpful. They were still sorting through her possessions, which was a slow and difficult process. What was *he* supposed to do with her gowns and her papers?

Despite Mary's admonition, there was no escaping the topic, thought Elizabeth. She hoped that Mr. Selby would retain command of his emotions. "I was so sorry to hear of her demise," she said. "As I said, I did not know her well, and I do not understand it."

Neither did Mr. Selby, who, in a quiet way, expressed his bewilderment at the recent and devastating event. Miss King and he had been happy; he was convinced of that. He loved her, and she had loved him. During their courtship, she had told him that he was the only man that she had ever truly cared for, and to prove it she had made out the will even before they married. They had had less than a month to wait before the nuptials. So why had she ended her life before their marriage began?

Elizabeth supposed that it would be worse for a man to have his bride take her life just after their wedding, rather than just before – for then the blame, if not the guilt, would fall even more heavily on the new husband. However, she did not believe that this reflection would offer Mr. Selby any consolation, so she kept it to herself. "I do not know," she said, sympathetically. She added: "My father is of the opinion that it is impossible to completely know another person," she offered.

Mr. Selby agreed that it seemed to be so, yet, going through her things, he had not discovered anything that would cast his dear Miss King in a different light.

"I am so sorry," Elizabeth said, then asked what he planned to do with her remaining possessions.

He said that he would keep some things, perhaps sell a few others, and give some items away. Mrs. Philips knew of several poor families that were deserving of charity.

"That is very good of you," Elizabeth said. She hesitated. "We heard – and my apologies, Mr. Selby, but you must understand that this sad affair is being much talked over – we heard that some of Miss King's jewelry was missing."

He confirmed that as far as they could tell, several items did appear to be missing, although there was a faint possibility that they were at her uncle's house in Liverpool – but her uncle had written to say that he had also been unable to locate Miss King's jewelry.

So far Mr. Selby had told Elizabeth very little that she had not already heard, although she had satisfied some of her curiosity in simply speaking with him. He did not seem to know why Miss King had taken her life, but even if he did, why would he share that reason with her? She had just met him, and she had not been close to Miss King; really, the matter did not concern her at all. Elizabeth was a little ashamed of her inquisitiveness; she only hoped her manner had not betrayed her dishonorable motives.

"I am wearying you with my words," he said, for Elizabeth had fallen silent while contemplating her own imperfections.

"Not at all," said Elizabeth.

Mr. Selby explained that it was inappropriate for him to be at a social gathering, but what was he to do? He knew so few people in Meryton, and it did not help to sit in a room at the Meryton Inn staring at four walls by the light of a candle.

Mary Bennet and Mr. Morris finished their game in time to listen to this comment and to agree with Mr. Selby. "Although grief is both expected and natural in such a situation," said Mary, "one should take precautions to keep it from becoming overwhelming."

"You should sell the property," advised Mr. Morris, "or perhaps let it, till the market improves. Mrs. Darcy – Mr. Selby – I have beaten Miss Bennet at backgammon, so one of you must play me next. Who will it be?"

Elizabeth suggested to Mr. Selby that he should be Mr. Morris's next opponent, and although he attempted to yield to her, her polite insistence compelled him to take his place at the board. Elizabeth was glad to see that the rolling of the dice, and the movement of the pieces, distracted him a little. She also attempted to converse with her sister Mary, and resumed the subject about a pianoforte. "Perhaps a small one would fit," said Elizabeth.

"I do not think so," said Mary, who explained that she had measured the room, the furniture and the stairs and had determined it was impossible. Mary then resumed watching the game between Mr. Morris and Mr. Selby, and made no effort to engage in additional conversation with her sister. Elizabeth began to regret not having taken a place at one of the game-tables. She looked up, and caught Jane's eye.

"We can make room for you, Lizzy," said Jane, "if you wish to join us."

So Elizabeth, much to Mrs. Philips's relief, sat beside Jane and played Vingt-Un. She still wondered about Mr. Selby and Miss King, but it seemed that there was nothing more to be learned this evening.

Mrs. Smith and Mr. Clarke were the great winners at cards. Completely fatigued, Jane and Elizabeth thanked their aunt, and the two sisters returned in the Pemberley carriage to Netherfield Park.

CHAPTER XI

At breakfast the next morning Jane and Elizabeth were greeted by Miss Bingley. Miss Bingley's headache had completely vanished; her spirits were excellent. She smiled at Jane, hoped her sister-in-law had suffered no ill effects from the late hours of the prior evening, and was cordial to Elizabeth.

The same pleasant mood could not be attributed to Mr. Bingley, who arrived from London in the late morning. His trip had been without incident, he said; his business had gone as expected and planned; Mr. and Mrs. Hurst sent their love; yet his irritability was evident in his abrupt, distracted way of speaking. He hurried to his library to put away his papers, and did not emerge for hours. Jane went in to take him a cup of tea, and discovered that he was drinking port, alone in his library.

She reported this to Elizabeth. "He was not really cross with me, not such that any other woman could complain, but his temper was not as sweet as usual. He thanked me for the tea, but said that he preferred port for the moment – at this time of day! – and that he wished to be alone."

"I am sorry to hear it," said Elizabeth.

"Oh! Lizzy! What if he is still brought low by whatever was distressing him before?"

Elizabeth feared the same thing, and was frustrated that she had not been able to resolve her sister's problems. All she could do was to listen and to be supportive, but she was not the panacea that her father had expected her to be. Aloud she wondered if Bingley could be tired from the journey and if that could be affecting his temper.

"That is a possibility," Jane acknowledged, "and in fact it is what he told me. Charles told me to forgive him his ill humor and he promised to be in better spirits tomorrow."

It was strange for Elizabeth to find Miss Bingley more agreeable than Mr. Bingley, but so it was that day, at least till Miss Bingley teased her brother about wishing to be alone to the point that he even snapped at her. At that point Miss Bingley, now vexed herself, joined Jane and Elizabeth for a three-handed card game, and wondered aloud how Charles, who had been by himself all day on his horse could possibly prefer solitude in the evening as well. "I do not understand it," said Miss Bingley, "he never behaved in this manner before." She seemed to imply that either Jane or Elizabeth was responsible.

"Perhaps he was disappointed in the purchase of the estate," Elizabeth suggested.

"Charles told me his trip to London had nothing to do with the purchase of the estate," Miss Bingley said.

Elizabeth, watching Jane deal the cards, reflected that Miss Bingley was too angry to realize that the information for which she had made such a point of triumphing before, had, in fact, been faulty. But Elizabeth, deciding that Miss Bingley's humor was already sufficiently sour, refrained from gloating.

The next day was Sunday, and a measure of normality was restored to the inmates of Netherfield Park. Bingley's temper was improved, as he had promised. They went to church, which gave them a glimpse of the new grave on its north side – Mr. Selby and Maria Lucas stood beside it – and the opportunity to exchange words with many members of the community. Afterwards they all, including Miss Bingley, went to a family dinner at Longbourn House. Mrs. Bennet spent much of the time advising Jane, and telling her to be patient – advice that Jane, of all people, hardly needed – and speaking on other matters concerning the coming child. Elizabeth suggested that she might want to keep some of the more intimate details to themselves, but Mrs. Bennet pointed out that they were all family, so what did it matter? Mr. Bennet rescued his son-in-law by inviting him into his library for a drink, but Miss Bingley was unable to escape with the men and instead was trapped between Mrs. Bennet and Mary.

Spending the day at Longbourn should have made the comparative sense and tranquility of Netherfield more appealing, but it did not have the desired effect. Jane retired early, while Mr. Bingley, apparently cross again, withdrew once more to his library. That left Miss Bingley and Elizabeth to each other's company, but they avoided conversation. Miss Bingley wrote a letter to her sister, while Elizabeth leafed through a book.

After some time, Miss Bingley put down her pen and excused herself, carrying her finished letter with her. Elizabeth turned the last page of the book she was reading and decided she might as well determine if the second volume was in the library. She was also, she realized, curious about Mr. Bingley and whatever distressed him. If he would not confide in Jane, it was unlikely that he would confide in *her*, but she might find a way to suggest that he consult either with Mr. Bennet or Mr. Darcy. Or even with Mr. Philips, if there were a legal matter.

But when Elizabeth approached the library, she discovered that Miss Bingley had preceded her; the voices of the brother and sister carried.

"Charles, Jane is a sweet wife and I am sure that she will be a devoted mother. But her relations! The afternoon at Longbourn was intolerable."

Elizabeth felt her cheeks burn and paused outside the door. Even though she was sensible of her mother's faults, and she should not, in fairness, object to others having the same opinion, it still pained her to listen to the effect that they had on others. She reminded herself that the conversation she was overhearing was private – in fact she really ought to depart.

But then Miss Bingley continued, on a topic more neutral and yet of interest to Elizabeth. "You must purchase an estate, Charles. If Rushburn is impossible, then choose another."

"My dear Caroline, I assure you that it is not practicable at this moment."

"Why did you go to London? If you do not tell me, then I will ask Louisa."

Elizabeth now understood the reason for Miss Bingley's letter to Mrs. Hurst.

"It was a matter of business that concerns neither you nor Louisa," said Charles. "And as for the purchase of an estate: my wife is about to bear a child. This is not the time for a removal. And as much as you may not care for some of Jane's relations, they will be a support to her during the coming months."

"When would the time be better, Charles? When you have an infant and another on the way?"

"If you do not like it here, Caroline, you can always go live with Louisa and Hurst."

Elizabeth, shocked by Bingley's cold words, slipped noiselessly down the hall, and stepped into the unlit breakfast-parlor, where she was unlikely to be discovered. How could Mr. Bingley speak so harshly to his sister? Sisters depended on their brothers, especially sisters without husbands or fathers. Elizabeth had always admired how protective and considerate Darcy was of his sister.

But Miss Bingley, if she wished it, *could* go to stay with the Hursts in Grosvenor Street, while Jane, as his wife, could not flee Mr. Bingley's bad temper. Was something particular distressing him, and it was yet unresolved? Elizabeth could not imagine what it was; the only clue was the purchase, or rather the non-purchase, of Rushburn Manor. Was that something on which he had set his heart? It did not speak well for his temper, if he could be so discomposed by such a disappointment, for, as Jane had said, other eligible estates would come on the market.

Or had Bingley always been of an uncertain temper, and they had misjudged him? First impressions could be wrong; Bingley's temper could have been softened by the euphoria of his initial love for Jane. Elizabeth was still convinced that Bingley loved Jane, but perhaps that love was not enough.

She finally felt as if enough time had passed so that she could leave the shadows of the breakfast-parlor without causing suspicions. Still carrying the book, she first went to the library, intending to speak to Bingley and to ask him what was wrong – but although candles burned, he was not there, and so conversation was impossible. She waited a few minutes, but Bingley did not return, and so Elizabeth, after locating the second volume, exchanged the books and went to her room.

CHAPTER XII

Elizabeth resolved, during the night, that during the following day she would write to Darcy to ask his advice, but while at breakfast she herself received a letter from her husband. He informed her that the local vicar had been in a carriage accident and was not expected to survive. Mr. Darcy had been planning to join her at Netherfield soon but now he had to remain where he was for the others in the parish.

"Dr. P— from Lambton has examined Wallace and said that all we can do is to make him comfortable and wait. The reverend is a dear friend and too young to die," Mr. Darcy wrote, "but alas, we are all mortal, and it seems as if he will not last long. You are attending life, Elizabeth, while your husband is preoccupied with death. So I must stay here to take care of the situation, to comfort my friend in his last days and to prepare, as I expect, to seek a new vicar for the living."

Elizabeth shared this dreadful news with her friends, who all expressed how shocked and grieved they were at this information. However, Mr. Bingley and his sister barely knew the man, whereas Jane had never met him at all, so the expressions of sympathy did not last long, and they turned to wondering who Darcy would find as a replacement.

"What about your esteemed cousin, Mr. Collins?" suggested Miss Bingley. "Mr. and Mrs. Collins will be visiting soon, will they not? You could mention the living to him."

Elizabeth knew that Miss Bingley meant to remind her of yet another embarrassing relation in her large collection of them.

Jane, however, responded as if Miss Bingley were serious. "Mr. Collins is a respectable man, and I am certain you it would be pleasant to have Charlotte near you, Lizzy."

Elizabeth followed Jane's lead. "Yes, Mr. Collins is eminently respectable, and he is assiduous in his duties. But much as I would love to have Charlotte near me, I do not think that either Mr. Darcy or I would care to deprive Lady Catherine de Bourgh of her clergyman."

"You can mention the living to Mr. Collins if you like, Caroline, as I am sure he will call on us soon," said Mr. Bingley. "Unless you decide to have another headache."

And with that Mr. Bingley excused himself, saying that he had an errand to run in Meryton but that it would not take long. He gave orders for his horse to be readied, and although Miss Bingley petitioned to go with him, saying that she would appreciate some exercise on horseback, he adamantly refused her company.

CHAPTER XIII

Miss Bingley refreshed her spirits by sketching a faithful representation of a yew tree, which Jane and Elizabeth dutifully admired. Mr. Bingley was in a better temper after his errand into town. He still vanished into his library for an hour, but he did not remain there, and he came out and played piquet with his sister. The four of them were sitting companionably when a chaise approached the entrance; they were being honored by an early visit from Mr. and Mrs. Collins and their little son, accompanied by a nursery maid, who had all arrived at Lucas Lodge just around noon.

"Mr. Collins, there was no need to call at Netherfield Park," said Jane after all the ladies and Mr. Bingley had admired the serenely sleeping baby. "We know how limited your time is in Hertfordshire."

"Mrs. Bingley, far be it from me to neglect to pay the attention due to any of my fair cousins. Especially when I was informed that Mrs. Darcy was also here, I felt compelled to make the effort."

"Also, Lewis likes riding in the carriage," added Mrs. Collins. "The motion puts him to sleep."

Elizabeth inquired after the ladies of Rosings Park: Lady Catherine, her daughter Miss Anne de Bourgh, and Mrs. Jenkinson, Miss de Bourgh's companion. Mr. Collins assured her Lady Catherine de Bourgh and her daughter Miss de Bourgh were in good health but rather distressed, because Mrs. Jenkinson was seriously ill.

"I am sorry to hear it," said Elizabeth.

Mr. Bingley demonstrated his general good nature by taking the pompous bore away. As Mr. Collins would be confined to a carriage again very soon, perhaps he would like to take some exercise?

"I thank you, Mr. Bingley; that is most attentive of you. Most attentive indeed; walking is the best exercise. Yes, I am certain that Mrs. Bingley and Mrs. Collins have much that they wish to discuss." Mr. Collins accompanied Mr. Bingley out of the room, and could be heard holding forth, with as much eloquence as he possessed, on the subjects of motherhood and fatherhood and the difficulties and delights that awaited the Bingleys.

As soon as the gentleman departed, Lewis Collins awoke, an act which necessitated another round of admiration. Now that his eyes were open, the ladies discussed whether or not he resembled Mr. or Mrs. Collins most. Miss Bingley thought he looked like Mr. Collins; Elizabeth thought he resembled Mrs. Collins, while Jane was of the opinion that he took after both parents but the salient point was that he was a complete darling. After this praise, this darling, the future heir of Longbourn, first fussed and then wailed at the top of his lungs. Joan, a young woman from Hunsford hired by Mrs. Collins, entered the room to take care of the baby, and removed him discreetly to another room.

"I have been seeking a nursery maid," said Jane. "How did you find yours, Charlotte?"

"Oh! There has never been any experience so vexing!" cried Mrs. Collins. And she explained how they had originally hired a woman called Mrs. Ford. Mrs. Ford was a widow, and had seemed a plain sensible woman. She was a little older than many nursery maids, but not so old so that Mrs. Collins would be worrying about the health of her nursery maid as opposed to her infant, and Mrs. Collins had been of the opinion that an older woman with some experience might be useful.

"Perfectly reasonable," remarked Jane.

"You mean Lady Catherine has not been willing to share her experience?" asked Elizabeth.

"Lady Catherine has been most attentive," said Mrs. Collins, "but even though she has shown great interest in and generosity towards Lewis, she can hardly assist with feeding, changing and washing my son on a daily basis."

"Tell us more about Mrs. Ford," pressed Jane.

Miss Bingley suppressed a yawn and said, "Yes, Mrs. Collins, do tell us."

Mrs. Collins did so. She assured them that Mrs. Ford had come with good rates and excellent references. She had been capable in her duties but she had only remained a few weeks and then had abruptly given notice.

"Why did she leave?" inquired Jane.

"At first Mrs. Ford said the work was too much for her. We offered her higher wages – which she really deserved – and less onerous duties, but nothing would induce her to remain, even though at the time we needed her desperately. Mr. Collins and I both had colds, and Lewis seemed to stay awake half each night. These may seem like trivialities, but at the time my fatigue was severe."

"Perhaps she was exhausted too," said Elizabeth. "And if, as you say, she was a little older, she may not have had the stamina to care for an infant."

"Yes, that I could understand, and that is why we offered to reduce her work. But Mrs. Ford told me, just before she departed, that she had no problem with Lewis – her difficulty was with Mr. Collins!"

This time Miss Bingley struggled to suppress a laugh instead of a yawn, while both Elizabeth and Jane politely said they were sorry that Charlotte had been forced to listen to anything unpleasant about her husband.

"But Eliza, her accusation made no sense! Mrs. Ford hardly ever saw Mr. Collins! I run the household, not he. And then *he* told me that Mrs. Ford had explained to him that she was leaving because of *me*."

This contradiction on the part of Mrs. Ford caught the attention of all of Mrs. Collins's audience. The ladies all agreed that her words had been most peculiar.

"I agree," said Mrs. Collins. "Mr. Collins and I nearly had an argument about the matter. You can imagine that we were especially cross and out of sorts. Then we realized that for some reason she was trying to provoke discord between us."

"She sounds like a most suspicious character," said Elizabeth, although she was trying to keep from laughing. "At least she did not blame the baby."

"No, she did not. Perhaps she realized that that would be too much!" Mrs. Collins shook her head. "Seriously, looking back on her short time with us, I cannot understand why she came in the first place, or why she left when she did. We wondered if she might have taken something, but no money was missing, nor any jewels nor any silver. At one point Mr. Collins thought some correspondence had vanished – he even asked her if she had seen it – but he discovered it several days later."

"Where was it?" Jane asked.

"Just where it should have been, under a few other papers in his desk in his study. I asked him if it were possible that he had simply overlooked them before, but he said that it was impossible. They were two notes from Lady Catherine de Bourgh, about some improvements that she was recommending to the gardens around the church, and he said he could not have just misplaced them. Yet why would anyone else, especially Mrs.

Ford, borrow them? It is not as if she or anyone else is particularly interested in whether we plant marguerites or lavender."

"Every male I have ever met has misplaced one possession or another and then blamed the women in his family," said Miss Bingley. "Charles never knew where his books were when it was time for him return to school, but even though he accused Louisa and me of moving them, we never did."

The other ladies, all married, did not agree aloud with Miss Bingley – but neither did they disagree. They all believed that Mr. Collins had overlooked the correspondence, or had perhaps moved the pages without realizing it. Jane suggested that a new father could easily fall prey to a moment of disorder and distractedness.

"So, Mrs. Ford did not take the papers," mused Elizabeth. "Perhaps she was unwell, or simply cross about being a nursery maid. It does appear that many people these days are out of sorts."

Mrs. Collins did not press for examples, for which Elizabeth was grateful, for Jane appeared unhappy at this allusion to Mr. Bingley's bad moods – although Elizabeth could have offered another instance in another person if required. Instead Mrs. Collins nodded, as if she was remembering some episode of ill-temper herself, but then she smiled and said with her usual calmness: "Who knows? Why should not nursery maids be just as capricious as the rest of us? Now we have Joan, who costs a little more and who is less experienced, but so far she has shown no inclination to abandon her position."

"The other woman sounded too perfect to be real," remarked Miss Bingley.

"Yes, perhaps she was. Now, Jane, I hope you are already interviewing possible nursery maids. From my experience, one cannot start soon enough, even though if you do believe you have found one you may still encounter vexations."

"I am, but I have not decided on anyone yet. Kitty has offered to assist, and so has Caroline. I will make certain, Charlotte, not to hire anyone named Mrs. Ford!" Jane assured her. "Even if she does come with excellent references."

The men, returning from their walk, overheard the last part the conversation. "Oh! That Mrs. Ford!" exclaimed Mr. Collins. "I have just been warning Mr. Bingley about her, and explaining how she upset everyone at the Parsonage. Even though she had every appearance of goodness, she was truly malicious, like a snake in the garden, deliberately spreading ill will. She even removed and then returned some papers in my study. I do believe she was attempting to damage my relationship with Lady Catherine, but it is difficult to fathom why. Perhaps she has a son or a nephew who hopes to insinuate himself and to take my place. That would explain her behavior. My position is so advantageous, I can imagine that others may scheme to oust me from it and to acquire it for themselves."

The ladies repressed smiles at Mr. Collins's fantastical reasoning. Jane offered refreshment to the men, but Mr. Collins, after many thanks and apologies, declined. "My time here is so brief, that we really should not stay. I hope that you will have the opportunity to see much more of Mrs. Collins, however, during her visit with her family. I wish you all the very best, especially you, my fair cousins."

The Collinses departed as quickly as Mr. Collins's long speeches would permit, collecting their son and their nursery maid and climbing back into the chaise in order to return to Lucas Lodge.

CHAPTER XIV

The inhabitants at Netherfield Park played cards that evening; then Miss Bingley and Elizabeth each sat down to the pianoforte in turn. "We should invite the Lucases for dinner," Jane suggested to her husband, "or perhaps the Gouldings. You could use an opponent at billiards."

Mr. Bingley, his spirits restored by the half hour with Mr. Collins, for Mr. Collins's troubles had reminded him that his own situation was envied by many, said that he was willing to entertain anyone who Jane wished to invite. "If what Mr. Collins has told me is true about the demands of an infant, than it would be better to have your friends over sooner rather than later. But nothing too extravagant, Jane – I am not in the mood for extravagant."

Mr. Bingley said he would practice at billiards, while all the ladies, a little fatigued – the day had been warm and heavy, as clouds had gathered but no rain had fallen – retired relatively early. Just as Elizabeth was about to blow out her candle, Jane entered her bedroom. "I hope I am not disturbing you, Lizzy," she began, keeping her voice low.

"Not at all," said Elizabeth, and then saw the anxiety on her sister's face. "Is something wrong?"

"Perhaps. I require – that is to say I wish for – your assistance. I am still worried about Bingley."

"But his mood has been much improved today," said Elizabeth.

"Yes, today, tonight, but what if he is just maintaining a good appearance for a few hours? What if his ill-temper returns tomorrow? I would not ask, except that I saw something suspicious and I believe you can help."

"I will do whatever you command, Jane. Tell me what it is that you desire."

Jane explained that Bingley had *not* been practicing billiards this evening as he had said that he would, but that instead she had passed by the library and had seen him poring over a book.

Elizabeth tried hard to take this seriously, but she could not help asking: "Why is that strange? He has a library, why is it odd if he uses it?"

"It is not just that, Lizzy. I think he was looking at something else, and that he is keeping it hidden in one of the books. We have volumes that no one ever looks at. Lizzy, I am not a great reader but you have a reputation for loving literature. Could you search among the books? No one would suspect you."

"You believe your husband has hidden something in one of the books?"

"That is what I believe. He shut the book when I entered, and it is possible that I am just imagining it – he could simply be using an old letter to mark his place – but he looked so upset when he saw me that I need some peace. Will you look into them, Lizzy? And later tell me what you see?"

"Perhaps I will find a copy of Lady Catherine's recommendations for the garden of the rectory at Hunsford?" Elizabeth teased, and then, without levity, she added: "Do not be troubled, Jane; I will do what I can. Do you have any idea which book I should examine? Netherfield's library may not be the size of Pemberley's but there are enough volumes that examining all of them would take several hours at least."

Jane was not certain, but she had noticed an empty space on one of the higher shelves to the left of the green baize curtain.

"Is it better if I go early in the morning or do you advise me to look tonight?"

Jane said Bingley had already come upstairs, so she recommended making the search just then. "Bingley will not see you, and if anyone else does, that would not raise any suspicions." So, after the sisters wished each other good night, Elizabeth waited a quarter of an hour and, carrying a lit candle with her, crept down to the Netherfield library and to the area that Jane had indicated. The section of the bookshelf did not get many users, as it was both a little high and contained volumes in other languages, including several in Latin, Greek, German and French. They were not texts that Mr. Bingley would consult often; Elizabeth could understand why Jane's curiosity had been provoked.

With which should she begin? Elizabeth decided to be methodical, going from left to right. She had to reach high above her to pull off the first volume. It was a popular work by Goethe, but in German, with print that was difficult to read, which accounted for its banishment to an inaccessible position. Elizabeth opened it and at first tried turning each leaf, but the procedure was tedious and she accidentally made small rips in a few of the pages. Her initial approach was too inefficient. She held the book up and rather guiltily shook it – how disapproving her father would be if he saw her treating a book this way! – and waited for something to fall out. Nothing did. She returned Goethe's *Die Leiden des Jungen Werthers* to its original spot, and pulled down the next book, one in Latin – Caesar's *De Bello Gallico* – and shook it gently as well. But it was only with the third attempt that she discovered anything: two sheets of paper, folded and tucked into a volume by Voltaire.

Was *this* what her brother-in-law had hidden? Glancing consciously around, but not seeing anyone, Elizabeth hastily scanned the pages, which were difficult to read by the light of a single candle, especially with her heart pounding so hard. She saw that it was a letter to a Miss Hightower, written in what appeared to be Bingley's hand. Elizabeth quickly glanced at the salutation and the close where she found his signature. Should she read it or not? To read another person's private correspondence, without permission, was a terrible breach of trust. There might be some excuse for a husband to read a wife's letter, or for a wife to read a husband's, because the mutual dependency and responsibility demanded full information. A parent had reason to make that argument with a child, too. But Charles Bingley was only her brother-in-law, which was not a relationship which allowed indiscriminate perusal on her part without permission. She had no right to read it.

And yet, Jane wished her to read it; Elizabeth was sure. Which principle was more important: sisterly loyalty or honoring the privacy of another's correspondence? So far her actions could be considered innocent and could certainly be easily explained. Elizabeth *could* have had a desire to read Voltaire's *Candide* and the witty pronouncements of Professor Pangloss. She *could* have opened the book and the letter *could* have fallen out by accident. But to continue – no, that was too much. Jane might even be upset by her reading this. Elizabeth decided that she should content herself with what she could scan when slowly picking it up and putting it away.

Yet had she not traveled from Pemberley to determine what was distressing Bingley, and through Bingley, dear Jane? It seemed foolish, even cowardly, to allow a few scruples to prevent her from reading the letter, especially when this could provide the answers that she needed to assist her sister. Elizabeth moved her candle over it, but the light was so poor and the penmanship so careless that she wished that she had waited till sunrise. Nevertheless, she persisted and ascertained that it was a letter, definitely from Mr. Bingley to a Miss Hightower, with phrases that were most shocking because they professed both affection for the recipient and alarm for her situation. Elizabeth searched for a date, but all it said was Tuesday – which Tuesday? she wondered – and that it had been written in London.

Before she had finished she heard footsteps in the passage; someone, probably one of the footmen, was coming. Discretion was definitely the better part of valor and so Elizabeth hastily began the process of putting everything away, first locating the approximately correct page in the book, then folding the letter back into the position in which she had found it.

Someone opened the door just as Elizabeth was replacing *Candide*, with the letter back inside it, on the high shelf.

"Ah, Eliza," said Miss Bingley. "I suppose I should not be surprised to find *you* in here. Are you missing all your books at Pemberley?"

"Not at all," said Elizabeth, hoping the dim light of the candle would keep Miss Bingley from detecting her flushed face and hence her desperate embarrassment. "The library at Netherfield Park is excellent. But I discovered that although I am fatigued, I could not sleep, so I was looking for something to help me slumber."

Miss Bingley sauntered over to the bookshelf and with her superior height glanced easily at the section of the shelves where Elizabeth had been searching. "I do not recall, Eliza, do you read German? Or French? Although they might be good choices for summoning Morpheus."

"A little French. But I think I would prefer something in English this evening. Are you looking for something particular yourself, Caroline?"

"The same as you. Something to help me sleep tonight. Jane is so fatigued these days that it makes for early evenings, and what else is there to do but to read?" As Miss Bingley was more familiar with the contents of the shelves, she was able to make recommendations. "Fordyce's Sermons? Or *The Ancient Mariner*?"

Elizabeth accepted the Coleridge with thanks and departed from the library, but, curious, she shielded the light from her candle and lingered in the corridor. Why was Miss Bingley in the library? She was not a great reader. On the other hand, as she had pointed out, if she was wakeful, what other way was there to while away the time?

Miss Bingley paused before the books in German and French, and Elizabeth wondered if Miss Bingley also knew that her brother had hidden a letter, and had also come in search of it. But then Miss Bingley moved to a different part of the room, and took a light novel from one of the shelves.

At this point there was an excellent chance that Miss Bingley would leave the library. Not wishing to be discovered, and feeling guilty for her clandestine observation, Elizabeth turned and went lightly down the corridor and then up the stairs to her room.

The Ancient Mariner did not put Elizabeth to sleep that night, even though she dutifully turned many pages and read some of the verse, so that she could later encounter Miss Bingley with a clear conscience on that point. Even after she extinguished her candle she had difficulty falling asleep, for she was troubled, extremely troubled, by what she had seen of Bingley's letter.

It appeared that Mr. Bingley had a passionate and guilty connection with a Miss Hightower. Given that he was married to her sister, this was extremely distressing.

Yet there were aspects that puzzled. The letter that she had seen had been written *by* Mr. Bingley *to* Miss Hightower. If there were an active correspondence between her brother-in-law and this woman, then why had Elizabeth not found a letter *from* her *to* him? That would make more sense. Perhaps he had just written the letter and was planning to send it later. However, it did not appear to be a recently written letter; from the deepness of the creases, even the age of the paper, it appeared a little older. Furthermore, the date and place did not make sense. Mr. Bingley had just been in London; that was true, and perhaps he had taken the time to write a letter. But he had not been there on a Tuesday! Had he simply put down the wrong day? Why would he write such a letter and not send it? If he decided not to send it, then why would he not destroy it? He had to realize that such a letter, if discovered, would seriously destroy Jane's peace of mind.

And that led to the next critical question: should she inform Jane of what she had seen or not? Elizabeth wanted to protect Jane from anything that might distress her. She had once protected her from the fact that Bingley's love for her had been genuine, because at the time it appeared that he might never declare his feelings for her and propose, and Elizabeth had not wanted to raise hopes that might not be fulfilled. Now she had another, far worse secret to conceal, and it was the opposite: that Bingley could be having an affair.

However, concealing her knowledge with respect to this would be more difficult. Jane had told her to investigate the library, and she would certainly press Elizabeth for the results of her investigation.

It appeared that Jane's worst fears had been correct all along: that Bingley had fallen out of love with her. Or, if he were still in love with her, then he had also developed feelings for another.

Yet not everything made sense. If only there were some way to learn more about Miss Hightower! But she had to do this without involving Jane or alerting the suspicions of Mr. Bingley.

Only when Elizabeth devised a scheme to accomplish this could she finally sleep.

CHAPTER XV

The next morning, unsurprisingly, Elizabeth rose later than usual, and when she came downstairs the others were already in the breakfast-parlor. Miss Bingley teased her a little about reading late, which Elizabeth did not deny. An inquiring glance from Jane made it clear that she wanted to know if Elizabeth had discovered anything. Reluctantly, Elizabeth inclined her head.

She was determined not to share what she had learned till they were completely alone. It was imperative that they not be disturbed or interrupted, because not only was what she had to communicate confidential, and her own role in procuring the information highly irregular, the information was such that it might severely disturb Jane's composure. Even Jane would need time to return to her usual serene self.

Elizabeth conveyed this to Jane with a few short phrases, not to be understood easily by the others.

In the meantime the morning post was brought to them by a footman. Miss Bingley received a note from her sister; Elizabeth received a long letter from Mr. Darcy, in which the continuing decline of Reverend Wallace was detailed, and Jane received a parcel of baby linens from Aunt Gardiner.

Mr. Bingley received no letters at all, but that fact seemed to make him more cheerful rather than not.

"The weather looks pleasant today," observed Jane. "Charles, why do not you and Caroline go riding this morning?"

Miss Bingley was delighted by the idea; she and her brother had not ridden together for weeks.

But Bingley, even though the suggestion obviously appealed to him, expressed reluctance. "I do not like to leave you alone, Jane."

"But Lizzy is here," said Jane. "I will not be alone, and you should take advantage of such lovely weather."

"But perhaps Eliza would wish to come too?" asked Miss Bingley, with admirable self-command. "We have a mount that might suit you."

Elizabeth assured Miss Bingley that she was not a great horsewoman.

"Really? I thought you might have mastered it during your months at Pemberley."

Elizabeth had gone riding occasionally with Darcy and with Georgiana at Pemberley, so during the past year she had acquired some skill – but she still declined and said she would remain at Netherfield with Jane.

Mr. Bingley and Miss Bingley did not press Elizabeth further – Mr. Bingley because he wanted Elizabeth to spend the hours with Jane, and Miss Bingley because she wanted Elizabeth not to spend the hours with *her*. On Jane's recommendation, the brother and sister decided to ride to Oakham Mount. They ordered the horses, and Miss Bingley went to change, and then the two departed. As soon as they were gone, Jane said: "You have something to tell me, Lizzy. I know you do."

Elizabeth admitted that she did but she said they needed to be alone, absolutely alone, before she would share what she had learned.

So they went to a section of the drawing-room, at a distance from any of the entrances, so that they could not be overheard by any of the servants. Even then Elizabeth was still not sure what she should say.

"Please, Lizzy, ignorance is not bliss, not when I already know something is wrong."

"Very well, Jane, but you must promise me not to judge too quickly. I know that is usually my failing and not yours, but you must do your best." After Jane promised, Elizabeth told everything that she could about her excursion to Netherfield's library the prior evening, from a description of the letter that she had found in *Candide* to her encounter with Miss Bingley, as well as some of her thoughts about the letter during the night.

Jane struggled to remain calm, but Elizabeth could see that her sister was very distressed. "Miss Hightower, you say? I have never even heard of her!"

"I know no one in Meryton with that name," said Elizabeth. "Of course, the letter had 'London' on it. I am sure there are plenty of Hightowers in London."

"And the letter was *from* him, not to him?"

"Yes."

"That is very strange," said Jane. "Although many would accuse their husbands of infidelity given such evidence, I do not see how Bingley could have been unfaithful. Since we married, we have spent very little time apart. He went to London last week, but he stayed with the Hursts, and Louisa – I know you are not fond of her – but Louisa is also a married woman. She would not countenance such behavior; I know she would not."

"I do not understand it. I have always believed that Bingley was deeply in love with you." Elizabeth said these words, although last night she had wondered the contrary.

"That is very kind of you, but what if you are wrong? You are very clever, Lizzy, but even you are not always correct. What if he has fallen out of love with me? Married life is not the same as courtship, and even if it were, people change."

Elizabeth squeezed her sister's hand sympathetically.

But Jane returned to attempting to convince herself that all was not dire. "No, Lizzy, that cannot be. He has not had time to form an alliance with anyone else, and I have trouble believing, despite everything, that he has been so inclined. Perhaps it is an old letter, which he wrote before we met."

Elizabeth said that was absolutely possible, for *Tuesday* could belong to any week, indeed to any year.

Jane then said: "But why would he keep it? Oh, Lizzy, perhaps it reminds him of a happier time."

"Do you wish to go and look at it? *I* should not read it again – I am uncomfortable with my actions so far – but you are Bingley's wife and have a right to do so."

Jane hesitated, but finally decided that her spirit would not rest till she had perused the pages in question. The sisters repaired to the library immediately, choosing to do this while Mr. Bingley and his sister were still making their journey to Oakham Mount.

"It was in here," said Elizabeth, pulling down the volume of *Candide*, and opening it.

But the book did not contain the letter.

"Lizzy, are you sure?" asked Jane, taking down the next book on the shelf and leafing through it.

Again the letter was not to be found.

"Perhaps he moved it – or perhaps Miss Bingley moved it?" suggested Elizabeth, as they continued to look. "Yet Miss Bingley did not seem aware of the letter. And I do not think she is skilled at disguising her feelings."

But Jane did not reply to this remark, because she exclaimed that she believed that she had found the letter, or at least, what remained of it.

Jane was standing before the library's fireplace, pointing at the hearth. "Because of the summer heat, we have no fire in here, but I see some charred paper." She could not bend down easily, so Elizabeth stooped and retrieved the sooty scraps.

"Is that it?"

Elizabeth studied it. "Yes, I believe so. The paper is similar, and here is a section with the words, *Tuesday, London*."

She handed the scrap to Jane, who looked at it and said: "This is it, I am sure! He must have come in here this morning, when no one was around, and used the flame of his candle to burn the letter."

Elizabeth agreed that Jane's version of events was quite probable.

Jane appeared ready to burst into tears, yet her words contradicted her expression. "I am so glad!"

"You are glad?"

Jane did not cry; however, her voice trembled. "Yes, Lizzy. This means I cannot read whatever was in it and thus invade my husband's privacy. And the fact that he has burnt it – that means he loves me. It is not a letter that he wanted to keep, as a souvenir of prior affections. And we can see that he did not send it. He loves me, now, no matter what he felt in the past or what temptations he may have suffered in the present."

"You are a better woman than I. My own curiosity would not be conquered so easily."

"What is past is past, and what is burnt is burnt. There!" Jane dropped the scrap, intending for it to fall back in the hearth – but it fluttered to the carpet instead. Elizabeth, more agile than her sister, bent down again and replaced it in the fireplace.

Footsteps signaling the entrance of another party into the room made them both turn around guiltily. It was not Mr. Bingley or his sister, however, but a young housemaid.

The housemaid was perturbed by the scene before her. "Mrs. Bingley, Mrs. Darcy, I can take care of the hearth. That is my job, that is!"

Jane and Elizabeth glanced at each other. Both had fingers stained with soot and Jane had a black streak on her face.

"Please do that, thank you, Reeves," said Jane.

Jane and Elizabeth left the library; in the hall, they burst out laughing. They then continued to Jane's dressing room in order to wash their hands and to wipe the ash from Jane's cheek.

CHAPTER XVI

As Elizabeth said, *her* curiosity was not so easily satisfied. She remembered something that Mr. Darcy had told her about Bingley a long time ago. Before Bingley had met Jane, he had been attracted to other pretty girls. *I had often seen him in love before*, were Darcy's exact words, although he then conceded that Mr. Bingley's affection for Jane was more serious than any other flirtation that he had previously observed.

Elizabeth had great respect for her husband's opinions, but she did not think that Darcy's judgments were infallible. Darcy had, at one point, completely underestimated Jane's affection for Bingley. What if he had underestimated Bingley's affection for another woman in the past? For her sister's tranquility, Elizabeth decided to do what she could to learn more.

It was one thing to have the wish or even the intention to do something, but rather another to actually accomplish it. Elizabeth could not possibly question Mr. Bingley about Miss Hightower, and Jane obviously knew nothing. Given that Mr. Darcy remained at Pemberley, she could not bring the matter up to him. She was unwilling, furthermore, to send the question to him in a letter, as it would then attract too much attention and possibly expose Bingley, her sister, and even the mysterious Miss Hightower. She could not bring up the subject with any of the servants, for they might find the queries strange.

But there was one person at Netherfield who might be able to tell her something, one person whom she could question without it appearing as if she were prying too much – someone to whom Elizabeth did not mind dissembling (she could not bear telling even tiny falsehoods to her husband) – with whom she could make casual inquiries, one with whom she could exchange idle words without its rousing much suspicion.

So, rather unusually, Elizabeth found herself seeking the company of Miss Bingley. Elizabeth was not ready to invite the other woman for another stroll in the shrubbery, but she did believe that she could endure sitting for a quarter-of-an-hour with her. So, later that day, after she had written to Darcy to say how she grieved she was about Reverend Wallace's situation, Elizabeth sat down with her sister's sister-in-law.

Miss Bingley raised an eyebrow but did not object to Elizabeth's company. She was in an excellent mood after the morning's ride with her brother – perhaps she just needed more exercise to improve her disposition, thought Elizabeth – and even offered, voluntarily, a few words of praise for the view from Oakham Mount, and that she wished that she had brought her sketch book with her.

"I am glad you liked it," said Elizabeth.

She had decided to approach her topic discreetly, first by speaking of something entirely different. "I see you are looking at music," she observed, for the sheet music to an Italian song was indeed in Miss Bingley's hands. "Tell me, Miss Bingley, what do you think of metronomes? Do you think they are useful for musicians?"

Miss Bingley, who had taken many pains to master the pianoforte, actually did have an opinion on the subject which was not an echo of someone she was trying to flatter or a sneer designed to denigrate someone she despised. Metronomes, in Miss Bingley's opinion, were useful for learning to play in time, but obviously should not be used in any actual performance. At that point the artistry of the performer needed to be paramount.

Elizabeth then complimented Miss Bingley on the reasonableness of her notions and added that someone named Miss Hightower would agree with her.

"Miss Hightower?" asked Miss Bingley.

"Do you know any Hightowers?" Elizabeth asked, hoping her manner appeared casual. "I am afraid that I am not certain of her first name."

"I once met a Miss Margaret Hightower," said Miss Bingley. "However, I find it hard to believe that *she* would have had an opinion about metronomes."

"Margaret Hightower," mused Elizabeth, as if she were trying to recall the first name. "That *might* have been it, but I am not still not certain. Can you tell me about her? How do you know her?"

"Miss Margaret Hightower," Miss Bingley continued, "was a young lady with whom my brother unfortunately became acquainted in Bath, after being introduced to her in the Pump Room."

"Why was the acquaintance unfortunate?" Elizabeth asked, hoping that she did not sound as intensely curious as she felt.

"The Pump Room is supposed to be reserved for those of distinction, but unfortunately, mistakes are made and inappropriate people sometimes manage to enter. It is impossible to be certain of backgrounds and breeding in such a place. The Pump Room is full of fortune hunters."

"I did not know," said Elizabeth. "I have never been there."

"It is a most dangerous place. A valet may be taken for a gentleman and a gentleman for a lord." Miss Bingley spoke with such warmth that Elizabeth wondered if Miss Bingley herself had been misled.

Miss Bingley continued. "I expect that Mr. Darcy is too aware of the distinction of class to frequent the Pump Room, although the waters are salutary and the ancient baths are interesting."

"And is that where you met your Miss Hightower?" Elizabeth asked.

"She was not *my* Miss Hightower," said Miss Bingley. "But the young woman I met was very pretty, rather short, with soft blue eyes. She looked well, I will admit – and my brother was a bit infatuated with her. But she was quite poor, not well educated and had no accomplishments worth mentioning. All she could do was paint tables and net purses. We kept him from making a fool of himself, however – even Charles agreed that he was too young to make such an important decision. And that was fortunate, for later she proved that her character lacked all decency and virtue."

"Why, what did she do? Did she marry someone else?"

"No, she did not, and she never will. Miss Hightower is dead," said Miss Bingley.

Elizabeth had not anticipated this, and so her astonished apology was genuine. "Excuse me, I had no idea! I did not mean to remind you of a death."

"*I* was never in love with her; I only met her once or twice. After Charles stopped going to the Pump Room, Miss Hightower managed to get herself into a difficult situation – without a husband – and then died during confinement. I understand that the child died too."

Elizabeth's mind flew quickly, exploring possibilities, and then she stopped herself, deciding to keep her speculating for later, when she was alone. "I am so sorry to hear of this befalling any young woman. When did all this take place?"

"More than a year before Charles first took Netherfield. We were all a little upset when we learned of it – Charles especially – but really, given her low background, who could be surprised?"

"I do not know," said Elizabeth. She decided it was time to finish the discussion of this subject; she did not trust herself not to say anything indiscreet. "At any rate, this Margaret Hightower cannot be the Hightower who had an opinion about metronomes, and even if there is a connection, given what happened, it is better not to mention it." She then continued to speak of the Italian song that Miss Bingley was studying, and hoped most earnestly that Miss Bingley would perform it for them all later.

CHAPTER XVII

The next day, the weather was again so fine that Mr. Bingley and his sister were again persuaded to take out the horses – although they promised not to be gone as long, as the Bennets were expected that evening – and Jane and Elizabeth went out into the gardens. Each sister was eager for a tête-à-tête.

Although Elizabeth was an excellent walker, and would have happily explored all the paths in the wood, Jane was not. So instead they went to a bench, in the shade of an oak tree, far enough from the house to make sure that they were not overheard.

As they sat on the bench, Jane said, "Lizzy, you will be ashamed of me."

"I do not see how that is possible, but pray tell me what you have done."

Jane shook her head. "This morning, even though I intended not to ask Bingley about Miss Hightower ..."

Her sister hesitated so long, that Elizabeth found herself obliged to supply the words. "You have asked him?"

Jane shook her head. "No – no. I have not. But I am considering it, Lizzy, because I cannot stop thinking about that letter. And I am afraid that I was as cross this morning as Bingley has been the past few weeks."

"I am glad to hear it."

"Why is that? How can you be glad to know that I am in such turmoil?"

"Because sometimes you have too much of the angel about you, Jane, and it is impossible for the rest of us to live up to your example. But as it happens, I have information about Miss Hightower that may spare you from having to have this conversation with Bingley."

"How can you have information about Miss Hightower? Did you question Bingley? Oh, Lizzy, that could make things even worse!"

Elizabeth assured her sister that she had not brought up the subject to Mr. Bingley, and that she had done her best to be discreet. That instead she had brought up the name Hightower in a different context with *Miss* Bingley, and then managed to elicit information from her. Then she told her sister all that she had learned.

Jane listened intently to Elizabeth's narration. "So the Miss Hightower of the letter is dead?" she asked, when her sister had concluded.

"Apparently she is. Perhaps Bingley's letter was to another Miss Hightower, but I doubt it. How many Miss Hightowers can there be – real or imaginary?"

Jane's mood was too grave to appreciate her sister's levity. "Then I believe that I understand what happened. Miss Hightower may have died two years ago, but someone only recently discovered the letter that Bingley wrote to her. That person did not feel comfortable destroying the letter, and so located Charles and sent it to him."

"That is certainly possible," said Elizabeth. "In fact, I believe you have hit on it, or have come very near. It is also possible that the person who went through Miss Hightower's things only located Bingley recently."

"True, true!" Jane exclaimed, and then continued. "When Charles received it, of course he was upset – it brought back memories – and he did not think that he could discuss it with anyone, especially not me."

Or his sister, thought Elizabeth, remembering the scornful way that Miss Bingley had dismissed Miss Hightower's plight. "I agree with everything you have said," Elizabeth said earnestly, hoping that her sister's imagination would be content with going this far, and stopping.

But Jane, although she generally tended to think the best of people, went a little further in her suspicions. She confirmed first that Miss Hightower had been with child out of wedlock and had died in consequence.

Elizabeth replied hesitantly. "If we are to believe Miss Bingley, who admits that she met Miss Hightower only once or twice, that is so."

"Then, Lizzy, I must ask – who was the father? What – what if it were Charles? Was there anything in the letter that you saw that implied that it could have been so?"

Elizabeth was sorry that even Jane's mind had discovered this possibility, yet she would not assuage her sister's doubts with a comforting falsehood. "Jane, I do not know. Nothing in what I read would contradict your hypothesis. In fact, the language rather supported it."

Jane blushed and blinked away a tear. "Lizzy, do you know what you are saying?"

"I do."

Jane was silent for several minutes, contemplating this possibility. Still, her faith in people prevailed. "Lizzy, I simply cannot believe it – no, I cannot. I *know* my husband. If Charles had been the father of Miss Hightower's child, he would have married her, no matter what his sisters and his friend said to him."

Elizabeth liked and esteemed her brother-in-law, but her confidence in him was not as strong as Jane's. When Mr. Bingley had fallen in love with Jane, he had first yielded to Mr. Darcy and his disapproving sisters by staying away from her instead of making an offer. Elizabeth also believed that his character was firmer now than it had been a few years ago, in large part due to Jane's love and support. That implied that Bingley's resolve in the past must have been weaker. Nevertheless, although she could not concur with Jane's theory, she did her best to offer one of her own. "There is so much we do not know. Perhaps there is a reason that Miss Hightower did not want to marry Bingley?" But as soon as she uttered these words, Elizabeth dismissed this idea, and Jane did too.

"No woman could refuse to marry a sweet man like Bingley," said Jane.

"Few would do so," Elizabeth agreed.

"And my husband would never have abandoned a woman carrying his child, not even if she were of a lower class or if she were ill-bred. So he could not have been the father. It is impossible."

Elizabeth only said, "You know him better than I."

"All of this is best forgotten. I will not trouble my husband with it. He received the letter that he wrote in the past, and it reminded him of some unhappy memories and soured his temper for a while. However, he has recovered his equanimity and he has burned the letter himself. He obviously does not want to think about it, and he certainly does not want to distress me with it. Poor Miss Hightower is dead and I should not be jealous of her – nor should I think ill of her."

De mortuis nihil nisi bonum, thought Elizabeth. Aloud she said, "You are both wise and sensible."

She hoped that Jane would be able to forget this had ever happened, and that she would not suffer the doubts that Elizabeth already experienced about Mr. Bingley's character. What if Bingley had seduced poor Miss Hightower and had subsequently abandoned her? It would mean that Bingley was not to be relied upon in a crisis, and was not the upstanding man that she wished for as the husband of a beloved sister and the father of a nephew or niece.

Jane continued to express her relief. "Lizzy, I am so glad – so grateful – that you have been with me through this. And you were so clever, asking Caroline in that roundabout way. My mind is now at ease, quite at ease. I am composed, absolutely composed, and I can have faith in my husband as one of the most tender-hearted of men."

"I am happy to hear it," said Elizabeth, and hoped that this time Jane's resolution would prove equal to the task, as she had not been able to quell her previous curiosity.

"I only hope Charles forgives me for being short-tempered with him this morning. I am ashamed of my behavior."

"I am sure he will forgive you," Elizabeth said. "Now to change the topic to one that really is different, and a happier one, what names are you considering for the baby? Charles, if it is a boy? And Jane if it is a girl, or perhaps Caroline or Louisa?"

"Yes, Jane Elizabeth, if it is a girl, but in that case we shall call her Jenny. If we have a second girl we will call her Caroline Louise. We are not completely settled on a name for a boy. Charles is a possibility, but we are also considering Bennet. What do you think of Bennet?"

"That will please Papa," said Elizabeth.

"And it will compensate for Mr. Collins's neglect. We are considering Bennet Charles Bingley. Or Charles Bennet Bingley. Unless you wish to use Bennet, if you should eventually have a boy."

Elizabeth said, "Darcy and I have not reached the point where we are discussing such matters, but his affection for his father's memory is so great that I imagine he would prefer to honor his father by naming his son after him – if and when we have one, that is. However, if we were to consider the name Bennet, that should not prevent you – there is room enough in the world for two cousin Bennets."

"Yes, indeed," agreed Jane, and there was a sparkle in her eyes. "We are taking over the country."

CHAPTER XVIII

With Jane in good spirits, Elizabeth considered making arrangements to return to Pemberley, especially as she was concerned about Darcy and his dying clergyman, but Jane and Bingley pressed her to stay. "I would so like you to be with me during the coming weeks," Jane said. "I want to introduce you to your niece or nephew."

"We would all appreciate your attendance during this time," added Bingley.

"Of course, Eliza, please stay at Netherfield."

Those last words were from Miss Bingley, and uttered without enthusiasm or feeling. Still, Elizabeth credited Miss Bingley for having said them, although perhaps Miss Bingley only viewed her as the lesser of two evils. If Elizabeth were staying at Netherfield, her presence might prevent Mrs. Bennet from moving in to assist with the baby.

"That is, if Darcy can spare you," added Miss Bingley, her tone implying that she thought Darcy ought to be able to spare Elizabeth easily.

"Mr. Darcy and I discussed the possibility of my remaining till the baby arrives, but I will write to him at once."

That morning Elizabeth received a letter from her husband, explaining that Wallace still lingered after his carriage accident. "Wallace is taking so long to die, that I am wondering if he might survive this. Dr. P—, alas, does not think that a recovery is at all likely, and only regrets that Wallace continues to suffer."

She wrote back to say that she seemed to have assisted Jane through the problem that had been bothering her – all was well but she would not trust the details to a letter, something that he would understand when they met – but that Jane and Bingley wished her to remain till the birth of their child. "It cannot be more than a few weeks from now," she wrote, "although reckoning these things are always a little uncertain. Jane will not admit it, but she is apprehensive about what is to come. However, I miss you – and Pemberley – at a word I will return at once. Bingley also tells me to tell you that you are welcome here as always, and he hopes to soon be able to introduce his child to Uncle Darcy." Elizabeth was sure, with such a missive, that she would remain at Netherfield for several more weeks. The relief on Jane's face when she informed her of her intention was great;

every woman knew of others who had died while becoming mothers, and she wanted her favorite sister to be with her during her greatest joy or to kiss her goodbye, if goodbye needed to be said.

Unfortunately for Miss Bingley, Elizabeth's remaining at Netherfield Park did not ward off the other Bennets but actually seemed to attract them. Mrs. Bennet came frequently with Kitty, sometimes bringing with her Mrs. Philips, or some of the Lucas girls, or even Mary Bennet, who acknowledged that she should make an effort to support her sister in this time of waiting. Mary's inspection of the nursery was cursory, but she informed Jane that she was assiduously practicing several lullabies. Mary also provided them with the most current information about the death of Miss King and the situation of Mr. Selby. Mr. Selby had, with the assistance of Mr. Morris, continued sorting through Miss King's possessions. Her jewelry had not been discovered. No one knew the reasons behind her death, with the possible exception of the reduction of her capital, and even that could not be understood.

According to Mary's information, Miss King's fortune had been in a bank in London. Mr. Philips and his clerks had been in correspondence with Haggerston, a London attorney, who had verified the amounts with Miss King's banker – the correspondence was necessary in order to transfer the money to Miss King's betrothed – and the banker had explained that the fortune had been intact up till a month ago. Before that, Miss King had only accepted the interest. However, during the last month of her life she had considerably reduced the capital. The withdrawals had been made against the banker's advice, but he had not had the right to refuse to give Miss King her own money.

"Perhaps the banker is lying," said Mary, "but my uncle Philips says he is a well-respected, conservative man with an excellent reputation."

"Then what did she do with the money?" demanded Elizabeth.

"No one knows," said Kitty.

"Nearly five thousand pounds?" Even Jane was aghast. "How could anyone spend so much?"

"To think that Mr. Bennet reproaches me for being too liberal," said Mrs. Bennet. "And when I do spend a few guineas, at least I have something to show for it afterwards, such as a bonnet or a new pair of gloves."

"It is all extremely peculiar," remarked Miss Bingley.

"Mr. Selby plans to leave the area on Monday," Mary concluded her narration.

"How do *you* know all this, Mary?" Elizabeth inquired, for in general the other ladies were better informed with respect to neighborhood gossip. Mary tended to be a source of quotes and paraphrases from great books, and not the details of the local, current occurrences.

Mary explained that she had walked to Clarke's Library in order to exchange some volumes for her and Mr. Bennet, and while there she had met Mr. Clarke, Mr. Jones and Mr. Morris. Mr. Morris had sat with her for a few minutes, which was when he had informed her of the correspondence with Miss King's banker. Normally they would keep such details confidential, but after consultation with Mr. Selby, they had decided that it was better to let the neighborhood know what had happened, because that would improve the chance of retrieving the money.

"Unfortunately I had no information about Miss King's expenditures that I could share with Mr. Morris," Mary said regretfully. "I could only promise him that I would share the details with my family and with the Lucases, which I have now done."

Elizabeth was confident that her sister's sharing of these details with the persons mentioned would spread them throughout Meryton, Longbourn, the other surrounding villages and far into the county. "Has anyone has come forward with information?"

But Mary had nothing more to report; no one knew what had happened to the dead woman's money.

"Or her jewelry," said Kitty.

"Jewelry would be easy to hide," said Elizabeth.

"So would bank notes," said Miss Bingley. "And they are more difficult to identify."

"It was Hannah," opined Mrs. Bennet, referring to Miss King's maid. "She was in the best position to find Miss King's money and her jewels, and, as you say, they are very small. By the time her place was searched, she had either sold them or hidden them some place no one would look."

Kitty protested. "But, Mamma, Maria Lucas reports that Hannah is extremely distraught. She has lost Miss King, she has lost her position, and now she has lost her reputation. She has been compelled to move in with her aunt, and her aunt is unkind to her as she has four young children and considers Hannah a burden."

"It is all an act," pronounced Mrs. Bennet. "The unkindness of others will be Hannah's excuse for moving away, at which point she will use Miss King's bank notes and earrings to start a life of comfort. Five thousand pounds! No one should pity her."

The hour was late and so Mrs. Bennet ordered the carriage. "Time to go, Mary, Kitty – Jane, dear, if you are uncomfortable, put more milk in your tea, or try a spoonful of vinegar and then a spoonful of honey."

The ladies from Longbourn women departed. The ladies at Netherfield were just deciding that they would be free of visitors for the rest of the day, when another carriage rolled into the lane.

"Is it my brother?" Miss Bingley inquired, for Mr. Bingley was paying a call on the Gouldings.

"Charles did not take the carriage; he went on horseback," said Jane.

Elizabeth moved to the window. "It is Sir William's carriage," she informed them.

Although it was the Lucas carriage, Sir William did not appear: only his two oldest daughters, Mrs. Collins and Miss Maria Lucas. Jane welcomed them and invited them to the drawing-room.

After the usual inquiries about health, Mrs. Collins explained their reason for coming. "I know it is late to make a call, but my mother had the carriage before this. We will not stay long, but I felt compelled to see you, Elizabeth, because Lewis and I expect to leave much sooner than originally planned. Mr. Collins is arriving in Hertfordshire tomorrow and shortly afterwards I will return to Hunsford with him."

Elizabeth was surprised. "Did he not just return to Hunsford?"

"Is there any reason for ending your visit so soon?" inquired Jane.

"It is a matter of convenience. He is coming in her ladyship's carriage," explained Mrs. Collins.

"That is most generous of Lady Catherine de Bourgh," observed Jane.

"Lady Catherine de Bourgh is coming with him," said Maria Lucas.

"Oh! Well, if Lady Catherine has decided to travel this way and has offered to bring Mr. Collins with her, I understand completely," said Elizabeth. Mr. Collins deferred in every possible way to her ladyship's wishes – he was diligent in inventing new methods of deference – and if Lady Catherine had decreed that Mr. Collins should accompany her to Meryton, then Mr. Collins would comply. "Is she on her way somewhere in particular?"

"My understanding is that she wishes to speak to *you*, Eliza."

This information was neither expected by nor welcome to Elizabeth. She felt her cheeks color.

"Is she not very angry with you?" inquired Maria Lucas. "I should be terrified if Lady Catherine de Bourgh were angry with me."

Elizabeth's last encounter with Lady Catherine had been extremely unpleasant. During their conversation, Lady Catherine had forbidden Elizabeth to marry her nephew Mr. Darcy, and when Elizabeth had defended her right to do as she liked and had protested that Lady Catherine should not interfere in her concerns, Lady Catherine had proceeded to insult her and to remind her of the inferiority of her relations and her situation. Elizabeth had only confided in a few about what had occurred during that meeting, but Lady Catherine had been frank in her disapprobation of the marriage to anyone who would hear her, so the world was generally aware of her opinion of Elizabeth.

"You are her niece by marriage," said Jane. "It is only natural that she should wish to see you."

No one attempted to argue aloud with Jane's charitable view of the situation, but silently they all disagreed with her.

"Perhaps you would care to read Mr. Collins's letter," said Mrs. Collins, withdrawing it from her reticule.

"May I read it aloud?" Elizabeth asked, and as Mrs. Collins gave permission, Elizabeth shared the following:

My dear Charlotte,

I will make this letter short because I expect to soon join you and little Lewis. If the travel goes according to plan, I will be reunited with you on X-- next, around 3 in the afternoon.

I will have the honor of being conveyed to Lucas Lodge in her ladyship's carriage, and even of having the honor of escorting Lady Catherine de Bourgh, herself. I was a little surprised that she should choose to make this journey now, as Miss de Bourgh is so distressed by Mrs. Jenkinson's illness. Nevertheless, even though Lady Catherine has reasons to remain at Rosings Park, she has decided to undertake this journey – she has intimated that she has a pressing matter of business – and has informed me that she absolutely requires my company.

She has expressed a great interest in Meryton, asking about the town and its inhabitants and its buildings. She even inquired about bridges, fields and trees, which rather surprised me, but her ladyship is always interested in everything. Unfortunately, even though I am the heir to Longbourn House, my knowledge of the neighborhood is extremely limited. I wish you had been here, my dear; you could have answered her questions with greater precision. She was not pleased that I could not tell her more.

When I informed her that Mrs. Darcy was in the area, visiting her sister Mrs. Bingley at Netherfield Park, her ladyship was originally displeased. However, her attitude soon changed and she is determined to call on Mrs. Darcy as soon as possible. I hope you will convey this information to my cousin Elizabeth and to the Bingleys, so that they can undertake whatever preparations required to receive their noble visitor.

"Does she plan to stay *here?*" Jane interrupted, aghast. She had never met Lady Catherine de Bourgh, but she had heard much, and nothing that would indicate that her ladyship would make an agreeable houseguest.

"No – no, she has made her own arrangements," Mrs. Collins assured them. "She will stay at the Meryton Inn."

"That is what the remainder of the letter contains," said Elizabeth, scanning it. "Do you know why she wishes to see me, Charlotte?"

"I cannot give you any details, because I do not know them, but I do know that she was distressed about something just before Lewis and I came here. Even Miss de Bourgh intimated that her mother's temper was – not good." *Not good* was as far as Mrs. Collins, cognizant of the source of most of her husband's tithes, would venture in her criticism of Lady Catherine.

Elizabeth required no effort to imagine Lady Catherine's being angry about something, or to imagine her being ill-tempered if something crossed her, but she could not imagine Lady Catherine inflicting her irritability on her daughter. Lady Catherine doted on Miss de Bourgh.

Mrs. Collins continued. "Eliza, I know Lady Catherine is not always the most agreeable of women, but she really does wish to see you. I hope you will be available. I expect she will call either late tomorrow or the morning after."

"Of course," said Elizabeth. She was not pleased by the prospect of being visited by Lady Catherine, but the woman was her aunt by marriage, and due some courtesy just because of that relationship. Besides, Elizabeth was determined to do everything to ease Lady Catherine's temper, as her friend and her cousin were at the mercy of her ladyship's whims. "I will remain at Netherfield Park till she has either called on me or till I am informed that she will not be coming."

Mrs. Collins and Maria Lucas, having completed their errand, departed.

CHAPTER XIX

All the inhabitants of Netherfield Park were ready to meet Lady Catherine and agreed to remain at the house during the time that she could be expected.

"Is that her carriage, Eliza?" inquired Miss Bingley, who had a great curiosity to see an aunt of Mr. Darcy's.

Elizabeth, glancing out the window, stated that it was, indeed, Lady Catherine's carriage.

"It is considerate of her to come here so soon," Jane said, for it was the earliest possible hour. "This way we are not forced to wait for her long."

Elizabeth would not agree that Lady Catherine was particularly considerate of others, but she could confirm that her ladyship, when she had an objective, was most direct in doing everything she could to attain it. However, despite much speculation about Mr. Darcy's aunt ever since Mrs. Collins's call, Elizabeth still could not comprehend what objective that Lady Catherine could have that involved *her*. Lady Catherine could no longer prevent Elizabeth's marriage with her nephew, as they were already married.

And Lady Catherine, after Elizabeth's marriage to Mr. Darcy, had written him a letter in which she abused his choice of bride in the frankest terms. Could Lady Catherine intend to apologize for her rudeness? Yet apologizing did not seem a part of Lady Catherine's character.

The grand carriage stopped before the door, and Elizabeth decided to cease speculating; her curiosity would be satisfied soon enough.

Her ladyship was ushered in immediately, the footman only serving to direct her towards the drawing-room. The Bingleys and Elizabeth all rose, while Lady Catherine made her entrance and seated herself in the room's best chair.

Lady Catherine, as the person with the highest rank, had to be the first to speak. She frowningly glanced around the room, studied its occupants, and finally addressed Elizabeth: "I hope you are well, Mrs. Darcy."

Elizabeth, noting that with those words, Lady Catherine had acknowledged her marriage, replied that she was indeed, quite well. She then inquired after her ladyship's health, and about Miss de Bourgh and Mrs. Jenkinson.

"I am well. My daughter is in her usual health, but is distressed by the condition of Mrs. Jenkinson, who is very ill." Lady Catherine surveyed the Bingleys. "These people are?"

It was an ungracious way to request introductions, but Elizabeth nevertheless complied, presenting first her sister, then Mr. Bingley, and, finally, Miss Bingley. Afterwards the Bingleys felt permitted to take seats in their own drawing-room.

Jane inquired whether or not her ladyship wished for any refreshment after her journey, but her ladyship declined.

Mr. Bingley then asked how her journey had been that day and again her ladyship answered concisely, only letting them know that she had already dropped Mr. Collins off at Lucas Lodge.

"I understand you are a tenant here, Mr. Bingley," said Lady Catherine.

Mr. Bingley acknowledged that he was. He meant to purchase an estate one day, but till he found one that pleased him he had to be somewhere.

"You do not intend to purchase Netherfield then?" asked her ladyship.

Elizabeth, who was familiar with Lady Catherine's impertinence on matters that did not concern her, was not surprised by the pointedness of this inquiry, but Mr. and Mrs. Bingley were a little taken aback and even Miss Bingley raised her eyebrows.

Mr. Bingley nevertheless answered the question. "Netherfield Park is not for sale, so the decision has been taken away from me."

Lady Catherine was not one to let a decision, whether it concerned her or not, be taken from her without a struggle, but she accepted submission in others. "That is just as well. There are much better neighborhoods."

Her ladyship's dismissive statement annoyed three of her four listeners: Jane and Elizabeth, who had grown up in the area, and Mr. Bingley, who had elected to live at Netherfield Park. Mr. Bingley defended his chosen home: "The neighborhood is not so bad. There is plenty of sport; the people are friendly, and the scenery is quite pleasant!"

Miss Bingley, however, was not in the least offended. "*I* quite agree with you, Lady Catherine. I have told my brother many times that he should purchase an estate somewhere else, preferably in Derbyshire."

Elizabeth decided to be as direct as Lady Catherine. "I wonder that you have traveled to Hertfordshire, if you think so poorly of it."

"I did not wish to make this journey, especially now, but it was necessary."

Lady Catherine gazed at Elizabeth so steadily and so angrily that Elizabeth felt herself color with irritation and embarrassment, even though, for all that she knew, she had no reason to feel embarrassed.

Jane asked: "Lady Catherine, what is it that you find wanting? Does the air seem unhealthy to you?"

Lady Catherine de Bourgh said she was concerned about some of the people. "I am fond of Mrs. Collins but there are others in Meryton who behave as they should not."

This was truly insulting. "If you are referring to me, I now live in Derbyshire," said Elizabeth. "And as for the Bingleys, you have not met them before today, so I do not see how their behavior could offend you."

"I did not mean the Bingleys," said Lady Catherine, "but others. I am sorry, very sorry, that Mr. Collins will find himself here one day. Some people are too interested in money and not sufficiently concerned with truth."

Elizabeth was too confused by this pronouncement to make any reasonable reply, while Mr. Bingley and his sister likewise appeared puzzled. Jane was the only one who sufficiently retained her composure to respond. "I am afraid, your ladyship, that mercenary, dishonest people exist everywhere – not just in this neighborhood."

Elizabeth was impressed by her sister's remark – for Jane, who generally saw goodness in everyone, to recognize the universality of wickedness was a step forward indeed – and that she should make it to Lady Catherine!

"There is something in what you say, Mrs. Bingley," Lady Catherine acknowledged grudgingly.

Lady Catherine rose to her feet; everyone else did likewise, out of deference for their noble guest, but she told them to sit back down. "I am not leaving, not just yet. I just wish to take a turn around the room. After sitting so long today in the carriage I find a little exercise beneficial."

All the ladies retook their seats as commanded, but Bingley remained standing. Lady Catherine said nothing as she toured the room. She inspected a few books, and then paused by the desk and actually picked a sheet of paper off of it and peered at it through her lorgnette. Elizabeth, familiar with her ladyship's autocratic impertinence, was not surprised, but the Bingleys exchanged shocked glances. Before Mr. or Mrs. Bingley could object to Lady Catherine's reading their private correspondence, her ladyship shook her head and put the sheet of paper back down on the desk, then continued exploring the room. Her next pause was before the mantelpiece – given the warmth of the day no fire burned in the hearth – where she examined some artwork. "These are rather fine," she pronounced reluctantly. "Did you draw them, Mrs. Darcy?"

"No, your ladyship, I do not draw."

"Really? Are you sure?"

Elizabeth thought the question was so preposterous that she did not answer it.

"That looks like a 'B' in the corner. Perhaps you did them, Mrs. Bingley?"

"No, they were done by my sisters-in-law. The one you are holding, of Mr. Bingley, was drawn by Miss Bingley here, and several others were sketched by Mrs. Hurst."

"They are not bad, although the lines could be stronger," said Lady Catherine. "I am an excellent judge of drawing. Every young lady should learn to draw, if her health permits."

"I completely agree," said Miss Bingley. "No woman can be considered truly accomplished without the ability to take a good likeness."

Elizabeth and Jane, neither of whom had learned to draw, exchanged an amused glance at this. Elizabeth could not help remembering, too, that Lady Catherine's daughter, the rather sickly Miss de Bourgh, had not learned it either – and Lady Catherine herself lacked any skill with a pencil, and she did not have the excuse of ill-health.

Her ladyship exchanged several other words with Miss Bingley, then told Mr. and Mrs. Bingley that the drawing-room would be improved if they exchanged the positions of the tables and the chairs. Finally she took a deep breath and addressed Elizabeth.

"I should appreciate a few words alone with you, Mrs. Darcy. There is a garden where we could walk, is there not?"

Elizabeth would at last learn the reason for this visit. With a little apprehension and much determination, Elizabeth said that they could take some exercise together. She sent a housemaid to fetch her parasol – while they waited, Jane asked again if she could prepare some refreshment for her ladyship upon their return to the house, but her ladyship steadfastly refused – then Elizabeth and her aunt by marriage went through the doors.

Elizabeth let Lady Catherine lead the way. The older woman leaned on a cane as she walked, and settled on a seat in the shade.

"Well, Mrs. Darcy. As I said before, you are looking well. Are you content? You should be content, in marrying Mr. Darcy, but I can see that you are not."

Elizabeth, who remained standing, was at a loss. "I assure you, that Mr. Darcy and I are very happy together."

"You are spiteful. Not only do you wish to ruin him, and display your bitterness towards me, but you are taking it out on my daughter. Anne, with Mrs. Jenkinson's poor health, and her disappointment over Darcy, is suffering greatly. Have you no pity? Do you wish to ruin all her prospects?"

"Lady Catherine, please believe me when I tell you that I wish Miss de Bourgh the best health and every happiness in the world."

"If that were so you would not have married Mr. Darcy. Do you mean to say that you are not conspiring to ruin my dear daughter?"

"I do not have the slightest idea what you are talking about. I am at a loss to understand why you have taken the trouble to travel to Hertfordshire, and I have no comprehension of how I am supposed to be injuring Miss de Bourgh. You generally do not hesitate to be frank; if you wish to be intelligible, please speak more plainly."

"And am I to believe that your presence here – *now* – is merely a coincidence?"

"A coincidence with what? I am visiting my sister, who appreciates my company at this particular time, for reasons that should be obvious."

"Perhaps you are innocent. Or perhaps you just play your part well." Lady Catherine sniffed. "Tell me, Mrs. Darcy, what do you know of Mr. Radclyff?"

Elizabeth shook her head. "I am unfamiliar with the name. Is Mr. Radclyff a suitor of Miss de Bourgh's?"

Lady Catherine hesitated before saying, "Not Miss de Bourgh, no." She then continued in her usual dictatorial manner: "I would prefer it, Mrs. Darcy, if you would not mention that name to anyone. I know that you did not show me any allegiance in the past, but now that you are married to my nephew, I hope I can rely on your discretion in a family matter."

Rather unwillingly, for her curiosity about the unknown Mr. Radclyff was great, Elizabeth nevertheless promised that she would not discuss the Mr. Radclyff with her friends.

Lady Catherine rose to her feet. "Very well. I am still not convinced that you are entirely innocent in all this, Mrs. Darcy, whether by design or not. I will be staying for the next day or two at the Meryton Inn. If I wish to see you again, I will send for you."

They walked the short distance to Lady Catherine's carriage; the footman assisted her ladyship inside.

"Good-bye, Mrs. Darcy. You may give my compliments to your sister and her family."

Elizabeth watched her husband's aunt depart, then returned to the house and reported on what she could of the conversation to the Bingleys without breaking her word. Lady Catherine had come to Meryton on some sort of business, but she had not explained what it was. "All I can tell you is that it does not please her. However, it appears that she will be staying a night or two at the Meryton Inn."

Miss Bingley, whose artistic ability had been praised, and who still, perhaps out of habit, admired anything or anyone related to Mr. Darcy – with the exception of Mrs. Darcy – was better disposed towards Lady Catherine than anyone else in their party. "It is strange that Lady Catherine would prefer staying there to staying here."

The others were grateful that Lady Catherine had not invited herself to Netherfield Park.

Miss Bingley then inquired about the accommodations at the Meryton Inn; however, Elizabeth and Jane could not give informed opinions, as neither of them had personally stayed there, but they knew of few complaints. "I am sure it will not compare with Rosings," said Elizabeth, "but Lady Catherine will certainly manage to get the best service that Meryton Inn can offer."

The others resumed their conjectures on Lady Catherine's business in Meryton – the general consensus was that it had to involve the Lucases, for they did not know of any other connections that Lady Catherine had in the area – but while the suggestions that they made were interesting, none of them had the ring or feel of truth. They were all left as dissatisfied and ignorant as before.

As Elizabeth had promised discretion to Lady Catherine, she contributed little to the speculation. She wished, very much, to discover something about Mr. Radclyff, and was determined that she would manage it somehow, despite her promise, but now was not the appropriate moment. Besides, if it was a family matter, a matter involving the de Bourghs and the Darcys and the mysterious Mr. Radclyff, it was unlikely that any of the inhabitants of Netherfield could enlighten her – a realization which made it easier for Elizabeth to keep her word to Lady Catherine.

Elizabeth contemplated writing and asking her husband if he were familiar with the name Radclyff, but then decided that this was another matter better not committed to paper. She wished that she and Mr. Darcy could speak, if only for a few minutes. How inconvenient distances were!

Mrs. Collins might know something, but Mrs. Collins was returning with Mr. Collins and Lady Catherine to Hunsford in a day or two. Unless

Elizabeth managed to find a moment alone with her friend before she departed – and Elizabeth doubted that such an opportunity would present itself – she could not ask at all. And if she was reluctant to mention Mr. Radclyff in a letter to Darcy in a letter, she dared not attempt it in her correspondence with her friend. Elizabeth was certain that all her letters to Mrs. Collins were read by Mr. Collins, and although Mrs. Collins could be relied upon to be discreet if asked, Elizabeth did not have the same confidence in Mr. Collins. As Mrs. Collins quite depended on the good will of Lady Catherine, Elizabeth would not do anything to compromise her friend's position.

Poor Charlotte! To have her time away from Hunsford – and away from the tiresome Mr. Collins and the autocratic Lady Catherine – so abruptly terminated! Elizabeth believed that this was her friend's first occasion away from Hunsford since the birth of her son, and she had expected her visit to last at least six weeks, and not less than two.

After the evening meal the group at Netherfield sat down to play quadrille. It was a tribute to her ladyship, Elizabeth explained, for it was Lady Catherine's favorite game.

CHAPTER XX

The next morning, while the Netherfield party was at breakfast, the post arrived. Mr. Bingley, to whom the letters had been handed, distributed them to the ladies. The first was to Jane, from Mrs. Wickham. Jane opened it and observed that Lydia was finally sending a note of thanks for the time she had spent with them.

"Or she is asking you for money," said Miss Bingley, who had a low opinion of Lydia Wickham, and nearly every other person not as rich as herself.

As both Jane and Elizabeth generally only received letters from their youngest sister when she needed funds, they did not dispute the point – but then Jane, reading it, said that this time Lydia had made no such request. "Admittedly it is rather short – she thanks us for the visit and she hopes that I am well. Then she suggests that we call the baby Lydia if it is a girl or George if it is a boy."

"Perhaps a page is missing?" asked Miss Bingley.

"It is not," Jane said, waving the letter in front of them.

Elizabeth wondered if there might be hope for Lydia, after all. She had been pleased by the improvements that she had noticed in Kitty. Perhaps her younger sisters had only needed time apart – they were a bad influence on each other – and a few more years to mature.

"Two letters for Mrs. Darcy," announced Mr. Bingley. "The first is also from Mrs. Lydia Wickham, and the second is from Pemberley," and he handed both to his fair sister-in-law.

"Mr. Darcy is such a faithful correspondent," observed Miss Bingley.

"It is not from Mr. Darcy, but his sister," said Elizabeth, opening that one first.

"Ah, Georgiana," said Miss Bingley, who had once planned for Miss Darcy to be *her* sister-in-law, and was not pleased to realize that Elizabeth was now on far more intimate terms with her. Still, she attempted to remain civil. "How is she? What does she say?"

"She is writing to me to let me know that her brother cannot write himself just now – he is extremely busy with Reverend Wallace in Kympton, who still lingers in terrible pain. Georgiana also has an idea about where to place a bench in the park and she desires my opinion," said Elizabeth.

"And the letter from Lydia?" inquired Jane.

"Perhaps she did not ask you for money, Jane, because she sent that request to Eliza."

Elizabeth opened the letter from Lydia, and glanced through it. She was a little embarrassed by her sister's childish, poorly formed hand, but she could report that the contents were innocent enough. "It is not very long, but it contains no request for funds. Instead she asks me to write a long letter back, and to tell her all about you and your condition, Jane. It seems that she does not trust you to give an honest report on yourself." She resolved that she would do this right away; it was important to encourage Lydia's unselfish sisterly impulses; even though Lydia's letter was short, she would write the lengthy response requested. Elizabeth always felt a little guilty about Lydia; if only she had warned her about George Wickham, Lydia might not have eloped with him, and so fixed her life's course when she was but sixteen.

"And, you, Caroline, have received the most interesting envelope of them all," continued Bingley, holding up the letter for them all to see. "Look at this fine stationery – this crest! You are corresponding with nobility? An admiring duke, whom you have neglected to mention?"

Miss Bingley turned a faint pink.

"It is from Lady Catherine," announced Elizabeth, recognizing the crest.

"You are honored," said Bingley, handing her ladyship's note to his sister with a flourish.

"And you are not honored, Charles," retorted Miss Bingley. "How is it that you are the only one not to receive a letter this morning?"

"I am not disappointed, I assure you," said Bingley. "Letters often mean work."

Elizabeth studied her brother-in-law; his relief seemed genuine. Well, he had had that unpleasant reminder of Miss Hightower, which had presumably arrived in the post. "My father feels the same way," she said.

"Papa does not mind receiving letters," Jane amended mildly. "He just does not like to write them himself."

"So, Caroline, what does Lady Catherine have to say?" asked Mr. Bingley.

"Lady Catherine wishes for me to dine with her this evening at the Meryton Inn," reported Miss Bingley. "She will send her carriage to fetch me this afternoon."

"That is an honor, Caroline," said Jane.

"But why did she invite you and not Elizabeth?" asked Bingley.

"That is true; it is an insult to you, Lizzy," said Jane, who was capable of indignation only when one of her dearest was being slighted. "She should have invited you as well as Miss Bingley."

Miss Bingley could not help smiling at the idea of Mrs. Darcy being slighted by Lady Catherine while she herself was complimented; it compensated a little – just a little – for Elizabeth's having received a letter from Georgiana Darcy.

"I assure you, I am not the least offended," said Elizabeth, struggling not to laugh. If she had been invited, she might have had to conjure up one of Miss Bingley's headaches.

"But what does she want? Why invite Caroline at all?" asked Bingley.

Miss Bingley had no answer to this.

Elizabeth, who knew Lady Catherine best, suggested that her ladyship appreciated company and that as Miss Bingley was least familiar to her ladyship that would make her the most interesting. "The best way to learn the reason for the invitation is to accept it, Miss Bingley – will you go? It will also give you the opportunity to judge the Meryton Inn yourself."

"And you will miss a visit from my mother," said Jane. "I am expecting her later today."

That settled it. Miss Bingley sent a reply to Lady Catherine at the Meryton Inn, accepting the invitation to dine.

The rest of the day was spent as usual, with the exception that Elizabeth, in addition to her notes to her husband and to her sister-in-law, penned a long letter to Lydia. In due time Miss Bingley dressed and her ladyship's carriage arrived, although it was not early enough for Miss Bingley to completely avoid Mrs. Bennet. The carriage from Longbourn arrived before, this time transporting Mrs. Bennet and her sister, Mrs. Philips.

Mrs. Bennet was most interested in Jane, of course, and had more ideas for the nursery and more opinions of potential nursery maids, but early in the visit she took Elizabeth aside and spoke in a half-whisper. "Be especially kind to your aunt Philips. She is rather low these days. It seems that she has had a falling-out with her friend, Mrs. Smith."

So Elizabeth made a point of sitting beside her aunt and asking about mutual acquaintances, and encouraged Mrs. Philips to speak. Mrs. Philips told her that Mr. Selby had concluded his business with Miss King's estate and departed. Unfortunately Miss King's money and her jewelry had still not been found, so Mr. Selby's inheritance from poor Miss King was limited to the house in Meryton and what remained in her bank account. Mr. Selby and Miss King were not of paramount interest to Mrs. Philips, however; other matters troubled her more. Mr. Clarke and Mr. Morris were not getting along. Mr. Morris complained that Mr. Clarke was usurping his friendship with young Mr. Jones – he even warned Mr. Jones against Mr. Clarke – claiming that Mr. Clarke was not trusted. This meant that inviting them both over for an evening was difficult and even Mr. Philips said the tension in the office was unpleasant.

But the chief of Mrs. Philips's woes centered on the apparent defection of her new friend Mrs. Smith, who had recently repulsed every effort at amity. "I wished to introduce her to Mrs. Collins, but she refused, and she has refused every invitation since."

Elizabeth wondered if Mrs. Smith, like Miss Bingley, had decided to develop headaches in order to avoid undesirable social commitments.

Mrs. Philips continued. "At my time of life, it is so important to have female friends – something you will learn to appreciate when you are older, Lizzy. I was delighted with Mrs. Smith, who was always agreeable and amusing. And now she will not accept any invitation at all, from an evening of casino to a game of cards to mere afternoon tea. I have asked her if something is wrong but she will not say."

"Perhaps she is not feeling well," said Elizabeth. "That could make her disinclined for engagements."

"Or perhaps she has decided that she has had enough of Meryton and wishes to leave it, as Mr. Clarke hinted – then we shall have to go through the annoying business of having to find another tenant. You, who have so much, cannot understand how important every little bit of income is to us, Lizzy. If only the war office would quarter another regiment here – then every room in the town was full, and we could charge whatever we wished!"

Elizabeth attempted to console her aunt, suggesting that either Mrs. Smith would recover her good will towards Mrs. Philips, or if Meryton truly displeased her, then another tenant would come, someone more consistently agreeable. "I am sure that Mrs. Smith's desertion has nothing to do with you, Aunt," said Elizabeth, "but is due to something that you do not know about Mrs. Smith."

But Mrs. Philips was determined not to be consoled. "Why does she not like Meryton?"

"It is a cross summer," Elizabeth said. "Maybe something will happen that will shake our friends out of their bad humor."

CHAPTER XXI

Something did happen. The very next morning Mr. Bingley was not at breakfast, and his wife reported that shortly after dawn an urgent message had arrived from Mr. Bennet, summoning Bingley to the Meryton Bridge, which connected the village of Longbourn to the town of Meryton. Bingley had saddled his black horse and departed at once.

"Is Papa unwell?" Elizabeth asked, alarmed. Their father's health had seemed quite usual the last time they had met, but good health three days ago did not guarantee good health today.

"Lizzy, the note came from him," said Jane, showing it to her.

Elizabeth anxiously read it. It contained no more than what Jane had reported, but his handwriting seemed firm.

Miss Bingley was likewise curious. "Lady Catherine's carriage took me past that bridge last night."

The sisters asked if Miss Bingley had noticed anything unusual, but she replied that she had not.

They all wondered why Mr. Bennet would summon Mr. Bingley to the bridge, but that curiosity was certain to be satisfied later. So instead they questioned Miss Bingley about her evening with Lady Catherine. Had anyone else been present? Had she enjoyed herself?

Miss Bingley replied that it had been an interesting, if not exactly an agreeable evening. Lady Catherine wanted to know what she thought of the denizens of Meryton, but Miss Bingley's information had not been as complete as she would have liked. She had questioned Miss Bingley about her artistic skills and wished to know if Mrs. Darcy had had any skill in that area – she had then asked about Mrs. Darcy's penmanship.

"Lizzy's penmanship?" Jane repeated.

Elizabeth was also taken aback; she could not see how her handwriting could matter to anyone except a correspondent, and she did not expect to write many letters to her ladyship in the future. "Perhaps she hopes I will write to Miss Anne de Bourgh?" she speculated, but then, recalling her conversation with Lady Catherine just the day before yesterday, and how her ladyship had been convinced that she was attempting to *ruin* Miss de Bourgh, that seemed unlikely. "How did you answer?"

Miss Bingley had said she had only seen Elizabeth's handwriting once or twice, and that there had been nothing particularly remarkable about it.

Elizabeth was tempted to ask if Lady Catherine had mentioned the name Radclyff but she decided not to risk it. Instead she pursued a different topic and inquired about Miss Bingley's opinion of the inn.

The Meryton Inn was reasonable, Miss Bingley reported; as there was nothing else, it would do. The food, at any rate, had been excellent; Lady Catherine would tolerate no less.

"Do you know when she returns to Hunsford?" Elizabeth asked, wishing that she could see Charlotte again before she departed but fearing that it was impossible.

"I believe her ladyship is departing today. She was to collect the Collinses late this morning and then continue on their journey. They may have already left."

The ladies of Netherfield finished breakfasting and moved to the drawing-room. The morning seemed most tranquil, till they heard hoofs galloping to the house. Jane peered through the window. "Why is Bingley in such a hurry?"

"Jane! Caroline! Elizabeth!" Bingley called, his loud voice and his footsteps announcing his swift approach through the house. He arrived in the drawing-room and paused just inside the threshold. "There you are!"

His eyes were large; his face reddened from exertion, and he was breathing hard.

"What is wrong?" cried Jane.

"Mr. Collins is dead! His body was found beneath the bridge."

CHAPTER XXII

All the ladies expressed consternation, but none of them had the presence of mind to engage in the reactions so often attributed to young ladies: no one burst into tears; no one fainted; no one even screamed or shrieked. They were, however, grieved and shocked and, after a few moments, burst forth with questions.

Elizabeth was the first. "Mr. Collins is dead! How can that be? Are you absolutely certain?"

Mr. Bingley assured them that he was certain. One of the servants from Longbourn House had been running an early-morning errand and had discovered the body herself. As Mr. Collins had occasionally stayed at Longbourn, and was generally known as Mr. Bennet's heir, she had informed Mr. Bennet immediately. Mr. Bennet was shocked enough to be provoked out of his usual lethargy. He dressed hastily and went with her and several other servants to inspect the situation. After confirming that it was indeed Mr. Collins, he dispatched the servants in several directions. He sent for the apothecary, the senior Mr. Jones, who would know what to do with the body. He sent another servant in the direction of Lucas Lodge, to inform Mrs. Collins and to fetch Sir William. And finally, he sent a servant to Netherfield Park to summon Mr. Bingley.

"Poor Charlotte!" Jane exclaimed. "She must be extremely grieved. What will she and her little boy do?"

Miss Bingley wished to know why Mr. Bennet had summoned Mr. Bingley. "What good could you do?"

"As I am married to a cousin of Mr. Collins, Mr. Bennet felt that I should be there," replied Mr. Bingley. "He then asked for me to call on Lady Catherine at the Meryton Inn. From his visit to Hunsford, Sir William Lucas is better acquainted with Lady Catherine, but Mr. Bennet believed that Sir William was needed at Lucas Lodge for his daughter. Even though Lady Catherine once called at Longbourn House, Mr. Bennet had never met her. He asked me to bring her the news, as he did not think this task should be left to a complete stranger."

"So you went to the Meryton Inn and informed her ladyship?" asked Elizabeth. "How did she react?"

Mr. Bingley confirmed that he had gone at once to the Meryton Inn. Lady Catherine, who had been planning to leave this morning, was already dressed and so had received him immediately. She had been horrified to learn what had happened to Mr. Collins, had demanded many details and then had finally insisted on being escorted to the bridge so that she could see for herself where the tragedy had occurred.

"She wished to see the body? Why? Did she not believe that he was dead?" asked Miss Bingley.

"She wished to understand how he died. When we reached the bridge, Lady Catherine looked around and brought up several puzzling points. Her ladyship asserted that Mr. Collins always drank very moderately, so he could not have stumbled from it in a drunken stupor. His health was excellent, and so it was unlikely that he had had some sort of fit and had fallen. In fact, she did not see how he could have fallen over the side of the bridge at all. The walls are tall enough to prevent from someone making that sort of error, even a tall man such as Mr. Collins."

"So Lady Catherine does not believe his death was an accident?" inquired Elizabeth, aghast at the implication.

"Lizzy, what are you suggesting? That Mr. Collins jumped?" cried Jane. "I cannot believe it. He had a good position, an excellent wife, and a little boy."

"And the expectation of inheriting Longbourn House," Mr. Bingley added.

Miss Bingley remarked: "His would not be the only suicide in Meryton."

"I am only attempting to understand what happened," said Elizabeth.

Mr. Bingley shook his head. "The bridge is not that high. I made a few inquiries of the crowd that gathered – everyone uses that bridge; it was impossible to keep people away – and learned that many of the boys, and even some of the girls, have jumped off it without injury. If Mr. Collins wished to take his life, jumping off the bridge would be an unreliable method."

"I remember that when the regiment was quartered here, a private who had been drinking decided to walk along the wall of the bridge," said Elizabeth. "He fell off, but he did not die. He only broke a leg, and then was rescued by his friends, and I believe he recovered. Like you, Jane, I cannot imagine that Mr. Collins would wish to kill himself – not only does he have a good position, a young son and expectations, but he would consider the act completely unfitting for a clergyman."

"So it must have been an accident," said Jane. "Perhaps Mr. Collins heard something and had some reason to be on the wall – and then he slipped and fell off and his fall was terribly unlucky. Or possibly – *possibly* someone pushed him, intending it to be a prank, but then it went horribly wrong. And then when whoever it was realized what he had done and left out of guilt and fear."

"Those theories are plausible. What does Lady Catherine say?" inquired Elizabeth.

"She did not reveal her thoughts on the matter," said Mr. Bingley. "She *did* say that this is a most unfortunate and unhappy neighborhood."

"I completely concur," said Miss Bingley.

"Lady Catherine also said that because of Mrs. Jenkinson's ill health, she cannot delay her return to Rosings Park for more than a few hours. She said she would first call on Mrs. Collins at Lucas Lodge – she expects that Mrs. Collins, under the circumstances, would not be returning with her – and that her ladyship then intends to come here."

"Oh! Then we cannot go to Lucas Lodge or to Longbourn," said Jane, "in order to condole with Charlotte or Papa."

"Not till later," agreed Mr. Bingley. "And Mr. Bennet said it is unlikely that Mrs. Bennet will be able to venture to Netherfield today; he wished to keep the carriage at hand in case he needs it for something urgent."

Jane and Elizabeth said that they understood perfectly, while Miss Bingley repressed a smile at the prospect of a day without Mrs. Bennet.

Even though Jane and Elizabeth could not depart from Netherfield themselves, they could dispatch a servant with notes to carry to Longbourn House and to Lucas Lodge and also to the Meryton Inn, in case Lady Catherine had not yet departed. When this first task was done, Elizabeth had longer letters to write, in this case to Mr. Darcy and his sister, while Jane decided to share the news with Lydia and with Mr. and Mrs. Gardiner. Even Miss Bingley wrote about the dreadful event to her sister in Grosvenor Square.

CHAPTER XXIII

Lady Catherine did not keep the inmates of Netherfield Park waiting long, but arrived about four hours after Bingley had returned to the estate with the news of Mr. Collins's death. When she appeared, her posture was as erect as ever, but the pallor of her skin signaled how perturbed she was by the morning's discovery.

"I am most sorry for your loss, Lady Catherine," Elizabeth said sincerely, after Lady Catherine had been shown into the parlor and had usurped the best chair.

The others also expressed their sympathy.

"He was not my relation. He was your cousin," stated Lady Catherine.

"Because our fathers had quarreled, we only met Mr. Collins for the first time about two years ago," Jane explained gently. "He has been a much greater part of your life than of ours, Lady Catherine."

"Perhaps," Lady Catherine acknowledged, her features tightening as if she were attempting not to weep.

Elizabeth added, "Lady Catherine, Mr. Collins valued your opinion more highly than any other person's in the world, and was very grateful for your patronage."

"A sensible and dependable young man. One rarely meets one like him," Lady Catherine pronounced.

They all agreed that Mr. Collins had been a man of unusual talents; Elizabeth then asked about Mrs. Collins.

"Mrs. Collins is handling the news very well, although naturally she is prostrate with grief and shock," said her ladyship. "She will remain at Lucas Lodge for the next few weeks, but will have to return to Hunsford at some point to direct what is to be done with her possessions. The timing of her return has not yet been arranged." Lady Catherine sat more upright than ever, and glared at each person in Netherfield's drawing-room in turn. "Even though we are grieving, I still wish to understand what happened. I must understand! Miss Bingley, *you* were in Meryton last night. Did you see anything or anyone? Did you look out the carriage window and see Mr. Collins?"

"No, I did not," replied Miss Bingley. "But the coach paused for a moment in the town. I thought your coachman spoke with someone – it might have been Mr. Collins."

"My coachman said he saw Mr. Collins, who asked if I were within the coach," said Lady Catherine. "When Mr. Collins learned that I was not inside, and that the coach was carrying someone – you, Miss Bingley – to dine with me at the Meryton Inn, Mr. Collins told Johnson that he would not disturb me this evening, but that he might have some important information for me that he would convey to me on the next day." Again she stared pointedly at each member of her audience. "Do any of you have any idea what that information might be?"

They all took a moment to consider, but no one had an answer to her ladyship's question. Elizabeth reflected that Mr. Collins's last and undelivered message could be absolutely anything, as her cousin had believed everything pertaining to Lady Catherine to be of the utmost significance, and so he could have referred to any matter, large or small, important or trivial. Yet Elizabeth comprehended her ladyship's urgent desire to know what he had wished to tell her. Even if the missing message had been of no real account – perhaps a suggestion regarding the garden at the Hunsford parish church – it was Mr. Collins's last message for her ladyship. Mr. Collins and Lady Catherine had, in their peculiar way, been a perfect match for each other: she so condescending and he so deferential.

"And what were you doing yesterday evening? I know where Miss Bingley was, but what about the rest of you?"

Her manner was autocratic and impertinent, but Jane answered calmly, explaining that they had all been together in Netherfield Park, receiving a visit from Mrs. Bennet and her sister Mrs. Philips.

Lady Catherine frowned, as if the report disappointed her, but she did not contradict it.

Elizabeth, reflecting, then said, "If Mr. Collins had something to tell you, it does not seem likely that he would take his own life."

Lady Catherine was affronted. "Take his own life! Nonsense!"

"What do you believe happened, Lady Catherine?" inquired Mr. Bingley.

But her ladyship did not answer this question. "This is a wicked place. I will be glad to leave it. In fact, I must depart immediately."

She rose and so did everyone else. The Bingleys inquired if she or her coachman, her maid or even the horses needed anything before the journey.

Lady Catherine refused all offers of assistance. She then addressed Elizabeth: "Mrs. Darcy, would you accompany me to my carriage? I wish to converse with you in private."

Elizabeth complied. As Lady Catherine only wanted her to accompany her to the carriage, rather than walk to a section of garden where they would not be overheard, she had hopes for a brief if not a civil exchange.

Lady Catherine began as soon as they were outside the house. "Mrs. Darcy, as both your relations and the Netherfield servants – yes, I have questioned them – confirm that you were here last night, I know that you were not involved, not directly at least, with the death of Mr. Collins."

"Lady Catherine, I know you think ill of me, but I am amazed that you could contemplate such a possibility. Why would I want Mr. Collins dead? And even if I did, how could I possibly manage it?"

"Mrs. Darcy, as I said that I believe you could not be involved, there is no reason to take umbrage. But pay attention to my words. Vigilance is absolutely necessary; you should trust no one; I was simply applying this principle myself. Something is terribly wrong here. I believe that Mr. Collins was deliberately killed. You are a clever young woman, Mrs. Darcy. You may, if you keep your wits about you, discover the identity of the perpetrator and keep others from being harmed."

"Deliberately killed!" exclaimed Elizabeth. "Other than your general dislike of Meryton, do you have any reason to believe that Mr. Collins was murdered?"

Yes, Lady Catherine did, thanks to her insistence on going to where the body had been found and her interrogation of those who had discovered it. Her ladyship explained that Mr. Collins had died from a blow to the head – apparently the back of the skull was bloody and broken – but the body had not been found near any large stones.

Elizabeth had to quell some queasiness as she listened to these unpleasant details. Then she posed questions of her own. "Was there any chance that Mr. Collins's body was moved by the flowing water? Could it have been near a large stone originally and then moved by the current?"

But to this suggestion Lady Catherine made two reasonable objections. First, the river was not that strong right now. And second, Mr. Collins's body had been discovered on the *upstream* side of the bridge, partly in the water but partly on the bank. She did not believe the water had moved his body at all.

Elizabeth shivered. Lady Catherine might be autocratic and meddlesome, but she was not at all unintelligent. She was, after all, Mr. Darcy's aunt. "If Mr. Collins did not break his head from the fall, he must have broken it before. Are you suggesting that someone killed Mr. Collins by hitting him on the head, and then threw his body over the bridge in order to make it appear like an accident?"

"Yes, that is what I believe."

"That person would have to be very strong, first to strike the blow and then to carry the body. Mr. Collins was not a small man."

"Or there would have to have been more than one person. As I said, there is evil in Meryton."

They had been standing near the open carriage door for several minutes; with these words Lady Catherine turned to go.

But Elizabeth detained her. "Does this have anything to do with Mr. Radclyff? I have honored your request for secrecy but if you wish me to be on my guard, then it would help for my information to be complete."

Her ladyship hesitated, as if she were considering what to reveal. "Mr. Radclyff has been dead more than ten years, so he could not have anything to do with this. But someone has been attempting to spread vile lies about him. That is all I will tell you, Mrs. Darcy. I must go; my daughter needs me. And Mrs. Collins will need you. You must show her every attention. Do what you can to console her, and even more importantly, to protect her. If Mr. Collins was in danger, she may be as well."

"But from what? From whom?" cried Elizabeth.

"I cannot answer you," said her ladyship. She stepped towards her carriage and indicated to her footman that he should assist her inside.

CHAPTER XXIV

Elizabeth watched the carriage from Rosings depart, and then turned and walked slowly to the house. The possibility that Mr. Collins could have been murdered was both frightening and sickening, yet Lady Catherine's remarks seemed to lead to that conclusion.

Before she reached the others in the drawing-room, she had to decide what of her conversation with Lady Catherine she should relate to the others. Elizabeth decided to reflect on her ladyship's speculations a little longer before communicating them, for what was said could not be unsaid, and Jane, in her condition, should not be perturbed more than she already was. Instead she explained that Lady Catherine had emphasized her concern for Mrs. Collins and her desire that she, Elizabeth, would do everything possible for her – the truth, but not the entire truth.

They consulted as to what they should do, now that their noble caller had come and departed. Despite so much having happened; it was only early afternoon. "I think that I should go see Charlotte," said Elizabeth. "Even if it is only for a few minutes."

"And I should call on Mr. Bennet, and determine if he needs any additional assistance," said Mr. Bingley. "Caroline, will you stay with Jane?"

Miss Bingley said that of course she would stay with Jane, even though Jane protested that she was not an invalid and did not need constant companionship.

Mr. Bingley ordered the carriage for himself and his sister-in-law, while Jane wrote another note to Mrs. Collins, including, on Miss Bingley's request, a few words of concern from her. In the meantime Elizabeth prepared to depart, changing her brightly colored gown for one in a more somber hue. Jane gave the note to her sister, and then Elizabeth and Mr. Bingley departed in the Netherfield carriage and headed towards Meryton.

"This is a dreadful business, an absolutely dreadful business," remarked Bingley.

"It is, it is," said Elizabeth, considering how much to share of Lady Catherine's conjectures.

"Her ladyship has a forceful personality."

"Indeed she does," said Elizabeth, smiling briefly before returning to the serious subject of the deceased Mr. Collins. "Before I call on Charlotte, is there anything particular that you can tell me about her husband's death? Is there anything that I should know before I condole with her?"

But Bingley had no observations besides those he had already given.

Elizabeth wondered silently if others had conjectured in the manner that Lady Catherine had conjectured. What if the murderer himself had returned to the scene of the crime, and had observed others making their observations?

"Why are you frowning?" inquired Bingley.

"I am wondering if Lady Catherine could be correct; and if there is something not right with Meryton. First Miss King took her own life, and now Mr. Collins is dead as well."

"I believe evil exists everywhere," said Bingley, which was a rather dispirited remark for him to make. Elizabeth would not dispute it, however.

The carriage took them to Lucas Lodge; Mr. Bingley told his coachman to continue to Longbourn House, which had a larger paddock; when Mr. Bingley and Mrs. Darcy were finished at the Lucases, they would walk the short distance on foot.

Then they were ushered inside and met by Lady Lucas. "I do not know if Mrs. Collins is receiving anyone just now," said Elizabeth, "but I felt that I had to condole with her if possible."

"I'm sure she will see you, Mrs. Darcy. Ah, Sir William! Here are Mrs. Darcy and Mr. Bingley, come to condole with us."

Sir William greeted them in a subdued manner and expressed his appreciation for their attention at this terrible time. He led them to the parlor where several of his daughters, including Mrs. Collins, were sitting. Maria Lucas was in tears, and being comforted by a younger sister. Mrs. Collins's eyes were dry, but she was pale, very pale, befitting someone who had received a great shock.

Both Elizabeth and her brother-in-law expressed their grief and concern for everyone at Lucas Lodge, especially Mrs. Collins. Elizabeth gave Mrs. Collins the note from Jane; Mrs. Collins read it, thanked Elizabeth and her sister, and then handed it to her father. The note was read and passed around the room till it reached Mrs. Collins once more; she glanced at it again, and then put it with other notes of condolence. Mr. Bingley offered his services, for what, he did not know, but he was ready to be active on the Lucases' behalf.

Elizabeth introduced the subject of Lady Catherine, and explained that her ladyship had called briefly at Netherfield on her way out of the neighborhood. The Lucases had always followed Mr. Collins's lead in the extent of deference shown to his patroness, and this deference survived his demise, so they were dutifully impressed by this information. Then, when

Elizabeth explained that her ladyship had given her a private message for Mrs. Collins, they were readily excused.

Mrs. Collins led Elizabeth to the breakfast-room, which they could have to themselves. They embraced and then sat down. "I am so grieved for you, Charlotte. It is a most terrible and unexpected thing to happen."

"It is. I know that not everyone thought well of Mr. Collins, Eliza, but he was a good husband – to the best of his abilities."

Elizabeth was heartily ashamed of her own expressions and judgments regarding her dead cousin, who had always treated her with kindness and respect. "You made him an excellent wife, Charlotte. As he once said, you made him the happiest of men."

"My poor little boy! What will we do?"

Elizabeth assured her that if she needed assistance, she was ready to offer, and Lady Catherine wished to convey the same message.

"You are very kind, but I am not distressed financially," said Mrs. Collins. "Mr. Collins and I were not extravagant. You need not concern yourself about that. And it is far too soon to make any sort of decision about the future."

"I understand," said Elizabeth, who was not certain that she did, but who wished to be as supportive as possible. "Charlotte, if it will not distress you too much, may we discuss what happened to Mr. Collins? We have both crossed that bridge thousands of times. How could he have fallen from it?"

"I do not know. I have been trying to comprehend it myself."

"Can you tell me what happened yesterday evening?"

Mrs. Collins was willing to relate all she knew. While Lady Catherine's carriage had traveled through Meryton on the way to Lucas Lodge, Mr. Collins believed that he had seen someone familiar. As he had not been completely certain – he had only glimpsed the person from a distance – he had told neither Lady Catherine nor Mrs. Collins the suspected identity. Late yesterday afternoon, when Lewis had settled down for a nap, Mr. Collins had walked into Meryton to look for that person again. He also said he might call on Lady Catherine to see if her accommodation was to her satisfaction and if he could do anything to ease her stay and to discuss the departure that had been scheduled for today.

"And do you know if he found that person? Do you have any idea who it could have been?"

Mrs. Collins said that she did not. She did not even know whether the person had been a man or a woman.

"And when did he begin this walk?"

Mrs. Collins reported that it had been about an hour before sunset.

"You were not surprised that he did not return to Lucas Lodge for dinner?"

"No, I thought that he had called at the Meryton Inn and that Lady Catherine had invited him to dine with her. I was too busy with Lewis and my family to notice his absence till quite late and even then I thought he might be on a sofa or in some other room, or even at the Meryton Inn itself. But I am only giving you my conjectures about his last night. What Mr. Collins really did after leaving here, I cannot say."

Elizabeth explained that Lady Catherine had invited Miss Bingley to dinner at the Meryton Inn and had sent the Rosings carriage for her. Neither Lady Catherine nor Miss Bingley had mentioned dining with Mr. Collins the previous evening – and given what had happened, if he had been with them, both women would have mentioned the circumstance. "I will ask for confirmation from Miss Bingley when I return to Netherfield, but I believe it is safe to presume Mr. Collins did not dine at the Meryton Inn last night."

"I expect you are right, Eliza – but then where did he go?"

But this question Elizabeth could not answer. She could only suggest making inquiries, to determine if anyone in Meryton had seen him yesterday evening. Mrs. Collins said she would ask her father and her brothers to make the inquiries and to see if they could learn anything about her husband's last movements.

Then Elizabeth asked: "Did Mr. Collins tell you why he and Lady Catherine came to Hertfordshire? I know she had some business here, something which distressed her greatly, but she would not tell me what it was."

"Yes, Mr. Collins said something similar."

"From something that her ladyship said, I believe it may involve Miss de Bourgh."

But Mrs. Collins only knew of one immediate concern that her ladyship had with respect to her daughter – other than the usual worry about Miss de Bourgh's indifferent health – and that was the grave illness of Mrs. Jenkinson.

An idea struck Elizabeth. "Is it possible that Mr. Collins might have seen Miss de Bourgh in Meryton?"

The notion was so startling that Mrs. Collins momentarily forgot her grief. "Miss de Bourgh? What business would she have here?"

Elizabeth could supply no answer to this, but she believed it could account for Mr. Collins's astonishment, and because of his deference for everyone associated with Rosings, could also explain why he did not mention her name before ascertaining that it was really Miss de Bourgh and what her purpose was in Meryton. Finally, Miss de Bourgh, despite her noble heritage and her autocratic mother, was both insignificant and small. If she put on the dress of an inferior, it would be easy for her to go about unnoticed.

Mrs. Collins acknowledged all these points, but raised some objections. She did not see how Miss de Bourgh could travel to Meryton without her mother noticing, and certainly not without her mother's servants noticing as well. Besides, Mrs. Jenkinson was truly ill and it seemed highly unlikely that Miss de Bourgh would leave her for several days.

"You are quite right," said Elizabeth. "Forget my conjecture."

"I think Miss de Bourgh is not possible, but Mr. Collins definitely saw *someone*," said Mrs. Collins. "*Something* happened last night. You are clever, Eliza; you must realize how unlikely it is that he fell from that bridge. And even if he did, how could it have killed him? My brothers jumped from it all the time when they were boys, and they never sustained anything worse than wet clothes and sprained ankles."

"So you believe...?" Elizabeth could not finish the question.

"I believe – I believe that someone must have killed him. As does Lady Catherine, and even you, Eliza, even if you are reluctant to mention it to me out of fear of distressing me. But I could not be more distressed than I already am, so do not concern yourself about that."

"Charlotte, I truly do not think that murder is the only possible explanation for Mr. Collins's death, because even that seems unlikely. I cannot imagine *anyone* wishing to harm your husband!"

"Nor can I. But I cannot imagine his taking his own life, or having a fit of apoplexy, or even how an accident could have led to his death – yet dead he is. So murder must be a possible explanation, in which case it is wise to be cautious."

"I agree with Lady Catherine that caution is necessary – she asked me to look after you, and to do what I can to protect you."

Mrs. Collins smiled sadly. "Lady Catherine is not an easy woman, but she is capable of kindness."

"She is certainly fond of *you*, Charlotte. And there is another point to discuss: Lady Catherine called Meryton wicked. Do you have any idea why? Could Mr. Collins have had any idea why?"

Mrs. Collins did not know but she believed that Mr. Collins might have had some sort of idea. He had hinted, upon his arrival at Lucas Lodge two days before that Lady Catherine was relying on him more than ever. Mrs. Collins had asked him to tell her what he meant but he had said that the matter was extremely confidential. She could have pressed, but the baby had needed attention, and Mrs. Collins had thought that she could ask him later. It had not occurred to her that Mr. Collins could be in any danger.

Elizabeth said that she completely understood.

The clock struck; their tête-à-tête had to end. Mrs. Collins said that she needed to tend to her son, and also to meet with others making condolence calls. Elizabeth rose to depart, saying that she and Bingley intended first to go to Longbourn House before they returned to Netherfield Park.

She shook her friend's hands, and then said before departing: "Lady Catherine must know more than she was willing to tell me. But she might confide in you, Charlotte."

Mrs. Collins promised that she would write to Lady Catherine at once, and if she learned anything of use, to share it with Elizabeth immediately.

CHAPTER XXV

Elizabeth rejoined Mr. Bingley and they continued on foot to Longbourn House. The walk was so short that they only had time enough to exchange a few impressions of what they had experienced at Lucas Lodge.

"Sir William cannot understand what happened," said Mr. Bingley. "Mr. Collins was always so careful."

Elizabeth had to agree.

"He wondered if Mr. Collins could have been on the bridge after sunset and was somehow knocked off by a carriage traversing it at the same time. If it were dark, a coachman might not have seen Mr. Collins, and if the coachman were a little deaf, he might not have even heard him over the sound of the horses."

"An accident, then," said Elizabeth, her heart lighter at this suggestion. Mr. Collins would still be dead, but Meryton would not be the wicked neighborhood that Lady Catherine averred that it was.

"Yes – but his two eldest sons do not agree; they think something sinister must have happened. Still, Sir William and his sons plan to query everyone in the neighborhood with a coach or a cart and to determine if anyone traversed the bridge yesterday evening."

"Even if that is what happened, they may not be able to discover the truth," warned Elizabeth. "The vehicle may have come from outside of this neighborhood. Or even if the driver is from this area, he may not wish to admit what happened."

Their discussion was ended by their arrival at Longbourn.

Mrs. Bennet was in hysterics, to which she had little right, as she had not seen the body and had claimed to dislike Mr. Collins when he had chosen to marry Miss Charlotte Lucas instead of one of her own daughters. But Mrs. Bennet rather enjoyed yielding to hysterics, and the occasion was too opportune for her not to take advantage of it. There were several strains to her volubility. First, Mr. Collins had been such an obliging man, healing the breach between the Bennets and the Collinses, and she had been very fond of him. It was shocking to think of Charlotte widowed so young, especially with a little boy. Second, there were too many funerals in the neighborhood this summer, especially of people dying far too young. Miss King! And now Mr. Collins! True, neither of them were officially residing here, as Miss King had only come for a few weeks and Mr. Collins had intended his visit to last only two days, but they had both managed to die here, which spoke even worse for Meryton. Third, the bridge! What if *it* were a danger to everyone? What if more people were to fall off and get killed? Mary, Kitty, her sister Mrs. Philips and even Mr. Bennet and herself – they were all at risk! Who could think that the bridge, on which they all depended, which they crossed more than once nearly every single day, could be putting them in such peril? Mrs. Bennet especially welcomed the arrival of her second daughter, to whom she could express all these thoughts afresh, as every other person at Longbourn House had already heard them several times.

The reactions of the rest of her family were not as loud but each member still had much to say. Kitty worried for Charlotte and her son; she asked Elizabeth how they were, and unlike Mrs. Bennet, actually attended to the answer. Mary reminded them all that in the midst of life they were in death, of whom may we seek for succor? – and that it was important to remember this: "at all times every man had but a short time to live. He cometh up, and is cut down, like a flower; he fleeth as it were a shadow and never continueth in one stay."

As for her father, he was less voluble, but the expression of his face showed that he was shocked and grieved by the demise of his much younger cousin. He stayed with his wife and daughters for a few minutes, then rose with the assistance of a cane – he explained tersely to Elizabeth that he had, while climbing the bank of the river when Mr. Collins's body was finally removed, badly sprained an ankle – and withdrew with Mr. Bingley into the library.

There was also speculation about where Mr. Collins should be buried. In his case there was little indication of suicide, so he merited a sanctified resting place – but where? With the deceased of the Lucases? He had been married to a Lucas, so there was reason for that notion. On the other hand, the Lucas family plot was extremely crowded. Mr. Collins had belonged to the Bennet family as well, so perhaps they should offer him a place in the Longbourn section of the cemetery.

Elizabeth suggested that if Mr. Collins were to be consulted he would wish to be buried in Hunsford, where he had served as rector. Near Lady Catherine, was what she thought but did not say. Elizabeth wondered what the expense might be, and then remembered that she could easily afford to pay for moving the body back to Kent if that was what Mrs. Collins wished.

They could make their offers, but the decision, ultimately, would belong to Mrs. Collins.

"Was the entail cut off?" Mrs. Bennet inquired hopefully.

Mrs. Bennet had posed this question several times already that day; Elizabeth's reply was as disappointing as the others. "No, Mamma, there is the son of Mr. Collins; he is now next in line."

Yet today even Mrs. Bennet could not voice any resentment towards young Lewis Collins. "Poor little fatherless boy! Well, at least he is not poor," she amended. "Still, life will be difficult for him, growing up without a father! You girls do not realize how fortunate you are, growing up with both parents still alive! Ah, Kitty, would you ring for tea? It is a little early but I am so thirsty."

Elizabeth, agreeing that it was useful to have a father and a mother, used the arrival of tea to join her father and Mr. Bingley in the library. After serving each of the men a cup, Elizabeth asked her father how he was. "It must have been terrible to see Mr. Collins's body this morning."

Mr. Bennet, his swollen ankle resting on a footstool, agreed that it was, but as Mary had been reminding them for the last few hours, they were all mortal.

"Your father handled everything very well," said Mr. Bingley admiringly. "He is a man for a crisis."

This was not the usual epithet for her father, but Elizabeth was aware that Mr. Bennet could be competent when compelled.

"I understand that you sent Mr. Bingley to fetch Lady Catherine, Papa."

Mr. Bennet explained his reasons. "As she had been so important to Mr. Collins, it was imperative to inform her. Mr. Bingley was the only one at the bridge who had met her, and he is also a friend of her nephew's. He seemed the most acceptable messenger."

Mr. Bingley said that in a situation such as this he was willing to do whatever was necessary.

"On her way back to Hunsford, Lady Catherine stopped to see us at Netherfield Park. Do you know what she suspects, Papa?"

Mr. Bennet sighed and placed his teacup on his saucer. "I expect that she believes that someone killed Mr. Collins deliberately. She did not declare that this morning, but her questions led in that direction."

"What is your opinion, Papa?"

"I agree that there are several things about the death that appear suspicious, but who could have done it? There are many who wished to avoid Mr. Collins, but I can think of none who hated him enough to want him dead – unless your friend Charlotte tired of being married to him. And as for your mother – Mr. Collins may be a favorite of hers today, but he was not two days ago – I can vouch for her being at Longbourn last night."

"Has Mr. Bingley told you Sir William's idea? How it might have been an accident?"

"Yes, but unless the driver of the unidentified cart or carriage was both blind and deaf, I cannot comprehend how that happened. Even last night – and although the moon was new, the stars were bright – one would see a large man like Mr. Collins when crossing the bridge. Even if the driver were inattentive or drunk, Mr. Collins should have had the time to get out of the way – no one can drive across that bridge at a gallop."

"Every theory seems impossible," said Elizabeth, "yet Mr. Collins is dead."

Mr. Bennet acknowledged that his daughter's statement was true.

"After consulting with your father, I agree that an accident of the type envisaged by Sir William is highly improbable," said Mr. Bingley regretfully.

"Yet an accident is preferable to the idea of murder," said Mr. Bennet. "Your mother is sufficiently anxious with the current products of her imagination – I expect it will be a month before she ventures across that bridge – I do not wish to give her another, even greater source of anxiety."

"Papa, I do not *wish* for Mr. Collins's death to be murder," said Elizabeth. "The possibility is terrifying. But should we not act on what is most likely to have happened and not what we would like to have happened? I appreciate that you do not wish to distress Mamma, but you and I and Lady Catherine are not the only ones who believe it could have been foul play. Charlotte is of the same opinion. If Charlotte conveys her belief to her family, then it will spread throughout the neighborhood. It will be impossible to keep this from my mother, Papa – or from Jane, Mr. Bingley."

Mr. Bennet acknowledged the logic of his daughter's point. "The question then becomes, what is to be done? Other than not crossing the bridge without protection?"

Elizabeth said that Sir William Lucas and his sons planned to query the neighborhood, to discover if anyone had traversed the bridge. "If we have other questions that we think should be asked, we should convey them to Sir William. And you should ask him what he and his sons have learned. You are clever, Papa; you may understand something that escapes the Lucases."

"You flatter me, Lizzy."

"If Mr. Collins was murdered, then these queries may warn the criminal," said Bingley, "and make him more difficult to discover."

Mr. Bennet believed that an investigation could affect the murderer's behavior in a number of different ways. "He could become desperate, and harm another. He could become extremely cautious, and not do anything more. Or he could decide that the best option is to leave Meryton – which, other than discovering and stopping him, would be best for the neighborhood. Of course, we would not necessarily *feel* safe, at least not for a long while, because we would not realize that he was gone – not unless he were so considerate as to leave a letter behind confessing to his evil deed." Which one of these course of events was most likely, Mr. Bennet could not guess, not without more information, although he had most confidence in saying that a letter of confession was highly unlikely.

"Yes, but these queries will also serve to warn the neighborhood and put people on their guard," said Elizabeth, "and although the neighborhood may not *feel* safer, it will actually *be* safer, because everyone will be more cautious. When I learned the truth about Wickham's character – and I learned of it before his regiment departed from Meryton – I did not warn anyone in the neighborhood, because I feared it would cause too much trouble – and because I had become privy to some information that I am still not at liberty to make public. I would prefer not to make the same mistake that I made with Wickham – keeping silent when I should speak out – especially when the lives of my family and friends could be at stake."

Mr. Bennet sighed. "Mrs. Bennet will be extremely anxious."

"I understand how you feel, Mr. Bennet," said Mr. Bingley. "I also have a wife whom I do not wish to worry."

Mr. Bennet returned to an earlier point, this time without any levity. "Who in Meryton knows Mr. Collins well enough to wish to murder him? Who else even knows him, besides us and the Lucases?"

None of them knew of any particular relationship that Mr. Collins had had with any of their neighbors, and certainly no one who had harbored any great resentments. Mr. Bingley pointed out that *Lady Catherine* had known Mr. Collins very well, and both she and he had been in Meryton last night. But Elizabeth and her father both raised objections to this conjecture. First, it was hard to imagine how Lady Catherine, who was tall but not that young, could have killed Mr. Collins, as the act would have required physical strength. Second, if Lady Catherine *had* killed him, then why would she have raised the possibility of his death being due to murder to Elizabeth?

"What about one of her servants?" asked Mr. Bingley. "The coachman or any of the others she brought with her? Do you know anything about them, Elizabeth?"

Elizabeth said that she knew their names but very little else about them. She suggested that this was another point to discuss with Mrs. Collins.

"Perhaps whoever did this was not trying to kill Mr. Collins," Mr. Bingley speculated.

Both Elizabeth and Mr. Bennet stared at him. "Explain yourself, please," said Mr. Bennet. "The injury on the back of Mr. Collins's head could not have been administered by accident. Or do you mean to suggest that the killer mistook Mr. Collins for someone else?"

"Perhaps. Or perhaps your cousin was simply in the wrong place at the wrong time."

"Do you mean someone who finds pleasure in killing people?" asked Elizabeth. For some reason that was more terrifying than the prospect of someone murdering Mr. Collins deliberately. The latter might be wickeder, but the former was more dangerous.

"Or perhaps someone who likes killing clergymen," suggested Mr. Bingley.

"That seems unlikely," said Mr. Bennet. "But, as we have already determined, all our conjectures seem unlikely, nevertheless Mr. Collins is dead. So I expect there is a murderer in Meryton."

"Has there ever been one before?" inquired Mr. Bingley.

Mr. Bennet described an incident from his youth, and a carriage accident that might not have been an accident, in which a wife died and the husband lived – but that was many years ago.

"Papa, what should we do? Besides warn people and ask for the assistance of the Lucases?"

Mr. Bennet said that they should consult with his brother-in-law Mr. Philips, the leading attorney in Meryton. Mr. Philips did not usually work on criminal cases, and Mr. Philips – stout, white-haired and red-faced – was not exactly energetic, but he had two young clerks who were eager to prove themselves.

CHAPTER XXVI

Mr. Bennet relayed their conclusions to those he needed to inform: Sir William and Mr. Philips, and the members of his own family. Sir William was terribly distressed at the idea that someone could have murdered his son-in-law, but he agreed that Mrs. Collins needed to be informed, for her own safety, just in case Mr. Bennet was correct. As Mrs. Collins had already reached the conclusion herself, she was not as perturbed by receiving her father's communication as he was in making it; in fact her anxiety was lessened, because now others would take precautions and she could more easily solicit her brothers and her father for protection.

Mr. Philips was skeptical at first that Mr. Collins could have been murdered – at *that* bridge? And why Mr. Collins? But as an attorney he was cognizant of the greed and foibles of human nature. He conveyed Mr. Bennet's theory to his clerks, who were both willing to do what they could to protect Meryton (and to increase their standing in the firm and in the town). Mr. Philips also told Mrs. Philips, and although she was not clear on the details which made murder rather than an accident more likely, the probability that it was murder was absolutely thrilling, and gave her reason to call on Mrs. Long, the reclusive Mrs. Smith (who allowed her in for half an hour in order to make this communication), the milliner across the street and anyone else who would listen. By telling Mrs. Philips, Meryton was warned.

The ladies living at Longbourn also had their reactions. Mary reveled in the proof that there was so much evil in the world, which she had always maintained, and not just the whole world, but in their very own neighborhood! Kitty resolved that she would never, ever cross this bridge alone in her life – at least not till the murderer were discovered and stopped, or if her aunt were giving a particularly enticing party, or if she had a pressing appointment with the milliner. The realization that she had so many reasons to cross that bridge rather distressed Kitty, and she asked Mary to cross the bridge with her – an act that only interested Mary if she already had another reason to go. Nevertheless, it appeared as if there would be at least a temporary cessation of hostilities between the two

Bennet daughters still at home – a benefit that even Mr. Bennet had not foreseen.

Mrs. Bennet was loud in her alarm, and she cried out at every noise, was positive that evildoers lurked in the shrubbery, and complained about the state of her nerves every hour. Of one thing she was certain: till the perpetrator was caught, *she* would not be crossing the bridge unless she could do it in the carriage. This was inconvenient to Mr. Bennet, who needed the horses in the farm, but he said he would see what he could do about their schedule, for it was even more inconvenient to have Mrs. Bennet without respite at Longbourn House.

Mr. Bingley did not like to alarm Jane with the communication, but his wife reacted far more calmly than Mr. Bennet's. Jane actually had trouble believing it – she thought the conjecture with respect to an accident far more likely – and even if it were murder, which it probably was not, she had complete confidence in Bingley's ability to protect her.

Miss Bingley suggested that they all remove to London, as, despite the reputation to the contrary, that large city was evidently safer than the little market-town of Meryton. Respectable clergymen were never murdered in London; London only killed those who deserved it. And then she repeated, as she had already repeated so often, that her brother should purchase or even hire an estate somewhere else. The murder of Mr. Collins, she argued, had to be grounds for breaking the lease early; no one could be expected to live in a place where clergymen were being targeted.

Mr. Bingley sighed, and said that he doubted that a murder two miles away would be considered grounds for breaking the lease. Even if clergymen were being targeted, no clergymen resided at Netherfield Park. Besides, Jane added, they were not completely certain that Mr. Collins had been murdered.

Elizabeth questioned Miss Bingley again about what had happened that evening, but she had no new information to give. She only confirmed that Mr. Collins had not dined with her and Lady Catherine at the Meryton Inn.

Most of Meryton was in an anxious state, and so when the Lucas sons and Mr. Clarke and Mr. Morris interviewed the neighborhood, everyone was willing to tell what they knew.

They ascertained that no cart nor carriage had crossed the bridge during the evening in question – or at least, no one was willing to admit it. Nearly everyone claimed to have been at home.

Although few facts were gleaned, many theories were offered. Old Mr. Robinson, who lived about a mile from the bridge, complained that a wheelbarrow of his had been moved that night – he had risen the next morning to discover it in the wrong part of his garden – but a wheelbarrow could not have knocked Mr. Collins off the bridge. The jailer's wife thought Mr. Collins was looking for treasure; the milliner thought a gust of wind must have blown his hat into the water, and that he had dived in afterwards; while the poulterer was certain that a vicious dog had chased the unfortunate clergyman, which had caused him to fall — but it turned out that the dog was detested by the poulterer, while the dog's owner swore the animal had been inside that entire evening. Finally, several wondered if there could be a connection between Mr. Collins's death and Miss King's missing jewels — but no one could fathom what it might be. Mr. Collins was dead, but he had not been robbed, and it was not even certain if the two had ever exchanged any words during their lifetimes. Luckily for Hannah, the late Miss King's former maid who had incurred so much suspicion, she had an alibi for the time of Mr. Collins's death.

Meryton had fewer parties in the evenings, and even fewer crossed the bridge at night. However, in the mornings half the town went to inspect under the bridge, especially the youths, in the hope of finding additional dead clergymen.

After some discussion, Mr. Collins was buried in the Longbourn family plot. Mrs. Collins thanked Mr. and Mrs. Bennet for their generosity and informed everyone she would remain a few weeks longer at Lucas Lodge. With Mrs. Jenkinson still in a serious decline, Lady Catherine was too busy to seek out a replacement for Mr. Collins. The vicar from the next parish was engaged to preach the Sunday sermons, and as no one needed the Parsonage, Lady Catherine could wait for Mrs. Collins to move out.

"I am still deciding where Lewis and I will live," said Mrs. Collins. She was considering renting a little house in the area, or perhaps one in Hunsford.

Mrs. Collins's brothers and Mr. Philips's clerks all asked her, now that her husband was buried, if she could think of anything that could have led to what happened, and if she knew any reason that Lady Catherine's coachman and other servants might have wanted to harm Mr. Collins. Mrs. Collins considered carefully, but she could not give them any clues. She knew of no quarrel between Mr. Collins and her ladyship's servants.

Elizabeth met with Mrs. Collins privately and asked if Lady Catherine had written her why she had traveled to Meryton in the first place, but Mrs. Collins said that her ladyship had not. Then Elizabeth decided to break her promise to Lady Catherine — her promise was important, but if Mrs. Collins was in danger, her safety took priority — and described what Lady Catherine had told her about Mr. Radclyff. Mrs. Collins said Lady Catherine had not mentioned him in her letter. However, now that she thought about it, she had heard of an Elinor Radclyff; she believed that Miss Radclyff was an old friend of Lady Catherine's. Perhaps Mr. Radclyff had been her brother?

Elizabeth said this was possible. She and Mrs. Collins tried to find a connection between the Radclyffs and the death of Mr. Collins, but without additional information, they had little confidence in their conjectures. Elizabeth kissed the baby, then embraced her friend. Before returning to Netherfield Park, she stopped at Longbourn and did her best to listen to everyone. She also asked Kitty to call on the young widow and comfort her when she could.

CHAPTER XXVII

A few days after Mr. Collins was buried, Mrs. Collins called at Netherfield Park. Jane and Elizabeth were surprised to see her because she was in deep mourning for the death of her husband, but they welcomed her cordially. They explained that Mr. Bingley and his sister were out riding.

Jane rang the bell for tea. After the usual inquiries about each other's health, which with the recent and the impending events necessitated longer and more detailed responses than usual, Mrs. Collins said she had a particular reason for coming to visit.

"I know it is not customary to make calls in my situation," said Mrs. Collins.

Jane said that they were such old friends and Mr. Collins had been their cousin, so there was no reason to stand on ceremony.

"My reason for coming is not purely social; I have something to tell you, Jane."

Elizabeth offered to leave the room if they needed privacy.

"No, no, it is nothing like that. It is not a confidential matter, but rather a warning, especially for Jane. Mrs. Ford is in Meryton. I saw her just yesterday."

This caused some confusion among the ladies of Netherfield Park, for at first they did not recall who Mrs. Ford was. "Do you mean the woman you hired, and who seemed a perfect nursery maid for Lewis, but who then departed without giving notice?" asked Elizabeth.

"Yes, Eliza, *that* Mrs. Ford."

The sisters née Bennet took a minute to understand this.

"How odd," Elizabeth finally remarked. "Charlotte, are you certain? Where did you see her?"

Jane shook her head. "I have never heard that name associated with anyone in Meryton."

Mrs. Collins said that she never had either, and that she had never seen the woman before meeting her in Kent, but that she found it extremely odd that Mrs. Ford, who had caused such trouble for her and Mr. Collins in Hunsford, should be here in Meryton. She assured Elizabeth that she had complete confidence in her identification. "My mother's eyesight is weaker than it used to be," she said, "but mine is excellent."

Elizabeth apologized for having expressed any doubt. "Why do you think she is here? You do not think – you do not think that she had anything to do with the death of Mr. Collins, do you?"

"I agree that it is most peculiar and I have wondered if she could have been the person whom Mr. Collins thought he might have seen when he arrived in Meryton. Mrs. Ford caused some unpleasantness between us, and so I now understand why he did not mention her to me on his last day. Although she is certainly not to be trusted or relied upon, I do not see how she could be responsible for my husband's death. She would not have the strength for such a blow, nor could she move a man as large as Mr. Collins. And, although I cannot recommend her as a nursery maid due to unreliability, she was always extremely gentle with the baby."

"Yet it is an extraordinary coincidence," said Elizabeth, and everyone agreed. "Where exactly did you see her, Charlotte?"

Mrs. Collins explained that the day before she had gone out in the Lucas carriage with her sister Maria and her son Lewis to call on Mrs. Long. It was necessary, she explained, to take Lewis out most days, both for his health and happiness as well as the health and happiness of all of those at Lucas Lodge. That was when she had seen Mrs. Ford. Her former domestic had entered a building on F— street, the house with the green casement, near Clarke's library.

Jane explained that those lodgings were owned by her uncle Philips. "He rented them out to a middle-aged woman, but she is not called Mrs. Ford."

"Her name is Mrs. Smith," said Elizabeth, and explained that she had met the tenant at a card game at the Philips's house.

None of the three ladies could understand what Mrs. Ford was doing in Meryton, or why she was calling on Mrs. Smith.

"Perhaps Mrs. Smith has hired your runaway nursery maid," said Jane.

"But not as a nursery maid!" said Elizabeth. "Not unless Mrs. Smith has a secret child!"

Elizabeth's words, uttered as a joke, caused the ladies to pause and wonder. It seemed impossible for Mrs. Smith to be the *mother* of an infant – she had not been expecting when Elizabeth had met her at her aunt's only a few weeks ago – but it was not impossible for her to have become responsible for one. She could be a grandmother suddenly left with a grandchild, or an aunt or even a great-aunt. And if the lease under which

Mrs. Smith had hired the rooms specified no children, that would explain why Mrs. Smith was avoiding Mrs. Philips.

"If Mrs. Smith has hired Mrs. Ford, it is likely that Mrs. Smith is being imposed upon. But what should we do?" asked Elizabeth.

None of the three ladies were inclined to call upon Mrs. Smith. Both Jane and Elizabeth had met her only once, and Mrs. Collins had never met her at all. Not only were none of them sure that they wanted to pursue the acquaintance, such a communication from a relative stranger would prove extremely awkward, if it did not offend her entirely. However, the solution was simple. Mrs. Collins's information would be given to Mr. and Mrs. Philips. Even if Mrs. Smith had recently ignored several of Mr. and Mrs. Philips's invitations, Mrs. Smith was still their tenant; they were best positioned to pass along the warning.

"I will call on Mrs. Philips immediately," Elizabeth promised. "Charlotte, do you wish to come with me? And perhaps describe this Mrs. Ford? I have never seen her."

Mrs. Collins expressed her regrets; she had to return to her little boy. "However, I can describe her to you."

Elizabeth listened carefully, but she thought that Mrs. Collins's description of Mrs. Ford would fit more than half the middle-aged women in England: medium brown hair that was turning gray, lines around the eyes, average height and a figure that once might have been good.

Mrs. Collins excused herself and departed.

Both Jane and Elizabeth discussed their friend and the mysterious Mrs. Ford. "Very strange," observed Jane.

"It is indeed," said Elizabeth. "But you have been advised – do not hire a middle-aged woman as a nursery maid! At least not till Charlotte has seen her and confirmed that she is *not* Mrs. Ford!"

Jane smiled at this and said that she had spoken to several candidates and none of them were middle-aged. Then she asked, more seriously, Elizabeth's opinion of how Mrs. Collins was faring. "Everything must seem more difficult for her now."

Elizabeth sighed. "Yes – but Charlotte is one of the most capable women of my acquaintance. She will manage."

They then discussed when Elizabeth should take her carriage to Meryton to call on their aunt. With Mr. Bingley still out riding with his sister, Elizabeth was reluctant to leave, but Jane told her she was being nonsensical. She felt fine, absolutely fine; she would only be alone for an hour or two at most; and finally, she would not be truly alone, for Netherfield Park was full of servants.

"I will go, only if you promise to defend me from Mr. Bingley if he is angry with me," said Elizabeth.

Jane promised that Bingley's temper would remain good – it had been so since a few days after they had found the remains of the burnt letter – so Elizabeth ordered her carriage and went to call on her aunt. Mrs. Philips was honored by this unscheduled visit from Mrs. Darcy, and quickly ushered her wealthy niece into the best seat. Her uncle and his clerks had come upstairs for tea, and so Elizabeth communicated Mrs. Collins's information to all of them, her delivery hindered by interruptions and misunderstandings.

"Who exactly is Mrs. Ford?" asked Mr. Clarke.

"Why does she even matter?" asked Mr. Morris.

Elizabeth explained that Mrs. Ford was a middle-aged nursery maid who had quit working for the Collinses without giving due notice.

Mr. Morris remained skeptical. "And what exactly does Mrs. Collins wish us to do? Sue Mrs. Ford for breach of contract? Or compel her to return to service?"

Mrs. Philips said, "Surely Mrs. Collins cannot want her back! This Mrs. Ford sounds most unreliable. It is a blessing when an unreliable servant leaves of her own volition."

Elizabeth said that she did not believe that Mrs. Collins was seeking any sort of recompense, but that she only wished to warn Mrs. Smith about her. As Mrs. Collins had never met Mrs. Smith, she hoped for someone else to deliver the warning.

Mr. Clarke sighed. "I suppose the death of Mr. Collins has made Mrs. Collins suspicious of everyone."

Mr. Philips remarked that the woman Mrs. Darcy had described hardly seemed dangerous.

Mrs. Philips agreed with the gentlemen, but she was still determined to oblige her wealthy niece. "Perhaps it is nothing, but I will tell Mrs. Smith, Lizzy. Even though Mrs. Smith has no reason to hire a nursery maid."

Elizabeth decided not to relate her conjectures on this point to her uncle and his clerks; what had seemed plausible to the ladies at Netherfield, seemed too fanciful to mention in this room with so many men.

Mr. Clarke explained that he handled Mrs. Smith's rent and that he could bring her the message, but Mrs. Philips insisted on undertaking the errand herself.

Then Mr. Clarke asked about Mrs. Collins. "Will she be returning soon to Hunsford?"

"At some point she must, if only to retrieve her possessions," said Elizabeth, but added that she did not know what Mrs. Collins's plans were; it was possible that Mrs. Collins did not know them herself.

"Poor Mrs. Collins!" exclaimed Mrs. Philips. "To be widowed so young, and to be facing life's challenges entirely alone."

Considering how crowded Lucas Lodge was these days, *alone* was not the best word to describe Mrs. Collins's situation, but despite being diverted, Elizabeth agreed with her aunt.

Mr. Morris cleared his throat. "If Mrs. Collins needs any assistance or advice, your uncle's firm is always available. You could tell her that, Mrs. Darcy."

"I will," said Elizabeth, then said she had to return to Jane. She was satisfied that she had done what she could to protect the reclusive Mrs. Smith, and now that her uncle's employees were attempting to use her to solicit business, it was time to depart.

CHAPTER XXVIII

Two days later, Elizabeth was sitting on a bench with her sister at Netherfield. They were discussing their aunt Philips's report of her visit to her tenant Mrs. Smith. It had, apparently, not gone well. Mrs. Smith did not know a Mrs. Ford, she was not planning to hire a Mrs. Ford, and she certainly had no intention of hiring a nursery maid!

Mrs. Philips had been diligent and had inquired at the other apartments, but no one in them had ever heard the name in question either. "I have done what I could, Lizzy."

Elizabeth thanked her aunt and wondered what she could do to compensate her for her trouble. Mrs. Philips did not stay long, and then Elizabeth and her sister went outside to enjoy the fine weather.

"Do you believe Charlotte was simply mistaken?" asked Jane. "Normally Charlotte is extremely level-headed, but these days she could be overwrought."

"Perhaps," said Elizabeth, who truly did not know what to think.

A servant then approached with a letter for Mrs. Darcy. It was not the usual time for the post so Elizabeth was a little surprised – and a little concerned, for generally bad news was the news that could not wait for regular delivery. Perhaps the vicar at the village of Kympton had died?

"From Mr. Darcy?" inquired Jane.

"This is not his handwriting," replied Elizabeth. She did not recognize the hand, which was very plain.

"From whom, then? Aunt Gardiner?"

"I do not know," said Elizabeth, inspecting the back. "There is no return address."

"You have a secret admirer!" teased Jane. With difficulty she rose and said she would return to the house. When Elizabeth said that she would return as well, Jane told her to stay where she was. "I know that you prefer to read your letters in private, and I also know that you would like to walk to the pond and that I could not manage it. Come inside after you have had a little exercise."

So Elizabeth remained on the bench and opened her letter; within she found two pieces of paper. The first was addressed to her:

Dear Mrs. Darcy,

Congratulations on your successful marriage. I hope you are very happy with your husband. If you wish to remain so, you will not want the following – and I have many other examples from your pen – sent to Mr. Darcy. To prevent me from doing so, you will need to comply with my instructions exactly.

The note then continued with the instructions to leave several bank notes at a certain spot in Meryton.

Mystified, Elizabeth turned to the next page, which was on a different type of paper, the type she had used when she was unmarried and living with her parents at Longbourn House.

My dearest Wickham,

began the letter, and continued with:

I have missed you so much.

The letter continued with expressions of affection, and with hopes that they would see each other again soon.

Elizabeth was horrified, for she recognized the handwriting: it was her own!

But *she* had never written such a letter.

Distressed, she folded up the pages and clutched them tightly. She took Jane's advice and walked to the pond – she had not intended to take the walk, as the day was warm and she was a little fatigued – but now it seemed important to get as far away from the house and any other sets of eyes who might perceive her shock and embarrassment. She reached the pond, seated herself on a stump near the water's edge and re-read the letter and the demand for cash.

Someone was blackmailing her! But was not blackmail usually applied to those who had done wrong? She had never written such a letter to Wickham. Yet how could she prove it?

She studied the letter that was supposed to be from her. Someone had managed to imitate her letter-writing style, from her handwriting to her expressions to the very paper and ink that she had used at Longbourn. Someone had somehow created a letter that would cause her terrible embarrassment if Mr. Darcy ever saw it. If she were not so upset she could almost admire the thoroughness of the criminal, who had showed tremendous attention to detail.

What should she do? If she paid the money – and she could afford it, although it would leave her rather short of cash – then perhaps the problem would go away.

But if she paid the money, what would she say to Mr. Darcy? He was as generous a man that she could hope for, but this sort of expenditure would have to be explained. There were all sorts of excuses that she could give: baby presents to Jane, money for her younger sisters, or better yet, some money to Mrs. Collins to help her with her expenses in this difficult time.

Elizabeth shook her head at her own folly. What was she thinking, coming up with lies to tell to her husband? She had never lied to him, and she did not want to start now. Besides, they were all such transparent lies, that they would not serve the purpose. Darcy certainly knew that most baby presents could not cost this much, and at some point he could ask Bingley about it. Even the excuses of money to her younger sisters or to Mrs. Collins were impossible; she could not count on their silence.

Besides, if she gave this forger money once, what was to stop him from returning to her with demands in the future? She would never be free.

A branch broke behind her; startled, she jumped and gave a cry of alarm.

Elizabeth turned and saw one of Netherfield's gardeners only a few paces away. He was tall and dark and he looked very strong; given what she had been thinking about, and the still-unexplained death of Mr. Collins, she was not sure whether to be reassured or unnerved by his presence.

"Apologies, Mrs. Darcy," said the man, bowing awkwardly. "Did not mean to frighten you."

"Of course you did not," she said, "I was startled, that is all." She glanced at the tools that he carried: a long stick and a veil, but noted that he did not proceed to his business. "Do you have something particular to do?"

"Yes, Mrs. Darcy. There's a wasps' nest in the tree over there," and he gestured. "I want to take it down, seeing as you and Miss Bingley keep walking here. But if you wish to stay here, I can destroy it later."

Elizabeth stared at the nest, and wondered how she could have missed it and the wasps buzzing in the vicinity. It was amazing that she had not been stung. "No, Brown," she said, finally recalling the undergardener's name, "you have everything you need with you to remove it. I will leave so that you can work."

He agreed that it was better to take care of it as soon as possible, but promised to wait till she was well away.

Clutching the letter and the demand for money she walked back to the house. The incline was gentle, but by the time she was back inside she was out of breath and a little dizzy. She must be very distraught to feel so faint, she thought, as she rested briefly on a chair in the vestibule.

A maid found her there and, alarmed by her pallor and the expression on her face, asked Mrs. Darcy if she were all right.

"I am well, quite well," Elizabeth said, rising back to her feet. "A little overheated, that is all." She then asked the maid to bring tea to her room, and went there immediately, barely acknowledging Miss Bingley as they passed each other on the staircase.

In the privacy of her room she read both pieces of paper again. She had been interested in George Wickham, for a few short months, when he first joined the regiment quartered in Meryton as a lieutenant several years ago. He was handsome, amusing and entertaining. She had been charmed by him; she had found him, for a time, to be the most amiable man of her acquaintance. At the time, when she had believed him to be an honorable man, he had appeared to like her too. Her interest in him had been so obvious that her mother and sisters had teased her about it, and then had comforted her when Wickham had begun to court another young lady from Meryton.

That was before she had learned that more than half of Wickham's stories to her were lies.

The letter was especially mortifying because she *had* had the feelings it expressed. She had not written it, but she *could* have written it.

What would Darcy say if he read a letter like this purporting to have been written by her? Would he ever have confidence in her again? He loved her a great deal; he had already forgiven much – her insolence, her misjudgments, her own sister's marriage to Wickham, a man whom he rightfully detested, and the tendency of nearly her entire family to expose themselves – and therefore him – to ridicule. He was capable of great forgiveness, but even the best of men had limits, and this – even though she knew she was not responsible – had to fill him with abhorrence.

Elizabeth paced back and forth, wishing that she felt better. She wondered if she were turning into her mother, for she had such tremblings and palpitations and spasms in her side and a sick feeling practically overwhelmed her. So much distress was not good for one's spirit or one's nerves! What should she do?

A breeze fluttered the curtains. She paused by the open window, breathing in the fresh air, and down below she saw the undergardener Brown returning to the house, his veil and long stick in hand. He was joined by the head gardener, who asked Brown if he had removed the wasps' nest. Brown replied that he had.

"Were you stung?" asked the head gardener.

"Yes, Sir, I was," said Brown, and showed his superior several places on his neck and hands where the wasps had fought back.

The head gardener was sympathetic. "Sometimes, to take down a nest, you have to get stung. Go see Mrs. Nicholls in the kitchen; she has a salve for burns and she can take care of you."

The head gardener's words inspired Elizabeth; she would seek assistance.

CHAPTER XXIX

Elizabeth, clutching the letters, left her dressing-room and went in search of her sister. She found her laughing with Bingley in the drawing-room. Elizabeth considered postponing this, but then realized that she could not postpone this; she had to take steps to resolve it as speedily as possible, while she still possessed the nerve to tell Jane. "Bingley, if you do not mind, there is something that I wish to consult Jane about."

Bingley, seeing the distress on his sister-in-law's face, made no objection to being told to leave one of the rooms in his own house.

"Lizzy, what is wrong?" Jane inquired, when they were alone.

Elizabeth sat down beside her sister. "I wish for you to take a look at this," she said, and handed Jane the paper that was allegedly from her to the man now married to her youngest sister.

Jane read a few words, then exclaimed: "Lizzy! When did *you* write to Wickham?"

"Keep reading," Elizabeth said.

Jane did so, and blushed. "I had no idea that your feelings for him were so strong."

"So that is what you believe," said Elizabeth.

Jane kept on thinking. "But if you sent this to him, why do you have it now? Did he send it back? Why would he send it back?"

"I do not know that he did."

"But who else would? Lydia? Did *she* send it to you? She must have been very upset if she read this letter. Wickham ought to have burnt it long ago – certainly as soon as they were married."

Elizabeth studied Jane. "So you are convinced that I wrote it?"

"It is your handwriting, Lizzy, and I know that you have used paper just like this. I also know that at one time you liked Wickham very much. I am sure you do not now, but – when did you write this? I see no date on it."

"We will come to that in a moment. Take a look, now, at this, Jane." Elizabeth gave her the page with the demand for money.

Jane read the demand once, and then again. "This is terrible, Lizzy. Who could have gotten ahold of these letters? And how many are there?"

"I do not know."

"How is it possible that you do not know? Did you write more than one letter? Lizzy, how could you?"

"The reason I do not know is because I did not write this. I have never written any letters to Wickham, not even since he married Lydia, and certainly not before."

Jane appeared skeptical. "But, Lizzy, this is *your* handwriting. And some of these expressions are your own."

"I agree that it is like, very like," Elizabeth admitted. "But I still did not write any of them. Someone is forging a letter by me in order to extort money."

Jane still frowned. "It is very strange! Who could be so wicked? Are you certain that you never wrote to Wickham?"

"I am absolutely certain, Jane. And if you do not believe me, no one else will – and then what shall I do?"

This appeal to her sister's confidence in her had an immediate effect. "Of course I believe you. You are my sister; I have every faith in you. What is wrong with me? Even if this sounds like you, you would never have written to Wickham like this!"

Elizabeth was so reassured by this that she burst into tears.

"Of course I believe you," Jane repeated warmly, as she found a handkerchief and passed it to her sister. "I know you, and I do not know whoever has written this letter or this demand for money. I will always take your word over a stranger's – indeed, I would take your word over nearly all my acquaintance. Do not distress yourself so."

After hearing this, Elizabeth was able to regain control of herself. She dried her eyes and then folded up the handkerchief. "Jane, I thank you. It means more than I can say. But I still need to consult you: what should I do about this demand? Should I pay the money or not? It is not so much, and it might prevent grief in the future."

Jane said, "What is to stop the person from asking for more? And if you pay once, then whoever it is will have you in their power. Because then you will appear guilty, even though you are not."

"You are right, Jane. It is difficult to think clearly, when someone is ready to tell such lies about oneself. In that case, should I warn Darcy? Before he receives any letters pretending to be from me? I hate to distress him so, when he is sitting at the deathbed of Reverend Wallace."

"You have several days before this person expects you to leave the money. I suppose he gave you the time because he could not be certain that you had so much cash on you. So you have a few days in which you can determine what you should do."

"Yes."

Jane was curious. "Could you pay that sort of money?"

"It would not be impossible, but it would be inconvenient, and would not spare me a conversation with Darcy – he might not demand an explanation for my extravagance, but I would feel compelled to give one." Elizabeth then had another thought, one that was absolutely odious. "You said that you would trust me over a stranger. But this cannot be the work of a stranger. This person knows my handwriting, my stationery, even my expressions. Oh, Jane! This must be the work of someone who knows me. Who could hate me so much?"

Jane was well-equipped to support Elizabeth, and to offer her strength and consolation. However, her generous nature made it difficult to suspect anyone, and especially not someone she knew.

Elizabeth, however, had fewer such inhibitions. "What about Wickham? Could he be responsible?"

It was painful to think that this could be done by their brother-in-law, especially as it implicated their own sister. But Mr. and Mrs. Wickham frequently needed money.

Jane, after a little consideration, was able to find some objections to Elizabeth's conjecture. "I cannot say that Wickham *would* not do it, not based on what we know of his character. But, Lizzy, I do not see how he *could* have done it. Could he have imitated your handwriting so well? And how could he have delivered the note? He is in Newcastle. He is not here to gather the money once it is paid."

"Are we certain of that?" asked Elizabeth. "Are we certain that he is in the north with his regiment, and not hidden somewhere in Meryton?"

"There have been no reports of Wickham in Meryton," said Jane. "And although I suppose that it is *possible* that he has returned, or that he would return, it seems unlikely. He is so tall – so handsome – and so well-known. Even if he arrived in a disguise, he would run the risk of detection. Besides, if Lydia and he need money, then why did she not ask for it? She has written to each of us without asking for any assistance."

"Perhaps she did not ask for any money because they were planning to send this demand."

"But Lizzy, do you really think Lydia would do such a thing?"

"Not personally; her handwriting is atrocious. But she is quick enough when she puts her mind to something. And this letter might strike her as being a joke, a very good joke. Or she might be revenging herself against me for having liked Wickham when he and I were first acquainted."

"I cannot believe it of her!"

"Jane, although I am grateful for your faith in *my* character, I still think you are too ready to accept goodness in other people."

"I have learned to be a little less trusting," said Jane. "But let us consider Lydia. Why would she not ask you or me for money if she needed it? Why would she be a party to sending this demand for money, and this forgery, when she must realize that there is a chance that you would refuse to pay it?"

This argument had more weight with Elizabeth than the suggestion that she should simply trust in the honor of their youngest sister. "If it is not Lydia or Wickham, then it must be someone in Meryton. Someone here who somehow knows my history, who somehow knows my handwriting and who is taking advantage of my visit to you to demand this money."

Jane considered, but could not come up with any objections to her sister's statements. "That is a terrible thought – to think that someone in Meryton is so mercenary and so cruel to compose such a letter. I can think of no one so dreadful among our acquaintance."

Elizabeth was not as charitable in her opinion of the people who had been their neighbors their entire lives, but even she had difficulty imagining that anyone could dislike and resent her so much.

Was this another consequence of having money? When she first met Mr. Darcy she had been repulsed by his reserve, his tendency to speak only to those whom he already knew, and his unengaging manner. Now *she* was the target of obsequiousness and swindlers. *He* had undoubtedly been importuned by both his entire life; no wonder he had always been slow to accept the overtures of strangers.

"It is hard, I agree, to think that someone we know could be so terrible." Elizabeth put the letters on her lap. "What do you advise that I do?"

"You mean, should you pay the money? I advise against it."

"That is not my only question. Should I tell Darcy? Showing him this letter could injure our marriage, and besides, he is already so distressed by the situation of Reverend Wallace."

"Surely he loves you too much to believe that you wrote it! And even if he did assume it was genuine, he must know that you have no feelings for Wickham now."

"Perhaps. What about other people? If I tell other people, then they may be able to help us determine who is behind it. On the other hand, our neighbors may believe that I wrote this and then my reputation will suffer." Elizabeth recalled how Kitty had once described her as being 'violently in love with Wickham' and again she felt queasy. If her own family believed that she had been violently in love, then what had her friends and acquaintances conjectured? "I should be able to trust Darcy with this information – but it is more difficult to have so much confidence in the neighborhood. For example, if the Lucases read this, then it would surely spread to Lady Catherine – and I am just mending the breach with her."

Jane said she honestly did not know. She wished that she could be of more help, but she could not determine what the appropriate choice of action was. "Showing this letter to our friends could damage not just your reputation, Lizzy, but it could be painful to Wickham and especially to Lydia."

Elizabeth thought that Jane was attributing the shame that *she* would feel if she were in this situation; she doubted that *Lydia* would react similarly. Lydia might even be triumphant in the idea that she had married a man whom one of her sisters had liked.

Elizabeth expressed these thoughts to Jane, but her eldest sister shook her head. "I am sure you are wrong, Lizzy. Lydia has more feeling than you give her credit for."

Elizabeth wondered and doubted but she did not dispute Jane's opinion. Jane had more recently spent time with Lydia; Elizabeth had not even seen that sister since just after her marriage to Wickham. "And what should I do?"

"The note does not expect you to pay the money for several days, does it?"

Elizabeth read the instructions aloud, to leave a named sum in the hollow of a horse chestnut tree in a particular field near the river. The date given was several days away.

"Then my suggestion is that you put everything safely away tonight, and do not consider it again till morning. We may have fresh ideas after a good night's sleep. Just now we are too distressed to think clearly."

Elizabeth believed that it was highly unlikely that she would sleep well that night, but she kept this thought from her sister. "I only ask that you tell no one about this, Jane, not till we have decided what to do. Not even Bingley."

"Of course. You may rely upon my discretion."

"I am so sorry to have burdened you with this, Jane. I cannot say that my heart is as light as a feather, but I do feel a little better for having shared this with you."

Jane told Elizabeth that she would always support her in everything, and then a maid arrived with tea things, followed by Miss Bingley. Elizabeth was unequal to facing Miss Bingley, and excused herself.

CHAPTER XXX

Jane sent her maid to inquire of Elizabeth whether she wished to join them for dinner that evening or to have a tray sent to her room. Elizabeth considered both options. Being with her sister and Mr. Bingley would be acceptable, but she did not think that she could endure the companionship of Miss Bingley for the evening. Miss Bingley was not a fool; she would realize that something was wrong, and even if she did not know what it was, she might indulge herself by making cruel hints and disparaging remarks about Mrs. Darcy's relationship with Mr. Darcy. Elizabeth told the maid that she would prefer a tray, and silently thanked her sister for her delicacy.

She read the letter and the demand over and over, wondering what she should do. She considered going to the horse chestnut tree and leaving an empty envelope and then watching to see who came by to retrieve it. But this plan presented many impracticalities. She could not stand for hours in a field to keep a lookout; it would attract attention of anyone who saw her – and when the culprit saw her he would simply not approach. The chances were that she would endure a lot of trouble and yet learn nothing in the end.

She also considered writing to Darcy and explaining the whole thing. But how could she put all of this into a letter? And would he believe her?

Elizabeth remembered a letter that he had written to her when *he* had had a great deal to explain, in order to defend himself against her ill opinion of him, as so much of which had been based on falsehoods. If he could write her such an important letter, when he believed that she hated him – and only hours earlier she had told him that he had been the last man that she could ever marry – then surely she could write him a letter when she had every reason to believe that he loved her.

Elizabeth sat down several times at the little desk in her dressing-room and attempted to write to her husband. The words, however, would not flow; her sentences sounded childish and petulant; and most of all, she hated what she had to say.

As she stared at a most unsatisfactory paragraph, her admiration for the man who was her husband grew. How had he, when he had been so perturbed by her refusal of his offer of marriage, been able to compose a missive so coherent? Of course, their situations were not exactly the same.

As she had disliked him so much at the time, a letter from him could not make her opinion of him any worse. But now Darcy loved her, and a letter such as the one she was attempting to write could damage the affection and the respect that he had for her.

Whoever had written this was very clever. Nothing, absolutely nothing was more important to her than Darcy's good opinion.

She tried writing that many things had happened in Meryton since her arrival: the deaths of Miss King and Mr. Collins, and then the strange angry visit of Lady Catherine. Those incidents she was able to dispatch in a few paragraphs, but when she wrote the name Wickham, her pen faltered. What if Georgiana were to read this letter? Elizabeth tried to convince herself that Georgiana surely no longer suffered over what had happened with her and Mr. Wickham by now; that it might even reassure her to learn that her clever sister-in-law had also been imposed upon and charmed by the same man who had both imposed upon and charmed her. That helped Elizabeth to persist, and to describe in full what had happened.

Yet, when she finished the letter, the candles burnt low, she was not satisfied. Had she explained herself? Would Darcy believe her, or would he believe that she really had written a letter to Wickham? In short, should she send this missive or not? She was not sure. She tried one in her father's style, merely telling Darcy that she needed to see him, and asking him to come without giving a reason.

But when she reviewed *that* letter, it did not please her either. It seemed so imperious – reminding her of the dictatorial Lady Catherine – and Darcy would be irritated to receive a summons without any words of explanation, especially given the sad situation at Kympton.

Neither letter suited her entirely, but unfortunately she could think of no perfect solution. Perhaps there was none. Elizabeth walked around her room a few times, wondering which she should send. She could not reach a decision, and she was extremely fatigued. Perhaps wisdom would come to her during the night. Or perhaps she would show both letters to Jane in the morning and ask for her advice.

Elizabeth hid both letters to Darcy beneath a book, along with the letter that she had allegedly written and the demand for cash. Afterwards she rang the bell for her maid. Jeanette helped her undress and took care of her hair.

"Will that be all, Madame?" Jeanette inquired. "Shall I take away the dinner tray?"

Elizabeth told her to do so, but as Jeanette was positioning the crockery and cutlery on the tray, she noticed that the writing materials were out upon the desk. "Have you a letter that you wish for me to post, Madame Darcy?"

"I beg your pardon? No. No, thank you, Jeanette," replied Elizabeth, a little ashamed of the disorder on the writing desk.

Jeanette departed with the tray and then Elizabeth blew out most of the candles, taking the one that was still burning over to the table beside her bed. With so much that had happened and such thoughts and threats tormenting her, how could she possibly sleep? Yet she was so fatigued!

Elizabeth extinguished the candle and lay her head on her pillow, but sleep would not come. Not all her thoughts were entirely desperate, however. Perhaps Jeanette could help her. Perhaps Jeanette could go to the field with the horse chestnut tree and watch for someone approaching the tree. It was an unusual task for a lady's maid but perhaps Jeanette would be of assistance. Elizabeth contemplated this scheme for several minutes before she was again plagued by doubt. If someone knew her sufficiently to forge a letter so well, then that someone surely was aware of her maidservant Jeanette.

Besides, what if Jeanette herself were involved? Elizabeth had hired Jeanette only since marrying Mr. Darcy – a woman in her position was expected to have a maidservant of her own, and she had engaged one from France in order to improve her command of the French language. Jeanette had always been pleasant and dependable, and Mr. Darcy and Elizabeth had checked Jeanette's references, but perhaps they had been misled. The maidservant could have easily found letters in Elizabeth's handwriting and have learned enough of Elizabeth's history to forge this letter.

Still, there were reasons *not* to suspect Jeanette. Jeanette's command of English was passable, but not sufficient to compose a letter of this nature. Nor had Jeanette struck Elizabeth as particularly cunning or ambitiously greedy. Perhaps the woman had dissembled all this time – Elizabeth had misjudged people before – but Jeanette would have had to maintain a façade for many months. Elizabeth decided she was not yet ready to suspect Jeanette, but neither was she willing to confide in her.

Perhaps the perpetrator was some other servant. Or some friend, or even, alas, a relative, who wished to partake of Mrs. Darcy's good fortune. Elizabeth trusted only a few implicitly. Jane, of course. Mr. Darcy. Her father, and even her mother. Her mother would *like* more money, thought Elizabeth, but she would never engage in such subterfuge; she would simply ask for it. Besides, Mrs. Bennet had a protectiveness towards her daughters that would prevent her from doing something this cruel. Nor could Elizabeth imagine Kitty or Mary being involved in such a scheme. Lydia's innocence was less clear, but Lydia was not in Meryton and Lydia lacked the ability to imitate handwriting. Elizabeth had not seen her sister for more than a year so she might have had the time to develop such skill in the intervening months – yet even then, the steady application that would have been required seemed inconsistent with Lydia's character.

Having found reasons not to suspect the nearest members of her family, Elizabeth relaxed a little. Not being able to trust all of them would be extremely distressing. The question then followed: whom did she not trust? Who had access to samples of her writing; who knew her history with Wickham; who was in a position to send her such a letter?

Miss Bingley? Miss Bingley was a skilled artist; perhaps she could also imitate others' handwriting. Beyond a brief note or two, Elizabeth had never written to Miss Bingley herself, but Miss Bingley, living as she did most of the time at Netherfield Park, could have easily studied letters that Elizabeth had sent to Jane. Miss Bingley was also in Meryton, which would make it easy for her to send the extortion demand, and to retrieve the bank notes from the horse chestnut tree. Furthermore, Miss Bingley had been riding frequently on horseback lately. And although Elizabeth did not believe that Miss Bingley *needed* money, Miss Bingley might take pleasure in damaging Elizabeth's relationship with Mr. Darcy. And perhaps Miss Bingley *did* need money, either for herself or for her sister Mrs. Hurst. Many people hid their financial circumstances when they were embarrassing.

Yet much as Elizabeth disliked Miss Bingley, she did not wish to condemn her too quickly. Although she and Miss Bingley had a strained relationship, that did not mean that Miss Bingley would behave in such an underhanded and heartless manner towards her. On the other hand, Miss Bingley's history was already stained with dishonesty and cruelty. When Mr. Bingley had first been interested in Jane, she had conspired to keep the pair apart, not letting her brother know when Jane was in London. Nevertheless this act, this letter demanding money, was so much worse! Could Elizabeth really believe it of her? Besides, if Miss Bingley had done this, and her involvement were discovered, she would anger those who were nearest to her excessively. Could Miss Bingley be so confident in her abilities to deceive that she assumed that no one would detect, or at least, suspect her? Or was Miss Bingley's grudge towards Elizabeth so great that she would think it worth the risk?

The truth was that Elizabeth still disliked Miss Bingley, and would prefer to suspect her to nearly every other person among her acquaintance. But she had learned, from experience, that it was perilous to form judgments his way.

"Yet this is foolish of me," Elizabeth said to herself as she adjusted her pillow. "I do not wish to suspect those whom I love, and I am reluctant to suspect those whom I do not love. Of course there are many people whom I do not know, to whom I am indifferent, but how could any of them have the information required to create such a letter? I must use reason and observation, and not be prejudiced by sentiment."

When she went beyond her closest connections, there were many people to suspect. Mrs. Bennet liked to boast of the number of families with whom they dined: what if some friend, or rather, some acquaintance, pretending to be a friend, had stolen a sample of Elizabeth's writing during a meal or party at Longbourn? Someone who was in debt, or someone whose prospects were poor. It could be one of Mrs. Long's nieces. One of the Gouldings? They seemed to have all the money that they needed, but how could she know for sure? Mr. Jones or Mr. Jones – the father or the son? Aunt Philips? Mrs. Philips had been rather concerned about retaining Mrs. Smith as a tenant; was it possible that she and Mr. Philips were in debt? While Elizabeth was unclear as to the state of her aunt and uncle's financial situation, she could not believe that Mrs. Philips would connive at defrauding her own niece. Aunt Philips had always been particularly fond of her nieces, and even if she no longer cared much about Mrs. Darcy's opinion, given that Mrs. Darcy lived so far away, Mrs. Philips was still especially dependent on her sister. No, Mrs. Philips would never risk the enmity of Mrs. Bennet, and besides, Elizabeth did not think that Mrs. Philips was cunning enough to concoct this scheme. Possibly Mrs. Philips had been used unwittingly by someone else – that was far more plausible – but as more than half of Meryton's population visited Mrs. Philips's apartment, the notion did nothing to narrow down Elizabeth's group of potential suspects.

She had to consider her dearest friends, the Lucases. Sir William and his wife Lady Lucas could never concoct such a scheme, but their daughter Mrs. Collins was more clever than most of the neighborhood *and* she had sketched when she was younger. Elizabeth had always been extremely fond of Charlotte, so the prospect of her as the perpetrator was extremely unpleasant, but she tried to consider the facts objectively. Mrs. Collins and Elizabeth corresponded frequently, and so she had many samples of Elizabeth's handwriting. Mrs. Collins also appreciated money; her reason for marrying Mr. Collins had been completely mercenary, as her best preservation from want.

But Charlotte, recently widowed, still suffering from the trauma of the death of Mr. Collins – even if she had married him out of prudence, he had been her husband – could she really be engaged in such an intricate scheme just now? How could she have the emotional fortitude? And yet the death of Mr. Collins might provide an incentive for such an act. Mrs. Collins might have reasonable expectations for the future, as her son Lewis was the heir to Longbourn – but that could be many years away, and she might need funds now.

Elizabeth did not wish to suspect Mrs. Collins – she was fond of Charlotte – but she also did not want to be blinded by her affections. Was there any reason not to suspect Charlotte, her friend of so many years?

Mrs. Collins might like having money – there were few who did not – but Elizabeth had never known her to do anything dishonest or unkind. Furthermore, Lucas Lodge was full of people these days: Sir William and Lady Lucas and their other children, not to mention Lewis Collins and all the servants. How could Charlotte could have managed, with so many people about, to forge the letter and to write the demand for money? The letter purporting to be from Elizabeth showed real craftsmanship; whoever had penned it had surely created several drafts. And how could Charlotte, with her young son to care for, even be at the horse chestnut tree to retrieve the money? She could only manage something like this with assistance, and whom could Charlotte trust with such an errand? Certainly neither of her parents would be complicit in such a scheme. Sir William, a former mayor of Meryton, prided himself as being a pillar of the community, and his wife would never do anything to jeopardize their position in the neighborhood. Besides, few of the Lucases could keep a secret.

Elizabeth was glad to be able to have solid reasons for moving Mrs. Collins off her mental list of possible perpetrators.

She needed to sleep. She needed to be clear-minded in the morning, so that she could decide on an appropriate course of action. Alas, it was one thing to resolve to fall asleep, and quite another to actually do it.

Her thoughts were interrupted by a knock on her door, so soft at first that Elizabeth was not sure if she had heard it or imagined it. But then the person outside knocked again, more loudly and a little more sharply. "What is it?" Elizabeth called.

"Elizabeth, please come." The voice on the other side of the door belonged to Mr. Bingley.

Her irritability changed to alarm. "Mr. Bingley, what is it?"

"Jane is in labor!"

CHAPTER XXXI

Elizabeth and Miss Bingley both attended Jane in her room, while Mr. Bingley was banished to the library. Both Elizabeth and Miss Bingley were anxious to do everything that they could to assist Jane, but they were unable to advise her whether she should sit or she should stand, whether she was better walking around the room or lying on her bed. They could only recommend that she should do whatever made her most comfortable, and at present nothing seemed to help.

"How useless we are," remarked Elizabeth, after she and Miss Bingley had inquired minutely after every twinge but were unable to make any suggestions with assurance.

"Are you in much pain?" inquired Miss Bingley solicitously.

But even this question Jane could not answer properly, because she had no basis for comparison. "I suppose it is bearable, as I have not cried out."

"Cry out if you wish to," said Elizabeth, "this is no time to be restrained."

"But I do not wish to – not really. I just feel peculiar. I just did not expect it to be tonight." With effort Jane walked around the room, then paused by the window to look out at the night sky.

"It appears it will be tonight, and that in the morning we will meet little Caroline Louise," said Miss Bingley. "Of course, I am teasing. I know you are planning on Jane Elizabeth. Unless the child is a boy."

"You have been saying that you wish it would happen soon," said Elizabeth, attempting to be encouraging. "So, here we are."

"I suppose. Perhaps – perhaps we should send for Mamma?" Jane turned back from the window, and her countenance was so anxious that both her sister and Miss Bingley realized how inadequate they were to this situation. To their credit, they did their best to reassure Jane by offering to find more competent assistance. Miss Bingley said that she believed that her brother already had sent the coach to Longbourn, and if Jane wished, she could send a man for one of the Mr. Joneses (she added, however, that she had little confidence in the local apothecaries). Elizabeth suggested that as fetching their mother could take two hours or more, that they should determine if any of the servants had any useful experience in these matters.

Miss Bingley and Jane considered and agreed that Mrs. Nicholls, the cook, who tended to the servants when they were injured or ill, might be a source of practical advice. Miss Bingley went to summon her, so Jane and Elizabeth were alone for a few minutes.

Jane trembled from a contraction; Elizabeth took her sister's hand and squeezed it sympathetically. "Jane – everything will be all right, I promise you. Both you and the baby will be fine."

"Of course we will," said her sister, when she could speak again. "And truly it is not as bad as I expected. But perhaps it will take many hours, and the terrible pain is to come later. Our mother has told me many times that first deliveries are the longest." She changed the subject. "I am so sorry to disturb your sleep – especially when you were so worried. Have you decided what to do about the letter?"

"Do not concern yourself with that," said Elizabeth earnestly. "And I would not be anywhere else tonight, Jane, but with you."

A knock on the door and more discomfort for Jane ended their tête-à-tête. Miss Bingley arrived with Mrs. Nicholls, middle-aged, stout and confident.

Jane apologized to the cook for rousing her in the middle of the night, and Mrs. Nicholls told Mrs. Bingley to think nothing of it; she had already instructed an undercook to bring some hot water and to make a pot of tea. Mrs. Nicholls then took command with as much authority as if Mrs. Bingley's bedroom were part of the Netherfield kitchens.

The cook ordered Mrs. Bingley to walk around the room; Jane obliged. Mrs. Nicholls told her to continue then asked how she was feeling – if the pains were more intense or less.

Jane replied, with hesitation, that they were less. "I understood that walking was supposed to hurry labor, not slow it down."

"Indeed it is. But, Mrs. Bingley, you are not in labor."

Mrs. Nicholls's pronouncement astonished all three young women. They protested, and described Jane's symptoms. Mrs. Nicholls was nevertheless adamant in her assessment. She explained that Mrs. Bingley would have a baby very soon, certainly within the next month, but not within the next day. The baby was not yet quite low enough, and several other symptoms were also missing.

Jane was mortified by the commotion which she had caused. Mrs. Nicholls, pouring out the tea that the undercook had brought, told her not to be. "Your time will come soon enough," she said, "but I expect it will be at least another fortnight."

The doors could be heard opening and shutting below. Mrs. Bennet had arrived in the Netherfield carriage, bringing with her Mary and Kitty; even though they were as far away as the vestibule, Mrs. Bennet's voice penetrated the walls and floors.

Mrs. Bennet hastened to Jane's room, Mary and Kitty yawning in her wake. Mrs. Bennet was at first reluctant to accept the diagnosis of Mrs. Nicholls, as Mrs. Nicholls was only Mrs. Bingley's cook and not Mrs. Bingley's mother. Moreover, Mrs. Bennet had been counting on holding her first grandchild that morning, which made her predisposed to prefer genuine labor. Yet Mrs. Bennet's priority was the safety of her daughter, and after a quarter of an hour she concurred that Jane's labor had not yet begun.

Jane apologized again for ruining everyone's sleep; the ladies united in telling her no apology was needed.

"Papa said he would not come till later this morning," added Kitty. "He said these things take time."

"As much as a fortnight, apparently," said Miss Bingley.

The fatigued women found Miss Bingley's remark extremely diverting; they burst out laughing. The sound brought Mr. Bingley to the door; he was expecting cries of pain, not peals of merriment; and he was confused and concerned. The ladies opened the door and explained that the baby had not yet arrived and was not expected for several days.

Mrs. Bennet, who had completely recovered her spirits, gave her opinion. "It will happen, dear Jane. I went through this myself. But perhaps I should stay at Netherfield till the child arrives."

Miss Bingley was alarmed by this suggestion. "Madam, that cannot be necessary. The baby may not appear for another two weeks and Longbourn House is not far. You may depend on my brother's carriage being sent to fetch you when the time comes."

Mrs. Bennet said that she did not like to put Mr. Bingley's coachman to trouble, which contradicted her usual attitude on the matter, for she usually maintained that coachmen existed in order to drive coaches.

Mr. Bingley and Jane also encouraged Mrs. Bennet to remain in the comfort of her own home at Longbourn while she could, for they would certainly impose upon her once the child arrived. Mrs. Bennet resisted these hints till Kitty reminded her of a dinner she had been planning to give at Longbourn; the local poulterer had some fat geese – she did not wish to forego that if she did not have to.

Miss Bingley, Mr. Bingley, Jane and even Elizabeth breathed a sigh of relief that Mrs. Bennet would not be moving in just yet. Kitty took a cloth and dabbed Jane's brow while Mary seated herself in a corner and slept.

Nicholls said she would make an early breakfast, an offer appreciated by everyone. Within an hour, those residing at Netherfield had dressed; within two, nearly everyone was seated in the breakfast parlor, the exception being Jane, who remained in her own room with Kitty. And within three hours, Mr. Bennet arrived in the Longbourn carriage, leaning on a cane and limping because of his sprained ankle.

Miss Bingley was rather put out at being invaded by so many Bennets, from both near and far – but Elizabeth thought she should not be cross at her father's arrival, as Mr. Bennet was bringing the means of taking most of them away.

"How is Jane?" he inquired anxiously. "Do I have a grandchild yet?"

Mr. Bingley informed his father-in-law of Jane's situation. Mr. Bennet's lips twisted with amusement, and he could not resist remarking to his wife: "You promised me a grandchild if I appeared this morning, but it appears that I was right to sleep till sunrise."

"And I was right to come, Mr. Bennet! I was summoned by a carriage from Netherfield Park!"

"I am the guilty party," said Mr. Bingley, particularly anxious, after a night of no sleep, to forestall a dispute between his wife's parents. "I misjudged the situation."

Kitty entered the room, and she suggested to Mr. Bennet that he go and see Jane for himself. "She has not come down for breakfast, but she is awake and dressed."

"I will do that," said Mr. Bennet. He spent ten minutes with Jane, then returned to the breakfast-parlor, where he joined them for some toast and tea. Then, sensibly pointing out that they were all tired and would need their strength in the very near future, Mr. Bennet herded his wife and younger daughters to the carriage so that anyone desiring a nap that day could easily take one.

CHAPTER XXXII

Later in the day Mr. Bingley and his sister decided to take some exercise by going out for a couple of hours on horseback, leaving Jane and Elizabeth together. They sat in the drawing-room with needlework.

Elizabeth yawned.

"I am so sorry for everyone's fatigue," Jane apologized.

It was at least the tenth time for Jane to apologize, thought Elizabeth. Sometimes one could tell that they were related to Mr. Collins – and then she mentally chastised herself for the unflattering thought about their dead cousin. "Given how worried I have been, I would have slept little anyway."

"What do you plan to do?" Jane inquired.

"I have attempted to compose a letter to Darcy, but I cannot; everything I have written is unsatisfactory. But I am determined not to give this person the money he demands. So I have written a letter asking for more time, saying that I cannot give him the money just yet, and I will put *that* in the horse chestnut tree."

"Do you think he will give you more time?"

"I do not know, and in fact, that is not my primary objective. Here are my intentions. In three days, the day on which I am supposed to leave the money in the tree, I will go to Meryton in my carriage, place my letter inside the horse chestnut tree, and then depart in the carriage. When we are out of sight I will descend from the carriage and send Wilson back to Netherfield. However, *I* will return through the woods and clandestinely observe who comes to the tree. In this manner I will discover who is to blame."

Jane admired her sister for the boldness of her plan, but she was also concerned for her safety. "You should not attempt this alone. You should take someone with you."

"I appreciate your concern, but I do not trust anyone."

"What about your coachman?"

"Wilson? Do you think I should trust him, or that I should not trust him?"

"I do not say that you should trust him particularly, but he will be involved. If you drive to that field with him, and then descend from the carriage to walk back, then he will realize that you are doing something. And even if he does not understand it, he will be curious and might mention it to someone."

Elizabeth considered. Wilson had been with the Darcy family for many years, which ought to be reason to trust him implicitly. Yet how could she be sure? Wilson might be mercenary. Or perhaps he was proud like Lady Catherine and disapproved of his master's marriage to her. Elizabeth did not elucidate her doubts about her coachman to her sister, instead she said, more generally: "I do not know. On principle I am reluctant to trust anyone besides you, Jane. It is only two miles in one direction, and the weather is fine. So I will walk there, place my letter in the tree, and then walk away and then slip back through the woods. Wilson need not know anything about it."

Jane still disliked the idea of her sister doing this alone. "Is there anyone who you trust? Our father, perhaps? Or Bingley?"

Elizabeth seriously considered both men. Mr. Bennet was still suffering from his sprained ankle and so would have difficulty walking the distance. She was reluctant to involve Mr. Bingley when she had not yet informed Darcy.

"That means you should inform Darcy," said Jane.

"I have every intention of doing so," Elizabeth assured her sister, "but some communications are better made in person than on paper. I will be extremely careful, Jane, I promise."

Jane begged her not to do anything rash. She could not convince her sister not to make this excursion but she did persuade her to agree to some precautions. Elizabeth would go but she had to promise to return before it became dark. "If you are not here before the sun sets, I will send both Bingley and Wilson after you."

Elizabeth agreed to this condition, which she thought reasonable, and over the next two days they decided on several improvements to the scheme. She would carry some bread, cheese and fruit, so that she would not be hungry or thirsty while she waited; she would wear comfortable, sturdy shoes; and she would dress in an old gown of green and brown muslin, so as to be less visible when she hid in the forest. Her French maid was not particularly impressed by her selected attire, even when she gave a reason for it – "Why do you wish to walk anywhere, Madame Darcy, when you have such a comfortable carriage?" – but Madame Darcy was known for her lengthy strolls through the grounds of Pemberley, so even if Jeanette could not comprehend the strange ways of Madame, Madame's decision to take a walk did not strike her as anything out of the ordinary. At breakfast, her letter in her reticule, Elizabeth explained that as it was a beautiful day – fortunately the weather had cooperated – she would take a long walk, and perhaps call on friends or family, and that she would be back in time for dinner. Miss Bingley raised an eyebrow but did not comment. Jane did not perfectly control her countenance and her unhappy expression caused her husband to offer himself as a walking companion to Elizabeth. She said no, she was inclined to a solitary ramble, and besides, Jane needed him more. And so, shortly after breakfast, carrying her parasol and her reticule, Elizabeth left Netherfield on foot.

The day was lovely, with a brilliant blue sky, cows in meadows and farmers in fields, and with all the golden glories of late summer. At first the exercise revived her spirits, but as Elizabeth neared the field with the horse chestnut tree her heart beat faster and even her hands shook.

She slowed her pace as she stepped off the dirt lane on to the field with the horse chestnut tree. She had strolled this way many times before, and she was pleased to see that her memory was exact. The large field was shaped like a triangle with sides that were not particularly straight. It was bordered on one side by the dirt lane on which she had walked; forest and shrubbery edged another side of the field, and the rocky edge of river, where a pair of boys fished, completed the triangle.

The forest was what interested her most; Elizabeth studied it, wondering if someone were in it watching her – and deciding where she should hide herself. She did not see anyone, but if someone *were* watching her – waiting for her to leave money in the tree – then she did not think her behavior would be unduly suspicious. She thought that most people in her situation would be seeking to discover the extortionist – and then wondered, distractedly, how many people had ever been in her situation?

Elizabeth did not detect anyone in the forest, which meant at least one of the following: that the forest was an excellent hiding place or that no one was watching. She hoped, when she reflected, that both were true.

She approached the tree, which rose tall and majestic in the middle of the field. Her heart fluttered with doubt: what if it were the wrong one? Then all of her effort, including the two miles she had already walked here, and the two miles she had yet to walk back, would be for nothing. But then she found the hollow and inside the hollow she discovered a wooden box. Whoever was doing this had left a box for the bank notes that he extorted, to keep them from getting wet, from being blown away, or even from being chewed on by an avaricious squirrel. With trembling hands she reached up and withdrew the box and examined it. Inside she found a note in handwriting that was exactly like her own, and on paper similar to what she owned. How annoying! Whoever was behind this had made his paper with its writing a worthless clue, but she removed it anyway. "Put the money in here, close the box and return it to the hollow of the tree," the note instructed. Frowning, she withdrew the letter from her reticule – the letter *without* money inside it – and put the letter into the box, then closed the box and replaced it in the tree. Feeling queasy and faint, Elizabeth glanced all around her but she still saw no one suspicious.

She closed her reticule, and then walked quickly away from the tree and back to the lane. At that point she stopped and turned to look – surely it would be natural to have some curiosity – but she discovered nothing. She returned the way she had come, till she reached a place on the lane where she was completely alone, with no one visible in either direction who could observe her. She stepped off the path and into the woods, pushing her way through brush and trees; Jeanette would have to work hard to clean her shoes and her petticoat. Elizabeth estimated that the horse chestnut tree had been out of her view about twenty minutes by the time she settled on a fallen log, reasonably hidden, to observe the situation. As far as she could perceive, nothing had changed.

When she sat down she was full of anxious apprehension. The anxiety remained, but Elizabeth soon found that her task was simultaneously one of tedium and dullness. She compelled herself to pay attention, as if she were a soldier on guard duty, but there was so little to see and to hear. A few butterflies flitted haphazardly a few feet above the grass. A dog barked in the distance. The boys continued to fish – this had been a favorite spot of her uncle Gardiner's when he was a boy – but she believed that he had

had more luck than the youths before her. As far as she could tell, they had caught nothing.

Elizabeth also observed the lane where she herself had walked just a few minutes before. It edged the field, then turned near the river and went downriver, and it, at least, was enlivened by occasional traffic. On it she spied several farmers, a pair of giggling girls, the manservant of Mrs. Long and several people whom she did not recognize. After about two hours she saw the familiar faces of Mr. Clarke and young Mr. Jones, who came with fishing tackle, crossed the meadow and were soon out of view as they went upstream along the river bank. The Lucas carriage appeared, and Mrs. Collins, her sister Maria and the nursery maid climbed out with Lewis. They spread a blanket on the field and stayed for about an hour. Mr. Morris walked by – Mr. Philips must have closed the office for the afternoon – and a while later Elizabeth thought she glimpsed her sister Mary. The greatest surprise was when Miss Bingley arrived on horseback, escorted by a groomsman. The coming and going of all the people could be explained by their pleasure in fishing, or the prettiness of the shady lane near the river, or simply because the route provided the most convenient path to their destination. No one, as far as she could determine from her position in the woods, manifested any consciousness of guilt – although perhaps the extortionist was so hardened that he would not – and no one approached the horse chestnut tree itself.

More hours passed. Elizabeth did not have a watch with her but she could determine this by the changing shadows. She consumed the fruit that she had brought with her and her other provisions. The anglers departed, both the men and the boys, and the lane was empty. Presumably everyone was at home drinking tea; Elizabeth longed for a cup herself. Surely the forger would come now for his money, or at least what he believed was his money? Or did he plan to wait till the cover of darkness? Yet the horse chestnut tree could be visited by anyone, and the cash which he was trying to extort from her could be found and taken by another person. The delay struck her as strange.

The shadows lengthened; if she did not leave soon, Jane would send the carriage after her. With great resolve, Elizabeth rose, pushed her way out of the woods, and with shaking legs and a fluttering heart, went to the horse chestnut tree.

The box was gone!

Elizabeth searched the hollow and the vicinity of the tree, even walking down to the river, but she did not find it. Someone must have taken the box out of the tree immediately after she put her letter inside, during the very few minutes that it had been completely out of her view. Where could that person have been hidden? In the woods, like herself? Or perhaps – and she looked up, and chastised herself for not having thought of this before – perhaps the culprit had been *in* the tree when she had put the envelope without the money in the box.

Tired and hungry, her shoes dirty, she turned back towards Netherfield. If only she had taken Jane's advice, and had enlisted the aid of another person in this endeavor! If that person had been hidden before, and had observed, then *she* would have learned who was behind this.

And, if the extortionist made good on his threat, he would be sending a copy of the letter that he had forged in her penmanship to Mr. Darcy. Possibly, nay probably, it was already posted. She counted the days that would pass before Mr. Darcy received it – he could receive it as soon as the day after tomorrow – and then wondered desperately what he would think of her after he received it. Sometimes she believed that he would understand that it was a complete falsehood, but then, the paper – the manner of expression – the very shape of the letters – all these things were against her! Sometimes *she* did not believe that she had not written it! Would her husband still respect and trust her after this? Or would she be doomed to a loveless marriage, forced to live with a person who despised her? During the long walk to her brother-in-law's hired estate – and the two miles seemed particularly long – her heart sometimes suggested one thing and at other times argued quite the opposite.

As she walked, she also considered all the things that she should have done and other things that she could have done. She could have enlisted the assistance of her father; even if, due to his injured ankle, he could not have accompanied her himself, he could have recommended someone discreet to assist her. Her father's judgment of character was not always perfect, but neither was hers. Together they might have decided on someone suitable.

Or else *she* should have sent an express to Mr. Darcy. She had not wished to distress him, but how much greater his distress would be now!

She almost hoped for a second letter from the extortionist. If he wrote again, then she could attempt a different solution to this terrible problem.

Footsore, berating herself for her shortsightedness, Elizabeth entered Netherfield and found her sister alone in her dressing room. Jane expressed relief in seeing her safe, ordered a tray of tea and bread and butter for her, and then asked if she had discovered anything.

Elizabeth explained her failure, and expressed her frustrations. "I wasted all that time!" she said. "But I was too proud – and too embarrassed – to involve anyone else but you, Jane."

Jane offered what comfort she could. "It is done, and whether or not it was the best course of action, your intentions were good. Instead of reviewing what you could have done, consider what you should do now."

"I will write to Darcy tonight," said Elizabeth. "I only hope that the words flow more easily than they did before."

"I think it would be wise. But, Lizzy," Jane began, but she did not finish her statement, for at that moment Miss Bingley opened the door and entered the room. From that point on the discussion was on the relative merits of horseback riding and walking as forms of taking exercise. Elizabeth argued that if one rode on a horse, it was the horse that was exercising. But she granted that Caroline Bingley's countenance was blooming, while she could see the dirt on her shoes and she was certain that her hair was a disgrace. She excused herself so that she could have order restored by the attentive ministrations of her maid.

CHAPTER XXXIII

That evening, instead of joining the others for cards and music after dinner, Elizabeth went directly to her room and sat down with renewed determination at her desk.

Possibly because she had been contemplating the letter that she had to write to her husband ever since she discovered that the box was missing from the horse chestnut tree, on this occasion after the words flowed more easily:

I postponed writing this letter, because I know how distressed you have been due to the sad situation of Reverend Wallace and I have not wished to augment your troubles – and because the following may come to nothing as it is.

A few days ago, I received a delivery, with a page forged by someone – I have not yet discovered who – and a demand for money. The forgery is of a letter, written by me to Wickham, using many terms of affection, and I suppose it is to have been written by me to him before you opened my eyes to his true character. Although the language and the paper and even the handwriting appear to be mine, I did not compose this letter! I have never written a letter to Wickham. It is a clever counterfeit and an attempt to extort money.

I was supposed to leave the money in a tree for the extortionist today. I did not. Instead I left a letter asking for more time to acquire the cash, claiming that I did not have so much with me (I do have the money with me; I have made a few presents but I have not been extravagant). My action, however, was in actuality a ruse, for my intention was to conceal myself in the nearby woods and to watch the hiding place for the money from a hiding place of my own, in the hopes of discovering what person or persons was behind this attempt at blackmail. Unfortunately, although I observed the horse chestnut tree for many hours, I did not learn anything, for my letter was somehow cleverly removed without my perceiving the person who took it.

As I did not leave any money, it is possible that the culprit has already sent you the forgery. Therefore I intend to send this by express to make sure that you are informed of the real situation.

The extortionist is clever, because he realizes that your good opinion is the most important thing in the world to me, and that I am loathe to lose even a tiny fraction of your esteem and your respect. Hence I can confess that I was actually tempted, for many hours, to pay the money. But that would mean putting my trust in him, a stranger whose character is based on exploitation and falsehood, instead of in you, who are both my husband and a man of integrity.

I realize that I should have sent this several days ago, as soon as I received the demand, but I did not want to worry you, especially given poor Wallace — I pray that he does not suffer much — and I confess that I was too perturbed to think or write clearly. I only hope that I am expressing myself clearly now.

Elizabeth perused this portion of her missive several times, and finally decided that it was the best she could manage. She signed it, addressed it and sealed it and resolved to send it by express the first thing in the morning.

Then she retired. After being outside all day, and her long walk, she was completely fatigued. Despite her mind and heart being in such tumult, she believed that she would sleep. She had done what she could.

Elizabeth did not wish to be selfish, but as she closed her eyes she hoped that Jane's baby would not arrive that night.

CHAPTER XXXIV

Elizabeth was not summoned by Mr. Bingley during the night, and she slept nearly as well as she hoped. When she awoke her resolve had not diminished, so as soon as she was up and fairly dressed she removed the letter she had written from its hiding place. Then she summoned a footman and said that the letter was to be sent express to Pemberley and gave him the money for the expense. In a few minutes Elizabeth could see him leaving the house with her message in hand.

The letter to Darcy was on its way. She had believed that knowing that she had done what she could to resolve the matter, she would be able to relax and to think about other things. She found, however, that tranquility did not automatically return to her. She kept wondering what her husband's reaction would be when he opened it.

After breakfast she joined Jane in the drawing-room and told her what she had done.

"I am glad," said Jane. "It was the right thing to do."

Elizabeth said she was grateful for her sister's approval and support. "Then why am I not calm? Worrying will accomplish nothing, yet I cannot seem to stop."

"And I keep wondering when this child will arrive. Yet that will not make it come faster!"

Their conversation was interrupted by the appearance of a chaise; Mr. and Mrs. Goulding were calling; Mr. Goulding in order to tell Bingley about a new gun, and Mrs. Goulding to make a present of baby caps. When Jane exclaimed that the caps were very pretty, but rather large for a newly born infant, Mrs. Goulding said that was intentional. "Your child will grow out of most of the gifts he is receiving now in only a few months, and then what will you do? Your friends may not be giving you presents then."

Jane thanked her for her generosity and consideration, while Elizabeth and Miss Bingley – the latter had also joined them – exchanged a glance of rare agreement. With such doting aunts, the child would want for nothing for sixty years at least.

The day continued with callers and companionship, so that Elizabeth, who had said she did not intend to worry about the letter that she had sent to her husband, involuntarily kept this resolution for many hours. Only late in the afternoon, after Mrs. Bennet and Kitty had departed – having invited everyone over to Longbourn to tea on the following day – did Elizabeth have an unoccupied moment.

With their visitors departed, Jane excused herself to take a nap; Mr. Bingley said he would shoot some billiards, and Miss Bingley had some music that she wished to practice. Elizabeth said she would take a little walk in the shrubbery – nothing as strenuous as the day before – in the sweet warm hour of the late afternoon.

She told herself that a stroll would calm her spirit, but instead of contemplating the leafy branches and the bracken, she indulged herself in distressing conjectures. She agreed with Jane in that by sending the letter she had done the right thing; that was to say, her head agreed, but her heart trembled.

Elizabeth realized that before yesterday evening she had wondered what Darcy would think *if* he learned about the letter to Wickham. Now she had to wonder what he would think of her *when* he learned about the letter to Wickham.

He had already endured so much mortification by making her the choice as his partner in life. He was a gentleman and she was a gentleman's daughter, which gave them equal rank in society – and yet no one would call them equal. In comparison with the Darcys, the Bennets were poor. Mr. Darcy had an income of 10,000£ per annum; while Mr. Bennet's income was only 2,000£. Georgiana Darcy had a fortune of 30,000£, while Miss Bingley and Mrs. Hurst each had 20,000£; Elizabeth could expect, at most, to inherit 1,000£.

Money was one thing; one could not help it, but what about accomplishments? Elizabeth played and sang – a little – but again, she had never practiced as diligently as she ought, and she was not skilled in comparison to Georgiana or even to Miss Bingley. And as for drawing, she could not. Perhaps she had read a little more than most other young ladies, true, but was reading especially useful?

But he loves you! her heart protested, defending itself from the onslaught of self-criticism.

The worst embarrassment was caused by her own family. Lady Catherine, insolent and dictatorial, was the only one among Darcy's relatives for whom anything ill could be said, while Elizabeth had so many relations to cause a blush. Lady Catherine was, however, completely respectable, while Elizabeth's sister Lydia had eloped with Wickham and had lived with him before their marriage – a marriage which Darcy himself had stepped in to coerce.

Again, her heart made a feeble attempt at argument. Georgiana Darcy herself had nearly eloped with Wickham, and Lydia had but been a few months older than Georgiana when she had been persuaded to the rash act. And even though Darcy repudiated Wickham, Wickham had been old Mr. Darcy's godson, raised with Darcy practically as a brother. Wickham, christened George Wickham in honor of old Mr. Darcy, was as much her husband's connection as hers. Yet it was Elizabeth's sister that had married Wickham; the world saw her family as having forced Darcy to have a brother-in-law whom he naturally detested.

This reckoning, what was the point? The question was, how would he react when he received her letter? Or the forged letter from the extortionist? It was possible that the latter had already reached him.

"But *I* did not write that letter!" Elizabeth protested aloud, as she sat on the bench by the pond. *She* had written a letter of explanation.

She tried to tell herself that she was being ridiculous, for there was a very good chance that he was not reacting to either letter. The extortionist might try with her again. If his goal was money, exposing her immediately would remove her reason to pay, so he might have not have sent anything to Pemberley. And it was too soon for Mr. Darcy to have received *her* letter, as she had only sent it this morning. She expected he was either at Kympton, sitting beside his friend's deathbed, or else back at Pemberley, taking turns with Mrs. Annesley in chaperoning the budding romance between his cousin Colonel Fitzwilliam and his sister Georgiana.

How he must have suffered, after she had refused his initial proposal of marriage. He had written a letter to her explaining and defending himself – and then he, although still in love with her, had not seen her for many months. He had believed, during all that time, that she despised him.

How surprised he must have been when he had run into her at Pemberley!

Visiting Pemberley had not been her idea, but a suggestion of the Gardiners, with whom she had been traveling. She would have refused to go, but the hotel chambermaid had told her that Mr. Darcy was not at home. She had not deliberately thrown herself in his way; still, the memory caused her to blush. Yet why should she be so embarrassed? He had been surprised to see her, but also glad, so very glad! And that meeting had given him the opportunity to show her that her reproofs had been attended to.

How wonderful it would be, if Darcy suddenly appeared and she could have the conversation she needed with him. But she was too impatient. He had had to endure months of suspense after handing her his letter; she had sent hers less than twelve hours before.

Perhaps she ought to leave for Pemberley immediately herself. At least there would be nothing scandalous or embarrassing about her going there now – she was Mrs. Darcy – Pemberley was her home. But Jane – she could not abandon Jane.

Having agitated herself completely with her wild, contradictory conjectures, intermixing them with painful memories and agonizing self-doubts, Elizabeth wiped away a tear, and then she started, for she heard voices. She heard Bingley say: "Let us take this path." Mr. Bingley was probably walking with his sister; they were certainly heading this way. She had to compose herself, for there was no escape, no alternate path, and she could not help wishing that Miss Caroline Bingley were not in the mood for exercise.

"Elizabeth! There she is – Elizabeth!"

The voice was familiar. It was not Miss Bingley's; it was not even Mr. Bingley's!

Heart pounding hard, Elizabeth rose and turned. The man striding towards her on the path was tall and handsome and very dear. "Darcy!"

CHAPTER XXXV

She had to be dreaming. She had been wishing for this yet certain that he was several counties away, two days of hard travel at best. "I do not believe it!"

He did not appear at all displeased to see her; in fact he smiled and gave her a kiss.

Mr. Bingley also looked pleased with himself. "I thought we would find your wife here. I will leave the two of you now. Unless you wish to take some refreshment in the house?" But Darcy declined, and said that he would eat and drink later, and Mr. Bingley departed, leaving Mr. and Mrs. Darcy standing together.

"How did you get here?" inquired Elizabeth, all astonishment.

"In a carriage, of course. Bingley's paddock is quite full. We should probably send one of the carriages back to Pemberley."

"But why did you come? Not that I am all displeased. Did you receive my letter? But that is impossible! I only sent it this morning."

"I received *a* letter."

"From whom?" Elizabeth was momentarily terrified; had the extortionist already written? Yet that seemed unlikely, for Darcy's behavior was as affectionate and solicitous as ever.

"I will show it to you," he said. He pulled a letter out a coat pocket – and Elizabeth nearly fainted – the paper was the same that they had used at Longbourn; had the extortionist acquired more Longbourn stationery? "Here, my dear, read it – it will not take long."

With trembling fingers, Elizabeth unfolded the page. The handwriting was familiar, but it was not hers – it was her father's!

My dear Sir,
Elizabeth needs you. If it is at all possible, come. Yours, etc.

And that, with Mr. Bennet's usual terseness, was the entire epistle.

"You seem perplexed."

"I am! I do want to see you, very much, because I have a communication to make that is rather difficult to make by letter. But I do not understand how my father could be involved – how could he even know, I have only discussed the matter with Jane – oh! – Jane, of course. Papa was here a few mornings ago; they obviously spoke then."

Mr. Darcy waited patiently for the matter to become intelligible to her, and as soon as it had, Elizabeth realized she had been negligent in her greeting. "What I have to tell you is important, but not so important that it cannot wait a few minutes." She invited him to join her on the bench, and asked about Reverend Wallace, Georgiana and the rest of those at Pemberley and also inquired about his journey.

Mr. Darcy explained that Mr. Wallace had died four days ago and had been buried the morning that Darcy had departed from Pemberley. He had stopped in Kympton for the burial. Everyone else at Pemberley, thank goodness, was in excellent health. His journey had been uneventful, and he had made good time. "Now, tell me why your father sent me this."

"Very well. Let me consider a moment, to get my thoughts in order," said Elizabeth, now wishing that she could simply hand him the letter that she had worked on so hard last night. But she did not delay the conversation for more than a minute and soon the communication was made. When she was done, Darcy was indignant and angry with whoever had done this; he wished to see the letter – it was hidden in her room, she explained, she would show it to him later – and told her that she had taken a great risk by maintaining a vigil at the horse chestnut tree.

"So you believe that I did not write to Wickham?"

"If that is what you tell me, yes, I believe you."

"But you may change your mind when I show it to you. It is a masterful forgery."

"Do you have less confidence in me than I have in you?" Darcy teased. Then, seriously, he explained that the wealthy were often the targets of the unscrupulous. Although he was sorry that this had happened to her, he was not particularly surprised. "I wish I could protect you from every situation, but I am proud of you for not yielding."

"The temptation was severe," she said.

Mr. Darcy was curious to see the letter, but even more interested in determining who might have written it. His first suspect, understandably, was George Wickham, but Elizabeth raised several objections – Wickham was supposed to be in Newcastle, and as far as they both knew, he did not have the skill for forgery. On the latter point, Darcy agreed. "If he did, I am certain that I would have learned of it before now."

A footman arrived, summoning them to dinner. The Darcys decided to postpone the continuation of their discussion till after the evening meal, for they were both hungry. Mr. Darcy, during his hasty journey, had eaten little, and Elizabeth, now that she had explained the matter to her husband, discovered that the sick feeling she had experienced during the past few days of anxiety was gone and that she was famished.

As they rose to return to the house, Elizabeth noticed that the wasps were busy rebuilding their nest, one tree over from where they had been before. This time their new home would be harder to reach and more difficult to destroy.

CHAPTER XXXVI

Mr. Darcy was welcomed by everyone at Netherfield. During and after dinner there was much conversation to be had, with everyone wishing to hear about all the news from Pemberley and especially about the death of Reverend Wallace.

"It has been a dreadful month for clergymen," said Miss Bingley archly after Darcy described his friend's death. Even though Mr. Darcy had been married for nearly a year, Miss Bingley had not relinquished her custom of paying attention to him.

Mr. Darcy expressed his condolences to Jane and to Elizabeth and inquired about Mrs. Collins.

"She is doing as well as can be expected, Sir," said Jane. "She and her little boy are staying with her family at Lucas Lodge."

"I would also be concerned about your aunt," Elizabeth added. "Lady Catherine quite depended on Mr. Collins."

"She did indeed," Mr. Darcy acknowledged.

Despite Miss Bingley's willingness to entertain them with several songs that she had recently mastered, the evening was not a late one. Jane, as usual, yawned early, and Bingley retired with his wife. Mr. and Mrs. Darcy also wished to be alone, and Mr. Darcy was fatigued from his long journey.

The next morning Elizabeth informed her husband that she had some rather disagreeable news for him: "We are invited to take tea today at Longbourn." He said that he believed he would survive it, and so later that day, Mr. and Mrs. Bingley and Mr. and Mrs. Darcy took the larger of the Pemberley carriages to Longbourn (the other Mr. Darcy sent back to Pemberley, but with word to the coachman that he could travel at a slower pace if he preferred). Even though Miss Bingley wished to devote as much time as she could to admiring and flattering Mr. Darcy, she decided that, given the large quantity of Bennets at Longbourn, her chances of any rational conversation there were slim and so she had a predictable headache that she thought she would best overcome by taking a horseback ride in the company of one of the grooms.

The Pemberley carriage arrived at Longbourn. Mr. Darcy's appearance was not a complete surprise; his carriage had been seen and recognized yesterday on its way to Netherfield, and as Mrs. Darcy was already in the neighborhood, the citizens of Meryton guessed, correctly, that she was being joined by Mr. Darcy.

Although Mr. Darcy was greeted with the utmost respect by Mrs. Bennet, and even with some pleasure by Mr. Bennet, concern for Jane took precedence. Mr. Bingley helped her inside, while Mrs. Bennet and Kitty hovered around, doing everything they could to make her comfortable.

"It will only be a few more days, dear Jane. You must be patient. I know of no one who is more patient, Mr. Bingley."

Mrs. Bennet, accustomed to praising her daughters to potential suitors in order to encourage proposals, had not given up this habit with the daughters who were successfully married.

"Truly, I am not that uncomfortable, Mamma."

"She is an angel," said Mr. Bingley.

"She is, is she not? I remember how difficult it was not to complain when I was expecting her," said Mrs. Bennet. "But I managed, and Jane is managing too."

Mr. Bennet cleared his throat, as if his memory of Mrs. Bennet when she had been in Jane's condition was a little different from his wife's, but he said nothing and contented himself with an amused glance at Elizabeth. Elizabeth was glad that her sister was absorbing all her mother's attention, for it was better to minimize exchanges between Mrs. Bennet and Mr. Darcy. She asked her mother about Mary, who had not yet joined them; Mrs. Bennet said that Mary was upstairs finishing something but had promised to come down shortly.

Mr. Darcy and Mr. Bennet settled into conversation, Mr. Darcy first expressing his condolences on the death of Mr. Collins, and second inquiring about Mr. Bennet's ankle, and finally thanking Mr. Bennet for the summons. All was resolved, he said, but his presence had been necessary. Some person – they did not know who – had been attempting to extort money from Elizabeth under false pretenses.

"I suppose wealth attracts fortune hunters of all types," said Mr. Bennet. "Do you wish to tell me more about what happened? My information came from Jane, not Lizzy, and Jane would not betray her sister's confidence."

Mr. Darcy explained that he would rather not, at least not at this time. Mr. Bennet said he had no objection to not hearing this information – his natural indolence made it easier for him to exercise self-restraint with respect to curiosity – and he turned the subject to the books that Elizabeth had brought him when she arrived a few weeks ago. Mr. Bennet understood that the volumes had been selected by Mr. Darcy himself. "May I compliment you, sir, in your excellent taste in many things – in literature as well as in wives! What is your opinion of *Waverley?*"

Elizabeth smiled as the two men discussed the relative merits of poetry and prose. She listened but said little; she was more fatigued by recent events than she had realized.

She next turned her attention to Mary, who was entering the room. Mr. Darcy and Mr. Bingley rose to their feet in acknowledgment of the arrival of their sister-in-law, but the ladies barely noticed the courtesy.

"Where have you been, Mary?" reproached Mrs. Bennet. "We have visitors! You must have heard the carriage!"

"I wanted to finish the chapter," Mary excused herself. "But I have just looked out the window. My aunt Philips is coming to the house with my uncle's clerk, Mr. Morris."

Elizabeth sighed. She could not protect Mr. Darcy entirely from her immediate family, but she had hoped to spare him from being importuned by Mrs. Philips. But she caught his eye, and he smiled at her. She realized that her husband did not need protection.

"Very well. Kitty, ring the bell for more tea," said Mrs. Bennet.

The door was opened, the pair could be heard entering, and Mrs. Philips's voice rang out.

"Sister! I have such news! Such terrible, terrible news!"

Everyone in the drawing-room stopped their conversation to exchange glances while the pair from Meryton rushed in. Elizabeth saw that her aunt did, indeed, appear to be extremely distressed, and she had a spasm of alarm regarding the health of her uncle Philips.

"Sister? What is it? Get up, Kitty, make way, and let her sit down," said Mrs. Bennet.

Kitty made room for her aunt, who was having what could be described as hysterics. Usually this was something in which her sister Mrs. Bennet was the virtuosa, but on this occasion, thanks to inspiration, Mrs. Philips outperformed her sister.

"I have such news! Such dreadful news!" She then paused in her outburst to acknowledge the presence of Mr. and Mrs. Bingley, and Mr. and Mrs. Darcy. "You are here as well. That is good. Everyone must hear what has happened."

Mr. Darcy bowed silently, while Mr. Bingley expressed his concern.

"What has happened, Aunt?" asked Jane, who was alarmed, but whose general serenity made it difficult for most to perceive her distress.

"A moment," said Aunt Philips. She could rarely expect to have such an audience; she wished to enjoy it to the fullest. "My smelling salts, if you would, Kitty," said Aunt Philips, holding out her reticule.

Kitty obligingly rummaged through her aunt's reticule, while Mrs. Bennet cried: "Oh! Sister! What is it? What has happened?"

"Do not keep us in suspense," urged Elizabeth, even though she was certain that the suspense would not last long.

"How is Mr. Philips?" inquired Mr. Bennet, whose thoughts had followed the same path as Elizabeth's. Mr. Philips's red face and corpulent figure could be harbingers of an apoplectic attack.

Mr. Morris, still standing, assured them that Mr. Philips was in his usual health, but then showed restraint and waited for Mrs. Philips to speak.

Kitty administered the smelling salts to Mrs. Philips, who then decided that she was sufficiently recovered to be able to explain why she had walked the mile from Meryton to Longbourn.

"Oh! Sister! Mrs. Smith is dead, and I found the body myself!"

CHAPTER XXXVII

The reactions of Mrs. Philips's listeners were both gratifying and various; they ranged from shocked exclamations of horror by Mrs. Bennet, to more gently expressed sympathy on the part of the Bennet daughters and Mr. Bingley, to the uninformed Mr. Darcy leaning over to Mr. Bennet and inquiring in a low voice, "Who is Mrs. Smith?"

While Mr. Bennet explained in undertones to Mr. Darcy the identity of Mrs. Smith – a middle-aged widow who was a tenant of Mr. and Mrs. Philips, information which did not stimulate Mr. Darcy's interest in the poor woman, but at least made the matter intelligible – the others demanded details from Mrs. Philips.

"When did this happen, Aunt?" Elizabeth inquired, while Kitty made sure that the newest arrivals had tea and Mary arranged for another chair to be brought into the drawing-room so that Mr. Morris could sit down.

"Only two hours ago!" she exclaimed.

"I believe it is more than four hours ago now," said Mr. Morris.

"Tell us everything!" demanded Mrs. Bennet.

Mrs. Philips was eager to do so, and although she was not the most methodical of narrators, the gist of her experience was soon conveyed, especially as she was assisted and occasionally corrected by the attentive Mr. Morris. The day before, Mrs. Smith had been expected to tea. Despite her expectations, a thaw in relations had occurred shortly after Mrs. Philips relayed the warning about Mrs. Ford.

The unfamiliar name prompted Mr. Darcy to inquire about the identity of Mrs. Ford. Elizabeth obliged by explaining that Mrs. Ford had been an unreliable nursery maid of Mrs. Collins's son Lewis. Mr. Darcy, still feeling as if he did not completely comprehend the situation despite his possession of these details, decided to let the information flow to everyone else without further interruption on his part.

Mrs. Philips continued her narration. Mrs. Smith, however, despite being expected yesterday for tea, had not appeared at Mrs. Philips's house; nor had she sent her excuses. Even when their friendship had been at its coolest, Mrs. Smith had always sent regrets when she declined invitations. Mrs. Philips, concerned, told a servant to inquire; the servant went, and then returned, explaining that no one had answered the door. Mrs. Philips had later consulted with Mr. Philips. Mrs. Smith was their tenant, staying in rooms which they owned. Could she be ill? Could she simply have made an unexpected journey? Could she have departed without paying?

Apprehensive, but with no idea what awaited them, this morning Mrs. Philips and Mr. Morris had walked to the building, taking the extra key with them. Mrs. Philips went in case Mrs. Smith were ill or required some sort of female assistance, while Mr. Morris accompanied her to give her moral fortitude, as Mrs. Philips was uneasy in this mission. They knocked on the door but there was no answer; they called aloud, but there was still no answer, and finally they decided that they would enter. So Mr. Morris unlocked the door and they crossed the threshold.

And thus they found her, dead on her own sofa! – or rather, what was even worse, dead on a sofa belonging to Mr. and Mrs. Philips, for the rooms had been let furnished.

"Oh! The sight! The smell!" exclaimed Mrs. Philips, and demanded that her smelling salts be handed to her again. Kitty, squeezed in beside her, obliged.

Once Mrs. Philips was a little recovered, everyone plied her and Mr. Morris with questions. When and how had Mrs. Smith died? Did they know? Who were her relations, if she had any? How did they plan to reach them?

Regarding when exactly Mrs. Smith had died, Mrs. Philips and Mr. Morris did not know. Perhaps the senior Mr. Jones, whom they had summoned, along with Mr. Philips and Mr. Clarke, shortly after the awful discovery, would be able to determine something, but Mrs. Philips believed that Mrs. Smith had been dead by the time of the missed tea appointment. "I last saw her three days ago," she said, "so it must have been after that," which certainly seemed reasonable to her audience, then she added the lament: "We will never get another tenant now. Those rooms will be empty for another year!"

Mrs. Bennet agreed that no one would now take the rooms, and mourned her sister's loss of income, but Mr. Bennet was less pessimistic. He pointed out that although Mrs. Smith's demise was certainly regrettable, and that Mr. and Mrs. Philips would wish to have the rooms cleaned, and perhaps they might want to dispose of the sofa (such a handsome sofa! Mrs. Philips remarked, remembering that she had had it reupholstered only two years before) people died every day, in houses and rooms all around the country. "Those lodgings do not remain empty," he said.

Mr. Bennet's words had little effect on his sister-in-law, who was enjoying her situation too much to be reasoned out of it. Moreover, Mrs. Philips was able to contradict him by saying: "Mr. Bennet, you do not yet know how she died, or why."

"Then how did Mrs. Smith die, Aunt Philips?" asked Jane.

"She took her own life!" was the answer.

They all exclaimed again in shock, with Mary remarking gravely that if these suicides continued, the north side of the parish church would become very crowded.

"How can you be sure that her death was a suicide?" Elizabeth inquired.

This time Mr. Morris supplied the relevant details. They had found a letter on the table beside the sofa. He could confirm that it was Mrs. Smith's handwriting; he had seen it before when communicating with her regarding the letting of the property, and Mrs. Philips had seen Mrs. Smith's hand before as well. In the letter Mrs. Smith plainly stated that she intended to take her own life.

As to how, they had found a tea cup containing what appeared to be belladonna in it, the same poison that Miss King had used, although this time they found no bill of sale. The elder Mr. Jones had identified the substance, explaining that he kept belladonna in his shop, because small amounts were useful against the headache, and said that he had noticed that a quantity of the very same medicine was missing from his cabinet. However, although the two facts made it *likely* that Mrs. Smith had taken the belladonna, the elder Mr. Jones could not confirm it with complete certitude. According to his records, neither he nor his son nor their shop boy had sold any belladonna to Mrs. Smith. He reviewed his accounts on a regular basis and certainly would have noted a new customer. Mrs. Smith could have had the medicine with her for a long time; she could have brought it with her from her previous abode; it was impossible to know.

"Could she have somehow taken the belladonna from Mr. Jones's shop?" asked Mr. Bingley. "Without being detected?"

No one in the drawing-room at Longbourn House could answer Mr. Bingley's question, as no one there had ever attempted to enter Mr. Jones's shop undetected. Mr. Morris, who knew Mr. Jones best, said that he believed that Mr. Jones usually locked the door, but he did not know if there were spare keys or occasions when one could enter unseen.

Jane suggested that Mrs. Smith's avoidance of Mrs. Philips during the past few weeks could be a sign of melancholia. Although Mrs. Philips exclaimed that this possibility was distressing and sad, her demeanor suggested otherwise, as it meant that Mrs. Smith's persistent refusal of Mrs. Philips's many invitations had little to do with Mrs. Philips.

With respect to locks and keys, there was more evidence regarding Mrs. Smith. The key that Mr. Philips had presented to Mrs. Smith when she paid her first rent was on the table beside the sofa on which Mrs. Smith had been found dead. This indicated that no one could have entered Mrs. Smith's apartment unless Mrs. Smith had let them in, and that she had been alone when she died.

"Why would you lock your door if you were trying to take your life?" wondered Kitty. "Eventually you would want your body to be found, would you not? Why make it more difficult for everyone else?"

"That is an excellent point, Kitty," said Mrs. Bennet. "This Mrs. Smith was most inconsiderate, especially of you, Sister!"

Mrs. Philips appreciated the sympathetic indignation, while Elizabeth had other ideas on the matter, suggesting that if one were truly determined to die, one would want to keep from being discovered before Death finished its course. "That could explain why Mrs. Smith locked her door. But that seems to me to be a much lesser question. Do you have any clue as to why she would take her life?"

Mrs. Philips said yes, there was more, and she gestured to Mr. Morris that he should continue and tell what else was in the note. Mr. Morris, not averse to dominating the conversation, explained that in Mrs. Smith's last letter, she confessed that she had been responsible for several recent crimes around Meryton. *She* had stolen Miss King's jewels, and *she* had even killed Mr. Collins!

"She wrote that she could no longer live with herself!" added Mrs. Philips. "That is why she took her life!"

The additional information completely astonished the entire Bennet family — as well as the servants of Longbourn House, who had discovered that something very interesting was being discussed in the drawing-room, and who had congregated in the vestibule to listen. Even the cook had come the roundabout way from the kitchen; only when a smoky smell reached their collective nostrils did she recall that the goose needed to be turned and everyone heard the sound of her heavy footsteps and doors creaking open and shut as she hastened back to her usual place.

"So Mrs. Smith stole Miss King's jewels!" exclaimed Mrs. Bennet. "And she killed Mr. Collins!"

Everyone expressed shock and disgust at both deeds, and Mary opined that now the north side of the church seemed too good a resting place for Mrs. Smith. It was a terrible sin to take your own life, but to take the life of another – of a clergyman! And it seemed inappropriate to put Mrs. Smith near Miss King for eternity, as Mrs. Smith had wronged Miss King.

"So that is why Mr. Selby could not find Miss King's jewels," remarked Kitty. "Did you find them in Mrs. Smith's rooms?"

Mr. Morris said they had yet to thoroughly search through Mrs. Smith's possessions, but no, they had not found anything that they could identify as having belonged to Miss King.

Elizabeth wondered exactly how the woman had managed to steal Miss King's jewels, and whether she had committed the theft before or after Miss King's death; missing jewelry could have contributed to Miss King's melancholia. As Elizabeth had not been intimate with either woman, she could imagine that there might have been opportunities of which she was unaware. (Miss King's former maidservant Hannah would be very thankful, observed Jane, and at least Mrs. Smith's confessional note would clear one innocent party.)

Everyone could understand why Mrs. Smith had taken Miss King's jewels; robbery, although a crime, was at least intelligible. But the other confession – the murder of Mr. Collins – was incomprehensible.

"Mrs. Smith killed Mr. Collins! Good gracious, why would she do that?" asked Mrs. Bennet.

"Did they even know each other?" inquired Mr. Bingley.

Mrs. Philips tried to remember if Mrs. Smith had ever mentioned Mr. Collins. Certainly Mrs. Smith had *heard* of the man, as she had met Lady Lucas more than once at Mrs. Philips's, but as far as she recalled, Mrs. Smith had never mentioned his name herself. Everyone then appealed to Elizabeth, to inquire if *she* knew of a connection between the two. Elizabeth had stayed with him and his wife in Kent for a six-week visit about a year and a half earlier, so of those in the drawing room, she knew Mr. Collins best.

Elizabeth, however, shook her head and said she was ignorant of any connection. "When I was in Hunsford I do not recall Mr. Collins ever mentioning anything of particular concerning a Mrs. Smith. There *was* a Mrs. Smith in the Hunsford parish, but she was not the Mrs. Smith that I met at Mrs. Philips's house – she was much taller and younger and had a completely different manner. You should address your inquiries to Mrs. Collins; her information would be far more complete."

Mr. Morris said that he planned to go to Lucas Lodge immediately after Longbourn House. Finally, Mr. Morris had brought Mrs. Smith's confessional note with him. "Mr. Bennet, as you are Mr. Collins's relative, I thought you should read this."

Mr. Bennet adjusted his glasses and took the piece of paper from Mr. Morris.

"We will need several copies of it," said Mr. Morris. "A copy should be sent to Mr. Selby, the betrothed of Miss King. I was hoping that Miss Bennet could make one to leave here," he said.

Mary was willing to be of assistance and went to fetch paper and a pen, then, when Mr. Bennet had finished reading it, she settled at a table in the corner of the room and commenced the task.

"I have observed that Miss Bennet has very legible handwriting," said Mr. Morris, while Mary worked.

Mary soon finished, then Mr. Morris said that he should take the original to Mrs. Collins at Lucas Lodge. He asked Mrs. Philips whether or not she wished to join him. Mrs. Philips was terribly torn. She was the center of attention in the Longbourn drawing-room in a way that she had not been for many years, indeed, in her entire life, so she was loathe to depart – yet she could not bear to think that Mr. Morris should deliver the news to Lucas Lodge without her. That consideration decided it, as well as the reflection that Mr. Philips and Mr. Clarke might have more news for them back in Meryton.

"Take care, Sister," said Mrs. Bennet, and Mrs. Philips retrieved her cherished little flask of smelling salts, so that she could employ it while having hysterics again at Lucas Lodge. Mrs. Philips and Mr. Morris then left Longbourn House, with many promises on the part of Mrs. Bennet that she would visit her sister soon to see how she was and to be informed of any developments.

The letter that Mary had copied was passed around, first to Mrs. Bennet, and then to the Bingleys and the Darcys. When Elizabeth scanned the letter she could not find anything in the words besides the information that Mr. Morris and Mrs. Philips had already relayed.

The sun was lower in the sky, and even though Mrs. Bennet asked them all to stay to dinner, Jane said she preferred returning to Netherfield. Mrs. Bennet, perhaps realizing that it was quite likely that the cook had burned the goose, did not insist. So the Darcys ordered the carriage, and soon the Darcys and the Bingleys were inside, still discussing the information that Mrs. Philips had brought to them.

"I am not surprised that you wished to remain in Hertfordshire," Mr. Darcy remarked to Elizabeth, "with everything that has been happening."

"That is not why I came," said Elizabeth.

"Of course; you are here for Jane."

"And I greatly appreciate it," said Jane.

"And I do not think these recent events have much to recommend them," said Elizabeth, "other than enlivening our conversations."

"But if this Mrs. Smith killed Mr. Collins, then the murderer is dead," said Bingley. "So we should be in no more danger here than in any other part of the country."

"Not only do I not understand why Mrs. Smith should have killed Mr. Collins," said Elizabeth, "I cannot understand how it is even possible. How could *she* have pushed Mr. Collins over the side of the bridge? Mr. Collins was a big man; Mrs. Smith was not a large woman and she did not look that strong."

Her fellow passengers agreed that Elizabeth had an interesting point, and as the carriage was approaching the bridge where Mr. Collins's body had been found, Mr. Darcy told Wilson to stop and wait for a few minutes. All except Jane climbed out and surveyed the area; she remained inside but watched and listened through the open carriage door. Mr. Bingley, who had been at the scene, described everything to them.

Mr. Collins had been only a little shorter than Mr. Darcy and much heavier, while Mrs. Smith had been about the same height as Elizabeth. "Elizabeth, do you believe that you could push me over the side of the bridge?"

Elizabeth protested at being asked to harm her husband, but he told her not to worry, and after a little effort on her part, she determined that his confidence was justified. "I could not do it."

"And you are younger, and presumably stronger, than this Mrs. Smith was," said Mr. Darcy.

Mr. Bingley added that Mr. Collins may have been injured, or even dead, before he was pushed over the side of the bridge. He did not know if that would make it easier or more difficult for Mrs. Smith to do what she had confessed to doing, but it was worth considering.

Deciding that there were no more clues to be gleaned at their current location, and mindful of Jane, they returned to the carriage and continued to Netherfield. Leaving the bridge did not cause them to leave the most interesting subject, and they tried to understand not just how, but why Mrs. Smith had killed Mr. Collins.

Elizabeth suggested that Mr. Collins had somehow discovered that Mrs. Smith had stolen Miss King's jewelry. "At least that would give her a motive."

But Mr. Bingley pointed out how improbable this was. Mr. Collins was rarely in Meryton; it seemed unlikely that he would recognize any of Miss King's possessions.

"Perhaps it was an unfortunate and peculiar accident," said Jane, "and Mrs. Smith felt so guilty afterwards that she took her own life."

"She also took Mary King's things," said Elizabeth. "If she had a conscience, she would not have done that."

"Stealing is wrong, but killing one's fellow man! Oh, that must be much worse."

"Perhaps if we speak to Mrs. Collins we will learn more," said Mr. Bingley.

"Yes," said Elizabeth, who wished that she could order the carriage to turn and call at Lucas Lodge. Her curiosity, however great, would have to wait for satisfaction. Besides, she reflected, it was very likely that her friend knew nothing; Mrs. Collins had said that she was completely unacquainted with Mrs. Smith.

When they reached Netherfield Park, the ladies changed for dinner. At that meal they were joined by Miss Bingley, whose headache had, as expected, completely disappeared after her horseback ride. Elizabeth noticed that Miss Bingley was becoming rather tanned.

Miss Bingley inquired about their visit to Longbourn, insinuating that Mr. Darcy must have been terribly bored and vexed by the company of so many Bennets, but Mr. Darcy replied that the afternoon had not been dull at all. Then Jane and Mr. Bingley explained how Mrs. Philips had arrived with the news of the suicide of Mrs. Smith and her confessional letter. Miss Bingley could barely tolerate Mrs. Philips and had never met Mrs. Smith, but even she was intrigued. "So this Mrs. Smith took Miss King's jewelry and she murdered Mr. Collins. Is that why she moved to Meryton? To commit these terrible crimes?"

No one could answer Miss Bingley why Mrs. Smith had moved to Meryton. Mr. Darcy had never even seen her; Mr. Bingley believed he had been introduced but could recall nothing about her; only Jane and Elizabeth had had any conversation with Mrs. Smith, and they had never posed this question to the now-dead woman. Still, all could speculate, and the conversation that evening diverted Jane from her discomfort.

.

CHAPTER XXXVIII

Elizabeth both hoped and feared that the night would be disturbed by Jane's going into labor, but Mr. Bingley did not summon her and they did not all meet again till the morning.

The topic that had animated everyone so much the evening before was barely mentioned at the breakfast table. Mrs. Smith had been scarcely known to them, and her letter of confession resolved two of the recent local mysteries. They might be curious as to why or how she had perpetrated these crimes, but they had no reason to doubt that she had. As Miss King, Mr. Collins and Mrs. Smith were all deceased, and it was unlikely that any witnesses existed who might bring more intelligibility to the circumstances, their curiosity might remain unsatisfied permanently.

It had rained during the night, so the morning was fresh and cool. Elizabeth and Darcy went for a walk; he gave her his arm and helped her over the puddles. She realized that she had not yet described her encounters with Lady Catherine, so she did so and inquired if Darcy knew anything about a Mr. Radclyff. Mr. Darcy shook his head. He thought his mother might have mentioned a Mr. Radclyff in connection with Lady Catherine, but that had been many years ago. It was possible that Colonel Fitzwilliam knew something, or his uncle the earl, but he was not certain that this was any concern of theirs.

Elizabeth added that Mr. Radclyff had been dead for more than a decade.

"I am not especially interested in Lady Catherine and men long dead," said Mr. Darcy. "Now, I have a question for you. How is your sister? Was it necessary for you to come here, or did your father exaggerate the urgency?"

Elizabeth told him that she believed her presence had been helpful. Her husband then naturally inquired about the nature of the problem. Elizabeth considered. She did not like to betray a confidence, but she had also discovered that keeping secrets from her husband was not the most sensible course of action. If she had written to him immediately about the extortion attempt, she could have spared him the journey from Netherfield.

They sat on a bench with a lovely prospect, shaded by the woods behind them, and she told him that there had been some anxiety and distress about a letter that Mr. Bingley had written to Miss Hightower, and did her best to explain what she had discovered about Miss Hightower from Miss Bingley.

"I do not understand. A letter written from Miss Hightower to Bingley?"

"No, the letter was definitely *to* Miss Hightower, written *by* Mr. Bingley."

"I beg your pardon, but that letter was *not* written by Mr. Bingley!"

Elizabeth colored to see Mr. Bingley and his sister emerging from the woods behind them. How much had they overheard?

Mr. Bingley had also reddened, and Miss Bingley, clearly irritated, took advantage of the moment to say, with sneering moral superiority: "Eliza, I do not know why you were asking about Miss Hightower, but it obviously had nothing to do with a metronome. I had not realized you were so sly."

"Did Jane see that letter?" demanded Mr. Bingley.

Elizabeth realized that her position was awkward with everyone, and moreover, that everyone's disapprobation was justified. Miss Bingley had the right to feel manipulated with respect to their previous conversation. Mr. Bingley could be angry with her for having read his private correspondence. Darcy might disapprove of her betraying confidences – as would Jane, for it was *her* confidence that Elizabeth was betraying. Jane, although she was least prone to it, had the most right to be angry – yet had not Jane counseled her to be completely honest with Mr. Darcy? Elizabeth decided it was better not to deny or dissemble; she responded first to Mr. Bingley. "No, Jane did not see the letter. I discovered it while looking through books in your library and the next morning I described it to her. We went together to the library the following day, but all we found were the ashes."

"I should not have hidden it in a book by Voltaire, not when you have hired a French maidservant."

Mr. Bingley was giving Elizabeth rather more credit than she deserved for application to improving her French, but she decided not to correct him by explaining that she had only opened Voltaire in a quest for that very letter. She focused on the critical matter. "I am sorry for the trouble that I may have caused. Jane *was* a little distressed by what I could describe of the contents of that letter, but as Miss Bingley tells me that Miss Hightower has been dead for some time, Jane decided it was best not to mention it. You wrote it years ago, but you have also destroyed it."

"But *I* never wrote it!"

"It was your handwriting," Elizabeth began and then stopped as understanding dawned in on her. "Oh!"

"A counterfeit," observed Mr. Darcy, nodding at his lady.

"Yes, it was a forgery. *I* never wrote it! But how can I convince Jane of that, when the handwriting is so like my own? I met Miss Hightower years ago, in the Pump Room. We flirted, that is true, but it was nothing more. And then, some months after I left Bath, I heard a rumor that – that she was in trouble. However, I was not responsible. Her – her lover was in the navy, and I am certain that he would have married her, had she not died with her child before he returned from the West Indies."

"I understand," said Mr. Darcy.

"I do not!" Miss Bingley complained.

"Even though I know I did not write that letter, how can I persuade Jane of this? How can I convince my wife that I will be a good husband to her and a devoted father to our child, when my own handwriting appears to show that I abandoned another young lady?"

"I believe you," Elizabeth assured him. "And Jane will as well. For I, too, received a similar letter."

When he heard this, Mr. Bingley took off at a quick stride, leaving his sister with Elizabeth and Mr. Darcy.

"Should we return to the house as well?" inquired Elizabeth. She was feeling wretched and culpable and wished to atone sooner rather than later.

"I think Bingley and your sister need some time alone," said Mr. Darcy.

Elizabeth sighed but agreed. Her penance for her indiscretion would be to suffer a little longer before she asked Jane for forgiveness.

"And while we allow my brother some privacy with his wife, you can let *me* know what you have been talking about," said Miss Bingley, with some asperity. "I refuse to be kept ignorant. Eliza, what letter did you receive from a lover in the West Indies?"

"I will explain what I can," said Elizabeth, shaking her head slightly, for Miss Bingley had put everything together wrong. Elizabeth then told about the extortion letter that she had received, about how she had decided not to pay, and how she had kept vigil at the horse chestnut tree but had failed to discover the identity of the culprit.

Miss Bingley curled her lip at the mention of a romantic letter to Wickham, for she had been scornful of Elizabeth's initial interest in that lieutenant. However, in front of Darcy she censured her remarks.

"I explained to Elizabeth that those with money are often the target of the unscrupulous," said Mr. Darcy. "There is no shame in it."

"I suppose Eliza would not have much experience with these base schemes," said Miss Bingley. "And what about my brother and Miss Hightower?"

Elizabeth believed that Mr. Bingley had been the victim of a similar extortion attempt; regarding what exactly, she would not say. "You should ask him for more information."

"I will," said Miss Bingley. "Dare we risk returning to the house now, or is it too soon?"

"I think we had better," said Mr. Darcy. "The weather is turning."

The heavens, which only thirty minutes before had been a halcyon blue, were filling up with clouds; several large drops had already fallen. Mr. Darcy offered one arm to Elizabeth and his other to Miss Bingley, and they hastened along the gravel walk.

CHAPTER XXXIX

Mr. Bingley and Jane were still in private conference in the library, so the others repaired to the drawing-room. Miss Bingley idly traced a sketch of a horse while Mr. Darcy wrote a letter to a friend who might be interested in acquiring the now-vacant living at Kympton. Elizabeth occupied herself with some needlepoint.

Several hours later the Bingleys, all secrets gone between them, joined their friends. Elizabeth glanced up anxiously; she was feeling guilty for having spoken to Darcy.

Jane did not appear angry, but neither did she seem pleased, while Mr. Bingley's countenance displayed embarrassment.

Elizabeth began to apologize, but Jane abruptly forestalled her. "It is all right, Lizzy." Elizabeth realized that Jane was far more perturbed by what her husband had said – or not said – than she was with *her*. Jane, although she was obviously not pleased, spoke seriously and calmly. "There is nothing to worry about," Jane said. "It is nothing – or rather it is a mere inconvenience, that will be got over in a while. But in the meantime I believe we should share information. Someone has been – has been attempting to extort money from us, and perhaps from others as well."

"Obviously it would help if we can determine who it is," said Mr. Bingley. "So we can stop him and expose him and either send him to prison or get him transported."

Elizabeth believed something else was distressing Jane, something that her sister was not yet ready to share. As she did not feel that *she* had any right to press for openness, she responded to Mr. Bingley's point. "He must be someone who knows us."

"What about Wickham?" suggested Mr. Darcy. "Could he have known about Miss Hightower?"

Mr. Bingley and his sister were the only two in the drawing-room who had known anything about Miss Hightower, and neither of them had ever mentioned Bingley's relationship with the unfortunate woman to either Mr. or Mrs. Wickham. Of course, it was possible that they had learned of the relationship some other way. Still, Mr. Darcy was certain that Mr. Wickham could not imitate the penmanship of anyone, while Jane and Elizabeth made similar statements about Lydia.

"What about servants?" asked Miss Bingley. Although her listeners did not share her prejudice against the lower classes, they were ready to consider her suggestion. If the extortionist were one of the servants, then that person probably worked at Netherfield. One of the Netherfield staff could have learned of Miss Hightower and her situation and would have been able to find an example of Mr. Bingley's handwriting. The culprit could have also known about Elizabeth's former interest in George Wickham – to Elizabeth's chagrin, that flirtation was well-known in Meryton.

"Oh! I cannot bear for it to be one of the servants!" Jane lamented, and she sought, as usual, to clear everyone from culpability, leaving them with no responsible parties. "The day that you went to leave a letter, Lizzy – just three days ago – were not all the servants in the house?"

Jane's question made them all, except for Mr. Darcy, cast their minds back to that morning. Jane and Miss Bingley had seen most of the household staff, while Mr. Bingley had been out with the groomsmen and had walked past the stables. "No one took a horse."

"What about the gardeners?" Elizabeth inquired. "Could not one of them have slipped off the estate and hurried to the horse chestnut tree?"

The inhabitants of Netherfield were so engrossed in this conversation that they did not hear the carriage approach; it was only when the footman announced Mr. and Mrs. Philips that they realized that they had callers. The visitors were accompanied by Mr. Philips's other clerk, Mr. Clarke. Jane and Mr. Bingley collected themselves and made them welcome, inviting them to sit down, asking them if they were dry (it still rained) and offering tea, while Miss Bingley looked in vain for a means of escape. Mr. Darcy leaned over to his wife and asked if she wished to hold Mrs. Philips's reticule in order to be ready to supply her with her smelling salts at the most interesting moments.

"I know that some of my relations are trying," Elizabeth said.

"As we are married, your relations are my relations," said Mr. Darcy.

But Mrs. Philips's behavior was not as extreme as it had been the day before at Longbourn House, possibly because she had her husband with her, or perhaps because she was less accustomed to such outbursts in the elegant drawing-room of Netherfield Park, or perhaps just because preserving such a level of hysteria was fatiguing. She had less stamina than

Mrs. Bennet. So during the pleasantries and the introduction of Mr. Clarke to Mr. Darcy, Mrs. Philips maintained, at least relative to their most recent encounter, a calm demeanor. Then Mr. Philips cleared his throat. "We have come to Netherfield in particular to see *you*, Mr. Darcy."

Everyone was surprised by this, as Mr. Darcy was barely acquainted with Mr. and Mrs. Philips. "Please explain," said Mr. Darcy.

"Mrs. Philips tells me you were at Longbourn when she brought news of the discovery of the death of Mrs. Smith."

"I was."

"Sir, did you know Mrs. Smith?"

Mr. Darcy was mystified, as was every other person in the drawing-room, but he did his best to answer the question. "I do not think so. Of course, over the years I must have met several Mrs. Smiths. But I know of none who would correspond to the description that I have heard of your late tenant."

"Are you sure, Mr. Darcy? Mr. Clarke and I found something," said Mrs. Philips, a little breathlessly. She usually was too awed by her nephew-in-law to speak to him, but the news that they had to share was so amazing that it gave her the courage her to address him directly.

The attorney Mr. Philips spoke more deliberately. "After Mrs. Smith's body was removed, I tasked Mrs. Philips and Mr. Clarke with sorting through some of the belongings of Mrs. Smith. Mrs. Philips was examining Mrs. Smith's more personal effects when she discovered some miniatures."

"One of them looks exactly like you, Mr. Darcy!" exclaimed Mrs. Philips. And Mrs. Philips had her moment of triumph, for none of her listeners expected this.

After many exclamations, and some speculation, and a little doubt, Elizabeth inquired if they had brought the miniatures with them.

They had. Mr. Philips withdrew his handkerchief from his pocket, unfolded it, and glanced down at the miniatures. "This, Sir, is the one that resembles you."

He passed it to Mr. Darcy, who carried it over to the window to examine it in better light; Elizabeth accompanied him.

"It does look like you!" she said. "I recognize that coat."

"Yes, it is hanging in my wardrobe at Pemberley."

Everyone else was nonplussed by this confirmation – Mrs. Philips delighted in their confusion – and they all begged to see the miniature. It was handed around and examined, first to Jane, then to Mr. Bingley, and finally to Miss Bingley, who studied it longest. "I recognize the artistry," pronounced Miss Bingley. "I believe this was made by your sister."

"Why would Mrs. Smith have a miniature drawn by Georgiana?" Elizabeth asked her husband.

But Mr. Darcy could not answer that question. "I can think of no reason for any of the Mrs. Smiths that I have met to have a portrait of me, large or small. And, as far as I know, I never met *this* Mrs. Smith."

"Mr. Philips, show Mr. Darcy the miniature of her!" cried Mrs. Philips excitedly; Mr. Clarke frowned slightly, as if disturbed by the volume of her outburst.

"We also found a miniature of Mrs. Smith," continued Mr. Philips, unwrapping another small portrait swaddled in cloth. "Perhaps you would be so good as to examine it."

Mr. Darcy took the miniature and returned to the window, where he examined the picture of the dead woman. He said nothing at first, but his features indicated utter stupefaction.

"What is it, Darcy?" cried Mr. Bingley.

"Do you know her? Who is she?" asked Elizabeth, joining him again by the window.

Mr. Darcy took a moment to recover, and then he turned and explained. "I *do* recognize this miniature, but the woman who called herself Mrs. Smith among you was known to me under another name – Mrs. Annabelle Younge. Even though it is considered inappropriate to speak ill of the dead, I must tell you that her character was not at all reputable. And the artist – I now recall sitting for the miniature, just after Mrs. Younge sat for this one – was my sister, Georgiana."

CHAPTER XL

Many exclamations followed Darcy's words, some of surprise, others of confusion; Miss Bingley reminded everyone that *she* had recognized Miss Darcy's handiwork first. When the initial astonishment subsided, Mr. Philips asked if Mr. Darcy could tell them more about this Mrs. Smith, or rather, Mrs. Younge.

Darcy returned to his seat, and hesitated as he considered what he should reveal. "After my parents died, my cousin Colonel Fitzwilliam and I became guardians to my sister Georgiana, who is more than ten years my junior. As you can imagine, we did not believe that two young men were the best role models for a girl her age – she needed female companionship and guidance. Mrs. Younge was recommended to us; she supplied excellent references, and so I hired her as a companion and chaperone for my sister when Georgiana left school. Unfortunately, we were deceived in her character, and I discovered later that the references were false. When I discovered her true nature, I dismissed Mrs. Younge immediately, and we were more careful the next time we hired someone to superintend my sister's education."

Everyone evinced sympathy, with Miss Bingley saying, "Poor Georgiana!"

Mr. Philip said: "You will not give us more details?"

"I will not."

Jane looked at Elizabeth and raised her eyebrows, for both of them knew the details that Mr. Darcy did not want to reveal. Mrs. Younge had been the one who had arranged for Miss Darcy to encounter George Wickham, when she was but fifteen. Georgiana, unaware of Wickham's debauchery and with pleasant memories of him from her childhood, had been persuaded to believe that she loved him. They had been on the point of an elopement when Mr. Darcy had arrived, just by chance, in time to prevent it and to keep his sister from a marriage that would have condemned her to a lifetime of misery. But less than two years later Mr. Darcy had found himself with Wickham as a brother-in-law after all, as Wickham had run off with Lydia Bennet, the youngest sister of Jane and Elizabeth.

Mr. Philips said that he respected Mr. Darcy's desire for privacy, then Mr. Clarke said: "Is there anything that you *can* tell us about Mrs. – Mrs. Younge?"

Mr. Darcy explained that the woman he had known had had a genteel manner, had appeared to have some knowledge in many feminine arts and had been fond of money. The last that he had heard of her, she had had a large house in London and had been supporting herself by letting lodgings. She had owned the house for at least several years before he had hired her to chaperone his sister; he could supply Mr. Philips with the address.

"Mrs. Smith was a landlady!" exclaimed Mrs. Philips, surprised to learn this about the woman she had considered her tenant. "Then why did she come to Meryton to rent our rooms?"

"And why did she murder Mr. Collins?" asked Miss Bingley. "Did they know each other?"

Mr. Darcy said that he knew of no connection between Mr. Collins and Mrs. Younge. It was possible, he supposed, that Mr. Collins had rented a room from Mrs. Younge at some point.

Mr. Clarke asked: "Feminine arts? Which feminine arts?"

Mr. Darcy explained that Mrs. Younge had spoken a little French, had played the pianoforte and had had a great appreciation for music, and was a passable artist. He could ask his sister for more details.

"Artist?" inquired Mr. Clarke. "We found paper and pens in her rooms."

"What types of paper?" Elizabeth asked, with urgency.

"Several different types of stationery," said Mrs. Philips. "One is just like the type that my sister uses at Longbourn."

"How peculiar," Jane remarked.

Elizabeth could not keep silent. "I do not think it was peculiar at all. What if she came here *because* of her connection to you, Darcy? What I have not told you, uncle, is that I received a threat of extortion." She gave an abbreviated version of the letter that she had received, not mentioning Mr. Bingley's own experience, for she realized that with her aunt in the room, everything that she said, along with embellishment and exaggeration, would soon be the talk of Meryton. "Through her connections to Mr. Darcy she could have been in a position to learn information about me. We know from her past history that Mrs. Younge was unscrupulous and avaricious."

Mr. Darcy and the Bingleys comprehended immediately the implications of Elizabeth's words, but the others required more time and more explanation before they completely understood: Mr. Philips because he was a little deaf; Mr. Clarke because he had the least knowledge of the original details; and Mrs. Philips because she was not as quick-witted.

"So, this Mrs. Smith – this Mrs. Younge – came to Meryton in order to extort money from you?" Mr. Clarke summarized. "And you believe that she did it by creating forgeries?"

Elizabeth said that was what she believed.

"How extraordinary!" exclaimed Mr. Clarke.

Mrs. Philips was utterly flabbergasted. "She always seemed so agreeable! Except when she would not talk to me, that is."

Mr. Philips cautiously raised an objection to his niece's conjecture. "We should recall that Mrs. Smith came to Meryton *before* Mrs. Darcy, when Mrs. Darcy was not even expected here. I am not saying that Mrs. Smith did not create the forgery; many circumstances point to her having done so, but I believe that blackmailing my niece could not have been her primary motive for moving here."

"But Mrs. Smith could hardly have traveled to Derbyshire to extort money from Mrs. Darcy," said Mr. Clarke. "If she had lived previously at Pemberley, she would have been recognized; she could not have hoped to escape detection. Mrs. Smith must have realized that Mrs. Darcy would eventually travel to this neighborhood to visit her family."

They all agreed that Mr. Clarke's conjectures seemed reasonable.

"Perhaps Mrs. Younge did not come to Meryton only to extort money from Mrs. Darcy," said Bingley, summoning the courage to recount his own experience. "I, too, received a letter and a demand. Before Elizabeth arrived."

"Will you tell us what your letter said?" inquired Mr. Philips.

"It does not matter; the charge was not true and the other party is dead," Jane said quickly.

"Mrs. Younge must have been an exceptional artist," said Miss Bingley. "A pity that she abused her talent so."

Mr. Philips said that he supposed this afternoon had cleared up some of the mystery with respect to Mrs. Smith. As the woman was dead, she could not be punished, but it might be possible to recover some of Miss King's jewels and money and to send them to Mr. Selby. Mr. Philips then asked if Mr. Darcy knew the names of any of her relatives.

But Mr. Darcy did not. "The references she gave me were false."

"I suppose she forged them too," suggested Mr. Clarke.

"I suppose she did," said Mr. Darcy. "I was unaware of that particular talent, but it is not one that she would advertise."

The clock struck the hour, and Mr. Philips put down his teacup. "We must return to Meryton; I have an appointment with a client and as you can imagine this affair with Mrs. Smith – I mean Mrs. Younge – is perturbing our schedules. I have left Mr. Morris alone these hours, but we have other business to attend."

Perhaps Meryton *could* support two attorneys in the future, thought Elizabeth; then Kitty could marry Mr. Clarke and Mary could marry Mr. Morris. Yet considering how little Kitty and Mary seemed to enjoy each other's company, arranging them to have husbands who were either partners or competitors might not be the best way to organize their future. Besides, Elizabeth reminded herself distractedly, she was resolved not to turn into her mother and to be preoccupied by matchmaking.

Mr. Darcy asked if he could keep the miniatures, and Mr. Philips agreed that he could, only that he would ask Mr. Darcy to sign for them. While Mr. Clarke prepared a brief document, and Mr. Darcy signed it, Mr. Bingley gathered his courage.

"What about the money?" he demanded. "Is there any chance to retrieve *my* money?"

Several occupants in the room gasped. Mr. Bingley had mentioned that he had been subject to extortion, but up till now he had not admitted that he had actually succumbed. Elizabeth had, however, guessed that was possible and she suspected that fetching the money from the bank must have been the reason behind Bingley's last journey to London. She looked sympathetically at Jane, but Jane was staring with determination at the carpet. Elizabeth then glanced at her husband, whose eyes met hers. Mr. Darcy nodded slightly, indicating that he, too, had guessed that Mr. Bingley had yielded.

Miss Bingley was less circumspect in her reaction. "Charles! Do you mean to say that you paid that woman cash?"

"Caroline—" began Mr. Bingley.

"How much? Is *this* why you are not purchasing Rushburn?"

"Caroline, please!" said Jane, with uncharacteristic sharpness.

Miss Bingley ceased her interrogation for the moment, but the anger in her eyes made it clear that she would continue later.

Mr. Philips, with so many years of practice as an attorney, appeared to ignore Miss Bingley's outburst, and replied calmly. "I regret to say, Sir, that we have not recovered any monies, just as we have not recovered Miss King's jewelry. However, we will continue to do what we can." He invited both of his nieces' husbands to furnish him with all the details that they could remember: Mr. Bingley, about how she had taken it and how much he had given her, and Mr. Darcy, everything that he could supply regarding the woman he had known as Mrs. Younge. "The more information we have about this woman and her crimes, the better are our chances of discovering what she has done with the property of others," said Mr. Philips.

Instead of staying to conclude the matter at the moment, the gentlemen made an appointment for the next day. Mr. Philips really did need to return to Meryton; Bingley and Darcy needed time to remember all the details; and finally, Bingley would find it easier to speak before a smaller audience. As they departed into the afternoon's gray drizzle, Mrs. Philips clutched her reticule and only then remembered that she had failed to make use of the smelling salts that she had brought with her, and that now it was too late. Even though she had forgotten about her little flask of salts, she was not disappointed by the afternoon: not at all! The visit had far exceeded her expectations and she looked forward to recounting the details in the many parlors of Meryton.

CHAPTER XLI

The inmates of Netherfield were not as satisfied with the afternoon as Mrs. Philips. Miss Bingley was especially vexed. First, Mr. Bingley had yielded to the extortionist merely to keep Jane tranquil, and as Jane was one of the most naturally tranquil women in the kingdom, that objective struck Miss Bingley as entirely unnecessary. Second, he had given away money that should have been used in purchasing an estate. As Mr. Bingley had inherited the money from their father, and as brothers were expected to provide for their unmarried sisters, Elizabeth thought that Miss Bingley's irritability had some justification.

Jane was not pleased that her own husband had not trusted her enough to tell her about Miss Hightower, and she even expressed some of her discontent to Elizabeth. "I can appreciate that he wished to protect me from not having confidence in his character, and that from one perspective he acted out of love for me. But Lizzy, he should have realized that I would have had more confidence in him if he had come to me with the truth."

Mr. Bingley, of course, was angry with himself for displaying such weakness, in perhaps destroying forever the possibility of a permanent residence, and in doubting the love and trust of his wife.

Mr. and Mrs. Darcy were not quite as vexed by their own behaviors; Elizabeth could congratulate herself for having not yielded to the extortionist, despite having been sorely tempted. But the Darcys still had their concerns. Elizabeth was anxious for Jane and Bingley. Jane would not tell her how much money Bingley had given away – perhaps she did not know the sum herself – but from the frowns and the sighs she was certain the amount was significant.

Mr. Darcy was especially perturbed by how all of this could have occurred – it seemed indubitable that Mrs. Younge had assistance in her blackmail compositions. Was it not likely that Wickham, Mrs. Younge's conspirator in the past, had abetted her in the present? He brought this up to the others, and although the idea was not pleasing, they did not dismiss the possibility. Then Darcy continued to the next point. If Wickham was involved, was it not likely that Lydia was also involved?

The notion that Lydia had colluded to steal from them was extremely unpleasant to her sisters. Jane could scarcely give it credence, but Elizabeth had little confidence in Lydia's innocence.

Mr. Bingley, grateful to shift blame onto others, actually hoped that Wickham was involved as that meant there was a chance to retrieve all, or at least some, of his money. He pointed out that Wickham and Lydia had recently stayed at Netherfield and they could have easily purloined samples of his handwriting.

Miss Bingley was also ready to condemn the Wickhams, and had additional observations. Had Lydia not written letters to Jane and to Eliza? Letters in which she did not ask for money? "We made a joke of it at the time, but what if she did not ask for money because she already had obtained some?"

"Oh!" cried Elizabeth, remembering. "Lydia asked that I write her a long letter! She could have then sent it on to Mrs. Younge so that she could imitate my handwriting. I was not blackmailed till after I sent Lydia that letter."

Jane conceded that the circumstances against Lydia and Wickham seemed very black, and was grieved to think that her own sister could be so guilty and so cruel. Jane, however, insisted that they should not assume that Wickham and Lydia were guilty, but should investigate further.

Elizabeth suggested that as they lacked confidence that Wickham and Lydia could be trusted, that they turn to other friends for assistance. Wickham was supposed to be with his regiment in Newcastle. Darcy, through his cousin Colonel Fitzwilliam, was acquainted with Colonel Thorne, the commander of Wickham's regiment. Darcy would write to Colonel Thorne and explain the situation, and ask for his assessment and his interference.

Lydia was in London with their aunt Gardiner. Mrs. Gardiner was not Lydia's favorite aunt, but London with its shops and theater and other amusements was inducement to visit. Elizabeth said she would write to Mrs. Gardiner, so Mr. and Mrs. Darcy dedicated the time till the evening meal in writing letters; even Miss Bingley wrote one to Mrs. Hurst.

Mr. Philips and Mr. Clarke were too discreet to let many details slip, but Mrs. Philips, in her apartment, had no inhibitions to prevent her from discussing what had been learned that day at Netherfield. She would have set off for Longbourn immediately, but Lady Lucas and Maria Lucas called on her as soon as she returned to Meryton. The news that the deceased Mrs. Smith had also been Mrs. Younge, a woman who had attempted to defraud Mr. Darcy, traveled through Meryton with wonderful velocity.

Rumors swelled, making Mrs. Smith far more glamorous in death than she had ever been in life. Some said she had been a *comtesse* who had narrowly escaped the horrors of the French revolution; others said she was the natural daughter of a governor of one of the colonies; and another set vowed that she had been an actress on the London stage. Kitty, after visiting the Lucases, reported these conjectures to her family.

"I cannot believe it!" exclaimed Mrs. Bennet, but her tone suggested that she did, even though it was unlikely that all, if any, of the rumors could be true.

"Perhaps, Mrs. Bennet, after you finish marrying off your daughters, you will take to a life of crime?" teased her husband.

Mrs. Bennet scolded her husband for implying that she would ever commit forgery and murder, while Kitty was amazed that anyone could tell so many lies.

"Lying is wrong," moralized Mary. "We must resist telling falsehoods, no matter how great the temptation, and it is especially sinful to bear false witness."

The Lucases, as Kitty had mentioned, were also speculating, and when Mrs. Collins heard about everything, she demanded use of the Lucas chaise, and journeyed again to Netherfield Park, just two days after the miniatures had been identified. They first went through the niceties, with Mr. Darcy expressing his regrets about the death of Mr. Collins, and Jane saying with patient impatience, that the great event would be any day now – "I know I have been using that phrase for a while, but eventually it must be true" – and her receiving calm encouragement from Mrs. Collins.

Mrs. Collins then changed the conversation to Meryton's current obsession. "I understand from Mrs. Philips that you have a miniature of Mrs. Smith, who was known as Mrs. Younge when she worked for Mr. Darcy. May I see it?"

Mr. Darcy fetched it at once. Mrs. Collins examined it in the light, and then said: "Just as I thought; *this* is a likeness of Mrs. Ford!"

Not everyone remembered that Mrs. Ford was the faithless nursery maid from the Hunsford Parsonage, so explanations were necessary, but when they were given everyone was astonished.

"Mrs. Smith, Mrs. Younge, Mrs. Ford!" exclaimed Mr. Bingley. "How many names did the woman have?"

The fact that Mrs. Smith had also been Mrs. Ford cleared up other perplexing matters. "So, Charlotte, when you thought you saw Mrs. Ford heading in the direction of Mrs. Smith's lodgings, you actually saw Mrs. Smith herself," Jane remarked, while Elizabeth said that she believed she understood why Mrs. Smith had refused so many of Mrs. Philips's invitations. "Mrs. Smith must have feared being recognized by *you*, Charlotte, and so she would not have gone to places where you might have met."

"Is it possible that Mr. Collins did see her and recognize her, and that explains why she murdered him?" asked Mr. Darcy.

"That – that is my suspicion," said Mrs. Collins, her voice trembling. She was generally calm, but this possibility was much even for her. For a few minutes, her friends focused on restoring her tranquility. Elizabeth squeezed her hand affectionately, Miss Bingley offered her a handkerchief, and Mr. Bingley poured her a glass of wine.

"This woman was far more evil than anyone could imagine!" cried Jane. "How could one person do so much?"

"Apparently she was very enterprising," remarked Miss Bingley.

Mrs. Collins soon regained self-command, and Mr. Darcy said that if Mrs. Collins were not too distressed, she might be able to give them some useful information. He had only had a few brief exchanges with Mrs. Younge, but as the woman had actually lived under the same roof as Mrs. Collins for a month, *she* might have more information about the woman.

"If that information can be trusted," said Miss Bingley.

"Of course Mrs. Collins can have no confidence in her references or whatever she said about herself," said Mr. Darcy, "but she may have clues to her habits and her preferences. Did you notice anything unusual about her? Perhaps some correspondence?"

Mrs. Collins said that Mrs. Ford had seemed a competent nursery maid, quite good with little Lewis, and that she had noticed nothing unusual.

Mr. Bingley asked if Mrs. Collins had received letters demanding money, but Mrs. Collins said she had not. Jane then asked if Mr. Collins might have received a demand that Mrs. Collins did not know about.

Imitating Mr. Collins's style of correspondence would require true artistry, thought Elizabeth, but she refrained from uttering this thought aloud. Jane's question caused Mrs. Collins to smile, and she said, "If I did not know about the demand that Mr. Collins received in the past, how could I know about it now, when I cannot ask him? But I do not think so. If he had received such a demand, I am sure that I would have detected an unevenness in his temper, and I did not. He was only distressed when Lady Catherine was distressed, and given how angry her ladyship was, and the fact that she came to Meryton when Mrs. Jenkinson is ill, I believe that *she* must have received some sort of extortion attempt. Besides, Mrs. Ford, as I think of her, targeted the wealthy. Although Mr. Collins had reasonable expectations, our means were relatively modest."

After some discussion, they concurred that this was likely the case. Mrs. Collins could confirm that some correspondence of Lady Catherine's had vanished, for a time, while Mrs. Smith-Younge-Ford was in the Parsonage. It had been found again, but it had disappeared long enough for someone to study the style and the penmanship. Extortion also explained why Lady Catherine had traveled to Meryton in the first place. Giving a lift to Mr. Collins had hardly seemed like a sufficient reason for such a journey; if her ladyship had wished to show him such attention, she could have lent him the carriage without her undertaking the trip as well. Moreover, she had stayed in Meryton, at the Inn, not just one night but two, even though she was vocal in her disapprobation of the town.

"I believe, from the way your aunt spoke to me, that she actually suspected me of being the instigator," said Elizabeth. "She was angry and suspicious and frankly, unintelligible."

Mr. Darcy was at first indignant that anyone could suspect his beloved Elizabeth of anything, but he calmed down when she pointed out that Lady Catherine's views were not so unreasonable. She and Mrs. Collins and she were both from Meryton, and so if Lady Catherine had been compelled to bring money to a certain spot in the neighborhood, her ladyship was likely to suspect the people she knew from that neighborhood. No one had connected Mrs. Smith with Mrs. Ford, so the real culprit had gone undetected.

"I will write to my aunt today and let her know that the extortionist is dead and that she can therefore relax," said Mr. Darcy. "And clear your name of all involvement."

"At least of that crime," said his wife.

Then Mr. Darcy posed another question. "Mrs. Collins, when this woman was with you, did you notice any letters that she received, or that she sent? Perhaps correspondence with a banker? If we track her contacts we may be able to retrieve some of the money that she extorted."

Mrs. Collins considered, then told what she remembered: the woman she had known as Mrs. Ford had not received any letters at the Parsonage; nor had she sent any. But Mrs. Collins added the caveat that she could not depend on her memory to be completely reliable. Mr. Collins often handled the post, and when Mrs. Ford had stayed at the Parsonage, she had been busy with her new infant and so many details might have escaped her. Furthermore, Mrs. Ford could have gone into the village to send or to retrieve any letters. Queries there might yield some information; she offered to undertake them, once she returned to Hunsford.

"If it is not too much trouble," said Mr. Bingley.

"Or Lady Catherine could make the inquiries," suggested Elizabeth. "I am certain that the men at the post would be make every effort to answer *her* questions. Do you think that she would mind, Charlotte?"

Mrs. Collins thought the suggestion was excellent – it was the sort of mission that her ladyship would enjoy – but its execution depended on the situation with Mrs. Jenkinson.

Mr. Darcy said that he would include this request in his letter to his aunt. He rose and repaired to the library to write the letter.

"What could Mrs. Smith have sent to Lady Catherine?" Bingley wondered.

"We should not speculate," said Jane, who could tamp down her curiosity easily when a matter did not concern her. "Especially as we know that Mrs. Smith operated by constructing falsehoods – which means that it could be anything."

Elizabeth had several ideas, but because of her promise to her ladyship, felt obliged not to mention them. "You are too good," she said.

Mrs. Collins said she needed to return to Lucas Lodge. Mr. Bingley escorted her to her carriage, and then went to the library to mention some details that Mr. Darcy might wish to include in his letter to his aunt. Elizabeth had planned to go for a walk, but rain threatened, so she remained indoors with the other ladies. "This Mrs. Smith-Ford-Younge was a very bold woman," she remarked.

"Do not tell me that you admire her, Mrs. Darcy," said Miss Bingley, who clearly hoped that Elizabeth would utter this opinion so that she could have the pleasure of despising her for it.

"Not at all. From what we know, she has committed many crimes, and has conspired to create lifelong unhappiness in many people. She apparently felt no remorse for what she had done. But if she generally felt no remorse for what she had done – then how could she feel enough remorse in order to take her own life?" asked Elizabeth.

"We do not know that she felt no remorse," said Jane. "Perhaps she did, and after the death of Mr. Collins, her guilt was too much for her to bear. Besides, my dear Lizzy, as you have never been a criminal, how can you know what she felt?"

Elizabeth thought that her sweet-tempered sister probably had even less insight into guilty hearts than she did, but she was not going to make this claim before Miss Bingley.

"Or else Mrs. Smith believed she was about to be discovered," suggested Miss Bingley, who, like Elizabeth, was not disposed to think well of everyone. "She may have expected that Mr. Collins's death would be taken as an unfortunate accident. Yet many in Meryton were convinced it was murder."

Miss Bingley, thought Elizabeth reluctantly, had made an excellent point.

CHAPTER XLII

Everyone was desirous to learn what would come back from the inquiries sent to London, Newcastle and Hunsford. Mr. Bingley was the most sanguine. "If there is a chance that I could retrieve the money…"

He did not complete his sentence, but everyone understood his meaning. The possibility of Mr. Bingley's purchasing Rushburn especially pleased Elizabeth and Miss Bingley. The former was eager to have Jane in the county next to Derbyshire, while the latter was eager to depart from the one she was in.

Jane was more cautious. "Although an estate of our own would be wonderful, it may not be possible to recover the money. We should not be too hopeful, only to be disappointed later."

"On what could Mrs. Smith have spent the money? Mrs. Philips's lodgings were not very dear and Mrs. Smith was not, from all accounts, living extravagantly," said Mr. Bingley optimistically.

Mr. Darcy had his doubts, because they did not know that Mrs. Younge had had the money. And if Wickham had the money, Wickham could have spent it on debts of honor.

They all eagerly awaited the post.

Mrs. Gardiner, located in London, was the first to respond. She reported that Lydia had been a little more generous lately, purchasing some presents for the children – but she did not believe that Lydia had somehow acquired a *very* large sum of money. Mrs. Gardiner had also told her niece of the suicide of Mrs. Smith, whom she had known as Mrs. Younge, as well as Mrs. Younge's confession to killing Mr. Collins. Lydia had been shocked by this, but she had not appeared guilty. Perhaps she was dissembling, but Mrs. Gardiner did not think so. She would, however, remain vigilant.

Colonel Thorne's letter arrived next. He, upon Colonel Fitzwilliam's request, had already been keeping an eye on Wickham, particularly his habits and his expenses. When Wickham had returned from Hertfordshire he had settled several outstanding accounts, but other than that, Thorne had not noticed anything unusual, and he had assumed that the extra cash had been a present from his brother-in-law. Thorne reported on his conversation with Lieutenant Wickham where he had informed him of the suicide of the woman he had known as Mrs. Younge. Wickham had appeared both shocked and grieved for the rest of the day, but he had not done anything especially unusual afterwards – he had only drunk a lot of wine, and to be truthful, Lieutenant Wickham drank a lot of wine even when he was not grieving. Thorne certainly did not believe that Wickham had suddenly become wealthy.

Mr. Bingley's spirits were dampened by the indications that the Wickhams did not seem to have his money; but then he put his hopes on to the response from Lady Catherine. Her ladyship had just as much reason as he did to discover the money.

Lady Catherine, as she had been contacted last, was the last to respond. Her ladyship wrote that she hoped that Mr. Darcy could assist her in retrieving her money, but with Mrs. Jenkinson on her deathbed she had to devote every moment to her daughter Anne. Nevertheless, she had made a few queries. She had gone to the Parsonage to interrogate the servants, who could tell her nothing, and then she had gone to the post office in Hunsford. The men working at the post office confirmed that Mrs. Ford had personally mailed letters and had received them, too, sending them to several addresses in London and to a Mr. Philips in Meryton.

"Mrs. Smith wrote to my uncle Philips!" exclaimed Jane.

"Of course she did," said Elizabeth. "She hired lodgings from him."

The innocuous explanation was rather disappointing.

"What about the letters to London?" inquired Bingley.

Mr. Darcy explained that Lady Catherine had pressed the men employed at the post office, but they had not been able to give her any addresses in the city.

"It will be difficult to discover my money in London," said Bingley, his spirits falling again.

"Difficult, but perhaps not impossible," said Mr. Darcy, and he said he would write to the London bankers and ask if they were aware of money that could have belonged to Mr. Bingley or to his aunt.

The Darcys rather wished that they could return to Pemberley, but Elizabeth would not go till she was certain that Jane was safe.

And Jane, sweet Jane, was becoming frustrated on her own account. Where was the child? She had never seen an elephant but she was sure she was as big as one! Perhaps she would be this size for the rest of her life!

Mrs. Bennet reassured her that she would not, and then destroyed the comfort that she had just given by wondering if Jane had miscalculated and if she might have to wait another month.

CHAPTER XLIII

The sun was setting earlier but the days were still warm. Mr. Bingley and Mr. Darcy went shooting together while Elizabeth and Miss Bingley took turns sitting with Jane. Miss Bingley had a respite from Mrs. Bennet's regular visits because the horses were needed for the harvest.

One golden day, Elizabeth invited Mrs. Collins to a little excursion with the baby. Elizabeth fetched her friend and her friend's nursery maid in her carriage and had Wilson drive them to the field with the large horse chestnut tree. They spread a blanket in the shade and entertained Lewis for about twenty minutes by blowing on as many dandelions as they could find. He then fell asleep and they could talk of other matters.

Elizabeth then pointed at the hollow in the horse chestnut tree. "That is where the box was hidden."

Mrs. Collins went to the tree and searched inside the hollow. "It is empty now," she reported. "I wonder what Mrs. Ford did with that box?"

"No one seems to know," said Elizabeth, who wished that she could find Mr. Bingley's money for him and Jane. She stared for a while at the tree, willing that it would yield its secrets, and then let her gaze wander towards the river, where two boys were fishing. "Charlotte, I am such a fool! I did not think that anyone could have observed Mrs. Younge going to the horse chestnut tree, but those boys were here; *they* might have seen her!"

Mrs. Collins said that she believed one of them was acquainted with her youngest brother and asked if Elizabeth wanted to speak to them; Elizabeth said she did.

So Mrs. Collins and Elizabeth left the baby with the nursery maid and walked down to the river, stepping carefully on the rocks, and spoke to the boys. The one with reddish hair, said Mrs. Collins, was Frank Perkins; he was the son of the local jailer. The other Elizabeth recognized as Jim Page, the son of the milliner whose shop was across from her uncle Philips's house and office in Meryton. Elizabeth asked them if they had caught anything that day.

Frank said that they had not.

"Not yet, anyway," added Jim.

Elizabeth then posed her question: "Have you ever seen anyone going to that horse chestnut tree? And either putting things into the hollow, or taking them out?"

"Yes," said Jim.

Her heart pounded with excitement. "Whom have you seen? And when?"

Jim gestured toward Mrs. Collins. "I seen her. About ten minutes ago."

Mrs. Collins's lips twitched as she repressed a smile; the answer was true but not helpful.

"Other than today. About nine days ago," said Elizabeth.

The boys glanced at each other. Frank shrugged, and Jim asked a question of his own. "You're Mrs. Darcy, the lady with the great estate, right? My mum has talked about you."

"I suppose I am."

"Well, then," said Jim.

"Well then?" repeated Elizabeth, puzzled as to why Jim was not answering her question. Mrs. Collins leaned to her and whispered, "I think he wants to be paid for his answer."

Elizabeth was embarrassed that she had not thought of this at first. What was the price of information? she wondered. She offered a shilling. The boys hesitated, then nodded. After she handed them the shilling – only one, she said, they would have to share – Jim explained that he had seen Mrs. Darcy go to the horse chestnut tree on the day she mentioned.

She felt rather cheated at having paid for information that she already knew. "Did you see anyone else?" she asked. "On that day?"

The boys glanced at each other again, and Jim Page said that he had not seen anyone. Elizabeth described Mrs. Smith and asked if they might have noticed her – if not near the horse chestnut tree, in the meadow.

"Is that the lady who drunk poison?" asked the jailer's son.

Elizabeth affirmed that it was, but even though it was clear that the boys would have liked to have seen *her*, they denied it. Disappointed in their quest, Elizabeth and Mrs. Collins turned away from the river bank, moving off the stones and back to the grass of the meadow.

"It is possible that Mrs. Ford was here but that they did not notice her," said Mrs. Collins. "She was easy to overlook."

"Or that someone else went to the horse chestnut tree and they missed him," said Elizabeth. "Or … one or both of them is lying."

"Why would either of them lie, Eliza?" asked Mrs. Collins. But before Elizabeth could answer, Mrs. Collins's nursery maid called to them. The baby was fussing, and Mrs. Collins said she needed to take Lewis home. They climbed into the carriage and left the meadow.

CHAPTER XLIV

Elizabeth related this conversation to Mr. Darcy, who said that it was very likely that the boys, engrossed by their fishing, simply had not noticed someone crossing the meadow. He fished himself and he understood how easy it was to be completely focused on the activity in the water.

Yet Elizabeth was not satisfied by this interpretation. Neither Frank Perkins nor Jim Page had *said* anything in particular, but their glances at each other suggested duplicity – or at least that they were not telling everything. She wished to know more. But questioning them by the river had not helped; she did not want to be wasting more shillings.

Elizabeth had no excuse for visiting the jail – Heaven forbid! – but it was perfectly reasonable for her to stop at the milliner's. So the next day, while the uncomfortable Jane was taking a nap, Mr. Bingley and Mr. Darcy had gone to the Gouldings in the Pemberley carriage, and Miss Bingley was idly leafing through some sheet music, Elizabeth said she wanted to visit the milliner's. Miss Bingley said that they could take the Netherfield carriage out together; she wished to make a sketch of Oakham Mount. But that would take some time; would Eliza mind waiting? Or did Eliza prefer to walk back?

As the distance from Meryton back to Netherfield was only two miles, and as the walk would take less time than Miss Bingley's sketch, Elizabeth said she would return on foot. So Miss Bingley gathered her pencils; Elizabeth changed her shoes; and, within half-an-hour, Miss Bingley and Mrs. Darcy were seated together in the Netherfield chaise. "It is not the prettiest day for a walk," said Miss Bingley, glancing at the overcast sky, "but I do not think it will rain."

"I agree," said Elizabeth, and by keeping their conversation to the weather, they remained civil for the duration of the ride into Meryton.

As the coachman helped Elizabeth descend, Miss Bingley politely repeated her offer to give Elizabeth a lift back to Netherfield, but Elizabeth just as politely and more earnestly declined.

Elizabeth entered the milliner's. Mrs. Page, who had been hoping for a visit from the wealthy Mrs. Darcy ever since her return to the neighborhood, and who had been disappointed till today, was delighted to welcome her and to assist her in purchasing whatever she wished (and more, if she could persuade Mrs. Darcy to it). Elizabeth browsed the fabrics and ribbons, hoping that while she lingered she would catch a moment with Mrs. Page's son Jim, but he did not seem to be in the shop.

Elizabeth did not see any item that she particularly desired. This shop had been always a favorite with her younger sisters; she had liked it herself, but she had never been able to afford all she wanted. Now that she had enough pin money to purchase whatever she liked, she discovered that nothing pleased her. Had her tastes changed so much in less than a year?

She asked Mrs. Page to show her baby caps. Mrs. Page was willing to show Mrs. Darcy anything, and brought out her selection. Elizabeth, her mind occupied, turned them over without seeing them properly. "I believe that the other day I saw your son, Jim, fishing by the river."

Mrs. Page agreed that it was quite likely; Jim was an avid angler. She added that it was useful to have a son who occasionally provided for the dinner table, especially given how much growing boys consumed. She then returned with determination to the subject of baby caps; Elizabeth surrendered and selected several that she considered least objectionable. The purchase was not of the quantity that Mrs. Page had hoped for – Mrs. Darcy ought to be more liberal to those in Meryton – but she did not complain. Just as she was wrapping the caps into a package, her son entered the shop.

"Jim, there you are! Look who is here! Mrs. Darcy has been asking about you."

The youth, who had been so brash in his bargaining by the river, was scarlet and tongue-tied now.

"Good afternoon, Jim," said Elizabeth.

He muttered hello – at least that was what she thought he said – and then turned to his mother. "Mum, could I have the key to the apartment?"

"What have you done with yours?"

He did not know, so after a brief remonstrance – which would have been much more explicit and vehement if Mrs. Page had not been waiting on a customer – she handed him a spare key. The youth quickly departed, and his mother said something about him going through a shy phase, which was not really like him, but boys were boys.

Elizabeth finished paying, said good-bye to Mrs. Page and then stepped out of the shop. Her brief encounter with Jim Page confirmed her conviction that the youth had seen more, or at least knew more, than he was revealing. She could not understand. If Jim Page had seen Mrs. Younge at the horse chestnut tree, then why would he not say? Something else had happened, she was certain of it. Yet she also did not see how she could convince him to tell her anything more – especially when he was nowhere in sight.

But the conversation between the youth and his mother had given Elizabeth another idea. Her uncle and aunt lived across the street; she would make inquiries.

Mrs. Philips was always happy to see any of her nieces, and especially honored that Mrs. Darcy would call on her so casually. She asked after Jane, and then without waiting to hear Elizabeth's answer, assured her that Mr. Philips and his clerks were doing everything they could to retrieve Mr. Bingley's money and that they could tell her about their efforts in a few minutes as they would soon arrive for tea. But with Lizzy here now, she would ring the bell immediately. After doing so she noticed that her dear Lizzy had a package from Mrs. Page's; and insisted on seeing the caps that Lizzy had bought for dear Jane, or rather dear Jane's baby; when was her poor niece ever going to have that baby? Jane must be so uncomfortable!

Mrs. Philips prattled on, not as voluble as her sister but keeping up a steady stream of observations. When the tea arrived, Elizabeth finally posed her query. "Aunt, there is more than one key to the apartment you let to Mrs. Smith, is there not?"

"Yes, of course, or else we could not have entered when we discovered her body. My heart still turns when I think of it! Why, Lizzy? Would you like to rent the apartment? So that the next time you come to the neighborhood you can have some privacy instead of staying at either Netherfield or Longbourn?"

Elizabeth, reflecting that everyone in Meryton wished to sell her something, politely steered her aunt away from this notion. She said that she was certain that Mr. and Mrs. Philips would find a more suitable tenant than herself, someone who not only wanted the lodgings, but needed them. And then she inquired where the extra key was generally kept.

"What an odd question! Let me think. When it is without a tenant, we usually keep one in Mr. Philips's office and one in the regular part of the house. When we rented it to Mrs. Smith we gave her one key and we kept the spare – but it was sometimes up here, and other times in Mr. Philips's office, depending on what was necessary – we were having carpentry work. Why do you wish to know, Lizzy?"

Before Elizabeth could explain, Mr. Philips and Mr. Morris came through the door. Greetings had to be exchanged, health inquired after, the men had to sit, and tea had to be poured and passed around before the subject could be resumed.

"Is Mr. Clarke coming too?" asked Mrs. Philips.

"He had a visitor," said Mr. Philips, "but that should only delay him a minute."

"Lizzy wants to know about the spare key to Mrs. Smith's apartment. I told her that it is sometimes in your office and sometimes here."

"Yes, that is true," said Mr. Philips.

Elizabeth then asked if someone could have borrowed the spare key.

Mr. Morris stared at her with his sharp dark eyes. "Borrowed the key? That is an interesting question, Mrs. Darcy."

"Why? Why is that interesting?" demanded Mrs. Philips, but before anyone could explain, Mr. Clarke arrived, excusing himself for his tardiness. Again their discussion was interrupted by an exchange of greetings.

"Have some tea, Mr. Clarke," said Mrs. Philips brightly, preparing him a cup and a plate. "My niece has asked a question that Mr. Morris finds interesting: could someone have borrowed the spare key to Mrs. Smith's apartment?"

"I am sure that Mrs. Darcy has an excellent reason for asking that question, but I cannot stay to discuss it. I have only come here to tell you that I have an urgent and sudden appointment, and cannot stay. You must excuse me."

Mrs. Philips was a little surprised, and asked if he would not stay for fifteen minutes, but Mr. Clarke refused and departed. Before anyone could wonder about his urgent appointment, they were joined by Sir William Lucas, who had just finished some errands in the town. After another exchange of greetings, he announced that he could not stay long, but that he yearned for a cup of tea and that he hoped that he could rely on the readiness and the generosity of Mrs. Philips.

With the entrance of Sir William, the topic of the key was dropped, although Mr. Morris frowned occasionally in Elizabeth's direction. She departed at the same time as Sir William, Mrs. Philips protesting that her visit had been too short. Elizabeth explained that she was walking back to Netherfield, information which would have surprised them if it had been uttered by any rich lady other than Mrs. Darcy.

The first little part of Elizabeth's and Sir William's route was the same, so they walked together. Elizabeth particularly wished to inquire about her friend. "How is Charlotte? Has she decided what she will do?"

They paused at one end of the bridge. Sir William needed to cross it to return to Lucas Lodge, while Elizabeth's direction was different. He took some time to answer her question, but from his words she extracted that Mrs. Collins had not yet reached a decision. Strange, thought Elizabeth, attending only superficially, that Mrs. Collins had taken less time to decide to marry Mr. Collins than she was taking to decide what to do now that he was dead.

"It is so terrible to think that he died – that he was murdered – on this very bridge," said Sir William.

"Was he?" asked Elizabeth.

"I beg your pardon?" asked Sir William, who was expecting a flowing response full of sympathy and sorrow, and not an abrupt question.

"Was Mr. Collins murdered *here*? How?"

Sir William hesitated, but obligingly attempted to answer. "She – that woman – said that she killed him. She hit him on the head and pushed him over the side."

"With what? With what did she hit him? Where is the weapon?"

"I do not know, Mrs. Darcy – a stick, a stone – does it matter? And as no one found it, and this area was well searched, she must have taken it with her. Mr. Collins is dead; his murderer is dead; it is best to let them rest in peace."

Perceiving that her curiosity made him uncomfortable, Elizabeth changed the subject. She said that she needed to go, and added, "Give my regards to Charlotte."

"You will not come with me to see her at Lucas Lodge? Or allow me to escort you to Longbourn?"

But Elizabeth, who had an idea she wished to pursue, excused herself. She told him that she would walk back to Netherfield, but first take the lane by the river. The route was a little longer, but the evening was pleasant and lately she had been indoors too much. From there she would continue to Netherfield.

Sir William wished her well and they parted.

CHAPTER XLV

The lane from the bridge continued for about three-quarters of a mile in close proximity to the river till it reached the large meadow with the horse chestnut tree. At that point the lane swerved away from the river, and forked, with one route leading back to Meryton while the other would be her path to Netherfield.

As she walked along the river, upon a lovely, wide path, Elizabeth's mind worked busily. Sir William and the rest of the neighborhood believed certain things about the deaths of Mr. Collins and Mrs. Younge, but what if those things were not true? What if the deaths had been arranged to *appear* a certain way, like a director staging a play, or an author creating a story? What if that someone still existed, someone who had taken Miss King's jewels, Mr. Bingley's money, and Mr. Collins's life?

When Elizabeth reached the meadow with the horse chestnut tree, she did not continue immediately towards Netherfield; nor did she approach the horse chestnut tree to reexamine it. This time she went to the edge of the river, where Jim Page and Frank Perkins had been fishing.

She studied the stones leading down to the water, wondering, and then turned to look back at the horse chestnut tree to see what the boys could have seen, had they been looking. And to her surprise, Mr. Clarke was crossing the meadow, heading from the lane in the direction of the spot where the forest came down nearly to the river.

He did not appear pleased to see her, then seemed to change his attitude and altered his direction to approach her. "Mrs. Darcy! Good afternoon!"

She greeted him and asked if he had managed to meet his appointment.

"My appointment? Ah, yes, I did." He raised his eyebrows. "What exactly are you doing here, Mrs. Darcy? Are you still searching for Mrs. Smith's spare key?"

"No. I was looking for rocks."

"Ah! Then you are in luck," he said, gesturing at the many rocks around them. "Is there something particular about these rocks? Are they better than the rocks in Derbyshire?"

"Mr. Collins's head was injured, possibly by a rock. What if the rock came from here? Or – what if he was hit with a rock here, and then moved him to where he was found under the bridge?"

Mr. Clarke appeared amused by her questions. "Why would Mrs. Smith do that? And how could she do that?"

Elizabeth said that the killer would have needed a cart, or a wheelbarrow, but it would have been possible. What Elizabeth did not understand was how Mrs. Smith had killed Mr. Collins in the first place, how a woman not taller than herself could have managed it.

"You have very good points, Mrs. Darcy, but I think I know how it was done." Mr. Clarke picked up a large rock and moved toward her, swinging it.

"What are you doing?" cried Elizabeth. "You almost struck me!" She had only been spared by a quick movement on her part.

"This time I will not miss," said Mr. Clarke, and he reached for her arm and lunged at her again with the stone.

But as her confusion shifted to horrified terror, Elizabeth wrenched her arm free and twisted out of his way. His second blow with the stone hit her shoulder, ripping her sleeve and causing her to cry out with pain. She scrambled away from the river, but it was difficult to move quickly enough. With her good arm she threw the package of baby caps at his face, but that distracted him only for seconds. She began to run. Elizabeth had been in the habit of running before she married, but since becoming Mrs. Darcy she had run very little.

Still, she was faster than her attacker had expected, and he was carrying a large stone. Why was Mr. Clarke doing this? *He* must have killed Mr. Collins! It was not Mrs. Younge; it had never been Mrs. Younge, or if it had been Mrs. Younge, then he must have been involved as well. But those details did not matter just now – just now she needed to save her life.

She raced across the meadow and reached the lane and turned left, away from the river, as she was more likely to find other people, and therefore safety this way, even though it meant running uphill. But it was at least a furlong till the nearest house, and even then, would reaching it do her any good? Knocking on a door was not sufficient security; someone had to open it and admit her. She could be struck down on a doorstep, her limp body then carried away. So she did not turn into a gravel drive that belonged to the Robinsons, but continued running up the lane.

Why were no people about? Were they all inside drinking tea? Mr. Clarke was gaining; she could tell he was gaining; she could hear his heavy breathing behind her. They were both running for their lives: she, to keep from being murdered; he, to keep from being hanged for his crimes.

She cried: "Help! Someone is attempting to kill me!" but she was almost out of breath, and even to her, her voice did not sound very loud.

And then she heard the sound of galloping hoofs.

Mr. Clarke heard the hoof beats as well; they both realized a horse was approaching. The clerk cursed her, but he did not come closer. He threw the stone he was carrying in her direction; Elizabeth jumped out of the way so that it only struck her in the foot. But Mr. Clarke did not stay to press his advantage; he continued running, away from the river and the coming horseman.

The horse arrived; its rider spoke. "Elizabeth? Elizabeth! I have been looking all over for you!"

Amazingly, marvelously, fortuitously, it was Mr. Darcy! With the sun setting and its rays in his eyes, he did not notice her distress: not her limp, nor her torn, bloody clothing, nor the expression on her face. And she was too breathless to speak and to explain herself.

He had news of his own. "Jane is in labor."

Elizabeth burst into tears.

CHAPTER XLVI

Smiling, believing that his wife's tears were of drops of joy for her sister, Mr. Darcy told her that Sir William Lucas had sent him in this direction. He then dismounted from his horse, and when he reached the ground he had a better view of Elizabeth's face. "Good God! What is the matter?"

In a few breathless sentences Elizabeth communicated the essentials. Mr. Darcy then had two objectives: to get his wife to safety, and to make sure that Mr. Clarke was stopped before he could escape. He helped Elizabeth on to his horse, and escorted the animal back into Meryton at a brisk walk. During the twenty-minute journey, Elizabeth described more of what happened. There he delivered her to Mr. and Mrs. Philips, who were still drinking tea with Mr. Morris, and explained that Mr. Philips's other clerk, Mr. Clarke, had attempted to kill their niece.

Mr. and Mrs. Philips might have had difficulty believing this but Elizabeth's dress was torn; her arm and her leg were bloody; her face was scraped and her bonnet askew. Besides, Mr. Philips found it impolitic to doubt Mr. Darcy, one of Derbyshire's richest men. Mrs. Philips was rather confused by some of the details – was not Mrs. Smith the murderess of Meryton? – but she set about tending her niece's injuries.

Mr. Morris was not displeased to learn that his rival in the office was a violent criminal.

They all offered assistance. Mr. Philips was not a man who could move quickly physically, but mentally he was competent, and he knew which men to summon. In addition to Mr. Morris, he suggested the Lucas boys – the Gouldings – Mr. Robinson – and Jailer Perkins. He also thought of several actions to be taken immediately. They would search Mr. Clarke's rooms – he would be a party to that – and they should also go to Mr. Clarke's family and to his good friend Mr. Jones, because he might turn to one of these people for assistance in his desire to escape. Finally, Mr. Philips would send someone to Longbourn House, to apprise them of the situation. Mr. Clarke might appeal to Kitty Bennet, and endanger her.

"I expect that the Longbourn carriage will soon be on its way to Netherfield," said Mr. Darcy. "Tell Mr. Bennet that he should stop here to collect Mrs. Darcy and take her with them. Go at once."

Richard, the servant given these messages, departed.

"What about the post?" asked Mr. Darcy. "Clarke could hire a horse to take him away."

"An excellent suggestion," said Mr. Philips.

"We should warn everyone who has a horse," added Mr. Morris. "Given what you have said, I do not think that Clarke would be concerned about acquiring an animal legally."

The men allocated the tasks among themselves and Mr. Philips's male servants, while the female servants agreed to barricade the doors and to keep Mr. Clarke from forcing his way inside and slaughtering them all. The men then departed, with a promise from Mr. Philips to Mrs. Philips that he would be extremely careful.

Mrs. Philips's maid washed and bandaged Elizabeth's wounds – fortunately no bones were broken, but she did have scrapes and bruises. Elizabeth refused her aunt's offer of smelling salts, but she did accept a glass of wine and several biscuits.

"I do not understand what happened, Lizzy," said her aunt. "Why did Mr. Clarke try to kill you?"

"I am still trying to understand everything myself, Aunt," said Elizabeth. "But I think that he is responsible for the murder of Mr. Collins."

"Do you mean to say that Mrs. Smith was innocent? Why then did she kill herself? And why did she leave a note confessing?"

"I do not think Mrs. Smith was especially innocent," said Elizabeth. "And I am not certain that she did kill herself, and I doubt very much that she wrote that note."

"I do not understand," repeated Mrs. Philips plaintively, but then a housemaid announced that the carriage from Longbourn was come.

Elizabeth apologized, but said that she absolutely had to depart; Jane needed her. She kissed her bewildered aunt, and promised to call as soon as she could and explain all that she knew.

CHAPTER XLVII

Elizabeth, escorted by a guard consisting of her anxious aunt, the cook and the housemaid, limped to the Longbourn carriage and climbed within. Inside were her father and her sister Mary; her mother and her sister Kitty had already been fetched by the Netherfield carriage.

"You look terrible," Mary remarked.

"Lizzy, what has happened?" asked her father, and he related how Mr. Philips's servant Richard had arrived with an urgent message.

During the carriage ride to Netherfield Elizabeth explained as best she could – as she spoke, she realized she would be recounting her experience often – what had happened with Mr. Clarke, how Mr. Darcy had found her, and how he had escorted her to Meryton while he and other men searched for the murderer.

Mr. Bennet and Mary were likewise confused by what Elizabeth told them at first, but they were not as bewildered as Mrs. Philips had been. "I could not understand how a woman the size of Mrs. Smith could kill Mr. Collins," said Mr. Bennet. "But Mr. Clarke – that is far more plausible."

"Mr. Morris intimated that Mr. Clarke was not to be trusted," said Mary. "He told me that he warned my uncle Philips but could not convince him."

Mr. Bennet was still perplexed. "If Mr. Clarke is the actual murderer, that better explains *how* the crime was committed. Still, I cannot understand *why* Mr. Clarke would murder my cousin. Was Mr. Clarke also seen by Mr. Collins in Hunsford?"

"Papa, I am still too distressed to reason clearly," said his daughter. "If Darcy and the others are able to apprehend Mr. Clarke, perhaps we will learn everything."

Mr. Bennet took his daughter's hand. "I am grateful that your injuries are no worse, Lizzy."

In half-an-hour the Longbourn carriage reached Netherfield; the footman helped them descend. Mr. Bennet leaned on his cane, and Elizabeth leaned on Mary.

They were greeted by Miss Bingley in the dimly lit vestibule. "There you are, Eliza; I assume Darcy found you!" and then surveying those who accompanied her, asked: "Where is Darcy?"

"He had some pressing business; I hope he will return soon," said Elizabeth. "How is Jane?"

"Mr. Jones and Mrs. Nicholls and even your mother agree that it will be many hours yet. Jane will be grateful that you are here, Eliza," and then, in the candlelight, finally perceived her injuries. "What happened? You look as if you were kicked by a horse!"

Elizabeth said she would explain everything later; just now she wished to see her sister. So Miss Bingley directed Mr. Bennet to the library – "my brother will be glad for the company" – and then accompanied Elizabeth and Mary upstairs, with Elizabeth continuing to lean on Mary. Miss Bingley knocked, and then they entered Jane's room, which was rather crowded, containing, as it did, Jane, Mrs. Bennet, Kitty Bennet, Mrs. Nicholls and the senior Mr. Jones. Mrs. Bennet was the first to speak. "Lizzy, there you are! Where have you been, Lizzy? Look Jane, here is Lizzy; that should make you feel better!"

"Lizzy, it is happening. It is really happening!" Jane exclaimed, and then cried aloud as she was gripped by pain.

"There, Jane, there; it will be all right," said Mrs. Bennet.

It was only when Jane's contraction was finished that Kitty noticed Elizabeth's torn clothing, bandages and scrapes. Elizabeth, not wishing to alarm anyone, explained that she had had a little accident earlier in the day but that she was tolerably well. Mr. Jones turned his attention briefly to Mrs. Darcy and inspected her injuries (Mrs. Bennet, worried about her eldest daughter and her first grandchild, did not). The apothecary proclaimed that Mrs. Darcy was in no danger – "not now" thought Elizabeth – but that she would be well served by an infusion of willow bark, to dull the pain. Elizabeth was grateful for the suggestion; with the worst of her terror gone, her bruises had begun to ache. Mrs. Nicholls said she would prepare willow bark for Mrs. Darcy, and tea for everyone else – it would be a long night – and Mary said she would join her father and Mr. Bingley in the library.

"Tell me about your accident, Lizzy," said Jane, after several more contractions and after the arrival of the tea and the willow bark infusion. Elizabeth protested that she did not want to distract Jane; Jane said that she desired to be distracted.

"Your injuries appear to have been caused by falling against some stone," remarked Mr. Jones.

"Did you fall, Lizzy? I have told you not to go climbing and wandering about. There is no need for it, especially as you have a perfectly good carriage," said Mrs. Bennet. "Here, Jane, drink some tea."

"Tell us what happened," Kitty urged.

So Elizabeth related what had happened to her. Her information was so riveting that Jane was fascinated, and begged for her to continue. Kitty was horrified to learn this information about Mr. Clarke, with whom she had danced several times. The senior Mr. Jones was alarmed – Mr. Clarke was a particular friend of his son's – but Elizabeth could reassure him by telling him that Mr. Darcy and her uncle Philips had sent someone to his house.

Mrs. Bennet was especially voluble. To think that Lizzy had been in danger! She apologized to her daughter for making light of her injuries. And Mr. Clarke, who had seemed so agreeable! To think that she had considered him a possible son-in-law! So *he* had murdered Mr. Collins, not that tenant of her sister's with so many names. Where was the murderer now, anyway, and were they safe? If he wished to kill Lizzy, would he not follow her to Netherfield? They were all in danger, in terrible danger!

Elizabeth could assure her mother that Mr. Clarke was being sought in all the most likely places. They were also guarding the various stables, as Mr. Morris believed that Mr. Clarke could attempt to steal a horse in order to flee. Upon hearing of this possibility, Miss Bingley left the room to give orders to secure the Netherfield stables.

And then Jane gave another cry, and Elizabeth paused in her narrative, while Mrs. Bennet, assisted by Mr. Jones, tended to her eldest daughter.

Elizabeth asked Kitty how she was faring on hearing this news.

Kitty *was* perturbed, but not unduly. "It is shocking to think that someone who flirted with me could be so vicious, but my heart is not broken. I was never in love with Mr. Clarke. I thought I did not care for him because I did not want to stay in Meryton, but I see now it was because I did not trust him."

Elizabeth wished that she had been so sensible with respect to Mr. Wickham. She also commended Kitty for not claiming more attention in the matter, unlike their mother.

Two hours passed, during which time Mr. Bingley called anxiously from the outside of the door, and learned that his wife was faring well. The housemaids prepared several bedrooms in case anyone wished to sleep, but instead of retiring in rooms and on furniture designed for sleeping, everyone dozed off in chairs or stretched out on various sofas. Perhaps they felt that they were showing sympathy for Jane, by being as uncomfortable as they could, but why they would be of more use to her if they were just as fatigued as she was instead of well-rested was a question that could not be answered. Mr. Bennet, in fact, seemed to be the only one who asked it, and even he was not ready to close his eyes, not till he knew that his eldest daughter was safe.

Two hours after midnight, Miss Bingley reappeared. "Eliza, Darcy has returned. Mr. Clarke has been discovered. He was hidden in *your* stables, Mr. Jones, apparently waiting either for you or for your son to return, as no horses were inside. The housekeeper reported that your son was out on another call."

Mr. Jones exclaimed with relief; Miss Bingley asked Elizabeth if she wished to go to Mr. Darcy, but Jane cried out. The baby was really on its way, and Elizabeth did not feel as if she could leave her sister's side for an instant. Miss Bingley obligingly delivered this information to those waiting in the library and then returned for the great event.

Dawn was breaking as Jane's little girl was put into her arms.

CHAPTER XLVIII

Elizabeth yielded her place in Jane's room to Mr. Bingley, who was grateful that his wife was safe, still unnerved by the anxiety he had experienced on her account, and in awe as he met his baby daughter. "Hello, Jenny," said the new father tenderly. Mr. Bingley's use of that name prompted a sigh from Miss Caroline Bingley, but only from habit; in truth she was ecstatic.

Elizabeth excused herself.

She went to the library where she found her husband and her father playing chess, neither looking his best, with rumpled hair, unshaven chins and wrinkled clothes. Mary snored on a sofa, her spectacles askew, a thick book open on her lap.

Elizabeth suggested to her father that he should go upstairs to see his new granddaughter. Leaning on his cane, Mr. Bennet rose and limped out of the library.

Mrs. Nicholls and the rest of the kitchen staff had prepared breakfast. The number sitting down to the table in the breakfast-parlor was large: Mr. Jones senior, Mary and Kitty Bennet, Mr. Bennet, Miss Bingley, and Mr. and Mrs. Darcy. Only Mrs. Bennet and the master and the mistress of Netherfield were absent; Mrs. Nicholls carried a tray to them herself, so that she could admire the Bingley baby.

"I have much to tell you," Mr. Darcy said, when Elizabeth and he were finally alone.

"I am certain that you do," Elizabeth said, and added that she admired his patience in not bringing up the subject before this.

Darcy explained that he and the other men had set about searching the area, alerting the jailer who summoned additional men, and then going to houses and especially stables, as Mr. Morris had suggested. Clarke had been found hiding in the Joneses' stables. Clarke was no match for Darcy and for the two men who accompanied him, so they had easily subdued him and had taken him to the local prison. It was not large, but it was secure, and Jailer Perkins was eager to earn his salary. When he heard that Mr. Clarke had attempted to murder Mrs. Darcy and had told her that *he* had murdered Mr. Collins, the jailer assured everyone that Clarke would not escape so that he could be brought to trial. However; Perkins was confused on one point: he thought that Mrs. Smith had killed Mr. Collins. Why were so many people confessing to that capital crime? How many enemies had that clergyman had?

"Why did Clarke say that he killed Mr. Collins?" Mr. Darcy asked. "Are you certain that you heard correctly?"

"Yes, I am certain," said Elizabeth. "And I believe Clarke said that he killed Mr. Collins because he has, indeed, killed Mr. Collins. Clarke even attempted to demonstrate to me, with a large stone, exactly how he did it."

Over that day and those that followed, some facts came to light, accompanied by many theories – the theories were necessary because Mr. Clarke was generally refusing to speak, and when he did say anything, no one was confident that he was telling the truth. But some of the young men in Meryton had known Henry Clarke, a younger son in the Clarke family, while they were youths together. While a boy, Henry had complained that *his* prospects from Clarke's library, the family business, were not promising, as the majority interest would be inherited by his eldest brother, Mr. Thomas Clarke. The acquaintances from his youth also said that Henry had spent much time copying handwriting and learned to imitate it perfectly.

But Clarke maintained that he was not the only one who had imitated the hands of others – several of them had made a game of it – and even if he were *capable* of forgery, that did not prove that he *was* a forger. He had heard, for example, that Mr. Darcy was an excellent shot when he hunted. Did that mean he was guilty of shooting people? Jailer Perkins ought to arrest Mr. Darcy!

They learned, too, that when he reached sixteen, Henry Clarke had left Meryton for London in order to seek his fortune, but his opportunities to make money honestly were few. He had no desire to join the navy, as the one occasion he had been on a ship he had suffered from debilitating seasickness, while the experienced sailors around him laughed and told him that the waves at the time were nothing. Most routes to prosperity required both more capital and patience than the young man possessed. This information was supplied by Mr. Thomas Clarke, who had received letters from Mr. Henry Clarke at the time. The older brother also confirmed that his brother had taken a room in a large building owned by a Mrs. Younge.

Confronted with evidence of this fact, Mr. Clarke admitted that he *had* been a lodger at Mrs. Younge's in London, and that he had been rather surprised to meet her again as Mrs. Smith, a tenant in Meryton. But he could not see any reason that he should do anything to stop this, especially as Mr. and Mrs. Philips had been so grateful to let those rooms. For all he knew, the widow had remarried since he last encountered her, and then had been abandoned by her husband. The sorry tale that he conjectured had kept him from inquiring further, and as Mrs. Smith paid her rent on time, what did her name matter? How could he know that she had masqueraded as a nursery maid in Hunsford? He had some imagination but evidently not as much as Mrs. Smith, Younge or Ford or whatever her name was – nor as much as Mrs. Darcy. Mrs. Smith had confessed in a letter to killing Mr. Collins, and Mrs. Darcy was inventing things, by telling people that *he* had confessed. Even if she were wealthy and were now mistress of a great estate, that did not give her the right to bear false witness against those less fortunate, laboring to earn their living in Meryton.

This story was brought to Elizabeth and Mr. Darcy by Mr. Philips after an interview with his erstwhile clerk.

"Why did Mrs. Smith confess that she killed Mr. Collins?" asked Mr. Philips.

"I do not believe that she did confess. All we have is her letter of confession, but recall that we are dealing with an expert forger. I believe he killed Mrs. Smith," said Elizabeth. "I believe that *he* was the expert at imitating handwriting, not she."

"Do you mean to say that Mrs. Annabelle Younge was *innocent?*" asked Mr. Darcy, doubt in his voice.

"No – no. I believe that they were conspirators, and that they worked together to procure the histories and the handwriting samples of wealthy targets. For example, *she* must have borrowed that sample of your aunt's handwriting. And somehow Mr. Collins recognized her, and perhaps saw the two of them together – and so Mr. Clarke killed him – or perhaps Mrs. Younge and Mr. Clarke murdered Mr. Collins together. When everyone became suspicious about my cousin's death; when it seemed so unlikely for it to have been accidental; when people were investigating and asking difficult questions, then Clarke must have decided he needed someone else to be blamed for what happened. And perhaps Mrs. Younge knew what he had done and was planning to expose him. Perhaps they had a falling-out.

I believe that she may have come to Meryton to protect her investment in these letters – perhaps he no longer wished to share. So he borrowed my uncle Philips's spare key, and used it to lock the door after poisoning her and leaving another forged letter."

Mr. Philips and Mr. Darcy considered Elizabeth's theories plausible. They were conveyed to Clarke, who said they were absurd and more evidence of Mrs. Darcy's mad fantasy. He even denied throwing a rock at her; she had run and had tripped and fallen. As for where the money was, he did not have it, so he could not tell anyone where it was.

His rooms were searched. They found stationery and pens, but what did that prove? Anyone could have pens and paper.

The younger Mr. Jones confirmed having supplied belladonna to Mr. Clarke for his headaches, and confessed that it was possible that Clarke had procured more from the apothecaries' shop.

"There will have to be a trial," Mr. Philips said to his niece. He was extremely unhappy about all of this. *He* had hired Mr. Henry Clarke as a clerk, believing him when he claimed to have studied law, feeling magnanimous to be able to give a local youth a chance to return to Meryton to make his career. Certainly Clarke had had some familiarity with the subject, but now that Mr. Philips reflected, the young man's knowledge had seemed far more theoretical than practical, as if he had only read about the matter and had never worked in an office, as he had averred.

"Have you investigated *his* references?" inquired Mr. Darcy. He pointed out that if those were discovered to be falsified, then that would be evidence that Clarke was a forger, if not a murderer. Even if he claimed that they had been penned by Mrs. Younge, he would be at the very least complicit in the use of forgeries.

To Mr. Philips's chagrin, he had not researched Mr. Clarke's references. "They were excellent," he remarked, then added, "but of course, they would be."

Mr. Philips delegated this project to Mr. Morris. Mr. Morris was greatly in ascendance these days, and he went to London personally to investigate. Mr. Morris reported that the references were false. The firm that Clarke claimed to have worked at in London had heard of him, but only as someone who had applied for a position, rather than as someone whom they had actually hired.

Frank Perkins, the son of the jailer, had not been involved. However, Jim Page, the youth who liked to fish, and who had denied seeing anyone other than Mrs. Darcy take a box out of the horse chestnut tree on the day that Elizabeth had left a message saying that she would not pay, came forward and admitted that he had taken the box out of the tree himself, as soon as Mrs. Darcy had left the meadow. Mr. Clarke – whom the youth knew because his mother's shop was across the street from Mr. Philips's office – had paid him to do that. Jim insisted that he had not lied when he claimed that he had not seen anyone but Mrs. Darcy at the tree that day, because how could he see himself? He had given the box to Mr. Clarke later. And right after he had seen her in his mother's shop, he had gone to warn Mr. Clarke that Mrs. Darcy had been asking lots of questions. *He* had been the visitor who had delayed Mr. Clarke's appearance at tea at the Philips's house that day. Jim Page was very sorry for his misdeeds, and returned to her the baby caps – now rather soiled – that Elizabeth had thrown at Mr. Clarke while at the river.

"I suppose I alarmed Clarke even more by asking about the spare key," mused Elizabeth, when she heard this.

"Yes, that is when he must have decided to bolt," said Mr. Darcy.

Moreover, while in London, Mr. Morris fetched Mrs. Wickham, who had been visiting her uncle and aunt in Gracechurch Street. Lydia, now staying at Longbourn, was able to supply much more history based on her conversations with her husband and Mrs. Younge. Lydia, always willing to talk if she had an audience, was even more determined to do so now that Mrs. Younge was dead. Lydia had liked Mrs. Younge, and Lydia did not believe that Mrs. Younge had taken her own life. Did she have any evidence? Yes, in a letter that Mrs. Younge had written to her, saying that she had had enough of Meryton. Lydia's aunt Philips was pleasant, but she wished to leave the dull country and return to the excitement of the city and her own house on Edward Street.

Lydia said that Mrs. Younge supplied Mr. Clarke with clients, usually via the lodgers who came through her house. He had first begun by composing letters of reference for those seeking positions, and thus received pounds here and there for his creations. But this was not enough for his ambition. In order to truly become rich, he needed to take large sums of money from those who had it.

He had assisted Mrs. Younge in procuring her position as a companion and chaperone to Miss Georgiana Darcy, by supplying her with references. If that scheme had succeeded he would have had access to his share of Miss Darcy's thirty thousand pounds. The plot had failed and so eventually Mr. Clarke and Mrs. Younge turned to this conspiracy of blackmail, which had the disadvantage of being illegal, but the advantage of having many potential victims. They based their extortion on histories and vulnerabilities, and when no dark secrets were to be discovered, they invented them.

"There will still need to be a trial," Mr. Philips said, "but this information will make it much more difficult for Clarke to wriggle free. Thanks to Mr. Morris's efforts, Clarke has been proven to use forgery; he told you that he was the murderer of Mr. Collins – and given their relative sizes, he is a much more likely killer than Mrs. Smith. Finally, Lydia's story helps us put everything together."

"Lydia is not exactly a perfect witness," said Elizabeth, who was biding her time before attempting a serious conversation with that sister, "and from what I understand, much of what she has told you is hearsay."

"True, but as Mrs. Smith is dead, Lydia's statement may be allowed. Your sister's information is also leading us into directions which will enable the discovery of additional and better evidence," said Mr. Philips. He held up a letter from Newcastle. "She has even persuaded her husband to testify."

"Wickham is also not an exemplary witness," Mr. Darcy remarked.

"If men were perfect, then there would be no need for trials, and far less need for attorneys," remarked Mr. Philips. He said that he could understand that Mr. and Mrs. Darcy were not anticipating this trial with any pleasure, but he hoped that it would at least give them an interesting memory.

But there was no trial, for two days later, Mr. Clarke was found dead in his cell. On the previous day, he had received a visit from his friend, young Mr. Jones. Mr. Clarke had asked Mr. Jones to detail the evidence against him, which was bleak and strong (the conversation being overheard by the jailer). Mr. Clarke also said that he preferred to take poison in order to avoid the shame and pain of being hung. The young apothecary denied giving Mr. Clarke any additional belladonna, but said that if Mr. Clarke had had only a few leaves or a portion of the even deadlier root with him, he could have easily taken his own life.

CHAPTER XLIX

Many in Meryton experienced relief when they learned of the suicide of Mr. Clarke. His death meant that there could be no trial, and several had not wished to have their histories exposed.

The members of the Clarke family were sorry about his death, but as his guilt as a forger and a murderer seemed certain beyond a reasonable doubt, it was considerate of Henry to take his life rather than to wait for a public execution. Mr. Darcy was glad that Elizabeth was spared having to testify. Mr. Philips was grateful that his negligence in not making a more thorough review of Henry Clarke's references would not be revealed to all of Meryton, which would surely do his practice no good.

Some of the locals were less satisfied. Mrs. Philips, echoing her husband, *said* she was pleased, but a note of regret remained in her voice because the trial *might* have been interesting. Others were more openly sorry about the loss of the spectacle.

A few had reactions that were decidedly mixed. Mr. Bingley was glad that he would not have to testify and exhibit his weakness to the world. On the other hand, Clarke's death meant that the retrieval of his money was less likely, and Bingley's hope to purchase Rushburn seemed impossible. Bingley alternated between utter happiness as he spent time with Jane and their new daughter and angry frustration as he received a letter from the estate agent, asking if he were still interested in the purchase that he could no longer afford.

The hunt for the missing money continued. Mr. Clarke's premises and Mrs. Smith's rooms were searched repeatedly. Mr. Gardiner arranged to examine Mrs. Smith's (Younge's) lodgings in Edward Street, but the exercise yielded nothing of particular value.

Young Mr. Jones seemed the most downcast. He stayed in the shop, mixing potions and dealing with customers, for his father said he was too dejected and too distracted to visit patients. In addition to the loss of and betrayal by his great friend, some wondered if *he* had given belladonna to Mr. Clarke when visiting him in prison the day before he died. Young Mr. Jones was so despondent, that some claimed that it was impossible; he would never have abetted the death of Mr. Clarke – while others said that his ashen face and shaking hands were signs of a guilty conscience.

Mr. Henry Clarke was buried on the north side of the church.

Elizabeth decided to have a serious discussion with Lydia. She first approached her father about it, and asked him if he had spoken to Lydia about her behavior, as Mrs. Wickham had obviously known something about, and could have been involved in, the recent events.

"I have not," Mr. Bennet admitted. "Mr. Philips requested that we do everything possible not to upset Lydia, as her cooperation was necessary for the trial. Of course, now there will be no trial, but since the death of Mr. Clarke I have not been able to create an opportunity. She is always either with her mother or at her aunt Philips's. I confess I could have made more of an effort, but she is an energetic young woman, and I am too old to hobble after her."

"Do you have any objection to my speaking with her?"

None at all. He was their father, but they were both married women, and in consequence, adults.

So with the cooperation of her sisters, Elizabeth arranged the conversation at Netherfield. Mrs. Bennet had come with her three younger daughters to visit Jane and the baby. Mrs. Bennet and her youngest daughter were admiring little Jenny when Elizabeth called to Lydia and said she wished to speak with her in private.

Lydia consented and accompanied Elizabeth to a room where she had arranged for cake and tea. "Lord! Our niece is adorable, is she not? It almost makes me wish that I had a child of my own. But Wickham thinks it is too soon, that a baby would interfere with our amusement. Still, I was the first married; I should have been the first mother."

"I am not certain that that is the best reason for becoming a mother," said Elizabeth.

"Then what is? When will *you* have a child?"

"That is between me and Darcy," said Elizabeth, feeling her cheeks redden.

"Lizzy, you are blushing! We are sisters, and we are both married women; *we* can certainly talk about such things! And having a child need not interfere with *your* amusement at all; if you like, you can hire a dozen nursery maids." Lydia reached over and inspected Elizabeth's sleeve. "I must say, Lizzy, you have some very fine clothing."

"You are dressed well yourself," said Elizabeth, for Lydia wore a very pretty muslin. "Was this a present from my aunt Gardiner?"

"No, Lizzy, it is not; I paid for it myself. You know that Papa gives me an allowance."

Elizabeth did know that their father gave Lydia an allowance, but she also knew how much and she was familiar with Lydia's spending habits. She did not see how Lydia could have afforded the gown. "How do *you* know so much about Mr. Clarke and Mrs. Younge?"

"If you are planning to preach at me, you can stop right now. You cannot make me talk more than I already have."

"I believe that I can," said Elizabeth. "I will give you one pound if you hear me out and answer my questions as well as you can."

Lydia first frowned, and then she relaxed and laughed. "Very well! But make it two pounds and you are not allowed to preach or to scold."

Elizabeth agreed to the terms, then began. "Several weeks ago, I wrote you a long letter. What did you do with my letter? Did you give it away?"

"No," said Lydia.

This was not the answer that Elizabeth expected. "Then how did Mr. Clarke acquire a sample of my handwriting?"

"I did not *give* away your letter, Lizzy – I sold it! For a hundred pounds!" Lydia laughed. "I wish I had a mirror to show you the look on your face – I have never seen you appear so astonished. Now the expression is gone – you are full of disapproval. *That* is how I bought this gown, by selling a letter of yours. I only wish my scribbles were worth so much!"

Elizabeth struggled to keep the anger out of her voice. "And did you know what it was to be used for?"

Lydia shrugged. "It was a hundred pounds, Lizzy!"

"Did you give away – or rather sell – correspondence of Bingley's?"

"I think Wickham did that while we were here."

Again Elizabeth struggled to keep her countenance, for she had other questions to ask. "What about Miss King?"

"Wickham had several letters from her when they were planning an engagement. He sold them."

"So she was also victim of extortion," concluded Elizabeth. "Lydia, how many lives have you harmed? Miss King and Mr. Collins are dead!"

"You promised you would not scold," said Lydia, "and you did not like Miss King or Mr. Collins yourself, Lizzy. Besides, *I* did not kill them and *I* did not extort any money. I only sold one letter, written by you. As you sent it to me, it was my property. I had the right to do with it as I liked."

"Legally, perhaps, but not morally," said Elizabeth. "What about your friend, Mrs. Younge?"

"I am sorry about her, and so is Wickham; that is why I am helping you."

For a price, thought Elizabeth. "Did you know what would happen with those letters? How they would be used? How they have affected people, and are still affecting people? Including Bingley and Jane?"

Lydia waved at the rich furnishings in the room: the satin covered pillows, the deeply hued fabrics, the elegant screen in the corner. "It is not as if Jane is especially unhappy. She has all she needs and more. And what did Bingley do to deserve all his money? He inherited it."

"It was legally his, Lydia."

"Legally, perhaps, but not morally," retorted Lydia, echoing Elizabeth's own words. "Bingley did not earn his money, and if he does not have the sense to keep it, why is that my problem? As for you, Lizzy, what have you done to earn *your* fortune? You just married a rich man. Perhaps if he were disagreeable, one could say that you had earned it, but everyone says that Darcy treats you as if you were a queen."

Elizabeth was taken aback at such sophisticated reasoning – especially at hearing it from her youngest sister.

Lydia continued. "And what did *Darcy* do to earn his fortune? Nothing! He inherited it, just because his father was rich. Why should some inherit money and others not? Have you ever thought it was fair that Mr. Collins should inherit Longbourn? Just because he was male and we have no brothers?"

Elizabeth had heard her mother's complaints about the entailment of Longbourn on Mr. Collins all her life. Repetition, perhaps, had made her empathize, and so she rather agreed with Lydia's position on the entailment – but did her sister's notions have any merit with respect to the inheritances of Bingley and Darcy? And then she realized how Lydia had developed such peculiar ideas: from listening to Wickham, who had always resented the fact that Darcy's father was rich while his own had been poor.

Elizabeth's anger with Lydia grew, as she thought of all the grief she had helped facilitate – and even in her own family! Her sisters! But she still had an important question to ask. "Do you have any idea where the money could be?"

But Lydia did not, although she desperately wished that she did. She had only sent Elizabeth's letter to Mrs. Younge, at that time known as Mrs. Smith. Even though she had met Henry Clarke, years ago, at Clarke's library in Meryton, her personal acquaintance with him had been very slight. She knew nothing of his habits or his friends; she truly had no information to give. "Is that all, Lizzy? Because then I will take four pounds. You promised not to preach and not to scold, yet you did, so you can pay me twice what we agreed on."

Rather than dispute the matter, Elizabeth reached for her reticule and handed her youngest sister four pounds. Lydia pocketed the cash and then, completely unabashed, left the room, saying she wanted another peep at little Jenny, as she was starting her journey for Newcastle the following day.

"You may come out," called Elizabeth, when Lydia was gone.

Mary and Kitty emerged from behind the screen in the corner. Mary complained that she was stiff, while Kitty coughed – she had been stifling the impulse with some difficulty during Elizabeth's interview with Lydia. Elizabeth thanked them for listening; she had wanted witnesses to the conversation, and others in the family to hear what Lydia said.

As the sisters helped themselves to tea and cake, they expressed their reactions to the conversation that they had overheard. Mary was grieved and shocked at Lydia's callous behavior towards her own family. Kitty expressed the same sentiment, but then she fretfully added that she wished that someone would pay *her* four pounds to hold a conversation. Elizabeth decided that the right thing to do was to make both Mary and Kitty a present of five pounds each – they should receive more than Lydia, not less, given that they were not (as far as Elizabeth knew) profiting from by selling her letters to forgers. For this afternoon, at least, virtue would be rewarded more than vice.

Mary and Kitty then also went up to be with Jane and the baby, while Elizabeth sat by herself and reflected. Where had Mr. Clarke hidden the money?

CHAPTER L

Jane, when she heard the gist of the conversation with Lydia – her role had been to keep Mrs. Bennet to herself while Elizabeth interrogated their youngest sister – was philosophical about the loss of capital. "We have each other, the baby is healthy, and if we cannot purchase a property at the moment, then we cannot. Most people are far less fortunate than we."

Mr. Bingley, however, was not so content; he wished to bring up his children on an estate that was his, and not where they resided as mere tenants. Moreover, he had received a letter offering Rushburn Manor for a reduced amount, but he still did not feel as if he could afford it. The offer would be open for a few weeks.

Miss Bingley, the most anxious for a removal and aware that the days for negotiation were passing, sat down one morning with Elizabeth and addressed her: "*You* have proven yourself quite clever in this matter, Eliza. Do you have any idea where my brother's money could be?"

Elizabeth believed that Miss Bingley's compliment was almost sincere, even if her reason for paying it was provoked by an ulterior motive. Elizabeth did not see how she could help, however. She had not really known Mr. Henry Clarke, barely to nod to, and everything associated with him had been searched without the money's being found. Or, what was also possible, was that the money *had* been found – but the person who had discovered it was staying silent in order to keep the money for himself.

Jane, when she heard this theory, said she did not believe it. "How could anyone in Meryton be so wicked as to take money from their neighbors?"

"After all the murders in Meryton this summer, Jane, you do not believe someone here is capable of theft?" Miss Bingley retorted.

Jane sighed and told Caroline that she might be right, but then the baby opened her eyes and the new mother was lost to further conversation.

Mr. Darcy and Elizabeth, after the christening in which they became the godparents of little Jane Elizabeth Bingley, decided it was time for them to depart. Jane was healthy; the child adorable; and they themselves were only in the way. They wanted to return to Pemberley.

The only frustration pertained to Rushburn Manor. "If I could only *loan* him the capital," Mr. Darcy said to Elizabeth, but Bingley had refused him, just as he had refused assistance from Miss Bingley.

After church on the Sunday before their planned departure, Mr. and Mrs. Darcy made a tour of the graveyard. They went first to the Longbourn plot and stood before the resting place of Elizabeth's cousin, Mr. Collins. At that point they were joined by Mrs. Collins.

"Eliza! Do you have a moment? I wish to speak with you."

Elizabeth said that they did.

"First, I must tell you that Mrs. Jenkinson died last week."

Both Mr. and Mrs. Darcy expressed their sympathy, and Mr. Darcy said that he would send letters of condolence to his aunt and his cousin.

"I will be taking Mrs. Jenkinson's position, so I will be living at Rosings Park. Lewis and I leave for Hunsford tomorrow."

"Oh!" exclaimed Elizabeth. Mrs. Collins had a small competency; how could she bear to live with Lady Catherine when there was no need?

Elizabeth did not ask her question aloud, but as if she could read her friend's thoughts, Mrs. Collins answered it.

"I know that Lady Catherine is not always the easiest of women, but I believe she will be good to Lewis and to me. She has promised to arrange a first-rate education for him, too."

If there were anyone who could deal with the autocratic demeanor of Lady Catherine with equanimity, that person was Charlotte Collins. Elizabeth then wondered if little Lewis Collins, who was already the heir to Longbourn House, could somehow end up as the heir to Rosings Park as well. Lady Catherine liked to have the distinction of rank preserved, which was a reason for it not to happen, but time and affection might have their effect. In the meantime both Mrs. Collins and her son would live in luxury, with every advantage, in chambers far more spacious and elegant than any of the crowded rooms at Lucas Lodge.

Elizabeth collected herself sufficiently to say, "I am pleased to learn that she values you," and Mr. Darcy added that he was glad his aunt had made such a sensible choice in her selection of a new companion for her daughter.

Mrs. Collins had an additional disclosure. "Lady Catherine also communicated to me about Mr. Radclyff."

Both Mr. Darcy and Elizabeth were intrigued, and asked Mrs. Collins to explain. It turned out that Mr. Radclyff had been a suitor of Lady Catherine's when she was young (Elizabeth had to make an effort to imagine a *young* Lady Catherine). The forgery that she had received – a letter pretending to be from herself – was a letter to that man, claiming that *he* was the father of Miss Anne de Bourgh. The forgery had struck Lady Catherine in her Achilles' heel – her love for her frail daughter was paramount; she would do anything for Anne, and she could not bear to have her composure disturbed, especially not when Mrs. Jenkinson was on her deathbed. With Sir Lewis de Bourgh and Mr. Radclyff both long dead, and her own words and handwriting apparently against her, Lady Catherine had not known how to prove that something had *not* happened more than two decades ago.

"So that is why she came to Meryton with Mr. Collins," said Elizabeth, now understanding her ladyship's dreadful mood.

"Yes. However, now that it has been proved that this rumor was based on forgeries and falsehoods, she has no qualms discussing it. And if the money is discovered, she wishes to have hers returned."

"I understand. But we do not know where it is, and we plan to depart for Pemberley on Tuesday," said Mr. Darcy.

"I recommend informing my uncle Philips of the amount," suggested Elizabeth.

"I will do that now, and then I must return to Lucas Lodge to take care of Lewis. I hope we will soon meet again – perhaps even at Rosings Park." Mrs. Collins shook hands with Elizabeth and then hastened away in search of Mr. Philips.

"If your aunt will permit me to stay at Rosings Park," Elizabeth said to her husband. "I would not wish for my presence to sully the great chimney-piece."

"Perhaps Mrs. Collins can soften Lady Catherine's attitude towards you," said Mr. Darcy.

They moved to inspect the three newest graves on the north side of the church. Neither Mr. Darcy nor Elizabeth had much sympathy for Mr. Clarke or Mrs. Smith (the name under which Mrs. Younge had been buried), but they felt great pity for Miss Mary King, who had been driven to despair. "Poor Miss King," Elizabeth said, as they studied the plain headstone. "I should have made an effort to become better acquainted with her when she was alive."

"She should have shown her betrothed the letter," said Mr. Darcy. "If she had trusted him, she might be happily married by now, and her fortune intact."

"But I can imagine what happened," said Elizabeth, and explained her theory to him. The initial demand might have been small enough that Miss King decided that it was more prudent to pay it than to risk her relationship with Mr. Selby. Then, after she had paid one time, the fact that she had paid at all made her guilt seem more certain, and so it was easy for Mr. Clarke to demand more.

"She was trapped," concluded Mr. Darcy.

"Yes, and the more money she paid, the more culpable she would have appeared to Mr. Selby. But I do not think she took her own life."

"Why not?"

"Because her banker wrote to my uncle, asking him to talk to her and to advise her. What if Mr. Henry Clarke saw that letter first? And delayed its reaching my uncle by a day or two? If my uncle Philips had been able to gain Miss King's confidence, then she would have stopped paying. They might have even determined who was responsible for the extortion. So I believe that Mr. Clarke killed her, in order to stop her from consulting with Mr. Philips and starting an investigation."

"I think you are right, Elizabeth – Clarke was responsible. Poor Miss King!"

Elizabeth turned to see young Mr. Jones approaching the grave of Mr. Clarke; when he noticed them, he hesitated; he only continued when Elizabeth called out his name.

As they met, the young apothecary bowed stiffly. "Mrs. Darcy. Mr. Darcy."

"I am sorry for the loss of your friend," said Elizabeth. "I know you cared about Mr. Clarke."

"Friend!" said Mr. Jones, and gave a short laugh devoid of humor. "I *believed* we were friends. But he was a friend to no one."

The bitterness in Mr. Jones's voice showed how much he had been grieved by Mr. Clarke's betrayals. Elizabeth wondered how much Mr. Bingley would suffer if Mr. Darcy were to use him so; from what she perceived, Mr. Jones's affection for and dependence on Mr. Clarke had been even greater than what Bingley had ever felt for Darcy.

"Mr. Jones, do you know what Mr. Clarke did with the money?" Mr. Darcy asked.

Mr. Jones reddened. "Do you not think others have asked me that? Do you not think I have asked myself that many times? But I do not know, for I never knew that he had it. Henry's rooms have been searched – the library – his haunts. But nothing has been found."

Elizabeth said, "I do not say that you knew him well, but you knew him better than any other person did – excepting, perhaps, Mrs. Smith, and she is dead. Is there nowhere else?"

The young apothecary shifted from embarrassment to indignation. "If I knew, I would say – do you not understand? Everyone in Meryton is treating me as if *I* were culpable – as if *I* murdered people and ruined them financially. Even my father is furious with me. But I am not a criminal; I am only a fool, and that is how I will be known here for the rest of my life. I would leave the area if I could, but as I do *not* have Clarke's money, I cannot afford to go anywhere!"

This was more speech than Elizabeth had ever heard from young Mr. Jones in her entire life.

"Time will lessen the effect," said Mr. Darcy. "And many others were fooled and betrayed by Clarke. You are not as singular as you believe."

Mr. Jones shrugged; the movement remind Elizabeth of how Mr. Clarke and young Mr. Jones had come together out of the woods. "What about your fishing spot?" she asked. "The one you occasionally went to with Mr. Clarke? Could you show it to us?"

Mr. Jones demurred and said he had never seen Mr. Clarke hide anything there. But Elizabeth persisted and young Mr. Jones was unable to deny this request to Mrs. Darcy, who had not only condescended to speak to him but who was actually addressing him in a civil manner.

They made arrangements to go to the river. The coach transported Mr. and Mrs. Darcy and young Mr. Jones to the lane bordering the meadow with the horse chestnut tree; Elizabeth told Wilson to continue to Netherfield with Mr. Bingley and his sister and then to return to this place and to wait for them.

"You wish to take a walk? Why not return to Netherfield and walk there?" asked Miss Bingley, who was puzzled by Elizabeth and Darcy's plans, and especially by the inclusion of young Mr. Jones, whom she did not consider worthy of the Pemberley carriage.

Mr. Bingley did not request an explanation. "I will tell Jane to expect you later."

The carriage drove away, and Mr. Jones led them across the field towards the edge of the river. "What is your idea?" inquired Mr. Darcy.

"Mr. Clarke used that horse chestnut tree as a hiding place, but this meadow is frequented by many. To hide his treasure he would need a much more secret place."

"Somewhere outside? Then it could be found by anyone," Mr. Darcy objected.

"Clarke was *here* the day that he attempted to kill me. I believe that after my inquiries about the spare key to Mrs. Younge's rooms he decided that he would soon be under suspicion and so he needed to leave Meryton. What if he was trying to collect the money before he departed? And then, after you rescued me, he could not return to collect the money?"

"Clarke was not a fool; he would have put the money into a bank. Perhaps under a different name. Like Mrs. Younge, he may have been using aliases."

"He might not have trusted the bankers," said Elizabeth. "But I agree it is not the only possibility. That is why I did not mention it to Bingley; I did not wish to raise false hopes. But if the other places have been searched and nothing has been found, looking here will not harm us."

Their task, however, soon became much more difficult. The meadow ended; the forest reached to the river's edge; pushing their way through the trees and brush meant torn clothing and muddy shoes. Mr. Darcy revised his opinion about Clarke's hiding place being found by anyone when the spot was so inaccessible, and Elizabeth, as a branch slapped her arm and thorns tore her bonnet, reconsidered her assertion of the search not causing any harm. She also wondered what had possessed her to attempt this in her Sunday finery.

Just as Elizabeth was about to ask how much further they had to continue, Mr. Jones announced that they had reached the fishing spot favored by Mr. Clarke. It was not especially wonderful; there was only a slight decrease in the amount of brush, and a few large rocks on which one could sit, albeit not exactly in comfort.

Mr. Darcy suggested that they search by each taking a different direction from the spot. None of them returned in the direction from whence they had come, as they could search as they returned. Mr. Jones pushed farther along the river's edge and Elizabeth and Mr. Darcy both pushed their way into the woods. "What exactly are we seeking?" inquired Mr. Darcy, as he rubbed his gloved hands together to rid them of some dirt.

"The hollow in the horse chestnut tree contained a wooden box," Elizabeth explained, "but I do not know if Mr. Clarke used the same method here."

"If he hid anything here at all," said Mr. Darcy.

Elizabeth heard the reproach in his voice. He had some justification, for she had dragged him out in his Sunday finery as well. But as long as they were here she would do her utmost. She looked high; she looked low; she gazed up into trees and studied the trunks and leafy branches; she pushed aside stones and leaves with a large stick.

Then she noticed something: not exactly tracks; the ground was too thickly covered with leaves for those, but she detected a few broken twigs on some bushes. Had they been snapped by an animal, by Mr. Clarke, or by some other creature or person completely unassociated with all of this? She noticed ivy growing on a tree; it hung loosely, however, and she pushed it aside.

Behind the ivy curtain, and above her, beyond her reach, was a hollow; she called Mr. Darcy to join and to assist her. He did so, followed shortly by Mr. Jones.

Mr. Darcy was tall enough to reach inside the hollow; he did so, and pulled out a plain brown cloth bag; Mr. Jones exclaimed with surprise. Mr. Darcy withdrew a wooden box out of the bag and handed it to his wife. "Congratulations, Elizabeth. You have found *something.*"

"Oh! It is like the one that Mr. Clarke used in the horse chestnut tree," Elizabeth exclaimed, turning it in her hands. She then added: "Although I do not believe it is the same one." She tried to open the box but it was locked. She shook it gently; they could hear objects rattling within.

"Let us take it back to Meryton," said Mr. Darcy.

CHAPTER LI

Wilson had brought the Pemberley coach to the appointed spot, and without comment he drove his master, mistress and Mr. Jones back to town. Soon they were announced by the Philips's footman.

The drawing room was crowded, for Mrs. Philips had invited her sister and her family to drink tea with her and Mr. Philips after church. Hence Mr. and Mrs. Bennet, and Mary and Kitty were also present, as well as Mr. Morris, Mr. Philips's remaining clerk. Mrs. Philips was still too awed by Mr. Darcy to remark on her niece's untidy appearance, so she just welcomed them and told the servants to bring more tea and muffins. Mrs. Bennet, however, had no such inhibition. "Lizzy! What have you been doing? Your shoes and the hem of your skirt are dirtier than anything I have ever seen, and a twig is sticking out of your hair!"

"Have you been chased by another murderer, Lizzy?" asked her father.

"We have found this," said Mr. Darcy, and he brought out the locked wooden box.

Questions were asked; explanations given, and everyone was eager to see what was in the box. But the box could not be opened till Mr. Philips had a servant bring a hammer. Mr. Morris did the honors – one of his more unusual duties, but recently his tasks had encompassed far more variety – and soon he broke through the lid. The contents did not disappoint. The locked box contained many bank notes – Mrs. Philips gasped while Mrs. Bennet exclaimed, "Good gracious! Lord bless me!" – as Mr. Morris counted them out and Mr. Philips verified the reckoning. Mr. Morris wrote the total on a piece of paper, along with other details concerning how it had been found.

The wooden container yielded more than cash; it also harbored jewels. The ladies were particularly fascinated by these, and Kitty was positive that a pair of amber earrings had belonged to Miss King; she believed that the rest of the jewelry had as well. Everyone agreed that this seemed to confirm that the box had been used by Mr. Clarke, and that it was very likely that he had murdered Miss King, stealing her jewels after poisoning her.

"Well, Kitty," said Mr. Bennet, "it appears that I have been wrong to think your preoccupation with jewelry frivolous!"

Mr. Philips said that some formalities needed to be observed, but that Mr. Bingley could expect to be reimbursed for all that he had paid out. Lady Catherine would likewise have her money returned – Mrs. Collins had spoken to him on the matter that morning at the church – and they would be able to send some funds and jewelry to Mr. Selby.

Yet more money remained. "What is to be done with it?" inquired Mary. "If no one claims it?"

Mr. Philips then inquired who, precisely, had found the box: Mr. Darcy, Mrs. Darcy, or Mr. Jones?

Both Mr. Darcy and Mr. Jones agreed that Elizabeth was responsible. *She* had made Mr. Jones lead them along the river bank, and although Mr. Darcy had been the one to bring down the box from the tree and had carried it, it had been *her* sharp eyes that had first discovered the hollow containing it.

"If no one else comes forth with a legitimate claim," said Mr. Philips, "the contents belong to the person who found the box. Apparently that would be you, Lizzy, although as your husband, Mr. Darcy has rights to it."

Mr. Darcy explained that the money would belong only to Elizabeth, and she blushed as her entire family turned to stare at her: the other ladies surely did not believe that *she* required additional wealth. Her father, however, offered sincere congratulations. "Well done, Lizzy!"

The others then reacted. Kitty sighed and fingered the amber earrings with longing; Mrs. Philips declared that her niece was one of the luckiest young ladies she had ever met; and Mrs. Bennet conceded that such a sum would be worth a ruined pair of shoes.

Then Mary said: "I do not believe that *I* would be tempted to accept this money. These are ill-gotten gains, extracted from the misery of others."

"Nonsense, Mary!" exclaimed Mrs. Bennet, who had already been scheming for ways to unburden Mrs. Darcy of some of her excess cash in the form of presents to herself and her other daughters.

"What about Mr. Collins?" inquired Mary. "And Mrs. Collins, his widow?"

Elizabeth generally paid little attention to Mary's moralizing, but on this occasion her sister's words made her reflect. All those in the room, who had been enjoying the spectacle of so much treasure, were sobered by the reminder of how Mr. Clarke had assembled it.

Mr. Philips warned that it was too soon to be too concerned about what anyone should do with the residual cash. "At this point, we do not know if anything will remain to be sent to you, Lizzy. Those with legitimate claims must take precedence."

Elizabeth was satisfied with this; she did not need the funds, and given Mary's point, she preferred that it be returned to those that had suffered if that were possible. Mr. Darcy wished to know if he could carry the money due Mr. Bingley back to his friend; Mr. Philips and Mr. Morris insisted on the signature of several witnesses – Mr. Bennet and Mr. Jones in addition to Mr. Darcy – but everyone agreed that it should be done, to make sure that the cash was delivered to Mr. Bingley as soon as possible.

CHAPTER LII

When presented with the funds, Mr. Bingley's initial reaction was not what either Elizabeth or Mr. Darcy expected. "No! I cannot accept this."

"Good God, Bingley! Why not?" asked Mr. Darcy.

"Because I do not believe that it is mine."

"These may not be the exact same bank notes that you left for Clarke," said Elizabeth, "as the box that we found contained many more and we cannot tell them apart. But you, and only you, have a claim to this money."

But Mr. Bingley's skepticism had a different origin. He believed that the money came from Mr. Darcy, and that his friend had taken money out of his own capital to compensate for the shortfall in Mr. Bingley's. "I cannot allow you to pay for what was utter folly on my part. Jane and I and the baby are not suffering. Keep your money for those who truly need it."

"I am flattered that you could believe me so generous, disappointed that you could think me so duplicitous, and quite in agreement that you made an error in judgment and do not deserve or need my charity," said Mr. Darcy. "Besides, this was not the only money that was in the box. Do you imagine that I am so rich as to be able to compensate all Clarke's victims?"

"We also discovered the amber earrings that belonged to Miss King," said Elizabeth. "Kitty recognized them. She and my mother are coming to Netherfield tomorrow; they will confirm everything that we have told you. As will my father, my uncle Philips, young Mr. Jones, and Mr. Morris, when you have the opportunity to speak with them. My uncle Philips wishes for you to visit his office to confirm your receipt of the money."

Bingley's resolution faltered at the mention of Miss King's earrings. He had occasionally danced with Miss King, and he recalled those pretty earrings. If they really had found Clarke's cache – but it was too marvelous to believe.

Mr. Darcy added that it was generally wise not to trust others completely, but he would appreciate it if Bingley would show more confidence in *him*.

Mr. Bingley, with a little more pressing, was eventually persuaded that it was true. He accepted the money, and then excused himself to share the news with his wife and sister. Their reactions were relief and joy; Jane even took a few minutes from gazing at her baby to express her gratitude to Darcy and her sister for their efforts. Miss Bingley was ecstatic, as this meant that her brother would be able to complete the purchase of the property that was *her* heart's desire. She was able to remark to Elizabeth in genuinely amiable tones that she had developed a great appreciation for Elizabeth's tendency to walk and wander and almost promised that she would never mock it again.

Elizabeth's appearance was put to rights by her maid, Jeanette. This time only her attire had been injured, and that damage was easily repaired. The evening was spent most congenially, although all the parties had various tasks. Mr. Bingley wrote to his agent about his intention to purchase Rushburn Manor; Mr. Darcy composed a letter to his aunt, to inform Lady Catherine that it appeared that her money had been found; even Miss Bingley wrote to her sister. Jane and Elizabeth did not sit down to desks with pens, but their hearts were more occupied than anyone else's, as they sat admiring little Jenny Elizabeth.

Only when that most important person was asleep could their conversation turn to other subjects.

"I shall be so sorry when you depart," Jane said to her sister. "Your support during this time can never be repaid. Not only did you listen to me, but you risked your life."

"And my shoes," said Elizabeth, laughing. She told Jane how happy she had been to have been of some assistance; how much she would miss her, but then added: "But soon – if Bingley is able to complete the purchase – you will be so much closer. And then Jenny will be able to spend more time with her uncle and aunt at Pemberley. Rushburn Manor is only thirty miles away!"

The next day, Monday, arrived. In the morning the letters written the evening before were posted, and Bingley rode into Meryton to take care of his business with Mr. Philips. In the afternoon, Mrs. Bennet made one of her frequent visits to Netherfield, and on this occasion Mr. Bennet and their daughters came as well. Mary had an important announcement to make. "Mr. Morris has made me an offer of marriage," she said. "And I have accepted him."

Jane and Elizabeth and the others congratulated Mary, who, in her happiness, appeared almost pretty. Mr. Morris was not handsome, nor was he rich or even particularly charming, but he was respectable and steady.

They intended to live in the rooms which had been rented by Mrs. Smith – Mary maintained she was not the least superstitious – and that meant that Mrs. Philips's rent would be restored.

Mrs. Bennet was satisfied. "Mr. Morris may not have the income of Darcy, Bingley or even dear Wickham," she said, rather to the mortification of her three eldest daughters, who would prefer not to have such matters discussed, although Mrs. Bennet would have surely retorted that they were all family and everyone already knew everything anyway. "But since the undoing of Mr. Clarke, Mr. Morris's prospects are greatly improved. Mr. Philips thinks very highly of him."

"And unlike dear Wickham, Mr. Morris's expenses are not likely to exceed his income," said Mr. Bennet.

"I wish you every happiness, Mary," said Mr. Darcy, and Miss Bingley did her best to echo him, although she was conscious that four of the five Bennet girls had found husbands in the last two years, while she, despite her fortune of twenty thousand pounds, remained single.

Everyone congratulated Mary, and then Jane said that they also had news. Mr. Bingley informed his in-laws that he had made an offer on an estate, up in Cheshire, a county next to Derbyshire. Mr. Bennet was happy for them, but Mrs. Bennet struggled. For Bingley to be the owner of a property instead of a tenant was a significant step up in his status and hence in the status of her eldest daughter – but it also meant that Jane and her only grandchild would move far away. "Are you certain there is no property closer?" she inquired, and mentioned several in the neighborhood whose families would have been horrified at Mrs. Bennet's readiness to evict them. Mr. Bingley informed her that he had never heard of anything for sale in the area, and that Rushburn Manor was a fine place, very healthy, and that the neighborhood was excellent. He considerately did not mention that its great distance from Longbourn was one of its advantages. Jane was kind enough to say that she hoped they would all visit, and then added that she would like Kitty to accompany them when they moved, and help them settle in their new home. She told them, too, that she would be hiring Hannah, Miss King's former maidservant, as a nursery maid for little Jenny.

"But Miss King's Hannah is a thief!" protested Mrs. Bennet.

"No, Mamma, it has been proven that she is *not* a thief," said Elizabeth.

Mrs. Bennet supposed that was true, but that it was very difficult to change one's opinion of another person, simply because that opinion was based on wrong information.

"That is an astute observation, Mrs. Bennet," said Mr. Bennet. "And I imagine that is one reason Hannah wishes to leave this neighborhood."

The Darcys were to begin their journey early the next morning, so despite the desire of Mrs. Bennet to remain late, Mr. Bennet insisted on summoning the Longbourn carriage at a reasonable hour. "Lizzy, I will miss you," he said, and Mr. Darcy told his father-in-law that he was welcome at Pemberley at any time. "I cannot promise you that my neighborhood will be as exciting as yours, Sir," Mr. Darcy added, "but the library can provide some milder entertainment."

Mr. Bennet, still employing a cane after spraining his ankle when he had been called to investigate the death of Mr. Collins, assured Mr. Darcy that after the past few weeks, he was more certain than ever that he preferred his adventures on paper. He then gathered Mary, Kitty and Mrs. Bennet and limped to his carriage.

The next morning, the Darcys, after fond farewells and plans to see the Bingleys at Pemberley for Christmas, entered their own carriage. As the weather was fine, Jeanette rode on the box with Wilson and Elizabeth and Darcy could chat in private.

"How do you like being an uncle?" asked Elizabeth, as the carriage pulled away from Netherfield.

Mr. Darcy spoke at length at the wonder of an infant so small, and marveled at how such tiny people could grow into adults as large as themselves. Then he complained that, during his entire visit, he had managed to hold the child only three times. "An uncle, even an uncle who is a godfather, must yield his claim to parents, grandparents, and her many aunts. It is most unfair."

Elizabeth laughed, and said that she pitied him, but that she also admired him for his excellent manners, for she understood what a hardship politeness was in this case. She, too, had regretted how little time she could spend with her niece. "The way to overcome this obstacle," she said, "is to have a child of one's own," and she informed him that they could expect a little Darcy in about seven months.

The father-to-be was elated by this news, and he was both pleased and surprised to discover that his wife had told him before anyone else, even Jane. Elizabeth explained that she was still angry with herself for not having told him about the extortion attempt immediately, and was trying to make amends for her earlier failure.

"Besides, you did not wish to detract attention from your sister's situation," said Mr. Darcy, who knew his wife pretty well. Then he inquired minutely as to how Elizabeth was feeling, discussed the best doctors and midwives in Derbyshire, and recommended renovations that they could make to his old nursery. Elizabeth assured him that she was perfectly well, listened to his ideas and then suggested some of her own. Most of all she delighted in the heartfelt happiness that she saw lighting up his countenance.

During the many hours of driving to Pemberley, the coming child was their first subject of conversation. The murders in Meryton, the extortion attempts, Mary's engagement to Mr. Morris, Georgiana's probable engagement to Colonel Fitzwilliam, Mrs. Collins's position at Rosings, Bingley's estate, a new vicar to replace the unfortunate Reverend Wallace and even the money that Elizabeth might receive – these matters were not exactly forgotten, for in many instances they required action or at least some attention on the part of the Darcys. But nothing could compare to the interest, love and joy that they experienced for the coming child.

AUTHOR'S NOTE

Please do not read these notes unless you are willing to be spoiled!

I have done my best to be consistent with the characters and with what Jane Austen intended for them. She indicated, at the end of *Pride & Prejudice* that Kitty was kept away from Lydia and spent the chief of her time with her two oldest sisters and was greatly improved as a result. Furthermore, the Bingleys only remained at Netherfield Park for a twelvemonth, and then Mr. Bingley purchased an estate in the county next to Derbyshire (the purchase of the estate provides part of the plot for *The Meryton Murders*). I could not discover which county, nor the name of the estate, so these are my own inventions. Outside of the actual text, in correspondence, Jane Austen indicated the futures of the two as-of-yet unmarried sisters. Kitty marries a clergyman near Pemberley, and Mary marries one of her uncle's clerks and became a sort of mistress of Meryton. These possibilities have been set up; Mary is being wooed by Mr. Morris and Kitty, who ironically has expressed distaste for clergymen in general, is being invited to stay at her sisters' estates.

Note that *The Meryton Murders* is based as much as possible on Austen's text and hence may differ from the various screen adaptations. Austen describes Mr. Collins as tall and heavy, but the actors who play him, no matter how brilliant they are at capturing his manner, do not always match the character physically. The 1995 BBC/A&E adaptation also shows a pianoforte at the house belonging to Mr. and Mrs. Philips, but the actual book describes how the Bennet girls long for an instrument when visiting their aunt. In that adaptation Mrs. Bennet's first name is given as "Fanny," but as in most Austen novels, first daughters are named for their mothers, I have assumed it was "Jane."

In *Pride & Prejudice* Austen gives some information regarding the geography of Meryton and the rest of the neighborhood. Longbourn is about a mile from the town, and Lucas Lodge is quite close to Longbourn, with Netherfield Park being three miles away from Longbourn House. I invented a bridge and a small river. This is not a great stretch, as England is full of streams and rivers and lakes. Besides, the text indicates that Mr. Gardiner, the brother of Mrs. Bennet, is fond of fishing. In *Pride & Prejudice* he lives in London (Gracechurch Street), but when he was a boy he must have lived in Meryton. So, with all this evidence, I felt authorized to put in a small river and some people fishing in it.

I have used the names of many bit characters mentioned in *Pride & Prejudice*. Mr. Jones is the apothecary; Mr. Morris is the name of the man arranging for Bingley to rent Netherfield; Clarke's library is mentioned. The young men in this novel are supposed to be sons or nephews with the same last names.

I am aware of one potential discrepancy (readers may find others). Mr. Darcy describes Mrs. Younge as supporting herself by letting lodgings *after* he dismisses her. I have made her a landlady *before* her time with Darcys as well – which does not contradict *Pride & Prejudice*, but is not implied by it. Not only do I find this more convenient, but it also seems more logical. Furthermore, this gives her the opportunity to form alliances with Henry Clarke and George Wickham.

I have done my best to imitate Jane Austen's voice. I have suppressed some of my own habits, and have tried to use her vocabulary instead of my own. *The Meryton Murders* is set in 1814, so I was constantly checking the online version of Merriam-Webster to determine when a word became part of the English language. This meant I had to delete words such as fiancé and détente and sabotage and to find appropriate alternatives. Spelling, however, is modern as my many editions of *Pride & Prejudice* are inconsistent and I prefer not to do battle with my word processor.

Jane Austen was born about a month later than expected, rather to the embarrassment of her parents, George and Cassandra Austen. As she was the 7th of 8th children, her father acknowledged that they should have reckoned better. I have paid homage to this by making Jane Bingley rather late in giving birth to her first child.

As for the plot based on blackmail and extortion, remember that it was a time when reputation was much easier to sully than it is now, and the consequences could be more severe, especially for a lady. As Mary Bennet says in *Pride & Prejudice*: "loss of virtue in a female is irretrievable; that one false step involves her in endless ruin; that her reputation is no less brittle than it is beautiful … ."

I have something in common with Mr. Clarke. I am making up stories about Jane Austen's characters, and I am trying to use her voice, just as Clarke makes up false histories and attempts to use their voices and handwriting. But I hope that, unlike the unfortunate recipients of Henry Clarke's inventions, *The Meryton Murders* will please and not distress its readers.

Thanks for reading!

Victoria Grossack

ABOUT THE AUTHOR

Victoria Grossack, married with children, is the author of several novels and more than seventy articles on the craft of writing. If she is not hiking or gardening, she is working hard on her next project.

If you want to read more of her work, consider:

The Highbury Murders: A Mystery Set in the Village of Jane Austen's Emma (most like *The Meryton Murders*)

Academic Assassination: A Zofia Martin Mystery is a contemporary mystery with an emphasis on science. If you like the TV show *The Big Bang Theory*, this may appeal to you.

The following novels are based on Greek mythology and are written with Alice Underwood. They are different in voice and style from Victoria Grossack's other works, but they are entertaining, especially if you like historical fiction. The Niobe trilogy solves a mass murder that took place more than 3000 years ago:

Jocasta: The Mother-Wife of Oedipus
Antigone & Creon: Guardians of Thebes

Children of Tantalus: Niobe & Pelops
The Road to Thebes: Niobe & Amphion
Arrows of Artemis: Niobe & Chloris

And, if you want to know more how Victoria Grossack writes as she does — if you wish to author stories and novels yourself, consider:

Crafting Fabulous Fiction: Levels of Structure, Characters & More

Lightning Source UK Ltd.
Milton Keynes UK
UKOW05f2041190517

301611UK00006B/446/P